The CHINA DOGS

A THRILLER

Sam Masters

WITNESS

An Imprint of HarperCollinsPublishers

THE CHINA DOGS. Copyright © 2014 by Sam Masters. All rights reserved. Printed in the United States of America. No part of this book may be used or reproduced in any manner whatsoever without written permission except in the case of brief quotations embodied in critical articles and reviews. For information, address Witness, an Imprint of HarperCollins Publishers, 195 Broadway, New York, NY 10007.

HarperCollins books may be purchased for educational, business, or sales promotional use. For information, please e-mail the Special Markets Department at SPSales@harpercollins.com.

FIRST EDITION

Designed by Rhea Braunstein

ISBN 978-0-06-234313-0

14 15 16 17   OV/RRD   10 9 8 7 6 5 4 3 2 1

The
CHINA DOGS

PART ONE

*The best thing of all is to take
the enemy's country whole and intact;
to shatter and destroy it is not so good.*

SUN TZU

I

Gobi Desert, Northeastern China

*T*he silver buses drive across the land of endless sand. Onboard are prisoners from China's notorious Death Row. Rapists, serial murderers, and child abusers.

Twenty men about to be given an extraordinary chance to live.

To wipe the slate clean.

The long vehicles that carry them are equipped with lethal electrocution equipment, state-of-the-art technology designed to deliver on-the-spot executions. The inmates can choose to stay on board and be quickly put to death; their organs harvested there and then and sold to those needing donations.

Or—when the doors swing open—they can run for their lives. Run into one of the largest deserts in the world and take their chances with what lies out there.

Air brakes hiss, sand sprays, and the five buses come to a synchronized stop in the blistering heat.

Three army copters hover in the sweltering air. Military bosses watch like circling vultures.

On cue, automated locks clunk and the big doors of the vehicles slide open.

Clouds of hot sand rise as the bare feet of desperate men jump and run from the vehicles.

No one remains.

Six miles away—six miles north, south, east, and west—the doors of four armored personnel carriers also open.

General Fu Zhang peers down like God. Watches life and death play out. People reduced to black dots, scattered like dung beetles. He can't help but think it would be better for the men if they'd stayed on the buses.

Their deaths would be less painful.

The leader of China's armed forces follows each and every fatality on his video monitor.

Nonchalantly, he waves a hand to the pilot to return to base.

He is pleased.

Seldom has he seen such *efficient* slaughter. Such *economic* carnage.

Project Nian is nearing completion.

2

Sinuiju, North Korea

*I*t's minus 25 and a skin-stripping wind whips down the Yula River, lashing the crews on the icebreaking barges that crunch in the whitened mouth of the delta where the Yellow Sea, Korean Bay, and East China Sea meet.

Fifty-nine-year-old Hao Weiwei and his only child, twenty-six-year-old Jihai, light cigarettes near mounds of snow at the end of the Friendship Bridge. They smoke and shiver as they stare nostalgically across at their home town of Dandong, a place they may never see again.

To the soldiers photographing them from the military towers on the Korean side of the river, the men look almost identical. Both are slight of build, with round, gentle faces and soft brown eyes. The father has a little less of the black, thick hair, and the son moves with more vigor as they both stamp their feet to stay warm.

Those who know them would tell you that they're more than family. They are coworkers and close friends, made closer by the cancer that took Jihai's mother when he was only sixteen. They are kind men. Dedicated workers. Perfect citizens.

Hao throws the remains of his cigarette into the Yula. "Enough now. Come, we still have a long way to go."

Jihai takes a final look at the matte grayness posing as daylight, sinks the stub of his cigarette beneath the snow and walks back toward the waiting van. He shuffles down the boards past other workers and takes his seat next to his best friend Péng, the rock he leaned on when his mother died. Péng is broad and round, so he takes up at least a seat and a half, but Jihai wouldn't want to be anywhere else. Sitting behind them is the unit's research assistant, Tāo, a frail and shy young man who is still more at home in scholarly surroundings than the world at large.

The government driver shuts the door and begins the long journey south.

It's to a destination that few people in the world have ever been to and most would fear to go.

3

Washington DC

Jack and Jane Molton are about as excited as young kids can get. Mom and Dad—Clint and Sheryl—are pretty wound up as well.

America's First Family is getting a new pet. One that's had more medical examinations than the President himself.

"Emperor" is a red Tibetan mastiff pup, a gift from Xian, the great and honorable leader of the People's Republic of China, and to quote twelve-year-old Jane, the dog is "super cute."

Officers Rick Ryan and Darryl Heitinger carry the small white cage into a playroom in the residential wing and salute their President.

Ryan, a young Marine with a chiseled GI Joe face, passes over a small red book. "Emperor's medical papers, sir. All jabs, quarantine tests, and inspections are up-to-date and fully in accordance with Homeland and White House regulations."

"Thank you, Rick."

The officers dutifully disappear and the family descends on the tiny bundle of fur that has its face pressed against the plastic coated bars.

"Me first! Let *me* hold him first." Ten-year-old Jack is beside himself with excitement.

Forty-seven-year-old Chicagoan Clint Molton bends his six-foot-two-inch frame to unlock the door. With one big hand he scoops out the fluff bundle, accompanied by a chorus of "Oooohs."

"Oh my God, he's *so* pretty!" Sheryl kisses the pup's shiny black nose before Clint passes him to Jack.

"In Chinese the breed is called *Do-khyi*," says the President, not that anyone is now listening to him. "It means home guard or door guard."

Again no reaction.

Clearly now is not the time to try to educate the family.

Jack cradles Emperor like a baby and rocks him lovingly. Jane rubs the soft golden fur under his chin. "Okay, come on, it's my turn now. Let me hold him." She tries to prise the pup from her younger brother's grip.

Mom sees problems brewing. "Hey, be careful. He's an animal, not a toy. You guys are going to have to learn to be gentle and responsible or you're going to hurt him."

Clint finally has a chance to add a fact that might get their attention. "And remember, when this little fella is fully grown, he's going to be worth a million bucks."

Sheryl looks shocked. "You're kidding?"

"Nope. Pedigrees like ours are rare. This breed goes back fifty-eight thousand years and some dogs fetch more than ten million yuan."

"Sheesh. You'd best take President Xian a nice present when you next see him."

"I will. I'm in China for the G20 later this year. But I'll call him tonight and say how much we all love the pup." He lifts Emperor out of his daughter's arms. "Let's put him back now, give him a rest, then we'll show him his basket and you can feed him."

Molton raises the dog so they're eye-to-eye. "You really are handsome. Seems I have some competition in the house at last."

His daughter squeals with laughter, "Daddy, Daddy look."

Molton doesn't have to.

He knows what's happened.

"Well, that's a first," says his wife. "The President of the United States has just been peed on."

4

Six months later, Miami International Airport

*L*ost Luggage—a synonym for purgatory. A place of despair. A vortex of broken souls, eternal delays, and heartfelt losses.

Among the melancholic masses is Zoe Speed, twenty-six years old, five-foot-six, with spiky black hair and an attitude to match.

Exhausted and angry, she strides from the counter not at all convinced that her worldly goods will turn up via the next flight and be sent as promised to her friend's address. That big old brown trunk, plastered front-to-back with check-in stickers, has stayed loyally with her for years across countless countries and continents. It's survived a turbulent childhood, her parents' divorce, cross-state house moves, transatlantic holidays, and even boyfriend breakups. Nothing has shaken it from her side. Until now. Until a pissy flight from Maryland.

A-friggin-mazing.

She hurries outside the recently extended terminal, a daunting seven million square feet of aviation commerce. From her cavernous shoulder bag she produces her pouch of Drum Original and rolls together a smoke.

Goddamn United Airlines.

She was going to kick the habit, but this latest event has broken her resolve. Mentally, she ticks off what's missing. Makeup, sleeping tablets, birthday cards, favorite silk underwear a boyfriend gave her, dresses and shoes she bought for herself back in New York.

And her camera.

The center of her life.

The beautiful Hasselblad she'd won in a photographic contest while finishing her art and media studies degree. Everything else seems unimportant.

Zoe throws away half of her cigarette as she reaches the lower level ramp and catches the downtown bus. It's packed but she gets a seat near the luggage rack and tries to chill. There's no point getting wound up about things she can't control. She slips off her red cord jacket and takes long, slow breaths like her shrink told her to. With every exhalation a little anger disappears. Not as quickly as if she had some dope, but it goes nonetheless.

After fifteen stops, Zoe changes and catches the 22 out to Coconut Grove Station. She gets off at Nineteenth and Twenty-second, then starts to walk to the eastern end of Coral Way where her friend Jude lives.

The two women met at Johns Hopkins. Jude was doing straight ER studies and Zoe was on placement at the more exotically titled Department of Art (as Applied to Medicine), shooting features on reconstructive surgery.

It's as hot as hell out on the street and she's wishing she wasn't wearing jeans and the red Converse trainers that match her cord jacket. She makes another roll up as she strolls and is just licking the edge of the paper when an alarm sounds behind her.

It's the Citibank that she passed less than a minute ago.

A stocky man bundles his way down the sidewalk. His face is covered by a balaclava. A big black canvas bag is over a shoulder and a sawed-off shotgun in his hands.

Shoppers scream and scatter.

A young mom topples her baby's stroller trying to escape.

Zoe's feet stick to the sidewalk.

She's directly in his way.

5

Beijing

"Can you believe these people?" Pat Cornwell, Vice President of the United States, points at the television in the corner of the hotel's heavily guarded penthouse suite. "Do you have any idea what this program is about?"

Clint Molton looks across from the rosewood desk where he's revising his speech for the conclusion of tomorrow's G20 summit. "Some chat show, by the look of it. It's probably no worse than *Survivor* or *Big Brother,* Pat—and hey, don't even get me started on those other trashy reality shows we have."

"Well, unfortunately my Chinese is good enough to tell you it's worse. Much worse than that. This is *a pre-execution* interview show. Can you imagine? The guests go straight from this little tête-à-tête to their death. Some forty million Chinese sickos make a regular appointment to view this stuff."

The President takes off his reading glasses and stares at the TV. A well-dressed female presenter in her late forties is sitting uncomfortably in a scrubby room, flanked by uniformed prison guards. The camera cuts to a sobbing middle-aged man in orange prison overalls, manacles around his wrists and ankles.

"What's he done?"

The VP explains. "Killed his gay lover. It was a crime of passion. He came home and found his boyfriend in bed with another man. Everyone started beating on everyone and the guy cracked his head and died."

"Not Murder One—not even in Texas."

Pat continues his scathing commentary. "The prisoner's family has refused to see him before he's executed. They seem more ashamed of his sexuality than his crime."

"Well done, China."

The Vice President watches some more then turns to Molton, "Jeez, the prisoner just asked the presenter if she'd be generous enough to shake his hand before he goes to his death—said he dreamed of touching someone who doesn't want to hurt him before he dies."

"Emotional moment."

"You'd have thought so. Only this bitch says no. Says he deserves to suffer some more."

Molton shakes his head. "It's a different world out here, Pat. One that we've taken big bucks from, so we're going to have to get used to their ways."

"You can't get used to what's wrong—no matter how big their checks."

On screen, the inmate is hauled sobbing to his feet. The presenter turns her back on him to deliver a final address to the camera. A picture comes up of his dead lover. Then another of the two of them together. Finally, a shot of the place where he's going to be executed.

Pat opens the suite's minibar. "I need a drink or ten. You want one?"

"No thanks." Molton picks up the pen he's been correcting his speech with and looks across at his old friend. "You know, Pat, there are many Americans who would applaud that sentence. They are proud to back capital punishment, and a lot of our states are more than happy to throw the switch."

Pat pulls a Bud off a shelf and flicks the door closed. "These motherfuckers still execute more people than the rest of the world put together, and the numbers are going up, not down."

"Biggest population on the planet—one point four billion—I guess they're going to have more bad guys than the rest of us."

The VP pops the cap off his Bud and swigs it. Time to bite his tongue. He's said enough.

Molton watches the cold beer glug down. "Actually, I will have one of those. Thanks." He smiles at his friend. "By the way, if we showed execution chat shows, the audience would be at least twice what the Chinese get."

6

Miami

Zoe wonders how her day got so shit so quickly.

First the lost baggage, now she's caught slap bang between a fleeing bank robber and a brown getaway car that's just pulled out from a Taco Bell opposite the Citibank and flung open the passenger door.

She needs to step aside. Get the hell out of the way. And quick.

Only, giving ground is not in her nature.

She slips off her shoulder bag and the precious computer inside it.

The onrushing robber glances toward the car and the woman driving it.

Zoe lurches into a jump kick.

Her right foot cracks his chin. Hits him as hard as a baseball bat.

Blood and spit spatter through the balaclava mouth hole as his feet come up and the back of his head cracks the sidewalk.

His shotgun clatters across the ground toward the getaway car.

The guy tries to get to his feet, but Zoe's over him already. She drops knees first onto his chest. Knocks the wind out of him. Probably cracks a rib or two as well.

The getaway driver, a scruffy redhead in her late thirties, is out of the car by now and has her hands on the shotgun.

"Armed police! Drop it!"

Zoe is still on the guy's chest. She can't see the officer behind her, but given his booming voice, presumes the drama is now ending.

"Drop it, lady! I won't tell you again."

The closeness of the cop spooks the robber into one desperate dash for freedom. He wriggles free of Zoe and swings a desperate punch. She grabs his fist with both hands and twists the arm to breaking point. Self-defense training taught her that she needs to keep her grip as she shuffles her weight off his chest, spins him facedown and pulls his wrist painfully up his back.

The redhead sees her man is out of the game. She drops the shotgun. "Okay, okay don't fire that thing."

"Move away from the weapon and lie on the ground." The cop shuffles toward her, his gun extended, handcuffs trailing from one hand. "Do it quickly, ma'am. Come on. Facedown. Hands behind your back."

Zoe manages to turn her head. She sees the cop bent over the woman clicking cuffs around her wrists. He's freaky. Tall, white-haired, with very pale skin, wearing big dark shades and a smart light suit.

He looks at her. Picks up the shotgun. Reaches into his pocket for a pair of plastic standby ties. "Can you hold him a couple of seconds more?"

"No problem," she says. "This asshole's going nowhere."

"Glad to hear it." He walks over, puts a knee into the man's back and carries on talking as he yanks up the robber's wrists and ties them with the restraints. "That was quite a job you did." He gives her a second glance. "You hurt at all?"

"No, I'm fine." She catches herself staring at him. Everything about the guy is wonderfully wrong. He's too tall. *Way* too pale for Miami. Thin but athletic. And that white hair makes him look a whole generation older than the rest of his body suggests. She'd kill for her camera right now. For a chance to capture this cool white warrior in the middle of the sizzling hot action.

The cop sees her gawping but doesn't seem embarrassed as he casually hauls the prisoner to his feet and carries on chatting. "I'm Lieutenant Walton, Miami PD." He flips his ID for her. "I was close by when the call went out."

"Zoe Speed." She envisages him in a thousand shots—near a burst of neon signs, his whiteness against a zillion electric colors, or down on the beach, walking past racks of browned bodies, blue sky and blue sea as backdrops. The guy's a photographer's dream.

He nods suggestively toward her legs. "You might like to know that you've split your jeans."

She puts a hand down and feels that several of the fashionable frayed and stitched splits have torn into a gaping flap up the inside of her thigh.

He smiles and adds, "My guess is that unless you cover up, you'll soon be getting stared at even more than I am."

1

Beijing

*S*ixty-year-old Xian Sheng, President of the People's Republic of China, General Secretary of the Communist Party, Commander-in-Chief and Chairman of the Military Commission, clears the room of his minions. He wants to meet with Vice President Zhang in private.

Twenty years Xian's junior, General Zhang is the former leader of the Special Operations Forces and one of China's most decorated soldiers. His modernization of the army, crackdown on organized crime, and tolerance of "black jails"—secret detention centers for troublesome dissidents—have already marked him out as Xian's likely successor.

Zhang is more than happy to publicly display his cruel streak. Some weeks ago he invited news crews to film him personally flogging a group of young soldiers who'd been involved in petty gambling. When the elderly grandfather of one of the beaten men complained about the severity of the punishment, he had him publicly flogged as well.

The president's grand office doors are opened by flunkies. The general marches in. He is small and muscular, his black hair short, his dark eyes big and bright. There are no scars or wounds on his body, save a crescent-shaped burn across his chest, the result of a pan of boiling water his psychotic mother threw at him when he was a small child.

"Please sit," Xian motions to a chair.

Zhang obeys, legs and heels smartly together, shoulders back and spine straight. He wants Xian's job. Wants it now. But knows the only route to power is through obedience, patience, and a bold, name-making campaign such as Project Nian.

The president looks up from a fan of papers on his desk. "What progress do you have to report?"

"We are on plan and within budget. As you requested, we have fixed disinformation intelligence to ensure that if our deceit is uncovered, we will be able to make the world think it is solely the work of the North Koreans and nothing to do with us. We will be able to present ourselves as concerned intermediaries, trying to stop their reckless despotic ways."

Xian Sheng stares into the ambitious eyes locked on his old and tired ones. "I still have my reservations. Perhaps it is better to have sponsored this idea from afar, rather than with us insinuated in its development."

"Please do not have such doubts. Without our direct involvement, this idea would have been but a lotus flower strangled in a field of weeds."

"Have our scientists now reached the required standards and implemented the proper controls that we spoke of?"

"They are on course to do so, and still within the given operational timetable."

The president senses he is being economical with the truth. "I am relying on you to ensure there will be only minimal casualties, Zhang. *Minimal*. Do I make myself clear?"

"Yes, sir."

The words ring hollow. "The party has given you their full support, as have I. Nian creates a powerful weapon to use against our enemies—but we must be able to fully control it, or else we are like a sleepy child with a loaded gun." His face grows sterner. "Remember, I only supported this project of yours with the understanding that you could deliver the behavioral modifiers that you promised."

"I remember well. Work on the modifiers is advanced enough for us not to be held up. I will not let you down"

"I *know* you won't." Xian prays he is right. In truth, he realizes there is already too much support among the military council for the project to be stopped.

"Mr. President, with respect, I think the Americans will be more skeptical and stubborn than you expect. As a race, they are both arrogant and ignorant. They believe they will never be held accountable for their actions, that irresponsibility is allowable if it is gross enough and blatant enough."

"Do not underestimate them, Zhang. President Molton presides over a country in the midst of extreme difficulties. History has taught us that when people are in the greatest danger they are capable of the greatest victories."

"Yes, sir."

"You have done well. I will speak with Molton after the summit. If he is not open to our offer, then as planned you must go ahead and meet with the head of the NIA and tell him of the consequences of such foolishness."

"I understand, sir. I have arranged to see him in the morning just before our military escort takes the presidential party back to Air Force One."

"Let us hope it does not come to that." Xian waves him away. "Go now and prepare your actions, while I prepare my words. Tomorrow we will see which is to control the way forward."

8

Miami

Rubberneckers crowd the sidewalk. Police sirens scythe the sultry afternoon air.

Members of an armed response unit—dispatched somewhat unnecessarily, as far as Walton's concerned—argue with a handful of regular cops about who takes possession of the cuffed prisoners.

Eventually the weapons men win. They get to walk away without doing the paperwork on the robbery, which also means not being snagged for subsequent court time. Grudgingly, a couple of uniforms traipse off to start interviews at the Citibank. Others haul the offenders away in separate green-striped Crown Vics.

Walton finishes briefing a sergeant and looks for Zoe. He sees her over in a pool of shade, leaning against the gnarled trunk of a palm, her black canvas bag back over her shoulder. She's shooting pictures on a smartphone. Interestingly, not of the prisoners but of him.

He walks toward her with his hand up, blocking the shot. "I'd rather you didn't do that."

She frowns. "Why?"

"Because I'm in the middle of doing my job and it pisses me off." He finger jabs shades back up his nose. "There are some paramedics up there, treating customers and bank tellers for shock. Having a gun waved in your face is alarming to most people. Maybe it would be good to get yourself checked out before I ask you some questions?"

"I'm not most people and I don't need checking, but thanks." She snaps a final close-up, smiles and walks past him.

"I still need to ask you some questions."

"Then ask away." She carries on walking.

"Hang on."

Zoe stops.

"You want to go for a drink, or something?"

She turns and hits him with a mischievous grin. "You asking me out?"

He laughs at her cheekiness. "I just thought after your ordeal you might want some water or coffee while I ask you the kind of questions cops have to ask."

"I don't. And it wasn't an ordeal. What *I want* is to go to my friend's house, just off the bottom of Coral Way. How about you give me a lift there and do your question shit on the way?"

He pulls a quizzical look. "My question shit?"

"Yeah, your question shit." She notices he has a nice smile.

"I guess I can. Follow me." He turns and walks across to the other side of the road.

Zoe tags behind him and sneaks several more shots. This time, of the long shadows he casts on the blacktop.

Walton stops at the passenger side of a '58 Dodge, a great big boat of a car, full of dents, ginger rust, and tarnished chrome. It's what his colleagues call "a Dumpster on wheels."

"What the *holy fuck* is this?" Zoe tentatively touches the mottled door handle.

"Custom Royal Lancer—Swept Wing. Not many made."

"I can see why." She jerks open the door and cautiously slides onto the worn white leather front seat.

Walton gets in the other side and slips a key into the ignition. "One day I'll do her up, and then this baby and me are gonna cruise coast-to-coast."

"Yeah, and one day I'll be chief photographer for AP or Reuters and have a Manhattan loft bigger than a football field."

"That what you want?"

"Yeah, maybe. An old snapper in NYC told me to look him up when I qualified. I guess he's only after getting in my pants, but I figure in a few months' time I'll give it a try."

"Which bit? The getting sexually assaulted bit or the job lead?"

"I think they go together."

Classical notes spill out of hidden door speakers.

The choice of music takes Zoe by surprise. "Mahler?"

"Resurrection."

"I thought that all cops listened to was bad-ass rap and Armageddon rock."

"Kinda like that too." He grins boyishly. The rebuilt V8 coughs through smoky pipes as he hits the gas. "You said you'd come from the airport, where did you fly in from?"

"Maryland."

"No bags?"

"Not anymore. Carrier lost them somewhere. Supposedly, they're going to deliver them later."

"Yeah, good luck with that."

"Tell me about it. Got my camera in there. It's like losing a limb." She leans forward and examines the car's dash. "Is the air-con on?"

"Only air-con is the window. Roll it down for *cool*, up for hot."

"Sophisticated." She cranks the handle and the sheet of glass drops in heavy jerks. From being alongside Walton she can see beyond his shades for the first time. "You're albinoid, right?" She looks pleased with her diagnosis. "And the shades are prescriptive not decorative because your albinism is oculocutaneous."

"Ten on ten. Though I got lucky."

"How so?"

"Well, I'm light sensitive—very sensitive. So I need reactive lenses, but my vision is perfect, so they let me be a cop."

"That's unusual. Albinism usually comes with bad eyesight."

"Like I said, I got lucky. And I guess, because you know so much about this weird little twist of genetics, you were a med student from Johns Hopkins before you switched to photography. Which in turn, would explain why a girl with a New York accent is flying in from Maryland."

"You're close."

"What'd I get wrong?"

"Well, I never studied medicine. Always wanted to be a photographer. After this stay with a friend, with or without help from the old perv in NYC, I'm planning on going there and starting up as a freelance photojournalist. Did an arts degree but spent a lot of time snapping doctors at work—and patients too." She's done disclosing so she shuts her eyes and enjoys a blast of cool wind from the open window.

"And patients included albinos?"

"Aha." She opens her eyes and looks across the seats to him. "You know what?"

"Yeah, I know *'what'* intimately. What about *'what'*?"

"If that offer of a drink still stands, then I'd be happy to take you up on it."

9

Miami

*F*ew people hate their jobs as much as thirty-two-year-old Huey Dunbar hates his. The two-hundred-pound, former car salesman detests the beach, loathes local history, and couldn't give an owl's hoot for the famous wildlife that apparently is in abundance around him.

After he lost his sales position, the best straw he could pull was one as a lighthouse guide over at the Bill Baggs Cape in Key Biscayne. Dressed in white sneakers, a baggy white shirt, and shorts as brown as his crew-cut hair, he plods past the coconut trees and climbs the twisting spiral of metal steps inside the whitewashed tower.

Partway up he wipes sweat from his face with the pristine handkerchief that his wife pressed last night and popped into his pocket. He folds it back along the creases and tries to inject enthusiasm into the patter he plies to the party of Japanese tourists trailing him: "The lighthouse you're ascending is recognized as the oldest structure in South Florida and was placed on the National Register of Historic Places in 1971. It was restored in 1967–70 and again in 1992–96." As he pauses for breath, a lightning storm of camera flashes illuminates his face. Half blind, he blusters on. "*This* is the only lighthouse to have been attacked by Indians. A U.S. Army base was then built here to protect the land and sea from subsequent attacks."

Huey turns his back on more flashes. He heads up the stairs to the lens room and the outside observation deck. It's the part groups always like best. They get to gawp and wonder at life from on high, while he stares vacantly out to sea and dreams of doing anything but this.

The guide looks back at his obedient charges. "You're all going to have to be careful coming in here. Hold onto the rails and take it in turns. One at a time, until I usher you through. Be careful now and no pushing."

He points an educational finger, "From the platform you can see the park and the skyline of the city of Miami. The beach out there is one of the top ten stretches of sand in the United States— and look over here," he points away at forty-five degrees, "you can see a lot of new homes, built after Andrew blew through like the end of the world was coming."

The tourists file in and out. Huey gets a minute to himself on the platform. He swings up the binoculars that now perpetually hang around his neck and looks out to sea. Some rich guys are racing each other on Honda jet skis, cutting up white surf as they zig and zag without a care in the world. Out on the prow of a million-dollar yacht a supermodel blonde in a haute couture black bikini braces herself then performs a perfect-legs-together swan dive into the aquamarine water.

Huey swings the glasses toward the shore where the poorer people play. Kids are running around laughing and screaming. They splash each other with wild enthusiasm, completely un-aware of the shit that awaits them when they graduate and have to find jobs and pay their own way.

And dammit, there's a dog down there too.

An Alsatian or another big breed like it. He guesses some ass-hole has ignored the No Pets signs and let the thing roam free.

There are no lifeguards out on the beach these days, so rules never get religiously enforced.

Huey reaches for the radio on his hip and then thinks, What the hell? Someone brought a pet to the beach, so what? He's not going to call the Ranger Station and get them all the way down here just to chase a mutt.

The animal, a stupid one by the look of it, scampers through the surf trying to eat the waves. A group of teenage girls get spooked and shout a little as they head for the dry sand.

One of the other girls takes a tumble and the dog circles her, wanting to play. Maybe it's her pet. She's on her back now and it's climbing all over her, eager for a game.

Huey refocuses.

"Holy Christ!" The dog isn't playing. It's turned nasty and is snarling at her.

Huey radios the Rangers. "Control, this is the lighthouse, we have an emergency out on the beach, a dog looks like it's about to attack a female bather."

There's a hiss and sizzle of static before a female controller comes back to him. "We're on it, Lighthouse. Someone already called it in."

The girl is still on her back, kicking out as the dog snaps. People are standing around but no one is helping.

The animal lunges and finds flesh.

A vicious bite into her left leg.

She screams.

It shakes its snarling head and pulls her in the sand.

More screams.

The dog begins to drag her away, like a hunk of meat stolen from a butcher's shop.

Huey shouts into his radio "Where the hell *are* you guys? This thing is *killing* her!"

He refocuses the binoculars.

The animal bites into her neck.

The girl's head flops.

There are no screams now.

No sounds at all from her.

Or the beach.

Just the dog slobbering and chewing.

People around Huey are sobbing.

"Come on folks, let's go back inside." He ushers them through to the lens room.

As Huey pulls the door shut he hears the crack of gunfire.

One. Two. Three quick shots.

A pause.

Two final cracks.

"It's all over," he says without even looking, "The Rangers just shot the dog. So, everything's fine now."

10

Miami

*W*alton parks his Dodge at the corner of Twelfth and Third, closes her up and looks back with pride. It's not a car; it's automotive art. Just as Miami is not a city, it's a life installation.

He and Zoe grab coffee at Angelo's, a gourmet café that he's been coming to ever since he discovered the difference between instant and ground.

He takes her statement over his two espressos, her numerous extra-vanilla Crèmappuccinos, and a plate of home-baked brownies.

Once they are down to the crumbs, Walton hands over a Miami police business card. "This is me, and my numbers. Someone from Robbery will ring and follow up with you. They'll keep you apprised of court dates and such like." He signals for the check then gets to his feet. "Excuse me, for a minute. I need to visit the restroom, then I'll take you to your friend's place."

"Thanks." As he disappears, she looks at the card.

LIEUTENANT I. WALTON
Specialized Operations Unit

I.

She wonders what the letter stands for.

Most likely Ian.

Surely not something like Isaac or Ibrahim?

She can't think of any others.

Igor?

No, he's definitely not an Igor.

Zoe is still guessing when the cop comes back. He seems edgy.

"Sorry." He gestures with his cell phone, "I just got a call from Dispatch. I'm afraid I'm going to have to leave you here."

"What?" She looks distinctly pissed.

"There's an emergency at the beach on Key Biscayne."

She gets to her feet. "What kind of emergency?"

He sees no harm in saying. "Some dog has gone crazy. Killed a girl. I don't think anyone else has been hurt."

The photojournalist inside her surfaces. "Can I tag along?"

"Not a good idea." He shoots her a disapproving look as he goes to the counter to settle the check. "There will be enough ghouls down there without me bringing more." He turns to a small, dark-haired guy in his late fifties. "*Muchas gracias,* Angelo."

Zoe stands stunned by the insult.

Walton puts down an extra twenty. "Could you please call a cab for the lady? It shouldn't cost more than ten to fifteen to get her to her friend's."

"Sure. No problem." Angelo takes the bill and turns to Zoe as he reaches for a phone. "You ready to go now, lady?"

"Yeah, I'm ready." She watches Walton leave without even saying goodbye. "Not big on manners, is he?"

Angelo looks up and smiles as the door bangs shut. "Ghost? Ghost is a perfect gentleman—until you piss him off. Then you'd better watch out."

▌▌

G20 Meeting, Beijing

The twenty leaders of the largest economies in the world stand shoulder-to-shoulder on the stage of the conference hall. They shake hands vigorously and smile perfectly for the official end of summit photographs.

Between them, they control a staggering eighty percent of the world's trade. Along with their finance ministers and bank governors, they are what make the world's businesses tick.

At the center of the shot are the three most powerful men on the planet. Clint Molton, President of the United States; Xian Sheng, head of the People's Republic of China; and Vladimir Stanislaw, leader of the Government of the Russian Federation.

When the last click of the cameras has been taken, Molton and Xian retire to a guarded side room for a very private discussion.

They settle in soft executive chairs made from caramel-colored leather, and the American gets the niceties out of the way: "Sheryl and I want to thank you again for your wonderful gift. The kids *adore* the dog. He's already very much one of the family."

Xian Sheng seems pleased. "I am very glad to hear this. May you enjoy many years of happiness together." He looks down at the rich, rigid grain of the heavy mahogany table that separates them and seems to study it for a moment. When he raises his head, the warmth has gone from his eyes. "Mr. President, your words at the close of the summit today gave Chinese people little comfort. Your debt to my country is more than two trillion dollars—and it is rising all the time. Yet all you speak of is the need for more trade and more expansion."

Molton leans forward. "I hope you understand, we have to generate greater revenues and profit overseas to service our debts. Either that or we face a currency devaluation and further downgrading of our credit status. My words, Mr. Xian, were about ambition and optimism, vital qualities as we *all* strive for growth."

"Words are not enough. And the interest you pay on loans is also not enough. We are no longer confident you can settle what you owe."

Molton leans back in his chair. "The United States has always honored its debts, and always will."

There is an awkward pause.

The Chinese leader runs his hands slowly over his slick black hair, then delivers the lines he's been rehearsing for days. "Mr. President—I have a proposition for you. A radical but practical one."

"I'm always open to offers, sir."

"China wants to *waive* your debts. Forget them completely. Treat the money as a real investment in your country and help the United States grow."

"That's very kind of you." Molton smiles diplomatically. "Why do I suspect this isn't the altruistic offer it seems?"

"In return for our two trillion dollars of loans *and* the interest payable on them—we want to own ten percent of America."

Molton smiles—he isn't sure he's heard the Chinese leader correctly. "I'm sorry, what exactly do you mean?"

"Think of United States like a company. A company in big trouble. Think of China like an angel investor. Angel gives two trillion dollars to help the troubled company. In return, United States pays us ten percent of all future taxes raised—*in perpetuity*, forever."

"I know what in perpetuity means. And the answer is no. The whole idea is as ludicrous and insulting to me as it would be to the American people." Molton gets to his feet to leave. "Thank you again for your hospitality, here in Beijing. We already have a signed and executed financial arrangement and we intend to honor it, as must the Chinese government."

Xian doesn't rise. "Mr. President, United States's foreign debts are fourteen trillion dollars—that is now bigger than the United States's annual revenues. China has enough influence in Asia and across the world—especially with our friends in Russia—to control almost half of your debt holders. Maybe more. You should take China's offer now at ten percent, or in the near future you will be forced to accept a not so generous offer."

Molton is almost at the door, "What did you just say?" He strides back to the table; fully aware his manners have gone. "Only, I'm really hoping I misheard you, because that sounded a whole lot like a threat to me."

Xian finally gets to his feet. He stays perfectly calm in the shadow of a man almost twice his size. "It was no threat, Mr. President—it is a promise. We have the power to *save* your economy or *ruin* it. You have the power to choose."

Molton glares at him, then turns and storms out.

The leader of the People's Republic of China calmly sits again. With a steady hand he pours a glass of water.

Before he finishes his first sip, the door is opened by General Zhang. "It went as I predicted?"

Xian puts his glass down. "Yes, you were right. Molton is deaf to my words and has chosen the path of ultimate actions. You must speak with Director Jackson before he leaves in the morning and intimate what terrible repercussions follow in the President's wake."

12

Bill Baggs Park, Miami

*B*y the time Walton gets to the scene, police patrols have sealed off a crescent-shaped area of the beach, south of Cape Florida Park Boulevard. They've also closed the park entrances and are searching cars and questioning pedestrians in order to find the owner of the killer dog.

Away from the uniformed cops, two white tents stand out on the now eerily empty sand.

One covers the body of a seventeen-year-old girl just identified as Kathy Morgan, an only child from Richmond Heights out in South Miami.

The other contains the animal that ripped her to pieces.

Walton signs in with a scenes-of-crime officer, passes through the fluttering tape and starts across the beach. A sea breeze tugs his trademark linen suit, and he feels the sun uncomfortably warm on his thin, white hair and his milky, pale skin.

Miami's blue sky has turned gray and the sea looks slow

and sad now, as though it knows what happened and understands it would be wrong to be boisterous at a time like this.
Music strikes up in Ghost's mind. It's gentler than the Mahler
in the Dodge—the achingly painful violin solo at the start of
Rimsky-Korsakov's *Scheherazade* with its melancholy flutter of
harp strings.

Behind the stylish shades that he almost never removes, his
pink pupils scan the scene for clues. He follows the path CSIs
have marked across the sand with their iron poles and yellow
tape.

The front of the nearest tent opens, and he greets forty-year-
old Medical Examiner Gerry Stockman. "Man, this is too beautiful a place to witness an accident as ugly as this."

"Sure is, Ghost." Stockman is kitted out in full white Tyvek suit
and wears blue rubber gloves—a testament to his long-standing
allergy to latex. "And when you see what's in here, you may rethink
your definition of the word 'ugly.'" He holds back the tent flap.
"Look but don't step in. Forensics hasn't been here yet."

The music in the detective's head is gone now. All he hears is
the buzz of flies, drawn to the unexpected feast of violated organs
and drying blood. He absorbs the visual brutality, blots up its violence and all the emotional pain he imagines the girl's family will
endure, until the only thing left is the puzzle of what happened.
"Where's the rest of her?"

The M.E. lets the flap fall and points across the sand. "There
are flesh and bone fragments spread for twenty to thirty yards,
some blood pooling where the dog stopped briefly, and then this
mess here, right where it was shot. The thing ripped her limb from
limb. Would probably have attacked others if a Ranger hadn't
killed it."

"Dog shouldn't have been on the beach in the first place."

Ghost nods toward a sign. "Rangers should have been quicker in acting."

"Always good to be wise *after* the event." Stockman knows the lieutenant of old, Ghost's lack of tolerance as legendary as his physical appearance. The M.E. takes a slim video camera out of an overall pocket and starts filming. CSIs will shoot comprehensive footage, but he wants his own as well. "The vet is already here. She's in the other tent."

Ghost looks out to the waves as he walks away. Sharp lights glint from boats bobbing on the sparkling water. He knows instantly what they are.

Cameras.

When the beaches were shut off, the photojournalists took to the ocean.

Two white-suited CSIs exit the tent he's heading toward. They open steel cases and unfold sample bags in preparation for the grisly evidence that has to be recovered.

Ghost ducks into the plastic shelter covering the forensic vet.

What he sees stops him in his tracks.

The dog is massive. Much bigger than he'd expected. It has huge legs and a giant square face that looks like it's been fashioned out of steel.

A plump, dark-haired woman in her mid-thirties is on her knees, covered in forensic whites and with a blue mask around her mouth. She looks up at him quizzically. "Sandra Teale, and you are?"

He slides ID out of his jacket, "Lieutenant Walton."

"You with the Canine Section?"

"No, Special Ops. I'm just the guy in the wrong place at the wrong time—and apparently the one they give all the weird and crappy jobs to."

She laughs. "Me too."

He squats alongside her. "Any microchip that will give us the owner's address?"

"Might well be, but I've not had time to run a scanner yet. I'll do it back at the lab and let you know."

"Thanks." He peers quizzically at the animal. "What kind of dog is it?"

"Cross breed—though I'm not sure exactly *what* has been crossed with what."

"Mike Tyson and a wolf, by the look of it."

He dimly recalls a course about dangerous dogs that he attended as a rookie. "That thing has a broad, deep chest and muscular shoulders—aren't they traits of a pit bull?"

"They are, but this isn't a pure pit, it's a mutt. I suspect someone was kenneling pits and then when the breed became regarded as dangerous, they started to cross them with other dogs to try to make them more sellable. It looks part mastiff and part something else—maybe German shepherd."

Ghost points at a wound. "I need the bullets when you dig them out. Just a formality for when we bring charges."

"Of course." Teale puts a gloved finger and thumb around one of the entry holes. "I'll send the slugs to Ballistics as soon as we get this big guy back to the lab and start our tests."

"It's a *him*?"

"Oh yeah." She lifts its back leg to prove her point. "*Very definitely* a him."

13

Coral Way, Miami

*T*he cab drops Zoe at a small building on a block opposite a Greek restaurant. At the door, she presses a buzzer marked CUN-NINGHAM.

A tinny voice squawks out of a wall-mounted Intercom. *"Hello."*

"Jude, it's Zoe."

There's a howl of excitement, then the muffled thud of feet descending stairs. The brown front door bursts open and a beaming Jude Cunningham bounces out and smothers her in a hug.

"Let me breathe," jokes Zoe.

"Wow! I can't believe you're actually here." The chubby blonde looks her over, then stares quizzically at the sidewalk near her feet. "Where's your baggage?"

"Don't ask. Probably somewhere in Alaska."

"Come inside and tell me." She holds the front door and reveals a tidy hallway leading off to four doors and a short flight of stairs to another four. "I was getting worried—your plane landed hours ago."

"I know." Zoe starts the climb. "There was a robbery around the corner and I got caught up in it."

"Oh my God. Anyone hurt?"

"Only the robber." As an afterthought she adds, "And my Levi's. I split them." She lifts a leg to demonstrate.

"Not a good look, sister." At the top of the stairs, Jude lets her in through an open door to the left. "Here you are—home away from home, for as long as you like."

"You might live to regret that." Zoe stares into a bright open room with white walls and a big window. The floors are bare boards sanded and polished to make them look "olde world." Fresh flowers stand in a fat-belly glass vase on a junk wood dining table with leather benches either side. "It's nice. You've made it really homey."

"Thanks." Jude walks her along a short corridor. "Your room's through here. Barely big enough to fit a cat let alone swing it— but hey, it's got a new bed and fresh linen."

"It looks lovely." Zoe tries to sound convincing.

"It'll look a whole lot better when we've opened a bottle of wine or two."

They head into the kitchen laughing, and Zoe checks her watch. "Shoot, I didn't realize it's so late. Mind if I call my brother Danny in New York? I've been trying all day and we keep missing each other. I promised I'd ring when I settled."

"Sure, the phone's by the door."

"Nah, it's okay. I still got credit on my cell." She pulls the phone out of her jeans pocket and dials.

Danny's three years older but is a constant worry for her. He runs with a bad crowd. Always seems to be up to shady stuff. Never wants to talk about what he's doing or who he's doing it for.

Zoe virtually brought him up after the family broke apart. Dad ran off with a younger woman and Mom hit the bottle. Almost overnight Zoe became the anchor of her brother's life. When she moved to Maryland, she half expected him to trail in her wake. It was a relief that he stayed in NYC to live on his own.

His phone trips to voice mail: "This is Danny, I'm busy doing other stuff, leave your details after the beep."

"Shit." She kills the call and puts her hand out for the glass of wine that Jude is offering. "God knows what he's up to. One day that boy's gonna get himself in big trouble."

14

The White House, Washington DC

*T*he press corps is lapping it up. America's First Lady and her gorgeous kids playing on the White House's famous Rose Garden lawns with a million-dollar Chinese dog, while President Pop is away in Beijing battling with the Asian business bores.

It's a classic photo opportunity.

And the dog is a wow as well. The Tibetan mastiff practically poses for shots. Tilts his cute head and shakes his thick double coat of fur as the kids hang onto his big neck and all but ride him.

Sheryl Molton gathers the pet and her two children beside a lectern and microphone to say a final few words before disappearing back inside. "Thank you all for coming. Emperor, Jack, Jane, and myself all hope you managed to get the pictures that you wanted and had as much fun as we did."

A reporter raises a hand, and when a press aide gives him the nod, he calls out a double-edged question "Jan Bolz, *Modern Dog* magazine—can you tell us, has Emperor already had all his shots and been microchipped?"

"He has. The President and I are big believers in animal welfare and owner responsibility. He's up-to-date on all his inoculations and has been chipped and registered—though, as I'm sure you'll agree, the chance of us losing him are pretty thin."

The remark draws laughter from across the lawns and even a

smile from the Secret Service men standing guard in their suits and shades.

"Anna Arit, *Washington Post*. Could you tell us, ma'am, are Asian dogs trickier to tame than American ones?"

There's laughter at the double entendre before the First Lady even starts to answer.

"In my experience, *all* dogs are tricky to tame. Ask any wife or mom in the country and if she's got *a dog* in her life she'll tell you they're always out making a mess somewhere."

More laughter and a ripple of applause fills the gardens.

"Ian McLoughlin, CNN. How is the President getting along with his new foreign friend? Has he already managed to establish himself as its master?"

Sheryl Molton senses the allusions are getting a little too close for comfort. "Hey, for a start, the President knows there's only one boss in my house, and I can tell you it's not him or the dog!" She decides to quit while she's ahead. "Thanks again, folks, I hope you all have a good day."

The cameras click like crazy as the First Family and Emperor walk away, waving and smiling in the Washington sunshine.

Once back inside the privacy of the West Wing, Sheryl asks herself the same question, and suspects her husband is having a far more difficult time with President Xian than anyone expects.

15

Downtown, Miami

The distraught faces of Kathy Morgan's parents are still burned in Ghost's mind as he drives away from work.

Over the years, he's learned to objectify victims as much as possible.

He's taught himself to see them as the central part of a cryptic puzzle that needs total focus and clarity of mind to crack. But he's never been completely successful at blocking out the person, and with it, all the human pain. Personal empathy and emotion seep like acid through whatever professional barriers he erects. Right now he's aching for Derek and Amy Morgan, wishing they'd never had to stand in that cold morgue and had a sheet pulled back to reveal the remains of their beloved child.

He tries to shut off work as he lets himself into a three-bedroom penthouse in the city's Historic District. The prime real estate has been in the family for decades, passed to him when his very successful, elderly parents died a few years back.

Around him is a stretch of land and key buildings bounded by Miami Court, North Third Street, West Third Avenue, and South Second Street. Most of what catches the eye was built during the Florida land boom of the 1920s, including the building that dominates the view from Ghost's front window. The Freedom Tower over at the Miami Dade College is a prime piece of Spanish Renaissance architecture, built in '25 as a print works for the *Miami News*. In the 1960s the federal government took it over, in order to process documents and provide health support for refugees fleeing from Castro's Cuba. That's when it got the iconic name Freedom Tower. These days it's more famous for the art exhibitions held there. Ghost has spent many an hour mesmerized by the works of Dali, Goya, and Da Vinci.

The walls of his apartment are filled with an eclectic and ever-changing mix of paintings by upcoming artists. His dealings in this world, like his activities in the stock and bond markets, brings him an annual income more than five times his police salary.

The first thing he does after kicking off his shoes is put on music.

Not from an iPod in a docking station, or a computer with endless, digitally streamed tracks, but from a vintage Bang and Olufsen gramophone that copes with anything vinyl from 33 rpm right back to a good old-fashioned 78.

He gently places one of his favorite discs on the turntable. It's Mindru Katz's live performances of Liszt's Piano Concerto No. 2 in A Major.

The master composer's melancholic opening is momentarily lost in the culinary clatter that Ghost creates in the kitchen. He may live on his own, but that doesn't stop him eating well. Tonight he's starting with fried foie gras and chicken livers on French toast, followed by pan-roasted veal chops and spinach.

He opens a bottle of Châteauneuf-du-Pape, Domaine de la Janasse, Vieilles Vignes. He swirls it in a large, round-bowled crystal glass, smells and sips. It's an '04 vintage, and on reflection he wishes he'd kept it a little while longer. The Grenache is still a summer too young for his palate.

Ghost slides open a door and takes his food to a table on the muggy balcony. The sound of piano music follows him and flows off the edge of the penthouse down into the distant, humming sea of life forty floors below.

As he eats, he flips open the file on today's case.

Already he has multiple pictures of the poor girl who was bitten to death. Dozens of statements. Maps of the dead zone and surrounding area. And a summary that says no one has a clue who owns the killer dog.

It's the kind of murder puzzle he's pieced together many times before: Who did what and to whom? Where did it happen and when? But the conundrum has never been quite as strange as this.

Why?

That's the most puzzling question of all.

Why?

Why did a dog turn on a kid? Why did it get so vicious? Why couldn't anyone find the owner?

He changes the record. Picks Tchaikovsky. More fairy-tale than Liszt. More scope to open up the imagination and let the thoughts break free.

He picks up one of the photographs in the file and closely examines the head of the giant animal. It has teeth like spiked railings. Vicious. Merciless. *"Canis lupus familiaris,"* he says, reminding himself that the ancestor of man's best friend is not Lassie the Wonder Dog, but the wolf. A blood-hungry apex predator. Unhunted, except by humans. The king at the very top of the animal food chain.

16

Beijing

*A*ir pollution hits a record high in China's capital city as another day breaks and the world leaders begin to head home from their summit.

General Zhang, Vice President of the People's Republic of China, turns away from the window of the hotel suite and faces his breakfast guest, forty-seven-year-old Brandon Jackson, the youngest black man to become Director of National Intelligence and the principal advisor to the President, the National Security Council, and the Homeland Security Council.

"I'm told our leaders had something of a disagreement last

night," General Zhang says. "President Xian and I are keen you do not leave our city having misunderstood matters."

"Don" Jackson has been briefed, and more than expected a "final word" from Zhang, a man widely regarded as the future president of China. "I don't think there is any misunderstanding, General. You are concerned about repayments of our debts and you suggested an alternative method of financing them. A method we have politely declined. There is no *ill* feeling. We can all move on and continue to grow good relations between our great countries."

"Aah." Zhang wags a finger indicatively. "This is what we feared. Mr. Jackson, I invited you here because there are things you may understand better than your President."

"There is very little President Molton doesn't understand, General Zhang."

"Allow me to show you something." He walks across the room and motions to a black leather settee. "Please sit while I close the curtains."

Jackson eases himself onto the hard two-seater. The room grows black. A ceiling-mounted projector throws a pool of bright light onto a wall.

"We have discovered a new form of terrorism, 'genetic terrorism,' which we fear may be used against you. Please watch."

Video footage flickers onto the wall. Jackson can tell it's shot from aerial cameras, mounted in planes or helicopters. Men in orange jumpsuits spill from a number of parked buses. They start to run. First all together, then they divide into smaller groups. It looks at first like some army challenge. Maybe a competition like in the Japanese game show *Endurance*.

Then it's apparent this is no game.

Lionlike beasts are attacking men. It's a bizarre form of Roman torture updated and played out in a desert rather than the Coliseum.

The camera zooms in.

Jackson sees jaws sink into thighs, faces, sides, and stomachs. Blood spills and dries almost instantly on the scorching sand. Now it's clear that the animals are dogs. Some are huge and incredibly muscular, the likes of which he's never seen before. Others are small, terrierlike, but maybe even more aggressive than the larger ones.

There is a cut in the video, a second or two of black frames. The camera pans over dismembered, disemboweled, and decapitated corpses.

The screen goes blank.

Zhang flicks on the room's lights.

Jackson swivels around to face him. "What the hell was that?"

Zhang smiles comfortably. Nothing is more pleasing to him than seeing his enemy morally distressed. "It has come from military sources, intelligence we cannot disclose but we know to be reliable. The dogs you saw have been genetically weaponized by a terror group who are enemies of America. They are capable of carnage far worse than you saw."

"What terror group?"

"I cannot say."

"Cannot or will not?"

"Let me put it like this." Zhang paces slowly. "China can stop this third party threat. We have enough influence with the country behind the terrorists to protect America and its allies from it. That is, *should* China *want* to." He stops intrusively close to the American and leans on the arm of the sofa. "Should we have a long-term interest in doing so."

Jackson stares through him. "Are you somehow connecting

your crazy taxation demands to an even crazier story that we need your protection from some tin-pot terror state and a pack of rabid dogs?"

"No I am not." He couldn't look more smug if he tried. "I am telling you that this weapon has already been deployed. These animals are already in your country and killing your people."

"What are you talking about?"

"Open your eyes, Mr. Jackson. You have a death in Miami. A young girl killed by a dog on a beach. Do you think that was an accident?"

"What?"

Zhang can tell the American hasn't yet heard about it. "Look into it. You will find that this is no normal dog-related death. Then, think of these canines as though they are hidden like genetic bombs. Thousands of them lie gently on your floors, just waiting to explode."

"You're right; I have no knowledge of any such incident. But let me get this right, you're saying it's been caused by one of these weaponized dogs and there are more of them?"

"This is what I am told by our intelligence sources. Of course it might not be true. But if it is, then puppies that American children are petting today—" He sighs resignedly. "—may well turn into their killers overnight."

Jackson's temper boils over. "If you have information that can save American lives—if there is so much as *an iota* of truth in this craziness—then I demand that you tell me right now who is behind this."

Zhang laughs. "You 'demand'? The days when America 'demanded' anything of China are over, Mr. Jackson." He points dismissively to the door, "I think it's about time you made your way to your colleagues and reminded President Molton of the generous offer President Xian has made him."

The NIA chief stands two feet from the general and stares into his eyes as only a trained interrogator can. He's looking for bluff, bravado, and bullshit. Some human sign that explains all the nonsense he's just seen and heard.

There's nothing.

Nothing but an inscrutable coldness.

Zhang gestures to the door. "My office will fix a follow-up call with you—I know you *will* need it."

17

Coral Way, Miami

*T*he sun of a bright new day penetrates the spare room shutters and wakes Zoe from a deep sleep.

She squints at the window holding back the jagged heat, climbs painfully out of the hard single bed in Jude's spare room, pulls on her only T-shirt and her damaged jeans, then pads barefoot to the kitchen.

Jude is sitting in pink and white pajamas nursing a hangover the size of Russia. A small TV churns out news, the volume turned down low. She takes one look at Zoe and grimaces. "You look like the walking dead. Remind me to lend you some clothes."

"Thanks. What I *really need* is water and coffee."

"Yes, ma'am." Jude climbs out of her seat and heads to the pot bubbling away on a worktop. "Would m'lady like anything else before I make up the beds, clean the floors, and do the laundry?"

"Silence would be great. My head is collapsing."

"That'll be the vodka shots. You're becoming a lightweight." She pours a mug of black coffee and puts it down along with a glass of water. "I'll get you some pills."

Zoe sits at the table and squints at the TV. Dollar crisis. More states following Detroit and going bankrupt. More unemployed. No wonder people drink so much.

"Here, enjoy." Jude places a plastic tub of Ibuprofen on the table.

Zoe shakes out 600 mg of tablets and forces them down with the water. It's way above the recommended dose but she has a lead-lined gut and frankly anything less won't do the trick.

She squints again at the TV.

Some serial killer has been executed in Texas. Good fucking riddance. And in Miami, a schoolgirl's been killed in a dog attack. "Hey, I know that guy." She points at a six-inch Ghost walking the screen. Some good-looking male reporter is trudging beside him on a beach, sticking a microphone across his chest.

Jude turns the sound up. "That's the cop who took you for coffee?"

"Very same."

The male reporter is just starting a new question, "Forensic scientists and a pathologist were seen out on the sands yesterday. Are their investigations finished now or will they be coming back?"

Ghost walks as he answers, "Initial investigation of the scene has been concluded and the beach has been reopened to the public. We haven't yet identified the owner of the dog that attacked the deceased and we'd be grateful for any help the public can give us."

"Do you have any theories about what went wrong here?"

He hesitates for a second. "An increasing amount of people are irresponsibly abandoning animals that they've grown bored with. Pets they can't afford to feed or have treated at the vet's—so we may well be looking at the result of such an abandonment."

"Thank you, Lieutenant Walton." The reporter turns directly

to the camera to start a Q&A with the local studio anchor. A caption crawls across the bottom of the screen naming the dead girl as seventeen-year-old Kathy Morgan and gives a police number for people to call with information.

Jude guns the volume down. "Story's awful, but he's kinda cute in a freaky way."

"Yeah, I was thinking of calling him and asking him out."

"You're shameless."

"That's my middle name."

"I'm out tonight anyway, so best *amuse* yourself."

"Somewhere special?"

"Jake's parents' twentieth anniversary dinner, so couldn't cancel. Sorry."

"What is twenty—silver?"

"China."

"Shit, that's boring. Silver or gold is good, but china?"

Jude pulls an apologetic face. "We got them a picnic set—in *white* china."

"Please euthanize me before I get to the age when I think china's exciting." She gets to her feet. "I'm gonna find the card the cop gave me and call him—at least I know he won't be boring."

18

Bill Baggs Park, Miami

*G*host sits in the pine-smelling, log-walled Ranger Station and carefully studies the pistol used to kill the dog on the beach.

It's an old Smith & Wesson Sigma, a double action 9mm with stainless steel slide and polymer grip.

He looks across the wooden table to the man who fired it, a shaking twig of a young guy who doesn't look old enough to buy beer. "Five shots—how come you needed so many?"

Twenty-two-year-old Mark Hadley has come in specially to be interviewed and sits alongside his boss, Senior Park Ranger Dwain Tulocky. Hadley's red-rimmed eyes and skin, almost as pale as Ghost's, are signs he's not yet over the ordeal. "It wouldn't stop. It jus' kept comin' an' comin'." He drops his head and stares at the table as though he's looking around for words he misplaced.

Dwain gives him a nudge. "Tell him about the Taser, son. Tell him what you done first."

The young Ranger puts his hands below the table and sits on them to stop them from shaking. "Like Mr. Tulocky says, I Tasered the thing first. That's protocol an' all. But it didn't do nothin'. Animal just kept chewin' on the girl—on what was left of her. Have you seen it, officer? D'you know how big it was?"

"I have." Ghost looks into Hadley's eyes and can tell the kid's back on the beach facing down the dog, sickened by the girl's death and at the same time frightened for his own life.

"Go on," prompts his boss. "Tell what you did next."

"The wire from the Taser barb were just dangling there from its side, with enough juice flowing through it to make a grown man flip like a pancake. The dog wasn't the least bit bothered, so I had to use my gun." He nods toward the Sigma in Ghost's hands. "I reckon I was nervous, coz I aimed at the head but hit it somewhere around the left shoulder. It made a noise, man, a real growl, like nothin' I never heard before, so I shot it again, more out of reflex than anythin'." He puts the fingers of his hand to his throat. "Second bullet missed its head but caught it in the neck." Hadley's breathing becomes short and he looks anxious and angry as he continues. "I was saying, 'Fall, you son of a bitch, fall,' but no way was it goin' down. It was still standin', big eyes starin' at me, so I shot the fucker again."

He looks up at Ghost. "Pardon my language, mister. Got it in its head this time, jus' above the nose—and then it leaped at me. I near shit my pants. Three fuckin' bullets and the thing still jumped me." He pulls his hands out and clasps them together on the table. "I shot it twice more when it did that. It fell on the sand right in front of me but I kept far back till I were sure it was dead."

"You did well, son." The big Ranger puts a beefy hand over his young colleague's shoulder. "You done the right thing and saved a lot of lives. Ain't that so, Lieutenant?"

Ghost knew his lines. "It certainly is."

"So there'll be no trouble from the po-lice? He can rest easy on that?"

"He can." Ghost's cell phone rings as he puts the gun down and stands to go. "You guys got any M4s?" He glances at the calling number and doesn't recognize it.

Tulocky nods. "Three of them carbines right over in the gun rack. Why you ask?"

The phone trips to the message service as he walks to the door. "Because I'm betting this isn't the only wild dog that you're going to have to shoot." He looks toward Mark. "And you, my friend— you might not get five shots to stop the next one."

Ghost walks out of the Ranger Station and picks up the call he missed on his cell phone.

"Hi, it's Zoe—you know, Zoe Speed, the beautiful action hero you so rudely abandoned after yesterday's robbery." Her voice is full of bounce and fun and he can't help but smile. "I just saw you on TV and it made me wonder if you wanted to apologize by taking me out for a drink or even dinner tonight. I've not with-held this number, so call me and let me know either way."

He smiles at her cheek as he clicks off the message and gets in his Dodge. The girl's got edge. Something unusual and sparky about her. Gutsy too. He knows his unusual looks often catch the eye of many pretty women, but things generally end badly. Once the physical novelty of bedding an albino has worn off and they've discovered his personality is even more complex than his appearance, they tend to run for the hills.

Ghost puts her out of his mind and thinks again of the dog on the beach. Did it really need five bullets to stop it? It was certainly a muscular slab of canine. But five rounds?

His cell phone buzzes. It's a call from his office. He picks it up on a Bluetooth relay. "Walton."

"Lieutenant, it's Annie Swanson, can you speak?"

"Sure, Annie, fire away."

"Just thought you might like to know that the FBI is all over your dead dog case."

"The Feds are interested in a dog death?"

"That's right. Admin fielded a call to me from the office of the National Intelligence Agency, they wanted everything we had on the death."

"The NIA is not the FBI, Annie—it's part of the CIA."

"Okay, my bad. But why would the CIA want to know about a dog attack?"

"Good question. Is there a name and number to call?"

"Yeah—a Gwendolyn Harries left her direct line. You want me to read the number or put you through?"

"Put me through. Thanks for the heads-up."

"You're welcome. I'm dialing now. Sorry for that mix-up thing with the FBI, I feel dumb now."

"Don't. They're both cut from the same cloth."

The line is filled with bleeps, then a distracted and old-sounding female voice answers: "Gwen Harries."

"Gwen, this is Lieutenant Walton from the Miami police. You wanted to speak to me about the fatal dog attack."

"I did, thanks for calling back." She searches her desk for the details she took down earlier. "Seventeen-year-old girl, right? Bitten to death on some beach?"

"Schoolgirl named Kathy Morgan. Hey, can I start off by asking why the NIA is interested in this?"

She sees no harm in telling him. "NIA isn't. Director Jackson is. I think it's a personal thing. He's with the President as we speak. As you might have read, the Moltons got a new dog some months back, so I suspect that's what's sparked the interest." She finds her notes. "Here we go. What was the breed of dog that carried out the attack? Your office didn't seem to know."

"Vet wasn't sure. She thought it was a cross. Maybe a Staff, pit bull or small mastiff."

"You got any photographs you can send?"

"I can call the vet and get some to you. Do you also want the PM reports on the dog and victim when they're in?"

She thinks on it for a minute. "May as well. I've got your electronic mail details on my screen. I'm sending you mine right now, so you can zip it to me. Would be good sooner than later."

"You'll have it sooner."

The line goes dead.

Then the phone rings again.

Ghost clicks the Bluetooth and assumes the officious NIA woman got cut off. "You'll have to give me twenty minutes; I'm still in backed-up traffic."

There's an awkward silence.

Then Zoe speaks. "I'm keen to see you, Lieutenant, but twenty minutes is a bit soon."

"Shit. I'm sorry. I thought you were someone else."

"Nope. Still the same person you left in the café and who left you a message earlier. So how are you fixed tonight?"

"I'd love to meet up. Sorry I didn't get around to returning your call. You still at your friend's place?"

"One sixty-one Huffington, just off the bottom of Coral Way."

"Is there anything you don't eat?"

"Humble pie and bullshit. Aside from that, no."

"Then be ready for eight."

"Where we going?"

"That's a surprise."

"I don't do surprises. I end up wearing the wrong clothes in the wrong places. Where we going?"

"Then dress smart. Smart is always good." He pulls into the police station parking lot and hangs up. His mind is still on the call from the NIA and the crap about the President getting a new dog.

19

Coral Way, Miami

Zoe is left staring at the dead phone—and at a real problem. She has nothing to wear but what she's dressed in. Plus maybe whatever she can borrow.

"Jude!" She shouts through to the bathroom where her friend is sitting behind a locked door. "You got anything super smart in your closet that I can borrow?"

"Look for yourself, though on my wages don't expect Chanel."

Zoe wanders through to the front bedroom and pulls open the mirrored doors of an anorexic closet.

The racks are squashed tight with a lifetime of clothes—skimpy dresses, a rainbow of tops, a great bird-print number that looks miles too big, a vividly floral tunic dress that might do at a push, a rose-print prom number that looks terrific, a pleated-front dress that is way beyond hideous, and a black sequin maxi dress so clingy and tight it must have been designed by a gynecologist.

She pulls out the maxi and the tunic and holds them up side by side. "Okay, looks like one of you is going out tonight—who is it going to be, clingy and black or flowery and nostalgic?"

"Clingy and black," says Jude from over her shoulder. "You don't want too many pastel colors going on around albino boy. I guess that's who you were talking to on the phone."

"It was. And you're right." She hangs the floral one up again. "You know anything about cops? Ever been out with one?"

"Never. But I bet he's rough and rude. He'll want to get into your pants before you even get shown the dessert menu."

Zoe smiles and swishes the maxi around on the hanger. "Here's hopin'."

20

New York

*T*here's no alternative but to run.

Run until his lungs are on fire and he can't breathe.

Then run some more.

Danny Speed has got jammed up. It's down to a weasel named

Jason Bennett who works the Internet café Bean and Bite. He knows it is.

The young programmer pumps his arms and gets his weight on his toes, just like his gym teacher told him back in the fifth grade, but the two undercover cops are still hot on his heels as he heads along an alley off Monroe Street.

He opens a gap as he sprints under the thundering carriage-ways of Manhattan Bridge. Glancing up, he sees hurtling gray trains and fender-to-fender cars trundling back and forth. A scavenging dog breaks from the shadows and barks so loudly he almost falls. Heart hammering, he dodges left into a yard that stretches around the back of the old glass works.

Danny's cursing himself. Jason had begged him to make a dozen copies of electronic swipe cards for a friend setting up his own company off East Broadway. He should have smelled a set-up right from the start. The guy was a slime ball at school and is a slime ball now—probably a coke head as well.

There are several Dumpsters up ahead, and for a second Danny thinks about hiding in one of them, but suspects *that* only works in movies.

One of the two iPhones, two BlackBerries, and two cheap burner cell phones in his denim jacket rings.

He has no idea which.

Now the ring tone kicks in. "Just Don't Give a Fuck." The full-blooded kick-ass Eminem track he assigned to his bossy sister.

"Shit!"

Zoe's not going to take a voice-mail recording for an answer. She's going to keep calling until she finally gets him to talk.

He vaults the farthest bin and uses it to spring onto a high metal fence and clamber down the other side into an adjoining yard.

Danny hits the ground like a sack of wet sand and tweaks an ankle.

Barking breaks out.

Another mutt. Jeez, they're everywhere these days.

This is a brown guard dog, woken from its curled-up-with-bone happiness into full growling-snarling-pissed-off mode.

"Fuck!"

Back through the fence he sees cops climbing the Dumpsters. They're out of shape, red-faced, but closing in. The dog's on the move too. Fired up and thundering across the gravel.

He spots the open back door of a fast food restaurant, steam billowing through the hanging strips of a tatty, multicolored plastic blind.

Danny beats the Alsatian by less than a yard and slams the door shut, trapping half the colorful streamers.

A kitchen porter, elbow deep in a sink of filthy pan water, shouts at him. Hard abuse in a rough Slavic tongue. The whole place is tight and busy with red-faced, sweating men hunched over blisteringly hot stoves and fryers.

He bolts down one side of the galley and bumps a chef.

Hot liquid slops from a pan and sizzles on a six-burner. There's another outburst of foreign cursing. Someone throws a pan lid that clatters on a wall by his shoulder.

Danny pushes through swing doors into the air-conditioned restaurant before any staff can follow. Startled diners look up from greasy plates, chicken bones held between their fingers, as he clatters past and out the front door.

Eminem's still rapping in his pocket as he beats an exit across the restaurant car park into the maze of back streets. Breathless, he pulls the phone out and presses Answer. "Sis, I'm kinda busy right now. Call you back!"

The cops are lost and he's heading home.
Out of their sight. Out of their clutches.
But only for now.

21

Beijing

*T*he world's most famous Boeing 747 roars down the runway at Capital International and rises into the yellow, smoggy sky.

Only when Air Force One levels out and the pilot's voice says "Seat belts can be unbuckled" does Don Jackson get a chance to talk openly to President Molton and Vice President Cornwell.

They gather in the "office," a working area fashioned from the same woods and leathers as the White House's Situation Room.

Molton cuts to the chase. "You said Zhang threatened us?"

"Cleverly and indirectly, but yes, sir, that's what it amounted to." The whole scene is indelibly etched in Jackson's memory. "It was just before we left—we were in his hotel suite and he was charming enough to start with. Then he said he wanted to show me some video footage. The lights went down, and up came this reel of guys in the desert. They looked like cons. Anyway, they were running. Next thing you know, you can see why they were on their toes. These dogs, maybe a dozen of them, appear from nowhere and rip them to shreds. It was barbaric."

The VP is skeptical. "You sure this was fact not fiction?"

"It looked real. Footage was virtually unedited and appeared to be military quality—not TV or movie standard. Certainly there was no use of green screen or special effects."

The President is eager to hear more. "Go on."

"When the clip finishes, Zhang tells me what I'd been looking at was weaponized animals, a new form of genetic terrorism that China believes is about to be unleashed—no pun intended—on the U.S."

Cornwell can't believe what he's hearing. "The fucking Chinese are going to turn dogs on us?" He laughs mockingly. "I thought the fuckers had eaten them all."

Molton scowls at him.

"*Not* the Chinese," Jackson stresses. "Zhang clearly said a 'third party'—a terror group—had already introduced genetically modified dogs into the U.S. But hey, China could come to our rescue and prevent people being killed—if China wanted."

"I see a less than subtle connection," says Molton. "This is linked to Xian's crazy demands re debt repayment. He's basically saying if we don't give in and pay a slice of taxation to China, they'll encourage some terrorists to set these weaponized canines on us." He looks directly at Jackson. "It all sounds ridiculous, but it is what it is. Did he give you any idea how many of these dogs there are and where and when all this is supposed to happen?"

The NIA director shakes his head. "He said it already was happening. Apparently there was some dog-related death in Miami yesterday. Zhang pointed it out to me—said we should look into it."

"Pha!" Cornwell dismisses it with a wave of his hand. "Little bastard will have seen it on CNN. Don't attach too much credibility to this horseshit."

Molton isn't so flip. "Anything in it?"

"Too soon to say." Jackson looks as uncomfortable as he feels. "I could only get a brief outline over the phone. Big dog went mad on a teenage girl over at a beach in Key Biscayne, then a Ranger shot it. Sad but not unheard of. Could be the heat, could be a disease, could be a lot of things."

"Find out which." Molton stares out into the clouds. "I hope to Christ this is as crazy as it sounds."

22

Coral Way, Miami

*T*he sun-shaped clock on Jude's kitchen wall strikes 8:00 P.M. almost at the same moment the downstairs' doorbell rings.

Zoe is listening to the weather guy on the radio telling her tonight is going to stay way too hot to go out in the black maxi dress she's just put on. Now that her date has turned up, she has no time to change into something cooler.

Reluctantly, she trots through to the intercom by the front door and presses the button that opens the front lobby door.

While he's on his way up she sneaks a final check in the full-length hall mirror. The dress is so tight that wearing any under-wear was impossible, unless she wanted to look like a patched up bicycle tire.

There's a polite knock on the apartment door.

She pulls it open and is amazed to see a small Hispanic man in his late forties in tattered jeans and a blue shirt that is soaked under the armpits.

"Cab for Zoe Speed."

"I didn't order a cab." She can't take her eyes off the driver's sweat patches.

"*Meester* Ghost sent me."

"Who?"

"*Lieutenant* Walton. Said to say sorry he couldn't come in person but he's running late."

She leaves the sweating cabbie on the doorstep while she collects her things and works out what kind of guy sends a car on a first date. Seems the night's going to be full of surprises.

Zoe swings a borrowed black purse over her shoulder. "Okay, I'm ready, let's roll."

He leads her downstairs to a yellow car and plays jazz on the radio as he heads back into the city.

She catches the driver's eyes in the rearview. "Where exactly are we going?"

He smiles back at her. "*Meester* Ghost said you would ask."

"Hey, what's with this Ghost shit?"

He looks up at her in his mirror. "That's what everyone calls him."

"It's not very nice."

"He don't mind. He really nice." He smiles widely so she can see his sign of approval for her date. "He said I should tell you you're going to one of the best restaurants he knows." His eyes twinkle. "I think you are in for a night you will remember."

"Is that right?" She can't keep the irritation out of her voice.

Two more jazz numbers play out before the cab pulls over in front of a tall sandy building that seems a cross between offices and apartments.

The driver turns in his seat. "Apartment 4011—that's the penthouse floor. The concierge will show you up."

"Apartment?" She bends in her seat and cranes her neck to get a view of where she's supposed to be going. "Shouldn't you just take me to the restaurant where we're having dinner?"

"Meester Ghost said to bring you here." He shrugs. "I just do what he say."

She gives up. "Okay. What do I owe you?"

He shakes his head. "The fare's already paid."

"Thanks." She gets out and flaps the door shut. A cool breeze billows across the sidewalk, and Miami's lights twinkle in the city blackness. It ain't New York, but she can feel the place has its own special energy and buzz.

The lobby is filled with black and white marble and some big old terra-cotta pots sprouting palms. A courteous concierge in his sixties shows her to the elevator and swipes his security card over an electronic reader so she can get to the penthouse suites.

Apartment 4011 is just a few doors down on the fortieth floor. She knocks on the rich oak door and waits.

Ghost opens it. He's dressed in an immaculately cut black dinner suit, complete with bow tie. Zoe notes it's not the clip-on cheating type but the really difficult shit you have to fold and twist all by yourself.

And he's minus shades. He's there in all his albino glory.

"Hi, come on in."

She stands there a second, in shock. "You look like James Fucking Bond."

He laughs. "I'll take that as a compliment."

"Please do."

She's still rooted as she studies his eyes. They're amazing. Hypnotic. Fascinating. She wishes she had a camera to catch the meek milky irises and the threateningly deep pink pupils.

"You want dinner in the corridor?" The big lieutenant smiles as he holds the door wide. "Or you want to come inside?"

"Sorry." She floats past him. "Inside is good." She takes a quick look at the decor. "Fuck, inside is *very good*." She grabs her iPhone from her purse and clicks at a white wall filled with multicolored original art. "You mind?"

He shrugs at her bent back as she snaps. "No, why on earth should I? Unless you're an art thief, planning a heist."

Zoe stops. "Stolen a few hearts in my time, but nothing else." She slips the camera back into her purse.

Ghost finds himself staring at her for the first time. She hadn't been wearing makeup when they met at the robbery and her hair was scraggy. Now her lightly powdered skin showcases beautiful cheekbones and she looks like a shimmering pixie. "I, er—like to patronize up-and-coming artists." He waves a hand toward the paintings. "For obvious reasons I tend to go for the more vibrant and unusual works." He walks her toward a horseshoe of white sofas. "Would you like a drink?"

"I would. What you got?"

"I've chilled some champagne. Unless you'd prefer something else?"

"Hard for a girl to say no to champagne."

"And you look lovely." He blurts it out and disappears into the kitchen.

"Lovely?" She smiles as she weighs up the word. She can't ever recall being called that before.

Hot. Sexy. Even beautiful. But never lovely.

She takes advantage of the fact that he's not in the room and shouts through to him, "The driver called you Mr. Ghost."

"Ah, yeah. Lots of people call me that."

"You don't mind? I thought it was kinda rude."

"Stopped minding a very long time back. As a cop you get called a lot worse."

While he's gone she walks to the window and looks out at Miami's illuminated cityscape. Music starts to seep into the room from hidden speakers, the unmistakable crackle and hiss of an old vinyl record, something classical and smooth that she doesn't recognize.

He reappears, looking every inch a high-class waiter as he balances a round silver tray bearing two crystal flutes of champagne on one outstretched hand. "It's a seven-year-old Taittinger. I visited the vineyard a few years ago and it reminds me of a wonderful French summer."

She takes a glass and tastes it. The fizz tingles sensuously across her lips and tongue, then melts in her mouth like a gossamer-thin wafer of honey.

"Okay?"

"*Very* okay." She lets the flute dangle between her fingers, enjoying the pleasure of its coolness in her warm hand. "So, surprise time is over—where exactly are we going to eat, Lieutenant?"

"Here," he says as though he's already told her. "Well, upstairs, to be precise."

23

Presidential Residence, Beijing

*A*s the long day draws to a close, Xian Sheng sits alone in the dimmed light of his study and pours a shot of whiskey. It's a sixty-four-year-old Macallan malt, one of only four hundred in existence, distilled in five sherry butts made from Spanish and American oak and given to him by President Molton as a gesture of friendship, a thank-you for the dog they now call Emperor.

Around the decanter's neck is a handwritten message: *Everyone eats and drinks, only a few appreciate what they taste.* The quotation is apt but incorrect. It comes from the Confucian classic *The Doctrine of the Mean* and should read: "Everyone eats and drinks: yet only a few appreciate the taste of food." He sips the liquor and forgives the mistake.

It is undoubtedly the best malt he has ever tasted.

Not worth the $60,000 a shot he is told it sometimes sells for, but still exceptionally good.

As he sips he knows that tomorrow General Zhang will come to him, his ambition shining like a new medal, and demand that he push China closer to war by green-lighting a total deployment of the Project Nian weapons. He has already given the go-ahead for some selective strikes—a show of strength to the Americans—but he realizes it is not enough. Zhang is an all-or-nothing soldier. Crush and conquer the enemy so they can never rebuild, so they live in fear of the victor for the rest of their days.

But Xian has serious doubts.

Doubts that this newfound biological warfare can be as widely controllable and effective as he is being told. Doubts that the new arsenal of money and technology is really better than the old one of nuclear missiles and diplomacy. Even the greenest of hunters understands that if you wound a big animal and don't kill it, then unless you retreat, it will destroy you. And America is a big animal.

He sips again on the Macallan and thinks about Zhang. He is a great warrior. A distinguished soldier. But he is an untrustworthy brute and a sadist. It would be disastrous for China should he ever realize his dreams of becoming President.

Then there is the problem of momentum.

Zhang has momentum.

Momentum and the backing of powerful members within the party. For him to hesitate now would be seen as a sign of cowardice, not wisdom. Nian has been many years in development and is long past the point when it can be further delayed or once more revised.

Xian finishes the whiskey and recaps the elegant Lalique decanter. About now the man who gave it to him will be flying out of Beijing, talking with his advisors, trying to make sense of how a visit that was supposed to strengthen ties between nations has instead concluded with grave threats against his people. Threats that are already being enforced.

On Xian's desk is a photograph of his family. His wife Suyin and their one child, Umbigo. They are pictured on the slopes of Dragon Bone Hill in Zhoukoudian, one of the oldest and most important places on earth. The area's ancient caves contain skulls and human remains that date back more than a quarter of a million years.

History is important to Xian. Reading it, learning from it, making it.

As he heads to bed he thinks about tomorrow and how historians of the future will judge the momentous decision he is about to make.

24

Historic District, Miami

"*D*inner is upstairs?" Zoe takes a sip of champagne and looks untrustingly at Ghost. "That's a little presumptuous, isn't it?"

He smiles at her and puts his own glass down. "I mean on the roof." He walks toward the patio doors, "Come and have a look."

She follows him out onto the large balcony and glances at the glitteringly beautiful view of Miami. Ghost disappears down the side of the terrace and takes a metal spiral up onto a helipad.

"Wow." Zoe is pleasantly surprised by a large spread of artificial lawn fringed by potted palms and the sound of music wafting over the rooftop.

"I called in some favors," explains the cop.

At the center of the covered helipad is a round table covered in crisp white linen and cream leather chairs. In the middle of the table is an arrangement of cut white and pink roses and a silver candlestick.

Zoe laughs as she approaches the laid place settings. "Please tell me this isn't white china."

"Actually it is." He walks toward her. "Fine bone china from England. Victorian, to be precise."

"*Bone* china? Why is it called that?" She picks up a charger plate and inspects it.

"Because it's a kind of porcelain made from about fifty percent bone ash."

"Yuk." She puts the plate down. "What's the music? I know it's Liszt but can't place the movement."

"It's Ayako Shinozaki's interpretation of *Liebesträum*." He pulls back a chair for her and lets her settle before seating himself opposite her. "Would you like something more modern?"

"No. I'm very happy to sit and drink champagne and listen to harp music on a grassed-over helipad." She picks up her champagne flute by the delicate spindle, "I toast your wild and beautiful taste."

"Here's to things wild and beautiful—and long may I be around them." He clinks his glass gently against hers.

Zoe notices his eyes never leave hers as they toast and drink. His stare is mesmeric but unthreatening.

A small dark-haired man of about Zoe's age appears from the stairs and distracts her. He's wearing a waiter's white shirt, black vest, black trousers, and is carrying two plates of food.

"Good evening, Lieutenant." He smiles at Zoe. "Welcome, ma'am, to the roof of the world. I hope you both enjoy the food."

"Thanks, Benny," Ghost says, then makes the introductions. "Benny, this is Zoe Speed from New York City via Maryland. Zoe, this is Benny Clark, Miami via Mexico and Los Angeles. Benny normally does pizza delivery but took the night off specially to help out. I'm very grateful Benny."

"My pleasure, Detective." He nods and walks away.

Ghost waits until he is out of earshot before adding, "Our 'waiter' used to run with a bad crowd. Before the pizza job he used to deliver more lucrative takeouts, namely crack and dope. To stay out of prison he turned C.I. Now he runs straighter than a train on the Nullarbor Plain." He points his fork at her starter of raw fish and vegetables seasoned in spices and marinated in vinegar. "How's the ceviche?"

She nods as she chews and listens. "It's good. Benny is an excellent cook."

He doesn't even think about telling her that Benny can't boil water and that he'd made both the classic Miami appetizer and the main course of New York strip steaks, marinated for the past three hours in his own unique recipe. "Yes he is, surprisingly so."

She takes another sip of champagne. "Do you know what *Liebesträum* means?"

"Yes. It's German. It means Dreams of Love."

She listens to the ripple of notes and it makes her think of video she shot of soft summer rain breaking the stillness of a lily strewn pond. "You're very cultured—for a cop."

He laughs. "I'll take that as a compliment."

"You should. It was meant to be. Cops are supposed to be gritty, earthy, grubby, and hard, but you—you have a gentleness." She realizes she may have accidentally insulted him. "Hey, I'm not saying you can't be a tough guy—I mean, I saw you out on the street with the robber and you handled yourself good. I just meant—"

"I know what you meant." He's amused by her awkwardness. "As a kid I retreated into books and music. Until I became big enough and skilled enough to fight, knowledge was my chosen weapon of self-defense. Still is, given the chance."

"So you're a thinker?"

"Try to be."

"I'm more impulsive. Go with the moment. Roll with how you feel."

He leans closer and holds her eyes. "And how do you feel tonight? Out here, with this strange man in the middle of this strange and hopefully pleasant moment?"

A tingle of excitement runs down her back. "I feel—"

Her cell phone rings mid-sentence. She looks accusingly at Jude's borrowed purse hanging over her chair.

Ghost nods at the bag. "Feel free to take it."

She fishes the phone out. It's jangling rudely with Eminem's "I Am What I Am" and flashes up a head shot of Danny. "It's my brother. Excuse me." She gets up from the table and walks to the edge of the helipad. "Hey, big guy, I'm out on a date. Can I call you back?"

"Tonight, or in the morning?" He sounds bored.

It's a simple question but one that suddenly fills her with panic. It presumes she might be staying the night. A few hours ago, steamy, one-night-stand sex is exactly what she had in mind. But now it seems a bad idea.

There's a danger she might get to like this guy. Like him more than she should.

Staying the night would be a disaster.

For both of them.

Come to think of it, staying a moment longer could be a big mistake. "No, Danny, it's okay. I can talk now."

"Hey, it's not urgent. Later or tomorrow would be fine."

She turns around to look at Ghost as she raises her voice in faked alarm. "Oh my God, you poor thing. Listen, don't worry, I'll leave now and call you when I'm back at Jude's. Don't worry, we can sort it out."

She clicks off the phone before her brother can answer and walks back to the table. "I'm real sorry, but I've got to go." She braces herself for the lie. "My brother has problems with depression and I really need to go somewhere private and talk him through it."

Ghost takes a beat and looks her over.

"Sorry, he's been like this since he was a kid." She gives a what-else-can-I-do shrug.

"There's an office downstairs. You can call from there and I'll have Benny keep your food warm."

"Thanks, but I'd better go."

He gets up from his seat and follows her across the helipad. "What did I do wrong, Zoe?" He catches up with her by the stairs. "Did all this freak you out? Did I go too much over the top?"

"No. No. Not at all. It was—lovely."

"Then why are you running off?"

"My brother really—"

He puts a finger to his lips. "Don't. Please, don't. I spend all my days being lied to, I can spot one miles away."

She gives up her excuse. "It's me. I'm no good with relationships, and all this fuss, well—it all spells out the fact that you're the kind of guy who is going to want a relationship."

"You're wrong—"

She forces out a goodbye smile. "Honestly, I'm doing you a favor by going."

He stands between her and the steps. "No you're not. You're trying to leave for the reason I was trying not to call you back."

The remark throws her. "Which is?"

He shrugs. "I don't know. There's some kind of connection." He tries to read her body language but can't help but be distracted by how beautiful she is. There's a brightness in her eyes and a sense of vitality that he's never noticed in any other woman. "It's not physical, Zoe—it's more than that. I find you fascinating—complex—intriguing and—"

"Lovely?"

"Yes, lovely." He laughs. "But that wasn't what I was going to say. I was going to say, unique. And I love unique."

She steps close to him. Close enough to vaporize the air between them. "If I stay, I'll break your heart."

He takes her face in his hands. "Albino hearts are extraordinarily strong. I'll take the risk."

Zoe doesn't blink or look away as she kisses him. Softly, then firmly. It doesn't only feel as unhurried and as exciting as she'd hoped, it feels perfect. Heart-racingly dangerous and yet sure and protective. Like it is the kiss she's always been searching for.

25

North Korea

*A*cross the 38th parallel runs a corridor of earth 150 miles long and less than three wide.

It's all that separates North and South Korea.

The soldiers staring down gun barrels at each other know this godforsaken patch of space as the DMZ—the Demilitarized Zone.

It has split the peninsula since a cease-fire in the Korean War half a century ago, and technically the two sides could resume fighting at any moment, as was borne out in 2013 over the North's repeated nuclear missile testing.

The DMZ is a bizarre strip of land that contains a village or two, land mines, guards, and regular tourist trips to the Military Arbitration Commission building where the cease-fire was hammered out and where both sides still meet on an almost daily basis to settle operational problems relating to the neutral turf.

Beneath their feet, and beyond the DMZ, are more than a thousand secret bunkers. Some contain KN-08 missiles and the first of the country's truly functional ICBMs. Others are merely dummy silos, serving no purpose except to distract America and NATO. Many are filled to the brim with military equipment, arms, and uniforms ready to be picked up in a war against the West or South Korea.

But a small number—hundreds of feet underground—house the laboratories and test center of Project Nian, a top secret operation started by the North Koreans, sponsored by the Chinese, and for the past six months personally overseen by China's top scientist, Hao Weiwei.

A gifted geneticist and loyal Communist Party activist, Hao has dedicated his life and learning to his homeland. Three years ago he and other leading geneticists were drafted into the project to help create the "enemy within." Six months ago, as the final stage approached, he and his team moved to North Korea and spend all their working lives in these bunkers. Only the Chinese scientist and his son have swipe-card access to all rooms and clearance to the world aboveground.

Hao Weiwei and his son Jihai trundle the sedated dogs through the muted light of the reinforced tunnels in to the ultra-secure testing room with its sterile cells. Each of them is pushing an identical, electrically assisted rolling cage. It's a cell on wheels, made of iron bars stretching nine feet long by six wide and six high. The cages are the same but the dogs about as different as can be.

In Jihai's cage is a shih tzu, a delicate breed much loved by the Ming Dynasty. It's a tiny, silky dog that weighs just eleven pounds and at a cute stretch is barely eleven inches from paw to shoulder.

In Hao's cage is an American pit bull terrier, a seventy-eight-pound slab of fighting muscle that is twice as big as the Chinese breed.

The two men are met by Péng and research assistant Tāo. They help them maneuver the containers through an air-lock antechamber into the testing room's central containment area—a giant glass-walled cube that can be used as one large, open area, or divided into separate observation and experimentation cells.

The scientists slide the sleeping animals out of the cages and leave them side by side in a single cell, before they withdraw to the other side of the testing cube and lock them in.

Hao turns to his son. "Are all checks complete?"

Jihai has been diligent. As always. "Blood count. DNA profile. Calcium levels. Protein readings. All have been entered into the computer, sir." He never calls him Father, not unless they are alone and off work.

"Good." Hao is pleased. One day the boy will make a very fine scientist. Perhaps even his successor.

Audio speakers on the outside of the containment cell crackle and hiss into life. Supersensitive microphones gather the dogs' sounds. Whispery breaths from the shih tzu. Heavy snorts from the pit bull.

The tiny dog is the first to start to wake.

"Take your positions." Hao walks to a master control panel and triggers the live video links.

He's giving General Zhang what he commanded. Footage of a live experiment. Proof that he and his team are incredibly close to achieving their task of perfecting a modifying spray that will almost instantly pacify even the most aggressive of the weaponized dogs.

The three scientists slide onto high stools and flip-down computer panels attached to the unbreakable glass cube. Thirty-six 3D video cameras jerk into autofocus on the other side of the reinforced panes.

Hao takes a long, slow breath then exhales before giving the command: "Arm and aim both the hypotrajectors and overhead sprays."

"One is armed and locked."

A raw, guttural noise blows bass into the speakers. The pit bull terrier is awake and is angry. It senses another dog close by. It's disorientated by the drugs and fears being attacked.

"Two is armed and locked."

The shih tzu gets to its feet. It's yapping. Wide-eyed. Small shoulders ridiculously squared for a fight.

"Three and four are armed and locked."

The terrier raises itself and regards the noisy ball of fluff in front of it with contempt.

"All atomizers loaded and ready, sir."

Only in the shih tzu's eyes is there a hint of the fact that this breed goes all the way back to the Senji—the ancient Chinese wolf—and that it hasn't survived more than ten thousand years just by being cute.

The terrier makes the mistake of growling and opening its jaws wide.

The tiny, genetically modified David goes for the giant Goliath.

Hao quickly glances at his command console and presses the keys that release a mist of serum into the sealed cell.

The shih tzu has the terrier by the throat and is forcing it onto the floor. Its pupils have dilated to the size of black golf balls and it seems possessed with preternatural strength.

Weiwei hits the computer keys again.

Another mist of vapor, longer and denser this time, clouds the fighting dogs.

The pit bull manages to escape the vicious, piranhalike jaws. It lunges and snaps. But all its jaws claim is a sliver of silken ear.

The shih tzu is too quick. And too strong. As soon as it jerks away from the terrier's snap, it turns on a dime and rams the bigger dog against the cell glass.

The terrier whimpers as it thumps its head.

The Chinese dog goes for its throat again. Sinks its teeth into an already gaping wound.

Hao can't watch anymore. He looks across to his colleagues. "Shoot it! Shoot it, now!"

They trigger the hypotrajectors and deadly darts hit the shih tzu.

Within seconds it will be dead.

"And the terrier," shouts Hao. "Put it out of its misery."

Péng and Jihai turn the hypotrajectors on the dying pit bull.

In the corner of the testing cell is a giant monitor and on it the face of General Zhang, watching.

His displeasure is plain for all to see.

The atomized modifier was supposed to have placated the weaponized shih tzu, not enraged it.

Hao has failed him again.

26

Miami

*M*orning light the color of maple syrup drizzles down Ghost's windshield as he drives the old Dodge across the Rickenbacker Causeway.

A seven-thirty shout from Dispatch means he's had to leave Zoe in bed, and that might not be a bad thing. He's not great at "mornings after" and dreads to think what someone as highly strung as Zoe is like at that time of day. He was actually surprised he'd gotten her to stay last night. It had certainly taken all of his powers of persuasion.

Zoe's still trespassing in his private thought field as he parks at Crandon Golf Course. He shows his badge to local cops and catches a ride on a GPS guided cart out to the seventeenth hole. The course is known to be spectacular, replete with saltwater lakes, towering palms, bleached bunkers, and immaculate greens and fairways.

Egrets pass overhead as he ducks a tape and follows a trail of verbal abuse being uttered from the shadows of a mangrove forest.

Medical Examiner Gerry Stockman has his legs spread over thick coils of roots and is peering down at the hideously mutilated body of an early morning jogger found less than an hour ago.

"Don't suppose you have a flask of coffee over there, Gerry?"

The M.E. looks up from his straddled stance. "My bad, I completely forgot to make you one as I was dragged from my night's sleep." He gestures to the corpse. "I'm hoping like hell that this is another of your dog-related deaths. Otherwise we really have one sick bitch of a serial killer on our hands."

Ghost climbs over the spaghettilike roots and stands next to him to take a look.

Most of the facial flesh has been chewed off. Only a few scraps of skin remain on arm bones pulped by powerful teeth. Several fingers are missing. All internal organs and most of the muscles and flesh of the thighs are gone.

It's a sight too horrible to even comment on. Ghost eases past the body and walks deeper into the forest. He feels a need to get a different perspective on what happened. Weigh up the location.

The way he sees it, the body is just off a small shield-shaped green, right out on the eastern corner of the course, teetering over the waters of the bay and maybe thirty feet into a big clump of mangroves. Behind that there's a steep drop to the boats in the marina. Down there are some parking areas and a cluster of fishing chalets. Man and dog most likely have come by vehicle, across the Rickenbacker like he did.

While Ghost is sizing things up Stockman has perfected his balancing act and is now shooting video from a small camera. The M.E. adds commentary notes as he steps precariously around the layers of dense roots and human remains. "White male of average height and build, late forties or fifties, judging by the condition of his gums and teeth, a nonsmoker but heavy coffee drinker."

Ghost can hear the comments as he picks his way back over the tangle of ankle-breaking branches and is rewarded by finding a wallet. He searches through it then shouts to the M.E. "Gerry, our man is fifty-five-year-old Matt Wood from Grand Avenue, over near Peacock Park. He was a father and grandfather." He takes out a creased photograph from the centerfold. "Two beautiful little girls who will never be pictured sitting on grandpa's knee again." He looks at another one. It shows a sun-tanned, white-haired man and his plump blond wife playing golf on the very course where his body has been found.

Ghost puts the pictures back and walks on. At the edge of the copse he finds yellow flowering gorse and shreds of a green woolen jumper. Just beyond that, deep in a tangle of mangrove roots, he comes across several dimpled balls, all gray and weathered, long lost, not recent. He turns around and guesses the dog that killed him had been in a thicket a few yards away.

Then he spots it.

Grooves in the soil.

"There are drag marks starting from over here," he shouts to the M.E. "I can see where the vic's heels have scuffed roots, leading your way."

Stockman videos the lieutenant as he turns and walks toward him.

Ghost continues his commentary. "Look, there's blood on the coiled roots, probably from the victim's hands as he tried to grab something and get away from the animal." He treads carefully, anxious not to trample evidence into the ground. "And there's a lot of dried blood just here. Spatter and spill on the fallen leaves." He crouches to get a better look. "Mangroves lose leaves all year round. We're lucky the drips didn't hit the soil and just disappear."

"Somehow I don't feel lucky," says the M.E. from behind the lens. "Lucky would be if I'd hit a sixty-eight out there and was now in the clubhouse enjoying breakfast."

"Lucky would be if I were still in bed, but I'm not. I think this is where the dog lost its grip as it dragged him." He visualizes the scene. "It then turned back at this spot and locked its jaws on him again."

"Would explain the change of spatter," concurs Stockman. "I hate mangroves."

Ghost looks up and across the forest. "There's a whole mix in here, red, black, and white. I can never remember exactly which is which."

The M.E. finishes videoing and points. "*Avicennia germinans*, those are the black ones with the snorkel roots that are giving us all the problems. Over there are the reds—the *rhizophora mangle*, and on the other side you have the whites, the *laguncularia racemosa*. It's unusual to get them together like this."

"There you go, you got lucky again." Ghost looks down at the corpse. "Given he isn't dressed in golf gear and that no one has reported a golfer who didn't come in from a day on the links, I think we can presume that Mr. Wood here is the owner of the dog that killed the girl on the beach."

"Go on."

"Well, I guess he came out yesterday, to book a round, maybe have a drink in the clubhouse, and brought the dog with him. When he went back to his vehicle, he took it for a walk. While he was doing that, the animal turned on him and killed him. It then ran from here down to the beach, which is what, three miles away?"

Stockman looks across to the distant lighthouse at Bill Baggs. "Less. From here, a little over two."

"Death of Kathy Morgan was about five P.M. Would you place this TOD around there, maybe thirty minutes or an hour earlier?"

The M.E. looks through a swirl of flies at the bloodred remains. "There's not a lot to go on, but I guess from the shreds of organs and decomposition of the main torso, you're in the ballpark." He looks again at the dried remains. "Could be earlier too. Maybe even by a couple of hours."

"Thanks." Ghost walks out of the forest and heads back to his Dodge. He's willing to bet a year's salary that there's an SUV or station wagon registered in Wood's name and parked at the clubhouse.

27

The White House, Washington DC

*T*he long flight back on Air Force One and stressful days in Beijing leave Clint Molton jet-lagged and bad-tempered.

He showers and changes clothes, then heads straight to the Oval Office to tackle a desk groaning with work.

Don Jackson is the first through his door.

He's carrying a stack of files and a mood as black as the President's. "'Morning, sir. I've spent the last hour trying to rub China off the world map on my office wall. Like a nasty stain, it just won't go away."

Molton huffs out a laugh. "What's the latest on this dog nonsense in Miami?"

"The forensic vet working the case is pretty sure it's just a wild dog—"

"Rabies?"

"She thinks not but she's asked for extra tests, in case there's a mutation of the strain."

"Let's hope that isn't the case. How old was the girl?"

"Seventeen."

He shuts his eyes for a second. He can't help but think about his own children and how the parents of the dead girl must now feel. "Remind me, what kind of dog we talking about?"

"Crossbreed. Part pit bull, which kind of explains the aggression." He opens one of his files and slides over prints of the dead dog. "The animal is more muscular than massive, but the report I have says it took five shots before a ranger could put it down."

"Five?" Molton widens his eyes in surprise. "So if it's not rabies, then what's the explanation for this dog going almost supernaturally vicious?"

"Vet still hasn't finished her report—could be anything from the heat to something that it ate." This seems the right moment to add the latest bad news he'd been advised of. "I got a call a few moments ago from my office. The coroner has turned out another bite-related death in Miami, he thinks it's the dog owner."

"Jeez." The President shakes his head. "Is all this normal, Don? I mean, are there always dog attacks like this and we just don't notice them? Or do we have to start taking Zhang's threats seriously?"

Jackson has been asking the same questions. "Two deaths but it looks like only one dog was involved, so it could easily be coincidence, sir. I think we shouldn't get alarmed. Statistics show there are about five million dog bites a year in America, with a thousand people a day needing some form of emergency care."

Molton is shocked. "That many, really?"

"Afraid so." He passes over another sheet. "A quick data scan that we did in the office shows most bad attacks always come from pit bulls, rottweilers, and wolf hybrids. It was a kind of pit-cross that was responsible for the beach death and maybe this latest one of the owner, so I don't see any reason to get overconcerned. That said, I'm having the analysts do a nationwide sweep to see if there have been any recent increases."

"Sounds like a good idea. Let me know what they come up with and keep me apprised of what that vet says." He hands back the papers the NIA director gave him and gestures to the stacks of work around him. "I'd like to talk more about this but I'm kind of snowed in, so let's move on. I'm hoping we can quickly put all this nonsense behind us."

28

Crandon Golf Club, Miami

*P*arked in a bay near the clubhouse is a white, new edition Ford Explorer that's covered in more dust than all the other vehicles around it. It's a sure sign that it's been there for at least a day.

Ghost wipes a hand over the dirt and looks through the back window of the SUV. There's a scuffed-up tartan blanket and a well-chewed rubber bone inside. A pull at a door handle tells him it's locked. He wipes the passenger window and presses close to the glass. There's an envelope on the passenger seat, waiting to be posted to a Mr. Adam Wood over at Immokalee. He guesses it's a card of some kind for the dead man's brother or son.

The lieutenant walks inside the clubhouse and asks some local cops where he can find the manager. Carlton Henderson is just a few feet away and overhears them talking. "Can I help you?"

Ghost shows his ID to the smart-suited, gray-haired man. "Miami Homicide. Do you have a Matt Wood on your membership roll?"

Henderson stares at the picture a moment before replying. "We do. Mr. Wood is one of our longest-serving members and is a very good golfer." He looks up from the picture to the real detective and realizes that the news is bad. "Is he the man found on the course?"

"Maybe. Was he here yesterday?"

Henderson nods. "Yes. I saw him in the bar, when I was walking through to see one of the pros."

"What time would that be?"

He has to think. "Let me see. After three-thirty. I had a call at three-thirty. Maybe 3:45, going on four."

Ghost does the math. Wood would have left around four-fifteen and walked the dog, probably let it relieve itself in the forest—that could easily take till around four-thirty. Dog kills him, then goes off that couple of miles down to Bill Baggs, maybe wanders and meanders awhile. All that could push the timing close to just before five, when Kathy Morgan was attacked.

He sees Henderson staring at him. "Could you look in your records for me, please, and tell me two things. Did he make a booking yesterday to play and what is his current address?"

"You got it." The course manager walks to a PC in a curved reception area and bangs away at the keyboard with a single finger on each hand.

Ghost's phone beeps. He glances at it. An SMS from Zoe.

THANKS FOR LAST NITE. GONE HOME. CALL ME. Z

He manages a smile. It's good to be reminded of the sweeter things in life when you're up to your ears in death.

Across the room, Henderson slides paper into the printer and then hits Send.

Ghost wanders over to see how he's progressing.

The manager takes out two printed pages and passes them over. "First paper is Mr. Wood's address—over at Phoenix Park. Second is our bookings' log. He reserved a round for tomorrow morning."

A squawk of police radio interrupts them. A young uniformed officer from the local Biscayne station shouts across. "Lieutenant."

Ghost walks over.

The rookie covers his mouth so no one else can hear or notice what he's saying. "We've got a call from someone on Crandon Boulevard, says there was a wild dog snapping at people. It's disappeared into public parkland."

29

Beijing

*T*he army jeep rumbles down miles of cobbled side streets until the driver hand-brakes it on a steep hill at the end of a cul-de-sac. Sitting in the back seat is General Zhang, his blood still boiling because of Weiwei's failure. The damned scientist is holding him back. There are advancements to be made. Next steps to be taken.

Soldiers smartly dismount and march briskly to the front of a large dilapidated building.

They bang gun butts on the peeling blue paint of a tall metal door. "Open up! Open for General Zhang!"

The words chill the blood of the man in charge of the black jail. It's one of a network of unauthorized detention centers the party turns a blind eye to. Zhang sees them as a necessary filter in the system. They catch the dregs. The thankless complainers and treasonable protestors—the agitators who spread lies about local government and party corruption. Black jails are a necessary evil. Vile places for vile people.

The inside is shrouded in shadow. The stone floors are wet

from disinfected water liberally doused to ensure that the general doesn't dirty his boots or immaculate uniform.

With each sanitized step, Zhang smells fear.

Smells it above the iron tang of spilled blood, above the sewage stench of those who've soiled themselves while being beaten and tortured, above the reek of rotting corpses waiting to be spirited away in the dead of night.

The jailer takes him down an ever-darkening passage. Down steep stone stairs to the basement where *they* are being kept.

The latest ones.

The women who dared sing songs mocking President Xian and General Zhang. Young fools who thought they could hide behind plastic masks of the Dalai Lama's face and film their obscene chants on camera phones with a view to showing themselves on the Internet.

Idiots.

The jailer almost feels sorry for them as he unlocks the basement door and lets the general into the fetid darkness of the torture room.

The women are already stripped naked and spread-eagled on death boards. Their ankles and wrists are tied to the rough crucifix-shaped planks, their heads held in nooses.

"Go!"

The jailer takes his cue. He shuts and bolts the door, leaving the general alone with the women.

Zhang stands. Motionless. Quiet as the rodents watching from the corners of the infested pit. He listens. Strains to hear their hearts racing with panic, savors their raspy breath quickening in the fetid air.

Now he moves.

He circles them.

Looks down into their faces. Into their eyes. Into what remains of their courage.

He grades them. Ranks them by the fear they show.

The bravest will pleasure him first. The most frightened he'll leave till last.

Leave her so she can hear the screams of the others.

30

Village Green Park, Key Biscayne

*M*ost kids out at Key Biscayne play their ball games on the spread of sun-scorched sports fields squashed between the Galleria and Key shopping centers just east of the Community Church.

The four fields are marked out for both English soccer and American football, and ten-year-old Dale Shawcross and his buddies have beaten the Steiner gang at both all year long.

Right now a five-a-side battle is being waged with the round ball and the score is 3–1 to the Shawcrosses. Dale's brother Vic has scored twice, the last an absolute screamer, and he's added the third. Steiner's one goal was lucky. A toe-ender that hit fat Adam in the face and went in off the post.

"Foul!" shouts Dale as Joey Redfern upends his brother Vic.

"That sucks! I played the ball." Alfie Steiner holds up his hands in innocence. "He went down like a sissy."

Vic is clutching his ankle and is close to tears as Dale walks over to sort it out. If that mouthy bastard says another word, he's going to hit him. He picks up a bottle of water from where he'd thrown it and swigs on the way. One thing for sure, his brother is going to have to toughen up and stop bawling so easily.

Someone shouts, "No! Get off!"

Dale looks up just as he's kneeling down next to Vic. A dog is snapping at Steiner's ankles trying to get the ball. It's so funny it makes him laugh.

"Here, have a drink." Dale passes the water to his brother to stop him from blubbing and continues to watch the mutt. It's some kind of black dog, jumping at Alfie Steiner, and the jerk is getting all freaked out. He shouts across to him, "It just wants to play, you idiot."

Alfie's scream gives away the fact that he's not good around dogs.

Dale gets to his feet and guesses the thing might have nipped him. "Stop shouting, you pussy. Dogs can tell when you're scared of them. I've got one at home and—"

He stops in his tracks.

Blood is running from the dog's jaws and Steiner isn't making any noise.

He's flat out.

There's red all over his soccer shirt.

And where his face used to be.

31

Beijing

The leader of the largest army in the world showers in the luxuriously marbled bathroom that adjoins his spacious office.

He scrubs hard to rid himself of the smell of the women.

Of their sex. And their blood. And their crying.

General Zhang changes into a freshly laundered new uniform.

He stands soldier-straight and checks himself in the full-length mirror.

His hair is jet black and shows no sign of graying.

His eyes are clear and bright.

His body toned and hard.

He is as handsome as he is powerful. The personification of virility. Before he moves away, he thinks of his burns.

The scars his mother gave him.

He makes sure they are well hidden. The world must only see him as perfect. Unblemished.

Waiting in the adjoining room, on a small hard chair in front of his large, antique desk, is Geng Chunlin, Minister of State Security and Head of Intelligence. Chunlin is a man without muscle or hair. There is barely flesh on his scrawny fifty-eight-year-old bones. He wears suits as gray and lifeless as his skin, trousers that stop too short above gray socks, and rubber-soled black shoes that encase his small, narrow feet.

The minister stands as the general enters the office and settles in his big, leather executive chair.

"Sit, Chunlin." Zhang stares distastefully at the specimen opposite him. The excuse for a man who wouldn't last an hour as a soldier. Wouldn't survive ten minutes in a black jail. Dislike aside, he knows the minister is as masterful in his own dark line of work as he is in his.

"I have a final briefing today with President Xian. After that, Lieutenant General Xue—not you—will be announced as operational commander of Nian." He pauses so he can enjoy the disappointment spreading across the minister's face. "For my meeting, Xue will provide me with updated satellite sequencing from the United States, data of where the weaponized canines have been deployed and also where the country's indigenous stray packs are roaming. You will assist him with whatever field intelligence he requires from our operatives. Are you clear about what is required of you?"

"I am, General."

"Good." Zhang gets up from behind his desk and paces. There is much on his mind. Project Nian is his brainchild but he is too reliant on science and scientists for his liking. Academics make soft soldiers. Men with brains are men you can never be certain of. Men of science always have excuses for delays and imperfections.

He sits on the edge of his desk and leans forward. Big unblinking eyes bore into those of the minister. He doesn't see commitment or courage. He sees hesitation. Uncertainty. "What is it, Chunlin? What darkness festers inside you?"

The minister thinks about lying but knows the general would see through him. "My intelligence says the program to deactivate the dogs is still incomplete. It seems they can be turned wild but cannot then be pacified. And—"

"Disinformation." Zhang spits out the word. "People are briefing against me."

"With respect, the feed from the laboratory in Korea showed—"

Zhang slaps him. Flat-hands him. A blow so hard it knocks both man and chair across the floor.

Chunlin makes no sound, no complaint. He quickly repositions the seat and himself and resists putting a hand to the burning skin of his face.

"What the feed showed was a *success*, Chunlin." The general glowers at him. "If you are asked about it, what did it show?"

"Success, sir."

He waves a hand dismissively. "Now get out of my sight. Report to Xue and get your job done."

32

Village Green Park, Key Biscayne

*P*olice marksmen slide out of the weapons van.

The killer dog is less than ten yards from Dale and Vic Shaw-cross.

Cradled in the cops' hands are Heckler & Koch PSGs—Präzisionsschützengewehr rifles. Fast, accurate, semiautomatics. They were invented after the Munich massacre at the Olympic games. A time when German police found themselves unable to stop terrorists from killing hostages because they couldn't get close enough to intervene.

The boys on the ground are huddled together, the older one protecting the younger.

The dog advances slowly. Red drool dangles from its lower jaw.

Marksman Tom Barrett fills his Hensoldt telescopic sight with its muscular form. In the back of his viewfinder, rapidly going out of focus, is the body of another kid, so motionless that he'd be amazed if the boy wasn't dead.

Six yards.

He takes a breath. Stays rock solid still. Focuses.

Squeezes the trigger.

The twenty-five-inch barrel coughs out the first of the twenty rounds packed in the rifle's magazine.

Four yards.

The animal takes the bullet in a shoulder and merely flicks a gaze in Barrett's direction.

He pumps out two more rounds. The first hits the same shoulder, the second slams into its side and head.

Two yards.

The dog wobbles, then tumbles like someone just hand-braked its back legs.

A second marksman, Craig Barry, walks toward the youngster. His PSG is trained on the dog's head.

He drops a defining round into its skull.

A few feet back from the snipers, Ghost bends over the savaged child. He puts two fingers to what's left of his neck and isn't amazed to find there's no pulse.

The poor kid's been ripped to shreds.

He checks his wrist and puts his face close to the boy's mouth. Nothing.

Ghost stands up and tries to shrug off the pain, the enormity of what's just happened. He knows he can't let it settle on him. Can't let the agony of seeing a young life destroyed seep into his pores and soak down into his spirit.

He walks over to the dead dog and stares at it. Three fatal dog attacks in two days. That call from the office of the NIA director is starting to seem less and less ridiculous and more and more interesting.

33

The White House, Washington DC

It seems the perfect August evening, as Clint Molton leaves the Oval Office to enjoy an al fresco dinner with his family in the Jacqueline Kennedy Garden on the south side of the East Colonnade.

The President walks a brick-paved pathway bordered by bronze-colored chrysanthemums and immaculately trimmed low box hedging. Off in the distance he sees Sheryl and the kids engrossed in a game of ball with the pup.

Watching her still brings a smile to his face and a glow of love. They met twenty-five years ago, and there's never been anyone else for either of them. Nor does he imagine there ever will be. He's a lucky man and knows it. President of the most powerful country in the world, happily married and the father of two gorgeous children. How could life get any sweeter?

White House serving staff stand at attention alongside a linen-covered buffet table groaning with salads, jugs of juice, cut meats, fruit, fresh cheeses, and home-baked breads.

"Great right arm you've got there!"

The First Lady turns and smiles as she hears his voice. "It's aching like crazy. This little guy never seems to tire."

Jack and Jane come running over to hug their father, closely followed by Emperor, a gnarled tennis ball lodged between his spiky puppy teeth. Molton gets a grip and shakes it free, then hurls it a good thirty yards down the manicured lawn. The mastiff hurtles after it, and the President guides his children toward the food tables.

A waiter passes the leader of the Western world a sanitized wipe for his hands. "Thank you, Philippe."

Sheryl kisses him, "How's your day been?"

"Busy. I'm still jet-lagged so it's tough getting back into things." He glances at the food. "I don't think I'm going to eat much, my hunger clock is messed up."

She tries to fathom how lagged he is. "What was Beijing—ten hours ahead?"

"Thirteen. Though if you ask me, it feels like it's a century behind."

Emperor appears at his knees, well-slobbered ball in mouth.

"No more, mister. We just cleaned up. Go on; give us a break for a while."

The dog drops the ball at Jack's feet then looks up with sad eyes and pants hopefully.

Sheryl's heart melts. "Aw, look at him. Isn't he so cute?"

"He certainly is." Molton watches his son put his foot on the ball and drag it back and forth like a soccer player.

Emperor's big head shifts with every move of the ten-year-old's foot.

Then he snaps.

Clamps his teeth around anklebone instead of tennis ball.

"Shit!" Molton jumps forward and pushes the dog away with the sole of his shoe.

Jack looks more frightened by his father's movement than the dog. "He didn't hurt me, look—" He lifts his leg to show an uncut ankle. "He's just playing, that's all."

Molton feels his heart banging in his chest. "Sorry."

Emperor drifts back sheepishly.

Jack drops to his knees, hugs the dog and ruffles his coat.

"Jack, not at the table." Sheryl takes another sanitized wipe and hands it to him. "Don't play with the dog while you're eating."

Molton's eyes never leave the animal. He wonders if he over-reacted, or if maybe dogs are much more dangerous than he ever figured.

34

Greenwich Village, New York

*D*anny Speed's apartment looks like a trashed Radio Shack storeroom.

You can't see furniture for all the motherboards, hard drives, and memory chips scattered there.

Amid the mess, financial journalist Jeff Libowicz counts cold hard cash into the young hacker's hands.

"Four sixty. Four eighty. Five hundred." The thirty-five-year-old shakes his head. It only took the nerd a couple of days to get secret financial information that he'd been chasing for weeks. "Fifteen hundred in total. I need my head examined."

"I don't do brain surgery." Danny stuffs the bills into the frayed pocket of his low-hanging gray jeans.

Libowicz slides his near-empty wallet back into his leather jacket and picks the A4 envelope off the top of a workstation. "Tell me—how exactly did you learn all the geeky stuff?" He points at a trio of pimped-up Macs running screens full of codes. "I struggle to operate just one of them."

"My father bullied me into computer sciences at college, and I picked up a pile of know-how before I dropped out."

"You're good. You should go back and finish."

"And you shouldn't pay people to break the law."

"Like they say, 'To each his own.' Seriously, man—you *are* good. I mean, that stuff you got for me was Fort Knoxed behind son-of-a-bitch Russian firewalls. I'm truly impressed."

"You shouldn't be. Most of their online security is old-fashioned, copied from the West. The Asians are actually much tougher nuts to crack."

"That right?"

"Yep." Danny lifts a Coke off the desk and drains it through a long blue straw. "Ain't just the Japanese either. China's all but caught up with them on tech. Koreans too."

Libowicz is intrigued. "I was just thinking. If you're not going to go into honest employment and pay Uncle Sam his taxes, then maybe I can make you a deal."

"I'm always open to a 'deal.'"

"Something that gives you more regular cash and doesn't cost me quite so much."

"Like what?"

"Like a *retainer*. Say I give you 12K a year—a grand a month—two fifty a week in cash?"

"And what do I have to do for that?"

"Fish around some more of those BRIC-based companies, see what's in their accounts, internal reports, business plans. You never know—we might even be able to flutter a bit on the big casino they call Wall Street."

Danny's interested. "Yeah, I can do that. But listen, man, you fuck me—like asking me to work 24/7—and not only is the deal off, I promise you, I will mess you up so bad you'll still be saying sorry in your next lifetime."

"Won't happen."

"I mean it. I'll stick your name on sex offenders' registers and screw your credit rating worse than Bernie Madoff."

Jeff holds up his hands. "Okay, I get the message. No fucking with Mr. Genius here. Now, do we have a deal?"

"Yeah, we have a deal."

They bump fists.

"Good. Now I've got to go. I'll mail you some companies to look at." Libowicz taps the folder of info he'd come for. "There's a story to write. Bets to place."

35

Weaponization Bunkers, North Korea

*J*ihai finds his father straining over a microscope in a glass-partitioned office at the end of the laboratory.

He should be sleeping.

It is three days since the old man rested. Seventy-two hours since he shut his eyes and for just one second didn't toil over the creation of the mood modifiers for the Nian dogs.

"I have brought you some food." Jihai places a tray at the end of his father's long worktop. "Fish, rice, and fruit. With a flask of tea and some juice."

Hao doesn't look up. His brain is focused on the magnified slide and the intense biological world spinning and swarming within it.

"Father, you must stop. You must rest."

The scientist angrily jerks his head up from his work. "It is not for a son to tell his father how to behave at work. Here, I am your boss, not your parent."

The young man stands his ground. "Many times you have told me that a tired mind is a useless mind. Fatigue breeds failure. I worry for your health and—"

Hao slaps his son's face. "Don't you dare talk to me about failure!"

Jihai puts a hand to the sting.

"It is *you*—you and those idiots you work with who have befriended Failure and welcomed him into our workplace to ruin us."

Jihai can see his father is exhausted. Hand still to burning face, he bows and starts to leave.

"Wait!"

He stops and turns.

"Thank you for the food. Though you should not have brought it in here, you know that."

"If I had not, there would be no chance of you stopping and eating."

Hao smiles and feels a pang of guilt.

"Shall I take it away?"

"No. Leave it there." He realizes he must talk to his son. Build a bridge between them. "You know how important our work is?"

"Yes, sir."

Hao's not sure he does. "The Americans and the West have developed ways of infecting our dogs. We have more than twenty million in our country, Jihai. Twenty million—that is like a whole country of dogs. The West, with all its research into cloning and genetic modification, has found a manner in which to bring diseased breeds into our country and have them multiply, turn on us and destroy us. This is why we still have rabies and they do not. Why we have had to ban dogs growing above knee height, ban them from being allowed out during the day, ban them from all parks, public places, and—"

"Sir—"

"Let me finish. These are the reasons our work here is so important. We must fight back. We replicate the aggression in order to find the passivity. Each day that we fail, the Americans breed more and more of these dogs—"

"What if that's not true?" Jihai jumps in. "What if it's propaganda and lies?"

Hao doesn't understand, and his face shows it.

Jihai tries to explain. "I have read things on the Internet about the Americans being attacked by dogs. Killed by wild dogs—wild in the ways we have seen in our own experiments."

Hao dismisses his child's ramblings. "Dogs are savage animals, Jihai. Wolves by nature." Another thought occurs to him. "Have you been reading noncensored sites?"

The young man shakes his head in despair. "Everyone reads them—everyone with a brain. Government censors can no more lock a toilet door, let alone secure a global power like the Internet. These days there isn't a student in China who doesn't know how to escape 'the lock.'"

His father is surprised, and instantly realizes he shouldn't be. His son and friends were born into the technological revolution. It is clay in their hands, to be modeled and shaped as they wish. Whereas *he* had to encounter it in his later years, and the experience was like meeting an alien creature and needing to learn its languages and habits.

Hao points to the microscope. "I must finish. I have work to do."

Jihai understands he is being dismissed. "Please eat some food—and please think on what I have said—not as a foolish son, but as one scientist to another. What if things are not as General Zhang says? What if our work is not to stop lethal American dogs, but to create Chinese ones?"

36

Greenwich Village, New York

*T*he reporter's money is scorching a hole in Danny's pocket as he leaves his run-down rental and heads across town.

He has plans for it.

Crazy, *crazy* plans.

He glances over his shoulder and checks reflections in storefront windows. As far as he can tell, he hasn't been followed. The last thing he wants is anyone on his tail.

Next to the newfound cash is a set of keys. Keys to a second apartment. One that neither he nor the three other hacktivists he operates with can live in. This is strictly a workplace, stuffed with the kind of technology NASA would die for.

Danny was still at college when he was recruited and paid to put the hacking group together. He wasn't sure what was happening at first. It was just one of those things that started small and snowballed into something bigger.

Much bigger.

He'd been at a party and a friend of a friend introduced him to an Ivy League dude with a bad coke habit and money to burn. As a favor, he set up his 3D home media entertainment system for him. It was one of those obscenely expensive domestic networks that plays your videos, music, and Internet all over the house and gardens. Afterward, the guy says he has a friend who will pay him a fortune to screw up a competing company's computer system. It wasn't exactly a fortune, but back in college two grand seemed so. Next thing Danny knew, he's being introduced to other rich boys with grudges, no principles, and lots of money that they're happy to part with in return for some clinical and cynical cyber skulduggery.

Then came the envelope.

Five grand in cash and the keys to a loft in SoHo, with the message: "Go in the spirit of the Slaughterhouse." It was a cryptic reference to the Cult of the Dead Cow, a group of U.S. hacktivists who worked from a secret HQ known as the Slaughterhouse, which got burned down way back in the nineties.

Whoever sent it knew they had the right man. From the time Danny first turned on a computer he'd been interested in using it for mischief. He'd grown up learning about the antics of groups like CDC, Hacker con, Ninja Strike Force, and Hacktivismo. At a time when most kids adopted sports stars as their heroes, his were Omega, the Cult of the Dead Cow, and the "Hong Kong Blondes"—a group of dissidents who disrupted censored networks across the People's Republic of China.

Danny briefly reflects on it all as he walks around his group's new base. There's a large open hardwood floor dotted with generous-size desks and new high-end computers and servers. The place smells of the fresh leather of four brown La-Z-Boys, and there are a couple of giant sofas in zebra fabric to crash on as well. A screen hides an area to cook, and a big fridge is filled with soda and beer. By the front door there are boxes of Tyvek suits and latex gloves—the hackers know they should leave no trace in either the real world or the virtual one.

The place is perfect.

Danny can't wait to get to work.

31

Weaponization Bunkers, North Korea

*T*he noise and the jolt wake him

Hao had been asleep.

He'd dozed off at the microscope. Fallen from his stool. On the way down, knocked over the food Jihai had brought him.

Now he is on the floor, surrounded by spilled fruit, rice, and fish, feeling an ache in his elbow and the back of his skull.

For a moment he doesn't move. He just stays there in the mess and stares up at the strips of neon on the ceiling.

Failure.

Failure is exhausting him.

Failure is breaking him.

Jihai's doubts had been the last straw. They had broken his concentration and shut down his brain. He could not cope with the thought that all their work and sacrifice of the last years was to create something murderous rather than to counter it.

Such thinking has to be banished from his mind. And from Jihai's.

He focuses.

Reminds himself of his predicament.

He had been so close to perfecting a pacifier—then everything changed. For weeks nothing went according to plan. It was as though the progress he'd made had all been a fluke and couldn't be repeated. He'd rerun all the tests using exactly the same measure of chemicals and made sure they were added, mixed, and dispensed in exactly the same doses.

Failure.

He had gone back and done it all again, this time putting the errors down to a difference in the breeds of dogs.

Failure multiplied by failure.

But even in the face of defeat he'd refused to give up.

He wondered if variances in the dogs' weight, sex, or age might have been to blame.

They weren't.

So now he knows he has to go back to his formulas.

Pick himself up and start again.

Hao does just that. He slides his hands across the food-splattered floor, eases himself upright and brushes himself down.

He has to put Jihai's comments out of his mind. Such thinking was crazy.

Such thinking could get them killed.

38

Historic District, Miami

*G*host is too tired to eat when he gets home.

He's spent the evening starting up an Incident Room to manage information on the dog attacks, and now he's wiped out.

He kicks off his shoes, throws his jacket over a chair, and grabs two beers from the fridge. He's so tightly wound; it's going to take at least two to relax him.

He pops the caps and sprawls out on the settee. Days don't come a lot worse than the ones he's having at the moment. Two dead kids within twenty-four hours and a grandfather killed as well.

He's never known anything like it.

Seventeen-year-old Kathy Morgan. Ten-year-old Alfie Steiner. Fifty-five-year-old Matt Wood. He closes his eyes and sees all their faces. Their faces and their injuries. The terrible bites, the fractured bones, the missing flesh.

Ghost finishes his first bottle and puts the second to his forehead to cool it down. He's trying not to think of the relatives now. Of the children's parents, of Wood's wife, whom he'd only seen fleetingly at the station while Annie dealt with her. The poor woman looked even paler than him. Going through her husband's life and searching for a reason for the attack will be a horrible process that will feel like it never ends.

The thought makes him restless. He gets up and takes his beer to the window. Looks out at the sweltering city and its swirl of lights and feels desperately alone.

It's almost midnight when the second bottle is empty and he's finished plotting out which few people he can detail to which numerous tasks in the not-too-far-away start to the new day.

He finds himself dialing Zoe's number while simultaneously wondering whether he's going to make a fool of himself.

She must have gone to bed, because all he gets is her voice massage. "Hi, you're through to Zoe Speed, photographer, adventurer, and lover of life. Leave a message and I'll get back to you. That is, unless you're on my shit list, in which case go . . ." A long bleep fills the gap. ". . . yourself."

He's laughing as he leaves the message. "Zoe, you said call, so I'm calling. Sorry it's so late, I was just—"

She picks up. "Hi, it's me. The *real* me, I mean. I just didn't get to the phone in time."

He sounds startled. "Oh. Hi." There seems no point beating about the bush. "Listen, I've had a truly shitty day and I think you might be the only person who can make it all right. My head is full of stuff that I really don't want to think about. Do you fancy catching a late drink somewhere?"

"No, not really."

The answer knocks him back. "Oh."

"But I do fancy catching a cab to your place. And I'm confident I can make you forget your messed up head and sleep soundly. Would that work instead?"

He laughs again. "Yeah. I guess it would."

"Give me a minute to steal something from my friend's closet, then I'll be with you."

39

Beijing

*P*resident Xian Sheng sits at his large presidential desk, a spacious block of ancient camphor wood so wide it takes him several strides to reach either end.

General Zhang is already pacing outside, eager to see him.

Before Xian lets him in, he pours a cup of green peony tea and waits for his call to the White House to be routed to the President of the United States.

There's a click as Molton comes on the line. "Xian, an unexpected surprise. How are you?"

The Chinese leader detects a deliberate overfriendliness in his counterpart's voice. "I'm in good health, Mr. President. As I hope are both you and your family."

"They are indeed. Thank you for asking. To what do I owe the honor of this call?"

"I wanted to personally follow up on our discussions at the

summit. As I mentioned, China is keen to help America come to an arrangement over both its financial difficulties and the terror threat that it is facing."

Molton heads him off. "Well, thank you for your consideration, but I believe I dealt with this pretty directly when we spoke. We have a perfectly acceptable and official financial arrangement with China and I see *no* reason at all to alter it. And I am not aware of any terror threats that we need your assistance with."

Xian pauses while he pours more tea into the simple clay cup that he always drinks from. "General Zhang is concerned. He believes that the type of incidents he warned Mr. Jackson about in Miami will spread and cause an even greater loss of life."

Molton exhales wearily. "President Xian, I'll be honest with you. I am struggling to take this seriously." His tone becomes less cordial. "The whole notion that weaponized canines could be used to attack American people seems hugely preposterous to both myself and my advisors. We see no evidence whatsoever that this so-called third party threat has any credence."

The Chinese leader wipes a drip of tea from the camphor desk. "Then I will bid you good day, Mr. President. I wish you well and look forward to the time when we may speak again."

"Good day to you too. Thank you for your call."

As the line goes dead, Xian presses a button on his phone and tells his secretary to show General Zhang in.

Seconds later the door opens. The military commander enters and closes it in a swift and orderly motion. Aware that this meeting demands even more formality and respect than he normally affords, he marches to the edge of the desk, stands ramrod straight in front of his leader and salutes.

Xian nods his consent for him to sit. He weighs up the eagerness in his colleague.

A soldier *ever*-hungry for war.

A man desperate for power.

His power.

"There is an old superstition that if you hear a dog howl late at night, then someone somewhere is dying. Today you come to me, Zhang, seeking to make a whole army of dogs howl and many, many people die. Are you *certain* that this is the moment for such disturbance?"

"Our hearts train our ears to crave silence, but our minds know that discourse is the only way to secure true peace."

Xian cradles the clay cup and sips his tea. "And what words of wisdom are your scientists telling you about the control of these weaponized canines? I ask because it is clear from your reports that they can be activated at will, but to date I have seen no evidence of pacification. Any coward can find a moment to catch an unsuspecting person off-guard and deliver a duplicitous cut—only a respected physician can provide the means to heal."

"Physicians also need to cut. I believe we are ready to do both as and when needed." Zhang pauses and wonders if Chunlin has secretly been briefing the president, apprising him of the problems he's been having with the scientists.

"You hesitate, General. Is it because you are thoughtful or because you are worried?"

"Thoughtful, President Xian. We have all the control we need." He slides over three thick manila files, stacked with satellite photographs, charts, reports, data analyses, and summaries. "Only two weaponized dogs were activated in the area we warned the Americans of. One was shot on a beach. The second in a park. Those files also show you the locations and activation timetables of the other weaponized dogs."

Xian doesn't even glance at the documents, let alone examine them. "Command is a matter of trust and loyalty. Men who rise together also fall together. Tell me, Zhang—will our country stand on your proposals to me and reach even greater heights, or will the weight of such ambition cause us to collectively and personally stumble and fall?"

The general chooses his words carefully before replying, "Project Nian will bring even more greatness to China, President Xian. It will restore our position as true leaders of the world. We have waited long to strike the first blow. Now that our hands have been shown and our enemy has seen the intent in our eyes, we *must* deliver the blow quickly."

Xian lifts the classical Gong Fu style teapot and delicately pours more of the calming brew while he contemplates the bigger picture. Never again will America be so weak. Poor leadership and a gangrenous economy have drained them of their financial wealth. Badly fought wars on distant battlefields have left their military forces unpopular, underresourced, demoralized, and depleted. He knows that Zhang is right about momentum. The power of the moment is with him.

"You have my permission to escalate the deployment of Nian dogs, but not unconditionally and not throughout all of America."

"President Xian—"

"Do not interrupt me."

Zhang nods respectfully.

"Give the Americans one more show of strength. One they cannot this time explain away. Extend your operation from Miami to all of Florida, but no farther. Call Director Jackson and make it clear to him that what he is about to witness is the full wrath of weaponized canines, a loss of life he could have prevented."

The general knows better than to argue.

"One more thing, Zhang. The day after tomorrow is the eighth; this is the number in which we have the greatest trust. Wait until luck is on our side before you tempt fate."

PART TWO

What is evil but good tortured
by its own hunger and thirst?

KHALIL GIBRAN

40

Beijing

*A*nd so the time comes.

The world's newest and most insidious weapon of mass destruction is about to be deployed, without fanfare or ceremony, at precisely the moment President Xian believes it is most likely to bring success.

He is merely following an age old tradition that still sees Singapore Airlines reserve flight numbers starting with eight to China—and in Korea saw the Petronas Towers in Malaysia stop at the eighty-eighth floor.

General Zhang is in the military control room and gives the green light to Xue Shi, his most trusted lieutenant, the man he has placed in minute-by-minute charge of the campaign that will secure his place as the eventual successor to Xian.

At six feet tall and 180 pounds in pure muscled weight, forty-two-year-old General Xue cuts a distinctive figure in most places, but especially among his diminutive colleagues.

Zhang's protégé diligently visits row after row of intelligence officers seated at computer terminals. He gives each of them specific details about which dog needs to be activated and when to do it.

He returns to Zhang and proudly confirms their readiness. "We are operational. I will see that you are not troubled unnecessarily, General, and will update you only on major developments."

Zhang nods his appreciation then lifts the cuff of his uniform to check his watch. "It is time for my telephone conference with the American."

"The office next door has been prepared, sir. I will personally put the call through to you."

Zhang leaves feeling pleased. Xue is loyal and trustworthy. Which is more than can be said of Chunlin. One day he will have to remove that man from his position and put someone more reliable there.

He settles at a cheap bare desk in the adjoining communications room and waits for the call to be patched through to him.

A woman's voice comes on the line. "I have Director Jackson for General Zhang."

Xue answers. "I have the general on the line and I am putting you through."

Data capture machines in Beijing and Washington silently record the conversation as it begins at 8:30 A.M. Beijing time on August 8, and 8:30 P.M. Washington time on August 7.

"General, this is Brandon Jackson, what can I do for you?"

Zhang has no time for pleasantries. "My president instructed me to call you as a matter of grave urgency. You will recall my warning when we were together in Beijing?"

"Of course. You played me that *unforgettable* footage."

"And since then you have seen it for yourself in Miami. You have seen it yet you still do not believe it."

Jackson doesn't answer.

"From midnight tonight—your time—the weaponized dogs we warned you of will extend their terror across Florida. Let me be clear—this is your terror. Bred by your arrogance and unleashed by your ignorance. Do not make the mistake, Mr. Director, of ignoring this final warning. If you do so, then you will find all of

America chased by these dogs of war and then not even God, let alone China, may be able to help you."

41

The White House, Washington DC

Clint Molton leaves his family in the lounge on the second floor to take the hastily scheduled late night call in the study next door. If he's lucky, he'll get back in time to see who makes it through to the final of *The Voice*.

He picks up the secure line and slips behind the desk that he's certain innumerable Presidents have taken late calls at. "Hi there, Don—what's got you working so late?"

"I'm very sorry to trouble you, sir. I just spoke to General Zhang in China and he gave me another of his heavily loaded warnings."

Just the mention of Zhang's name makes the President grow tense. "Tell me the worst of it."

"Well, it was uncomfortably similar to last time. A heads-up that these weaponized canines are going to start killing people and—"

"Hang on, Don, didn't you and I agree that this guy had a screw loose and we were going to ignore him?"

"We did, sir, and I apologize. I trouble you because Zhang has been somewhat specific. He claims there will be more attacks tomorrow. He said, and I quote, 'You have seen it for yourself in Miami. You have seen it yet you still do not believe it. From midnight, the weaponized dogs we warned you of will now extend their terror across Florida.'"

"How did he sound when he said it? Speculative or sure?"

"Relaxed and cocky. Like some punk who has a card in his hand that we really didn't think he had."

The President examines the computer screen on the desk in front of him. "I've a space in my diary at eleven. I'm due to be with the VP. I think it would be good if you came over and talked to us both."

"Yes, sir. I'll be there. I'll also have my people extend their monitoring of police activity and ER rooms from Miami to all of Florida."

"Let's hope there's nothing untoward to report. Good night, Don."

"Good night, Mr. President."

42

Lake Jackson, Florida

A hard night of summery thunderstorms yields to a soft dawn sky that's a psychedelic mix of purples, pinks, and pallid blues. Beneath it a cool silver mist swirls over an eight-mile-long lake.

Thirty-year-old marathon runner Ellen McGonall has ninety minutes for her training run before the weather becomes unbearably hot and she begins her shift at the nearby aquatic reserve.

She starts out on the west side of the flat-bottomed lake that's brimming with bass, crappie, and bluegill and works her way clockwise. Her husband Tommy caught a large-mouth bass out here two weekends back and took home the Tallahassee Trophy Rod.

A beep from her wristwatch tells her she should already have done her first mile, and she hasn't. Ellen digs in and quickens her pace. She just got back in training since suffering from shin splints, and her schedule is geared to get her fit for the Bay Marathon in October, then the Pensacola and Space Coast marathons in November, before finishing the year with the Mangrove and Jacksonville Bank events in December.

Six miles out she's back on time and feeling good. The sky is clear and not yet too hot. She's thinking of the blue herons and wood storks they've spotted recently, and the big old alligator that scared the daylights out of a boat of fishermen at Meginnis Arm. More than anything, though, she's thinking how lucky she is to be alive. How fortunate to live in this awesome part of the world and have her good health, a handsome and loving husband, and two beautiful young babies.

Life is amazing.

As she bowls along Millers Landing her eyes roam over the vast water and back toward her house on the other side, at the bottom of Treeline Drive. She and Tommy bought the bungalow five years ago when it was little more than clapboard, and he's fixed it up just fine.

Her head swivels the other way, down the track leading to where her friends the Coopers keep some kennels. She does a double take. Strange that the dogs are still asleep. Usually there's a bark or two as she goes by. And generally Zack and Zef, their big old Alsatians, run down to meet her.

It's no trouble for Ellen to jog down the track and out the other end. It'll add thirty seconds or so to her mile time, but so what? She turns in and immediately sees Zack.

He's dead.

She doesn't need a longer or closer look to confirm it.

Something's ripped his throat out.

Ellen breaks her stride and starts to slow. Ten yards away to her right she sees Zef.

The sight of him stops her.

He's on his back, legs splayed and white belly fur bloodred.

It's a gator.

She just knows it is.

Those things grow to be ten feet long and weigh over five hundred pounds. They can chew-down a dog like a kiddie can crunch up a candy bar.

She walks tentatively down the gravel toward the house and the big old barn at the side where the Coopers keep the pups they breed

"Pete!" She wouldn't normally shout, but hell, what's gone on here isn't normal. "Lizzie!"

The barn door is busted open. It's splintered, like someone's driven a small truck clean through it.

Ellen's blood runs cold. Her bare arms come up in goose bumps and she rubs them as she walks toward the black hole in the timber.

"Hello!"

No way is she going inside. Not in a million lifetimes. She stands ten feet back and at first can't see anything. Then her eyes balance light and shade and she starts to see clearly.

There's nothing in there. No movement. No noise.

No pups.

They must have got out.

Blood.

A stream of it is running down the center of the concrete floor and into the drain her husband helped Pete put in so he could wash away any mess the dogs made.

Ellen feels spooked.

She spins around.

There's nothing there.

She breathes a sigh of relief. Those gators can move quick over short distances, twenty miles an hour or even faster, and despite all her training that's still a whole lot quicker than she can run.

A noise comes from over at the house.

Thank God.

Ellen heads toward the side door. She sees two Labradors standing there.

The dogs have their heads down. They're playing with something. Pulling it between them.

"Pete!" He can't be far away.

The dogs hear her and look around.

Now Ellen sees what they were playing with—and she knows Pete isn't going to be returning her shout.

She backs away. Hopes that if she moves slowly and confidently they're going to let her go.

But deep down she knows things aren't going to work out that way.

The dogs lose interest in Pete's head and prowl toward her. The one on the left bares its teeth and starts to growl. The other dips its shoulders.

And begins to run.

Ellen turns and sprints as fast as she can.

Gravel slips under her right foot.

She stumbles but doesn't go down.

Twelve feet away are the lower branches of an old hickory.

She veers to her right and then snaps left to throw off the dogs.

Three feet to go.

Ellen checks her stride and readies for the jump.

The first Labrador bites her left thigh. Takes out a hand-sized chunk of muscle.

She crashes head first into the old trees.

Mercifully, she's unconscious by the time the second dog bites into her.

43

Beijing

*T*wo hundred miles above the earth, silently drifting Chinese military satellites slowly buzz into life and alter their angles, tilts, and focus.

Cutting edge technology that's been copied, stolen, and modified has given the People's Republic the lead when it comes to snooping.

Gigantic lenses fix like beady eyes on Florida, especially a remote patch of land and buildings off the east side of Lake Jackson.

The optical imaging systems on the reconnaissance satellites are powerful enough to focus on the eye of a rat. But their targets today are bigger than that.

Much bigger.

Coordinates are being programmed by military operators in Beijing. Shiny, unblinking robot eyes in the skies follow the fresh movement of newly activated, weaponized canines.

Lieutenant General Xue Shi stares into the never closing eyes of the satellites orbiting the earth. They shift and jerk imperceptibly as they follow the transmitted coordinators of the weaponized canines.

The man in charge of Project Nian scans the streams of constantly changing data and the stacked banks of monitors recording constant video feeds.

The pictures of the dogs come in black and white, color and 3D. In long shots, close-ups, real-time, recorded, and slow motion.

They come with map and graphic overlays of streets, rivers, towns, and cities, with text boxes highlighting hospitals, police HQs, fire stations, ambulance bases, and army camps.

Xue pulls up an overview of the orbit schedules for the newest generation of recon satellites and the older, more basic fifteen-ton Lacrosse-class radar-imaging satellites. He compares past, current, and predicted positions of the animals and forms a model to demonstrate the shape and speed of the military progress he expects to be made.

The whole project is a marvel to him. The genetic engineering. The cutting-edge system of tracking all the weaponized dogs. The wonderful logistics and covert operations that went into moving the hounds into the right locations. It had been like training and mobilizing an invisible army.

The positions of China's secret soldiers show on Xue's matte black screens. All he has to do is pick which ones he wants to deploy, sit back and watch the devastation. More accurate than smart bombs. More insidious than napalm. More emotionally traumatic than suicide bombing.

Xue uncaps a bottle of water and takes a long, cooling swallow as he watches the Labradors finish off the last of the woman jogger.

44

Greenwich Village, New York

*T*he Village is still bathed in the cool of twilight as Danny Speed shuffles down the stone stairs of his old apartment block and approaches his motorbike.

The street smells comfortingly of summer blossom, and he can't help but feel the excitement of a new day.

Danny's up early. He's got lots of things happening. Big things. Serious things. World-changing things. Especially if anyone catches him doing them.

Not that they will.

He's cautious. More than anyone he knows.

He puts his helmet down on the sidewalk, drops into a press-up position and checks beneath the chained and alarmed super-bike before he even touches it.

Caution starts on his own doorstep.

After a visual check, he runs two handheld scanners around the entire frame. One is to detect any tracking device that may have been attached. The other will tell him of the presence of something more serious.

Explosives.

Only when he's absolutely certain that nobody has interfered with the machine does he disarm the alarm, unchain the wheels, and start it up.

The street is empty but he still checks all around him. Not out of a sense of road safety, but in case there are people slouched low in parked cars, ready to follow him or alert others to their movements.

Danny knows that when you do what he does, you break a lot of laws and make a lot of enemies.

He revs the black Kawasaki and enjoys the throaty growl of its engines before finally pulling away.

He always leaves his building with time to spare. Not because he's an arrive-early kind of guy, but because most times he goes back. He circles the block and returns to the outside of his apartment, almost as though he's forgotten something. Then he retraces his steps and goes through all his checks all over again.

It's like some kind of OCD madness. A compulsion, but one that keeps him out of trouble. The way he figures it, if someone were going to try to steal his computers, or worse still, the data in them, then they'd have to give themselves maximum time to do it. Starting the moment he leaves.

Half an hour later he makes it to Wall Street and begins another laborious set of checks.

Only when he's absolutely certain that he's not been followed or watched does he go up to the loft and begin his day of intensive criminal activity.

45

Historic District, Miami

*T*he digital clock beside Ghost's bed shows 6:59.

He reaches his arm over Zoe and tries not to wake her as he clicks off the alarm before it brings a rude end to their night together.

As quietly as possible, he shaves, showers, and dresses for work in a green linen suit and matching silk shirt.

He watches her as he buttons up.

She looks peaceful now but had been thrashing around in her sleep, mumbling and sweating her way through some kind of nightmare. It had been the kind of thing he was afraid of happening to himself when he called and asked her to be with him. See enough shit in your life and eventually it comes chasing you in your sleep.

Ghost stands at the end of the bed, unsure whether to wake her or leave her to sleep. Somehow, with messed-up hair and zero makeup, she's even more attractive than when she's in a pretty dress and all her paint and finery. He leans over, tenderly touches her face and whispers, "Hey, Zoe, I'm going—"

Ghost never finishes.

She grabs his hand, twists it and forces his fingers back so hard she almost breaks his wrist.

The move knocks him off balance.

Ghost tumbles onto the bed and across her legs.

Zoe sits bolt upright, still holding the wristlock. Her eyes are filled with fury. She's set to drive an elbow smack into the middle of his nose—when she comes to her senses and stops herself.

Ghost sees her change. The aggression dissolves and almost becomes fear. She must have been asleep, in the middle of another bad dream when he'd touched her. She'd mistaken it for violence. Maybe even a delayed aftershock to the incident with the robber in the street. "It's all right. You're okay."

She releases his hand. "What the fuck were you doing?"

He rubs his wrist. "I was saying goodbye. Seeing if you wanted anything before I left. Oh, and maybe I was trying to be *affectionate*."

"Then fucking don't be when I'm asleep." She slips naked out of the quilt and angrily scans the room. There's no gown in sight so she grabs a shirt off a laundered pile on his dresser.

"Suits you."

She starts to fasten the middle buttons.

"I'm sorry if I spooked you. I had no intention of hurting or frightening you."

"You didn't." Zoe finishes buttoning up and starts to feel stupid about getting angry. "I just don't like being touched—not unless I'm expecting it." She rolls up the shirtsleeves.

"That's sad."

"That's my rule."

"Then it's a sad rule. Why did you invent it?"

"Because men need rules."

"What's wrong, Zoe? Were you thinking about the robbery?"

"No."

"Then what? What's eating you so badly that it makes you this angry?"

"Memories. When I'm asleep they become all too real. That's what makes me angry."

46

Montgomery Correctional Center, Jacksonville, Florida

Folks used to call the place "City Farm Prison," and many locals still do, especially those who've got ancestors who spent time there. Ever since it opened, inmates have worked the soil as part of their stretch, and boosted the local economy in the bargain.

Back in '58, Jonboy Layton was one of the first admitted to a new, plaster-smelling cell as punishment for trespass, disorderly conduct, and assault, and Justin Cartwright was one of the wet-behind-the-ears "screws" who got to crack a stick around Jonboy's legs when he misbehaved in the crop fields. And so was born a spark of interfamily hatred that still burns brightly more than half a century later.

Montgomery has grown over the years and now covers 640 acres of northwestern Jacksonville. It provides close to $200,000 of crops and services to the community.

This fine August morning, Justin T. Cartwright is the officer-in-charge of the ten-man Landscape and Nursery detail working the prison's two-acre vegetable field. As usual, thirty-three-year-old Jax Layton is one of the slackers.

The big, dark-haired officer shouts across the soil. "C'mon, less chatter and more work, Layton. Those peppers aren't going to pick themselves."

"I need a minute." He bends a little, puts a soiled hand beneath his prison issue T-shirt and rubs at his heart. "I got a stitch."

Cartwright thinks he's faking. He walks around the row of dark green plants bulging with waxy orange peppers. Gets up close to the muscular inmate and issues his second and final warning. "It's stitches you'll be *needing* if you keep mouthing off. Now get those habaneros harvested."

"Give me a minute." He really does have a stitch. Or at least that's what he hopes it is. His old man died of a heart attack in his early forties and it's always at the back of his mind.

The big guard leans over Layton and shoves the rounded end of the baton into the soft nest of flesh under the man's chin. "Get the fuck up and start working."

Tension sparks across the plot. A guard dog barks. One of the officers slips the safety off his rifle. Other inmates stop working and watch in silence.

Stitch or no stitch, the way Jax Layton sees it, he's been left with no choice but to stand up for himself. If he lets Cartwright humiliate him now, then he'll never get over the loss of face.

He straightens up just as he was told to. Then he smashes his forehead hard into the bridge of the screw's nose. Before the blood even comes, he drives his knee hard into Cartwright's testicles. The second he does it, he knows he's only got time to swing one good punch before the other guards make their move.

Layton launches a jaw-breaking haymaker.

A warning shot goes off somewhere behind him.

The damned guard dog barks like crazy.

He straightens up. Steps away. Braces himself for the beating that he knows is going to come.

Only it doesn't.

The German shepherd is going mad. It's jumping all over its handler, George Jennings.

Only, it's not jumping.

It's biting.

The other guard, old man Foreman, waves his rifle back and forth but can't get off a shot for fear of hitting George.

Layton's glad they didn't set that damned dog on him. It's chewing up George real bad.

Foreman finally swings the rifle butt and manages to knock the mutt away for a second.

The dog shakes its big bloody head.

Someone across the soil shouts, "Jesus Fucking Christ."

Now, everyone sees what a mess the dog has made of Jennings.

It's ripped holes in the man's face and arms.

The guy is blind.

He's on his knees. Blood drips through his fingers as he holds his hands to his face.

Foreman's frozen with shock.

He looks like a kid who just whacked a hornet's nest and knows he's about to get his ass stung to death.

As the German shepherd jumps Foreman, Layton turns his attention to Cartwright. He's still moaning and groaning, while curled in a fetal position holding his balls.

His gun is there for the grabbing.

It would be a crime to look a gift horse in the mouth.

Jax Layton sticks a knee into the fallen guard's side and unholsters the weapon.

Now anything is possible.

Anything on earth.

47

Historic District, Miami

Ghost brews a pot of rich Colombian roast, while Zoe sulks in the shower and dresses. He hopes when she materializes she's calmer.

As he's getting white mugs from the cupboard, she walks into his kitchen of cool Italian marbles and brushed metals, wearing the tiny red dress she'd turned up in last night.

She looks self-conscious as their eyes meet. "Not quite the daytime look, is it?" She sits at a breakfast bar and fiddles with her phone.

"Oh I don't know—it still looks great to me. You want coffee?"

"Intravenously." She reads mails on her phone. "You know those dog incidents you've been covering?"

"Aha." He pours her a cup. "Cream and sugar?"

"Just black. I need the kick first thing." She scrolls as she talks. "They're not just in Miami—the attacks."

"What d'you mean?"

She looks up at him. "Well, I was interested in what you were doing, so after I saw you on TV, I set up a Google Alert on canine incidents, and look . . ." She holds out the iPhone so he can see. "There are dozens of them. All over America. All over the world."

Ghost puts her coffee down and looks over her shoulder. "There are a lot of dogs in the world, so I guess that naturally translates into a lot of bites."

"And *deaths*, see . . ." She puts the phone into his hand.

DOG ATTACK VICTIM TRIES TO SAVE OWNER'S LIFE
New York Times

A cyclist who was attacked by four dogs shook off her bite wounds and battled to save the life of the animals' owner after he suffered a heart attack trying to pull them off her. The 47-year-old woman was out biking . . . See all stories on this topic>

MASTIFF BITES PUT 7 PEOPLE IN HOSPITAL
Error! Hyperlink reference not valid.

Police shot dead a mastiff that turned on a family and their neighbors in what onlookers have described as a rabidlike frenzy. The group were enjoying a BBQ when the two-year-old hound jumped and snapped at them, causing three adults and four children to need more than a hundred stitches among them. See all stories on this topic>

Ghost reads then hands the phone back. "I don't know if it's the heat or the fact that the economy has dipped again, but over the last few days things seem to have gotten worse." He looks confused for a moment. "I really don't know what's at the root of all this. When Kathy Morgan died, I told the press that I thought the killer dog might be a stray. God knows there are so many roaming around these days. Then we found the guy on the golf course, and it looks like he'd been killed by his pet. Next we get the young boy playing soccer killed by a rottweiler."

"You think they're all connected somehow?"

"That's why we've set up an Incident Room—to discover if there's a common denominator. But I don't see how there can be. Different breeds. Different people. Different times, places, and circumstances." He glances at his watch. "Listen, I'm in danger of running late." He nods to her coffee. "If you drink that quickly, I'll drop you back at your friend's place before I head into work. That way you won't feel too self-conscious catching a cab looking like you stayed out *unexpectedly*."

She smiles. "Most considerate."

"Or I could just give you a key?"

"What?"

"A key. I could give you one so you let yourself in and out, when you want."

Zoe is speechless.

She feels like she's a little kid on a seesaw and some giant bully just sat down on the other end and is bouncing up and down.

"A lift would be great. Thanks."

48

Montgomery Correctional Center, Jacksonville, Florida

Jax Layton knows there isn't a member of his family who wouldn't stand up and applaud him if he put a bullet through Justin Cartwright's big dumb head. But as he's well aware, the punishment for that in Florida is the death penalty, and he has no intention of swapping his two-year stretch for a cell on Death Row.

Instead, he's going to do what Foreman should have done— had the old fool had the skill and nerve to do it. He's going to shoot the damned guard dog.

The German shepherd is ripping chunks out of the white-haired guard, and Layton reckons it's now or never. He rests Cartwright's 9mm on his left forearm, squints along the barrel and, because the dog's jaws are so close to Foreman, aims for its body. There's a crack of gunfire and the round disappears into a fuzz of black and gold fur.

Everyone holds their breath and waits for the outcome.

The dog jerks and stumbles but doesn't go down. Enraged, it bites hard on Foreman's leg.

The old guy falls to the dirt.

It's only a matter of time before the big dog chews him up.

Layton lands a second shot.

This time it's higher up, just under the shoulder.

The dog's front right leg gives way.

Layton knows that he has it now. All he has to do is get up close and finish the thing off.

He skirts a big harvest barrow already stacked with peppers. Moves around until he gets a clean shot at the mutt's head.

The pistol kicks in his hand.

The German shepherd goes down with a yelp.

For a second there's silence. Then the hot Florida air fills with whistling, clapping, and cheering.

Jax Layton, local car thief and habitual petty offender, takes a hero's bow.

49

Coral Way, Miami

*T*he famous clarinet opening of Gershwin's *Rhapsody in Blue* plays in Ghost's Dodge as he drops Zoe off and pulls away from Jude's apartment block.

The lieutenant is happily lost in the complex classical and jazz composition when his phone rudely beeps and, due to the horrors of Bluetooth, the music is muted and he's forced to answer it on the in-car system.

"Lieutenant Walton."

"Hi, this is Sandra Teale." In case he's forgotten who she is, she adds, "The vet from the beach at Key Biscayne."

He remembers her all too well. "Hi there, do you have some good news for me?"

"I have news—though I'm not sure you'll find it good."

"Try me."

"I've now examined both the dog that killed Kathy Morgan and Matt Wood and also the animal that killed Alfie Steiner and they have something in common."

Ghost's pale albino eyes light up. "They do?"

"Yes. They both had massively high levels of a type of epinephrine in their systems."

"That's adrenaline, right?"

"Correct. But these were of such high levels that at first I suspected both animals might have been suffering from Cushing's disease—that's a condition where the adrenal glands, which are situated at the top of the kidneys, produce too much of the stress hormone cortisol because of an adrenal or pituitary tumor."

"But that wasn't the case?"

"No it wasn't." Teale looks down at her notes. "Both dogs were perfectly healthy. No growths or diseases of any kind. No reason for them to have such high adrenaline rates."

"So they were doped?"

"I thought so but I couldn't see any signs of injection. It's possible to put some extra adrenaline down to the excitement in the animals' final moments and of course the reaction to the shootings, but levels still wouldn't be this high."

"So how do you explain such high levels?"

"For the moment, I can't. What's more, the boys in the tox lab say what they found is not normal epinephrine, it's an incredibly concentrated mutated version of it."

"Now I'm out of my depth. I know epinephrine is an adrenaline chloride, but beyond that I'm a fifth grader."

She tries to make it simple. "You've heard of the fight or flight mechanism, right?"

"Sure. The psychological trigger that makes us decide whether to run for our lives or become violent in order to protect ourselves."

"Right. Well, the 'trigger,' as you eloquently call it, is the autonomic nervous system, and it is divided into the sympathetic and parasympathetic branches. In general, these two systems oppose each other. When stimulated, the sympathetic system increases heart rate, blood pressure, and cardiac activity. What happened in the case of both these animals is that some highly concentrated drug homed in on the chemical receptors in their cells and sent them into an aggressive overload."

"So the dogs panicked and fought?"

"That's what I believe happened."

Ghost turns the Dodge into the police station yard. "Do you think they could have been experimented on somehow?"

She's been wondering the same thing. "I really don't know. There's no clear evidence of it. I've asked for the medical records of the Wood dog. It could be that it was being treated with some new drug that I haven't heard of. But from the autopsy, I couldn't spot any underlying condition that looked as though it needed treatment. Do you know yet who owned the other animal?"

He switches the car engine off. "I don't have a name for you, but I'm on my way into the office right now, so hopefully I will in a very short time."

"Will you let me know, Lieutenant?"

"Of course." He looks at his phone. "Is this the best number to get you on?"

"It is." She takes a beat, then adds, "It's also good for fixing dinner on, or just coffee."

Ghost is surprised by her suggestion. He can often go months without attracting *any* female attention, now he's suddenly got too much. "Then I'd really better make sure I don't lose it."

"You do that. 'Bye."

He hangs up and heads inside.

The AC in the station house is set to lower than a fridge. The place drives him crazy. It's either too hot or too cold. Somehow, they never manage to get it right. He's just about to clear reception when the desk sergeant, a big bull of a guy named Stefan, shouts across to him, "Yo, Ghost—you got a visitor."

The lieutenant looks toward the row of hard plastic chairs reserved for members of the public unfortunate enough to have to wander in off the street and ask for help. A smartly dressed white guy with well-cut, dark hair is playing Tetris on his phone.

He looks up as soon as the cop heads his way. "Lieutenant, Carlo Affonso from CBS."

"What can I do for you, Carlo, I'm in a hurry."

"Off-the-record comment on the dogs?"

Ghost smiles at him. "You guys don't do off-the-record."

"On-the-record, then."

He decides to give him a break. "Off-the-record."

Affonso nods.

"You need to have a look at bite rates—fatal and nonfatal. I suspect you'll find they're pushing a line to a new peak. Dogs are being more aggressive for some reason. Might be the recession. Might be the heat. Or maybe they've just had enough of being dragged around on a leash and having their butts kicked." He starts to walk to the security door that only cops can get through.

The reporter is catching his drift. "I want to do a piece that makes people take more care around dogs. You got any statistics, or pictures of attacks, anything that can help me?"

Ghost has his swipe pass on the electronic reader. "You got a card?"

Affonso pulls one out of his shirt pocket.

Ghost takes it and looks it over. "I get something the public needs to know, I'll call, but don't pester me anymore." He passes through to the other side.

He's pocketing the reporter's card at the top of the stairs when he almost walks straight into his captain, Bob Cummings.

"What the fuck, Ghost?"

"Apologies."

"Accepted. I was on my way to your squad room. There's some Little Miss Dazzlebutt from the CIA squatting in my office saying she ain't gonna move until she sees you."

50

The White House, Washington DC

*P*resident Molton's morning proves hectic.

Breakfast with speechwriters, a quick intelligence briefing, an Executive Office session on fiscal reform, and a tough one-on-one with the VP on internal budgets. He and Pat Cornwell are only just done when Don Jackson is ushered in for his slightly postponed eleven o'clock meeting.

"My apologies for keeping you waiting." Molton gestures to sofas around a low but large glass-topped table. "I've updated Pat on our conversation last night re General Zhang."

Jackson flips open his attaché case. "I've brought a transcript of the call, in case you'd like to scrutinize it."

"I'd like to scrutinize Zhang's head on a platter," says the VP. "'Morning, Don. How you doing?"

"I'm fine, thank you, sir." Jackson settles opposite the two politicians and hands over copies of the transcript.

Molton starts to flick through it.

Cornwell is still staring at Jackson. "You know, you don't look so 'fine,' Don. We're used to seeing you with a bit more spring in your step."

"Optimism doesn't come easy when you're talking to the Chinese, Mr. Vice President. I feel somewhat as though my spring is pretty much sprung at the moment."

Molton gets to business. "Tell us first, what are the hard facts on dog attacks?"

"Not good, sir. We've had two fatalities. One at a correctional center in Jacksonville and one at Lake Jackson. Given my name is Jackson. I can't help but point out they could have been deliberately targeted in order to send us a message."

"You serious?" The VP looks astonished. "You need time off, my friend, you're seeing shadows where there aren't any."

The President is too long in the tooth to jump to conclusions. "Maybe not, Pat. Don's right to point it out, now let's pick through the details."

Jackson hands out more sheets. "These are the case details. Millers Landing, Lake Jackson, early hours of this morning. A young couple who bred dogs and a local jogger were killed by animal or animals unknown."

Cornwell jumps in. "Animals unknown? That's gator country. Could easily be one of those big lizards."

The director nods. "It could be, but said 'unknown' also bust into a barn and ripped a dozen pups to pieces."

"Still possible." The VP sits back undaunted and crosses his arms.

"A couple of hours later," Jackson continues, "a correctional officer's German shepherd turned on him while he was out with a group of ten prisoners. Facts get a bit messy here, but it seems the dog killed the handler then attacked another officer before a prisoner shot it dead."

Molton's not sure he heard that properly. "A prisoner shot it?"

"Yes, sir. As I said, the facts are not really clear. It seems some kind of altercation had been under way when the dog kicked off;

a prisoner grabbed an officer's gun and shot it. Took three bullets to kill the thing."

"Hang on a minute." Cornwell sees another chance to be picky. "We've got three deaths by animal or animals unknown in one location and another by a German shepherd, which, unless I'm unusually mistaken, has actually been trained to turn violent when prisoners get rowdy and physical."

"Yes sir, but—"

"Don, regardless of them both happening in places that have Jackson in their names, I don't think either of these can seriously be attributed to Chinese war games."

Molton nods. "I agree."

"Sir, General Zhang specifically warned that—"

Molton cuts him off. "I understand that the call from Zhang last night flagged deaths in Florida, but I think we're being too easily spooked here." He sits back and puts the briefing sheets down. "To be honest, Don, I'm relieved that this is all you brought to us. My big fear last night was that you were going to come in here today and read off a long list of attacks and deaths."

"Add these deaths to those in Miami and I'm afraid you have your list, Mr. President."

Molton is still not buying it. "Hell, Don, you're starting to talk like a journalist. We've got a spike in dog-related deaths, that's all. Like someone said, these things are unpredictable. There's a bunch all at once and then none for ages. Over the year things even out."

The NIA director shuts his file.

He knows they're wrong.

He also knows that at the moment he doesn't have enough proof to make the two most powerful men in the country change their minds. "Thanks for your time, gentlemen. I'll update you if there are further serious developments in Florida or if there is any more communication from Zhang."

Cornwell has a point to make before the director goes. "Clint's remark about you talking like a journalist made me think." He glances toward the President, then back at Jackson. "The press are going to start panic stories about dog attacks. We need to make sure no one in our administration comments. Same with the law enforcement and medical people, we don't want them saying crazy things either. There can't be any leaks on our discussions or data compiled."

Molton nods. "Can you have the White House press team briefed accordingly?"

"Sure," says the VP. "Consider it done."

The President can tell Jackson is biting his tongue. "Don, I appreciate your diligence in bringing your concerns to us. It's always better to be safe than sorry. I've got the French president and his wife arriving this afternoon, and a state dinner tonight, so I'm going to be tied up, but don't hesitate to contact Pat if you need to."

"Thank you." The NIA director shoots Cornwell a look on his way to the door. "I suspect we'll be talking later, Mr. Vice President."

51

Miami

Ghost is usually pretty good at fitting faces to voices, but in the case of the CIA agent sitting in his captain's office, he's got it hopelessly wrong.

When he'd taken Gwendolyn Harries's call in his car, she'd been sharp, officious, and mature. He'd imagined her as one of the army of pencil-thin, mid-thirties, dynamic go-getters that the Agency likes to recruit.

Wrong. Wrong. Wrong.

Agent Harries turns out to be a small, chubby brunette with a boyish haircut. She's wearing an unflattering, gray suit and unfashionably chunky heels.

Cummings walks her to the door. "Agent Harries, meet Lieutenant Walton. Ghost is heading up our investigations into the recent dog attacks and he'll look after you now. Thanks for stopping by." He shuts his door after they shake hands,

"This needn't take long," Agent Harries says, then frowns. "Did your captain just call you Ghost?"

"He did. Let's go down the corridor, there's an interview room we can use. You want anything, coffee, water?"

"No, I'm good."

He shows her inside.

She takes a seat without being asked and flops her black leather shoulder bag on the table in order to fish out a pen and notebook.

"So what brings you all the way from Langley?"

"I'm not based in Langley. I was just over at the head office for catch-up meetings when this dog thing broke. I work from our field office in North Miami Beach." She clicks the top of her pen, "So what's the latest?"

"We've just started setting up a team—mainly admin—to process intel on the attacks. I got an interesting call from the vet who attended the Kathy Morgan case, the one we initially spoke about, and also the boy who died on the soccer field just down the coast—"

"This is Teale, right?" She glances down at notes she's taken from her bag. "Sandra Teale."

"Right." As he's answering, Annie Swanson passes the interview room window. "Hang on a second." He rushes out the door to catch her. "Annie, you got a name and address yet on the dog that killed the boy in Key Biscayne?"

"Came in half an hour ago." The blond detective sees he's got someone in the interview room. "You want it now or later?"

"CIA," he whispers. "Give me a minute."

"Got you."

"Thanks." Ghost returns to the interview room. "Where was I?"

"Teale."

"Oh, yeah. She thinks both dogs had too much adrenaline in their systems. It somehow made them hyperaggressive."

Harries scribbles a line of squiggles in perfect shorthand. "She say how that came to be?"

"No. I don't think she knows yet. She's checking the medical records of the first dog and will do the same with the second when I send her the owner details."

"Both dogs were microchipped?"

"Yeah. Responsible owners. And the vet said both animals were kept in good health too."

"I'll go see Teale straight after this."

"Does she know that?"

Harries smiles and closes her notebook. "I don't like appointments. I find people act differently when they know you are coming."

"That's true." Ghost turns to the door as Detective Swanson enters and slips him a folded piece of paper. "Thanks, Annie. This is Agent Harries—I think you both spoke on the phone."

The blonde sticks out a hand. "Pleased to meet you."

"Likewise."

Annie raises an eyebrow to Ghost as she drifts away.

He reads her note aloud. "'Rottweiler that killed the kid playing soccer belongs to a local character named Dwayne Artunes. He's a hip-hop artist, lives fifteen minutes from Teale's surgery.'" He looks at the CIA agent. "You want to come rap on his door with me?"

52

Merritt Island, Florida

*R*ealtor Fran Ennis eats her lunchtime pastrami sandwich and slugs from a bottle of Coke Zero as she drives to her first and only job of the day.

She has a good feeling about this one.

It's been a month since she sold anything of note, but in the last twenty-four hours she's booked four viewings for two of her biggest properties. That's nothing compared with five years ago, when she would sell three houses a week, but at least it's a clear sign that things are looking up.

And about time too.

The recession has seen the forty-year-old Fran divorced and forced to sell her own family home. So she's hoping the couple she's about to meet are what they say they are—cash buyers looking to do a quick deal.

The property she's selling is Old Temperance Farm. It's a spread of seventeen acres that has just become too much for Josh Whitting, the childless seventy-year-old who wants to sell up and move to somewhere smaller—about sixteen and a half acres smaller. Luckily for Fran, she's got just the place that would suit him too. And in her wildest dreams she's hoping to close both sales this week.

Josh is something of a raggedy curmudgeon. He doesn't have time for anyone but the horses, chickens, and dogs he keeps around the place, so Fran has persuaded him to let her do the viewing on her own, while he spends the morning in town. Only, as she pulls into the long drive, she realizes he seems to have forgotten. His filthy old pickup is there and it's left mud and manure all over the place.

Fran is just about to rush inside and ask him to move it when a black Range Rover Sport crunches its way into the brick-paved yard.

The Dixons are here.

Clive and Suzie.

He's a sports agent and she's a secretary. They live in Tampa and are looking for a place in the country as a second home.

Cash buyers.

The Holy Grail.

Fran reminds herself of all the basics as she gets out of the car and heads to the house with front door keys in hand.

"Hello!" she shouts to get their attention. "I'm Fran Ennis of Taylor, Cook, and Ennis." She beams her best sales smile as they wave and head her way. "What a great view! Did you see the beach on the way down? Isn't it amazing?"

"No." Thirty-year-old Clive Dixon is sullen-faced as he shakes her hand. "I was on a call."

"I saw it." Suzie Dixon sticks out a hand to shake, and with it Fran has a glimmer of hope that they aren't *both* assholes of the highest order. "Your office's directions were very good."

"I'm so glad." Fran smiles at them both. They seem an unlikely couple. Little and large. He's tall and heavy, sweating in a black suit, and looks like he spends a lot of late nights in bars. His twenty-six-year-old wife is just the opposite. Painfully thin, dressed in a little floral print dress, and wearing so much makeup she looks like she's been fashioned out of wax.

Fran opens the big round-topped front door to the farm and instantly wishes she'd sent a cleaning team around. She knew the old guy's place would smell musty but she never expected a stink like this. "Come on in. Forgive the smell; I think Mr. Whitting's septic tank needs emptying."

Suzie Dixon pinches her nose.

"Sorry about that." Fran professionally pushes on. "The stairs up ahead of you are made from wood off the land and have an interesting history. They're the main stairs for the use of the master and mistress of the house." She pauses to let the grandeur of the statement sink in. "Old Temperance Farm used to have servants, so they have another set at the back of the house, leading from the kitchen to an upstairs laundry and ironing room." She is about to pile on another layer of historic polish when she hears a thump on the floor above.

Heavy movement on bare boards.

Her heart sinks.

Josh is obviously knocking around and is going to ruin things.

Clive Dixon's heard it as well but jumps to a different conclusion. "Is that the owner? Is someone else being shown around?" He seems annoyed. "Your office promised me we were the only people interested. We've driven all the way over from—"

The agent doesn't get the chance to finish his rebuke.

The head of a big rottweiler appears at the top of the stairs.

Dangling from its mouth are strips of what looks like brown and pink rags that it's been shaking and playing with.

"Mr. Whitting's dog," explains Fran, with some relief.

A second black rottweiler appears. Pulling along half its master's bloody torso.

"Holy fuck." Clive Dixon turns and runs for the door.

The first dog bounds downstairs and leaps onto his back.

The second drops Whitting's remains and follows.

Fran Ennis pulls frantically at the front door.

She gets it open.

But only an inch.

There's a terrifying roar.

Both dogs are on them. Biting and snarling at their legs and backs. Ripping and clawing flesh and bone.

53

Miami Beach

$\mathcal{D}$wayne Artunes's place is like one of those you drool over on *Cribs*.

Long drive, big house, a pool large enough to breed whales in, and a driveway full of luxury convertibles, an SUV, Harley, and pink Hummer.

Ghost holds his ID in front of the rapper's mirrored shades as they stand at the front door. "Lieutenant Walton, and this is Gwen Harries. We've come to talk about your dog, Dwayne."

"Not my dawg no more, but c'mon in, man." He pulls the door wide, gold bracelets jangling at the end of a bare muscled arm bulging from a white vest.

Ghost and Harries walk a hallway of white walls and marble floor tiles.

The sound of gunfire stops them.

Dwayne sees them freeze and folds up laughing. "COD, man! My homies are online kicking ass." The barefoot rapper is still hooting as he leads them through to a lounge as big as basketball court.

A group of black guys are curled up on white leather sofas, gripping gold PS4 controllers and whooping every time they chalk up another kill.

No one looks at Ghost and Harries, not even the young girls in cropped tops and hot pants sitting on the white shag pile at the guys' feet.

Dwayne guides them into a conservatory that looks out onto his Olympic-sized pool. "So you found Melissa's fucking dawg?"

Harries fishes for the notebook in the shoulder bag. "Melissa who?"

"Melissa out-on-her-ass-bitch, for fuckin' around with Jimmy Jay, that's who."

Ghost tries to help. "Your ex. We talking wife or girlfriend?"

"Wife?" He doubles up laughing again. "Man, I'd never marry that bitch. Not if she was the last pussy on earth."

"And the dog was hers?"

"Yeah. I said that. I threw her cheating ass out and then she rang an' asked if Tyson had come back here coz he'd run off."

"When was this?"

He shrugs. "Fuck man, I don't know. Days ago. Two, I think."

Ghost reaches into a jacket and pulls out one of the less gruesome postmortem photographs from the soccer field. "Is this Tyson?"

Dwayne snatches the print and holds it up to the light but doesn't take his shades off. "Looks like it. What you do, shoot the ugly fucker?" He hands it back.

"Actually we did. But only after it bit a young kid to death."

"Fuck, man, really?

"Yeah, really. So we need to speak to Melissa. You got a follow-up address and number for her?"

"I got one." He nods to Harries's notebook. "Give me that pen and paper."

She flips the page so he can't see her note and hands it over with her rollerball.

Dwayne writes on the clean sheet. "She's a cheatin' bitch but she loved that fuckin' dawg. Go easy on her, man."

"We'll give her your regards," says Harries.

Ghost takes the notebook.

"That it?" asks Dwayne. "You need anythin' else before you go?"

Harries clears her throat with a hesitant cough. "Yeah, I do. Was that the latest *Call of Duty* your boys were playing?"

The rapper smiles. "Hell no. That was an unreleased beta version, sister. Guy who runs the studio's a friend of mine."

Her eyes light up. "Then I'd really like a turn."

54

Allapattah, Miami

*T*he nine-mile drive from Miami Beach to Melissa Clay's place takes Ghost less than twenty minutes.

He parks the Dodge outside the run-down shack and rings the front bell while Harries slides round the back.

There's no answer.

The CIA agent shouts around to him. "She's back here."

Ghost treads thin gravel down the side of the house and finds Harries staring at a young black woman in a gray tracksuit, crashed out on shabby rattan sofa on the back porch.

"Totally wasted, by the looks of her." She picks up a saucer full of stubbed out spliffs and holds it so he can see the cause. "Doped to the eyeballs."

Ghost slides the young woman's legs off the sofa and sits her up. "Melissa, I'm a cop. I need you to wake up and get yourself together. I have to talk to you about your dog."

Melissa's head wobbles, her eyes flicker open for a second and she smiles at him.

"She's not just baked," he says. "I think she's taken something else as well." He looks at her arms but can't find any track marks. "Probably Valium or some type of diazepam. Can you come and watch her while I look around inside?"

"Sure." Harries props Melissa upright and then sits alongside her.

Ghost pushes the screen door open.

The dark kitchen is buzzing with flies. They're feasting on a waste bin overflowing with takeout food. The sink is full of unwashed dishes and soiled pans caked in green mold. The small counter is stacked with unwashed plates and open tin cans that couldn't be pushed into the waste bin. There are dozens of beer cans lying on the floor, along with an empty tequila bottle.

On a wall opposite the sink Ghost finds several cute photographs of the rottweiler as a puppy, pinned to a corkboard. There's a signed photo of Dwayne Artunes too, with a big heart drawn in black felt tip. Melissa has stuck a small kitchen knife through the top of his head.

Ghost searches her cupboards and drawers. One is full of old guarantees for kitchen appliances and a mix of bills. In the middle of them all he finds the dog's vet records. Turns out it was chipped at Julio's Veterinary Practitioners in Overtown, the same place the Wood dog was done. He speed-dials Annie Swanson.

The young detective picks up within a couple of rings. "Yes, Lieutenant."

"Annie, I'm out at Allapattah, south of the park, near the

YMCA building. I need a young woman by the name of Melissa Clay brought in for questioning in relation to the dog that killed the Steiner kid. She's the girlfriend of Dwayne Artunes—correction, the *ex*-girlfriend of Artunes—and looks like she's the owner of the dog."

"I'll have uniforms there in a minute."

"Get a doctor to look at her as well. She's in orbit at the moment, which is why I can't interview her."

"Gotcha." Cheekily, she adds, "How's it going with your CIA friend?"

"Could be worse. Turns out she's a hotshot at *Call of Duty*. Kicked the asses of Artunes's homies. The ride was worth it just to see that."

"The world is full of surprises, Lieutenant."

"Mercifully it is." He hangs up and wanders outside.

Melissa is asleep again and Harries is on the phone. Ghost watches her and can see she's stressed. She writes furiously in her notebook and then looks surprised when she catches him staring. She finishes the call and walks over. "You find anything?"

He holds up the vet's records. "Julio's in Overtown—the same place the Wood dog was treated and the girl was attacked. I'm going to call in there as soon as a squad car comes for sleeping beauty." He nods to the end of the yard where Harries had been standing. "You looked busy over there."

"Yeah, I was." At first she's not sure whether to tell him what's on her mind, but guesses he'll find out soon enough. "Seems there have been a number of other dog-related deaths today in Florida. A correctional officer killed at a prison in Jacksonville, a jogger and two local Labrador breeders over Tallahassee way. And we've just had reports of some old guy, plus a realtor and a couple she was showing around his farm, being bitten to death on Merritt Island."

"Hell, there's some strange shit going down." He looks at her suspiciously. "Do *you* know what's happening? I mean, there has to be some reason the CIA were so quick to jump into this."

She poker-faces him. "I don't know any more than I told you on the phone the other day."

"Bullshit."

"No, really."

"I'm not buying that." He reads her eyes. She's good at blanking off, but not perfect. The fixed stare shows she's not being natural, which in turn tells him he's hit a nerve. "Tell me, Agent Harries, are there dog-related deaths like this all over the country, or only in Florida?"

"Far as I'm aware, only Florida." She walks closer to him, her eyes still not blinking. "But listen, you're right—it's strange as hell that I'm here on this fact-finding tour. Strange to you and even stranger to me. And if you're thinking that even if I did know what was going on I wouldn't tell you, then you're right about that too."

55

New York

*D*anny puts in six hours before the others arrive and settle down to work.

They're a motley crew.

Kayoz is a twenty-year-old black Kylie Minogue. A pocket rocket of edgy female attitude from Brisbane, who insists her singing voice is actually better than the Aussie star's. Those who've heard her on an open mic night in Greenwich Village would argue that she has a point. A Pepsi Max to her left is Word, the planet's most introverted twenty-five-year-old. His nickname comes from the fact that the long-haired, bearded six-footer can go an entire day not speaking a single word. Then there is Right, whose real name is Wong, a twenty-eight-year-old Korean computer genius with the body and chiseled looks of Bruce Lee, but sadly for him, none of the martial-arts expertise to go with it.

They're all working on "Jolly Roger," a campaign they started to further the cause of global piracy. They're creating free links into Hollywood pay-to-view film sites, distributing mail that advertises how to access the movies without paying a dime and breaking the geo-locks that prevent local TV programs and sports events from being shown freely all over the world.

Danny has personally been creating his own brand of chaos on an Asian content network, by disabling their pay systems and creating windows of free access that take the authorities weeks to shutter.

Now he's bored.

He grabs a soda from the fridge and finds a quiet corner to call his girlfriend.

"Hey, babes, what's up?"

"Not much."

Jenny McCann has taken the day off because it's her birthday and she is running on slow. *Real* slow. Right now she's soaking away her pains in bathwater hot enough to cook a lobster. "I'm just lying in the tub, listening to music, wondering what presents you got for me and *exactly* how much you're going to spoil me tonight."

"Yeah, well, I am gonna spoil you big-time, but listen, 'fraid I'm going to be a little late doin' it."

"Late?"

"Sorry."

"Oh come on, it's my *birthday*, Danny." She sits up in disgust and sloshes suds over the sides. "You *can't* be late on my birthday."

"I know. I'm really sorry. I'm going to make it up to you. I need an extra hour, that's all."

She sinks back in the warm water again and sulks. "An hour's okay. Providing it is only an hour and not a *Danny* hour."

"A regular sixty minute hour, I promise."

"Okay."

"Thanks." He takes a breath and says words he's only recently learned to say. "I love you. Love you to pieces."

"Do you? Really? Or are you just trying to get your sorry ass out of the shit it's in and get yourself in the running for the best fuck of your life?"

He laughs. "No. I really do. But don't get me wrong, my ass still wants to be in the running for that—you know, that *other* thing."

She's amused by his coyness. "For a *fuck*. Can't you even bring yourself to say it?"

"Yeah, I can, but it doesn't seem right saying it you."

"Why not?"

"Coz I don't want to think of it like that. I want to think of it as *love,* not sex."

"Oh my God, you are *so* sappy. Not that I'm complaining."

"Make no mistake, Jenny McCann, I really, honestly, love you."

She knows what he wants to hear. *Needs* to hear her say it back. "And I love you too, idiot boy."

"You'd better. I have to go, babes. Have a good day and I'll see you tonight. Then we'll go downtown somewhere special, okay?"

"Cool." She doesn't let him get off the line that quickly. "Where we going?"

He laughs at her nosiness. "I'm going to surprise you."

"Not Mexican. I don't want Mexican again."

"No Mex, I promise. I have to go."

He rings off and is still smiling as he goes back to the rest of the hackers. Soon they'll be gone. Then he can start his other work. The stuff they can't see. Must never see.

The stuff that does more than just pay the rent.

56

Eisenhower Executive Office, Washington DC

The whole world knows what the White House looks like, the iconic building at 1600 Pennsylvania Avenue that for two hundred years has been the center of the U.S. presidency. Few, though, are aware that there's an even more impressive slab of architecture right next door to it.

The Eisenhower Executive Office boasts two miles of black and white tiled corridors, eight monumental curving staircases of granite with four thousand individually cast bronze balustrades, four skylight domes and two spectacular stained-glass rotundas. It's got a four-story library, individual rooms of cast iron, marbled walls, extensive gold leaf ornamentations, intricately stenciled ceilings, and painstaking marquetry. When it was completed it became the biggest office building in Washington and home to the State, War, and Navy departments. It is from here that most of America's foreign policies have been drafted. But these days it's also used by the Vice President of the United States and his huge contingent of executive members.

Pat Cornwell has dedicated rooms in the West Wing next to

the President, but this is where he prefers to be. Not just because of the splendor of the building but because it gives him some vital distance from the President, enough space and privacy for him to form his own views on things.

It's here, in an office that in its time was used by sixteen Secretaries of the Navy, that he meets privately with Don Jackson. "I don't have long, Don. I have to put in a fleeting appearance for cocktails drinks before this French dinner then I have to go eat with the Board of Governors of the Fed."

The NIA director takes a seat on the opposite side of the large antique desk and gets straight to the point. "Going back to the cases I mentioned this morning, it *wasn't* a gator that killed the young couple and the woman jogger at Millers Landing. The Sheriff's Office shot dead a Labrador that had half chewed its way through an iron and mesh fence at a kindergarten and was snapping at people even while it was stuck. There was a collar on it saying it belonged to the Coopers at Millers Landing—they're the dog breeders who died."

"I wish it had been a gator."

Jackson plows on. "We did some phone interviews with the guard and the prisoners who survived the German shepherd attack at Montgomery Correctional. They all say the dog didn't respond to any attempts by the handler to control it. It even continued biting and attacking long after another guard laid into it with a rifle stock."

"Jeez."

"And all this from an animal that won obedience trials."

Cornwell puts a big hand to his shiny forehead in despair. "Anything else?"

"Afraid so. There have been several more dog attacks during the day." He takes a breath. "And these are even worse." He places a briefing sheet on the desktop. "A realtor, a farm owner, and a couple being shown around the property have been killed by rottweilers on Merritt Island. A delivery guy found their bodies inside the home. Or should I say what was left of their bodies. Local cops discovered the animals roaming the land and shot them. It looked like the dogs had chewed clean through the front door of the farmhouse to get out."

"Jesus Christ."

Jackson puts a final sheet down on the desk. "Last and least, this is a list of minor attacks in Florida, resulting in people needing ER treatment for dog bites."

Cornwell nods tiredly. "And the press is all over this?"

"They're getting there. For now, commentators seem to be blaming the heat wave. Goddamned temperatures hit 103 the other day. They'll work their way closer to the truth."

"Then we have to lead them astray. I'll have the White House press office brief on it. Have you met Jay Ashton, the new secretary?"

"No, sir."

"I'll fix for him to call you. Jay will get his spin teams to work. I'll talk to the President about how much we should tell him—re Zhang, etcetera."

"As little as possible, sir."

"I take your point, Don, we just have to make sure he has sufficient information to do his job properly and stamp out any fires that the news organizations might be lighting with their speculation." He drums his fingers on the leather inset of the desk while he considers what else needs to be started. "Right after this meeting, I'll get my office to roughly brief the White House heads of Science and Health and ask our advisors to give us some insight into whether this dog weaponization is actually possible. I'll try to fix an early session for tomorrow. I guess you've already got your intelligence people crawling all over China to see if there's anything to flag up?"

"Not just China, all of Asia, sir. As you know, we've been on high alert in the region since Obama's days."

The comment makes Cornwell reflective. "That sonovabitch was right about the next threat coming from Asia. Just a shame he cut the Defense and Intelligence budgets so fucking deeply we almost can't afford to stage a fistfight in a schoolyard."

Jackson places another briefing sheet on the VP's desk. "I've had an agent in Miami checking on the early dog deaths. The veterinary physician out there says that two of the canines that killed people had abnormally high levels of adrenaline."

"You got anything to compare that to?"

"What do you mean, sir?"

"I mean, wouldn't all dogs test like that right after a kill? They get all worked up during the fight, I suppose."

"Apparently not to this level. If you look at those notes, sir, you'll see that the vet believes the dogs may have somehow been given some highly concentrated adrenaline drug that tipped them into hyperaggression."

"You mean like an injection?"

Jackson shrugs. "We don't know. It could be intravenous, maybe given by a vet as medicines, or perhaps through foodstuffs that have been poisoned at the point of manufacture or display."

"Like baby food contamination on supermarket shelves?"

Jackson was cautious about committing himself. "Possibly. At this stage we're just shooting in the dark."

"Then we need to do better."

"I know, sir. But only this morning you and President Molton were dismissing Zhang as mad."

"Zhang *is* mad. Of that we're sure. We just can't take chances that his madness is limited to his mind. It may now have crept past Xian and into Chinese military operations as well."

57

Bar Francais, New York

*F*our French waiters are approaching the brunette at table twelve. There's a glowing birthday cake in their hands and on their lips the first chorus line of "Happy Birthday."

Twenty-three-year-old Jenny McCann buries her face in her fingers, "Oh my God. Oh no, I don't believe you did this."

"Happy birthday to you! Happy—"

She punches the shoulder of the man at her side. "Danny, you shouldn't have. Oh goodness."

"—birthday, dear Jenny, happy birthday—"

Candlelight flickers on her face as she leans across and kisses him. Cheers break out as she smooches the man in her life.

"—to yooooo!"

The whole restaurant is now clapping, immersing the couple in a crashing wave of sound that fizzles and disappears as quickly as it came.

Crimson-faced, she blows out the candles and makes her wish. The waiters move in and slice cake as quick as a corner kid cutting coke.

Danny Speed takes his girlfriend's shaking hand. They've been together for only a short time but he wants it to be for the rest of his life. No one's ever made him feel like she does. "I have another surprise."

Her brown eyes are as big as saucers. She's never been to a restaurant as expensive as this. Never had anyone other than friends and family sing "Happy Birthday" to her.

Danny dips into his pocket and conjures up the little square box of magic that his mom told him all girls dream of. He flips open the brown faux-leather lid and reveals a modest speck of diamond on a nine-carat band. "Jennifer Louisa McCann, will you do me the immense honor of being my wife?"

Her eyes fill with tears and her heart bounces like a jackrabbit in a carrot field. Danny's a great guy. Good-looking. Smart. There are so many reasons to say yes.

And as many to say no.

She knows what he does, the hacking and the wheeling-and-dealing—and she knows it's not right. The kind of *not right* that can end in jail time.

He can see her hesitation.

And so too can other diners.

People at surrounding tables have spotted the outstretched hand, the ring proffered on the sweating palm of the young man with a desperately expectant look on his face. What was once a white-clothed dinner table is now a stage, an intimate moment in a very much public performance.

Danny takes her hand and squeezes it. "Jen, I love you. I'd cut pieces from my soul to just spend the rest of my life with you."

She shuts her eyes and takes a deep breath.

The power of the words and pressure of the moment are too great to resist. She opens wide and smiles at him. "Yes. Yes! I'd love to be your wife."

58

Police HQ, Miami

Six hours after Melissa Clay was brought in for questioning, a police doctor rules she's fit to be interviewed.

Ghost does the Q&A with detective Annie Swanson. Partly because he wants her to watch and learn but also, because of Melissa's drug problems, he's keen to have a sympathetic female in the room for her.

They start off real slow, with all the formalities and chitchat, then the lieutenant lays out pictures of the dead rottweiler faceup on the table like they were picture cards. He looks across to the wreck of a woman in a yellow V-neck T-shirt and ragged blue jeans. "This your dog, Melissa? Is this Tyson?"

She stares but doesn't touch the print, or show any emotion. Drugs and depression have dried up all of her feelings. Her voice is slow and slurred, "Yeah, that T. Wad 'appened to him?"

He ignores her question. "When and where did you last see him?"

She closes her eyes and takes an eternity to answer. "Hell, I don't know. He gone, that all I figure."

"Try harder." He leans over the table and shakes her gently. "Melissa, stay awake and you might just stay outta jail. Dwayne said you drove to his place at Miami Beach and took the dog after you guys split up. Is that right?"

She nods. "Yeah. That motherfucker said he loved me." She licks dried lips. "Told me that over an' over. 'Love you, baby.' And what does he do? He makes up this shit that—"

Ghost doesn't want to hear it. "I'm not interested in you and Dwayne, Melissa. The dog, Tyson—you picked him up and then what?"

She lets her head loll to one side and scratches an itch on her neck. Mosquito bite that hurts like hell.

"Melissa, the dog!"

She gets herself together. "I let him go."

"Where? Miami Beach?"

Scratching has made her neck bleed. She looks inquisitively at the blood on her fingers. It reminds her of needles and smack and the wonderfulness of forgetting life's shit.

"Melissa, did you let Tyson go on Miami Beach?"

She looks up from her blood. "Naah. I let him out someplace else. I was jus' drivin'. I stopped and Tyson was yappin' and all. It was like he wanted to be free. So I opened the door and said, 'Get the fuck outta here' . . ." She smiles happily. ". . . and he did. He just fucking ran. Then I drove off."

Ghost's heard worse stories in his time, much worse, but he still can't believe the stupidity and selfishness of such an action. "Where, Melissa? Where was this?"

She thinks on it. Her face grows sad as she reconnects with the dog. With the little bit of tenderness she had. "Near the shoppin' center, out at Key Biscayne. I remember now."

Ghost nods to Annie.

She knows what to do. There are two other photographs, face-down in front of her. She turns them over and slides them across to Melissa. "This is Alfie Steiner. Ten years old. He was playing soccer with friends when Tyson bit him to death."

Melissa stares at the picture then looks away.

"The dog ever attack anyone else, Melissa?"

Wet eyes turn and fix on the cops. "That sad. About that boy—that real sad."

Annie stays calm. "It is. Especially for the boy's family. I asked you a question—has Tyson ever attacked anyone else?"

"No." She shakes her head several times to emphasize. "T—he was a gentle baby." She smiles as images of him as a puppy swim into her addled brain. "Was that why you shot him? Coz of the boy? Coz of what happened?"

Ghost answers. "It was, Melissa." He thinks about telling her that had she kept her car door shut that day, then both the dog and Alfie Steiner would be alive. But he doesn't. She'll find her own route to guilt soon enough. "Detective Swanson is going to wrap up here. You're going to get charged Melissa, with not having a license for the dog, not having it on a leash, and criminal recklessness." He lets it sink in, then adds, "I'm going to have to review the case with my captain and it may be that we decide to add second degree murder to that list as well, so you're going to need an attorney to represent you. Do you understand what I'm telling you?"

She's biting on a nail now and fumbling her way through a long fogged mind. "I didn't kill that boy. It was Tyson. Fuck man, you already been judge and jury and given *him* the death penalty. I want to go now."

Ghost gets to his feet. "Do you have an attorney, Melissa, or you want us to get one for you?"

She lets her head droop. Tired eyes find her lap, her feet, then the floor. "I ain't got no representation."

Ghost nods to Annie and heads to the door. He knows she's going to need a really good defense lawyer, and not just to fight the charges. Once Alfie Steiner's family find out the owner has been traced, they're sure to file civil proceedings that will take every last cent Melissa has.

59

Coral Way, Miami

Zoe spends much of the day unpacking her finally returned trunk of clothes

The other thing occupying her mind is Ghost.

She thought he might call or text but he hasn't. Nor has she. All that sudden shit this morning about giving her a key was too much to take. Way too scary.

A key?

What the hell was he thinking?

They barely know each other and *bam* now he wants to give her a key. That's creepy. Weird. Strange. Controlling.

Isn't it?

Or was he just being practical? Nice? Friendly?

Or more?

She spent most of her day *not* thinking about all these things. Plus what he might be doing, what he might be thinking about, and whether she's just completely misjudged him and is in danger of making a fool of herself.

He's definitely weird.

But it seems a nice weird. He's smart and weird. Stylish and weird. Strong and weird. Then again, wasn't that late call he made, asking for her company, a sweet flash of vulnerability? A strong, smart guy who isn't afraid of showing his vulnerability. Now that *is* seriously weird.

The evening news is all about new dog attacks, and to understand Ghost and his work a little more, Zoe finds herself checking stories on the Internet. It seems like the whole canine world is turning on the hands that feed them.

Jude is staying over at Jake's again and then they're off to the Bahamas for a few days, where his company is fitting air-con in a new hotel. It means she has the run of the place, and guiltily raids the snacks cupboard while she scribbles things down.

Two bags of chips and a Snickers bar later, Zoe knows that there are around eighty million pet dogs in the U.S., with about five million a year lost or abandoned, and close to three million euthanized by shelters. Like Ghost had said, the figure has been jumping year after year as the recession deepened. Fertile dogs have two litters a year and produce between six and ten pups. It doesn't come as a surprise to learn that big dogs are really popular. Labs come number one in the nation's Top Ten, German shepherds three. Retrievers four. Boxers six, and bulldogs ten. Then, just outside that elite group, come the mastiff and Doberman pinscher.

She pours herself a glass of wine from an opened bottle of Chilean red and digs some more. From what she can work out, pit bulls and rottweilers cause three-quarters of all attacks on kids and 80 percent on adults. Additionally, they account for 77 percent of *all* attacks that cause bodily harm, three-quarters of the maimings, and two to three deaths a week.

Zoe pours a second glass of red and is about to close down her computer when her phone comes alive with a ring tone she knows is Danny's. "Hi there, what you up to?"

Restaurant noise, laughter, and plate clatter all precede his answer. "Congratulations, Zo', you're about to get yourself a sister-in-law."

"What the fuck?" She sits in shock.

On the phone line, Danny sounds as wired as a speed addict. "I've just proposed and Jenny's said yes."

"You what?" Zoe can't believe it. What an idiot. He's going to *marry* some tramp she hasn't even met.

"Listen, sis, she's here with me, I'm gonna put Jenny on so you can say hi."

"No. Don't. I don't want to speak to her. Get serious Danny—you know what a fucking mess Mom and Dad made of marriage—"

Jenny McCann already has the phone to her ear and is listening to every word.

"—any girl who says yes to marriage after such a short relationship is even more stupid than you—"

"Hi, Zoe, this is Jenny. I can't wait to meet—"

Zoe cuts her off.

Fuck.

What a nightmare. Some freeloader she's never met is about to screw up her brother's life, and she's already trash-mouthed her.

And on top of that it's almost midnight and Ghost hasn't phoned.

60

Police HQ, Miami

It's past midnight when Ghost and Annie finish charging Melissa Clay with second degree murder.

He drives home feeling darkly depressed. Had the woman not broken up with Dwayne, she wouldn't have driven off with the dog, wouldn't have opened the car door and let it go. Alfie Steiner would be alive and she wouldn't be heading to prison and bankruptcy.

The woulds and would-nots are as thick and cloying as the humid Miami air. He showers, puts on shorts and a T-shirt, and feels desperately hungry.

In the kitchen he picks fresh fruits from a wooden bowl, cuts slices of cheeses he bought last weekend at the European Deli in Lake Worth, and decants a twenty-year-old port he got at a wine auction almost a year ago.

He takes the food and drink to a handmade oak dining table and then goes to the study to search for some specific volumes of the Encyclopedia Britannica. He has the same volumes online but prefers the touch and feel of real books.

Dogs are still on his mind.

Dogs that start as pets and end up as killers.

Dogs that ruin lives.

Ghost has to know more about them, has to study the history of this strange enemy in order to work out why man's best friend is suddenly turning into mankind's worst enemy.

Books in hand, he returns to the table and pours a luxurious dribble of Delaforce's aptly named "Curious and Ancient." As it breathes a little more, he slices off what he hopes is a complementary piece of Blue Shropshire Stilton.

At first he's not sure the creamy nuttiness of the cheese sits well with the port's sharp but jammy spice, then after a second tasting he decides it's a good choice.

Good but not great.

Ghost starts with the basics. The American Kennel Club recognizes 148 different breeds of dogs and splits them into seven basic categories: terrier, toy, working, herding, hound, sporting, and nonsporting. The smallest breed is the Chihuahua, the tallest the Irish wolfhound, and the heaviest the St. Bernard.

Trawling through canine history he finds that early Egyptians,

Greeks, and Persians all used dogs in their armies. The Romans specifically trained the big Molossus—*Canis Mollosus*—and sent packs into battle wearing crude metal armor and spiked iron collars. Similarly, Attila the Hun deployed the mastifflike creatures in bloody and brutal campaigns.

Further down the timeline, Spanish conquistadors trained armored dogs to kill and disembowel South American natives. The British used dogs when they attacked the Irish. The Irish in turn used their native wolfhounds to attack the horses and knights of invading Normans. All manner of leaders from Frederick the Great to Napoleon and Elizabeth I used dogs in battles.

Police first deployed dogs in Victorian England, when the Metropolitan London Police used bloodhounds in the hunt for Jack the Ripper. Most American cops didn't get canine units until post-WWII, after witnessing how the Nazis used military dogs for control and punishment.

Ghost cuts himself a generous slice of Brie de Meaux, which he eats without biscuits, and instantly wishes he'd opened champagne rather than port, or better still chosen the Camembert. Nevertheless, he still understands why Louis XVI's dying wish was for a spoonful of Brie.

He slices some green apple to clear his palate and reads that during the Second World War the Russians used dogs strapped with explosives to destroy German tanks, while during the Vietnam War the Americans used more than five thousand battle dogs. Back in 2011 the U.S. Navy SEALs used a Belgian Malinois war dog in Operation Neptune Spear, the strike that killed Osama bin Laden.

Across the room his phone buzzes with a text.

Zoe?

He walks across and picks it up.

HOPE U HAD A GD DAY.
HAVE INTRSTNG DOG STUFF 4U.
WILL MAIL 2MORROW.
Z

He's pleased to get the message. It means she forgives him for spooking her with the offer of a key. The look in her eyes had surprised him. Made him think she'd run for the hills. Maybe he should have behaved like he normally does.

Guarded. Closed. Impassive.

Only she doesn't make him feel like that. She makes him feel like he's known her for years.

THANKS

He sends the one word reply and then regrets it.

It wasn't enough.

He'd meant it to be cool. Grateful but not overeager. Warm but not pressing. He'd stopped himself from adding a kiss because that would have looked desperate. He'd pulled short of suggesting dinner tomorrow or later in the week because he thought she'd feel pressured. But now he stares down at the phone and THANKS looks more ridiculous than any or all of those other things.

Ghost tidies the remains of his dinner and drags himself off to bed.

Almost inevitably, he lies in the dark with his eyes open and his head banging.

When he shutters his lids, the faces of Kathy Morgan, Alfie Steiner, and Matt Wood await him. Lost souls stand in the dark tunnels that separate him and sleep.

And he knows that tomorrow there will be new, bloodless

faces for him to meet, new horrors to absorb, new puzzles to try to make sense of.

And he realizes one other thing. Life's too short to make stupid mistakes.

He picks up the phone and sends another text.

WOULD LOVE TO SEE YOU AGAIN WHEN YOU'RE READY. X

PART THREE

And Caesar's spirit, raging for revenge,
With Ate by his side come hot from hell,
Shall in these confines with a monarch's voice
Cry "Havoc!" and let slip the dogs of war,
That this foul deed shall smell above the earth
With carrion men, groaning for burial.

WILLIAM SHAKESPEARE, *Julius Caesar*, Act 3, Scene 1

61

*T*he two glamorous young women giggling in the ascending lift inside the Raffles Hotel regard themselves *baopo*—high-class hookers—who only sleep with VIPs and ultrarich businessmen.

Their "owner" tells them they have the natural beauty to one day reach the top of their profession and become *baoernai,* "second wives," to rich and powerful politicians, executives, and local government officials.

It's heading toward midnight as they are ushered into the seventh floor Presidential Suite of the hotel. They have no idea who their middle-aged client is. The teenagers know only what they've been told. He's important. Someone high up inside the party. Someone it's in their interests to pleasure to the *best* of their abilities.

And that they mustn't speak.

On no account must they utter a word, unless they're told to.

Their "owner," a former army colonel named Huan Lee, tries not to catch the eye of the man he's leaving them with. He bows respectively as he shuts the door, then waits outside in the plush Presidential Lobby.

General Zhang is in civilian clothes, not military attire.

He takes off the jacket to his plain brown suit and drops it on a chaise longue. He paces as he looks the girls over and imagines what he's going to do to them.

They are exactly as he ordered.

Young, plump specimens; generous in waists and breasts, shiny black hair in beaded pigtails, both dressed in crisp green schoolgirl uniforms.

They are perfect for venting his anger. For cooling the terrible rage that broils inside him.

He is a soldier. Like the dogs he is turning on the Americans, his instincts are those of an aggressor, a fighter, a conqueror.

He has a *need* to hurt.

"You!" He points to the more round-faced one. "Sit there."

The girl pads across the plush cream carpet to a dressing table chair.

As she sits, Zhang uses precut lengths of rope to bind her wrists and ankles to the wooden frame.

Hungry-eyed, he turns to the other girl. The one without any sign of fear.

He grabs her one-handed by the throat and slaps her face.

The shock in her eyes excites him.

Enough for him to hit her again.

Only when she cries does Zhang feel excited enough to want her. Aroused enough to squeeze her neck some more and haul her to the giant four-poster.

He keeps his grip while he sexually brutalizes her. His eyes never leave the girl on the chair. Watching her watching him raises his arousal. He is already intoxicated with the thought of what he's going to do to her.

62

Greenwich Village, New York

*D*anny's careful not to wake her.

He slips out of bed and gently folds the quilt back around the naked, sleeping body of the woman he's just asked to marry him.

His future wife.

Just the thought of it makes him feel different. More grown up. Almost complete.

Mrs. Jenny Speed.

He creaks his way across the apartment. First, to use the tiny bathroom, then to find postcelebratory Advil in the kitchen before settling behind his computers.

Then he does what most people do online. He scans the dailies. Checks his mail. Flicks through Facebook and wakes up.

After that he does what the *normal* people *don't* do.

He hacks.

Time to earn the retainer Libowicz is paying him. He works from the list he's been furnished with and launches invasive programming right into the central nervous system of some of the biggest firms in Brazil, India, China, and Russia. An hour from now he'll have access to all the mail accounts of their top executives. That's a good place to start. Execs file everything. And everything they don't want people to see, they very helpfully dump in recycle bins, delete file caches, or personal folders. All of which he can open quicker than they can say "Flash drive."

As his Macs work their magic he returns to the kitchen, this time for coffee.

A phone rings.

For a split second he hopes it's his sister, calling to apologize, to say what an ass she's been and how she's really happy for him.

But it's not Zoe's ring tone.

It's a buzz.

And not any old buzz.

It's the buzz of the new burner. The cheap cell phone he bought yesterday before he met Jenny. The one he'll throw away tonight right after he gets himself a new one.

It's in the bedroom.

With Jenny.

There's no question of being quiet now. He knows he has to get it. Quick. Before she does.

He walks straight into the room and sees the lit-up display glowing inside his jeans pocket. Thank God he didn't leave it by the bed.

Jenny stirs but doesn't wake.

He grabs it and looks at the message.

His heart thumps and his spirits drop. This is a tough one. A get caught, get badly burned one.

He dresses quicker than he's ever done and logs the Macs off. Libowicz's work can wait.

He has more important matters to attend to.

63

Beijing

*T*he first girl is still crying when Zhang throws her out of the hotel room.

He is not worried.

Her owner is waiting outside. An ex-army man who has been

paid well for his troubles and will make sure she keeps her mouth shut. Even if he has to permanently close it.

And now the other one.

The one who started bravely defiant and then screamed so loudly that he had to gag her with a belt from a hotel robe.

The general tilts the dressing table chair she's tied to and drags it across the vast bedroom to the bed. For a moment he puzzles about how to abuse and hurt her while she's still thrashing around on the chair.

To his astonishment his mobile phone rings. He gave the strictest of instructions not to be disturbed.

There can only be one reason for it.

And it isn't good.

He snatches if off the bedside table. "Yes."

"General, it is Xue. I am in the Operations Room and have just received word from the presidential building—Xian is on his way over here. He has decided to make an impromptu visit."

Zhang slams the phone down in fury. Xian means to catch him out. Visiting the Nian Command Center without informing him, intending to discuss it without him present—all this amounts to the ultimate military insult.

One he is not prepared to tolerate.

64

New York

JACKPOT

That was the one word message on Danny's phone. But it was enough to turn his life upside down.

He deletes it.

Powers off the device.

Removes the SIM and dumps it.

He slips a leg over the wild black Kawasaki waiting outside his brownstone and rips up the peace of the early morning all the way down to Wall Street. He drops the phone in a trash can full of flies and plastic at the McDonald's near the bottom of Broadway, turns into the garage of his building and makes his way upstairs.

The air-con inside the loft isn't working, but it doesn't matter. Danny's too wired to notice, let alone care.

The young hacker logs on to his terminal and enters the complicated series of alphanumerical codes he set up to protect his machine and hide its identity.

Finally, he gets to the program that he left running.

Jackpot was the key word for what he's been pursuing.

Danny feels tingles and shivers all over his body, an exhilarating biochemical cocktail of astonishment, excitement, and fear over what he's about to get himself into.

This is a biggie.

A noise spooks him.

A door banging in the corridor.

He races to the spyglass on his entrance door. Sees a fat guy in a blue Adidas tracksuit trying to do stretches before going downstairs for a run. Any other day he'd have been happy with that, would have gone back to his desk without a care in the world.

Not today.

Not Jackpot day.

He squints through the peephole until the jogger has lumbered out of view, then he chains the door and opens it a fraction. Enough to hear the lift *bing* and the car open up.

Danny stays motionless. Listens until he hears the doors close.

He rushes back inside and locks his front door. Bolts it top and bottom. Heavy dead locks slam solidly across its middle.

He dashes to his window and stares into the street below. The loft was chosen specifically so he can see everything out on the sidewalk.

He waits patiently.

The fat guy in blue waddles out of the front of the building, arms already pumping, big ass swinging as he crosses the road and heads to the patch of park on Rector.

Danny relaxes and returns to his seat.

Now for the hard part.

Cracking the code that Jackpot has thrown up.

65

Beijing

General Zhang slams yet another door.

He storms his way down the spiraling metal stairs toward the command bunker where Project Nian is being run.

His face is contorted with anger when he enters the room.

President Xian is standing in conversation with Geng Chunlin, the Minister of State Security, and Lieutenant General Xue.

It amuses Xian to see how hot and flustered Zhang is. The horrible man must have been forced to abandon one of his dark pleasures in order to get here so quickly. "General," he shouts across the room with a smile on his face, "I have decided Minister Chunlin should from now on be based here full-time. I want him to become an 'independent' observer, on behalf of the party. He will report directly to me and not to Xue."

Zhang can feel he's being outmaneuvered. Chunlin must have told Xian something about the failures in developing the mood pacifiers for the attack dogs. Now Xian is isolating him, making him feel exposed and undermined. "President Xian, may I speak privately with you?" He gestures to the corridor and the quiet, empty rooms that lie off it.

Xian nods his consent.

Zhang shoots the minister a look of pure contempt as he leads the way outside and into a room two doors down the corridor. A light comes on automatically as he enters. He waits until the heavy door swings shut behind his leader. "Mr. President, your unexpected appearance here—in the dead of night—makes me look foolish. I would have appreciated—"

Xian cuts him off. "You have fashioned your own foolishness, General."

The rebuff stings and he finds himself answering with more anger in his voice than he knows prudent. "What has Chunlin said to you? It is clear he came to you and has spoken ill of me. We had a meeting and a differing of opinions. Words were said. Voices raised. I suspect he is now briefing against me because of that and the fact that I appointed Xue as operational leader."

"You speak so much and say so little." The president pauses, in order that Zhang can see the disappointment in his face. "You are the opposite of Minister Chunlin, a comrade who said nothing ill of your meeting, only that he was concerned about the running of Nian and felt he should be more involved. Those words were enough for me. Geng Chunlin is a man of honor and one I have trusted for many years. It was his sign to me that he had my interests and those of our party at heart. Now what of you, General? Can I trust you to respect my decision and behave as honorably to me?"

Zhang is wise enough to know that in every defeat there is an opportunity to be seized. A victor always wants to show mercy. He seizes his chance and bows his head apologetically. "You are my president and also the Chairman of the Central Military Commissions. If I have offended you, or in any way shown disrespect to you through my behavior, then I most humbly apologize. If you no longer think me worthy of serving you, then I ask you to call a meeting of the CMC and have them remove me."

"You know that is not necessary. I seek to strengthen our bonds, not sever them."

Zhang looks up at Xian like a repentant son. "Then I promise to work honorably with Chunlin, but I need your trust to do so. The time has come for Nian to be run as a military operation, not as a political threat. Let Chunlin and me punish the Americans for their defiance. Grant me the freedom to use all the ferocity we have available to quickly bring Molton to his knees and have him beg to you. If you cannot trust me to do that, then I humbly beg you to present my case to the CMC and relieve me of my duties."

Xian keeps the anger from his eyes. Putting a dispute before the CMC would result in questions being raised over his own leadership and his ability to carry the support of the military. He has no choice but to loosen the leash on Zhang.

"You have my trust." He walks toward the door. "But guard it with your life. Because if you betray me, that is exactly the price you will pay."

66

Beijing

It's 2:00 A.M. when General Zhang returns to the Operations Room. He instructs Chunlin and Xue to follow him into an adjacent office.

Once the door is shut behind them he comes straight to the point. "President Xian and I have had a very pleasing discussion about the running of Project Nian." His gaze falls like a black cross on Chunlin. "He has informed me of your concerns, Minister, and I am indebted to you for volunteering to be stationed in the Operations Room." He nods to his trusted deputy. "Lieutenant Xue will keep you informed of all operational activity. You will be told of intended actions and the consequences of those actions."

Zhang takes a breath and lets it inflate the smile on his balloonlike face.

"I have been informed by President Xian that as of this moment I now have complete military control of Project Nian." He looks pointedly at Chunlin, "It is me—and me alone—who will decide what dogs are activated, when they are activated, and if—or when—any pacifiers need to be deployed to deactivate them." He lets the words sink in. "Is that clear, Minister?"

Chunlin feels himself redden. "Yes, General."

"Good." He pulls the door open and holds it for Chunlin to pass through. "Can I give you a lift, Minister? I would hate anything to happen to you as you head home."

67

Historic District, Miami

*G*host can't sleep so he runs.

His big feet slap out echoes down deserted streets where many have only just gone to bed and where it's still too soon for early risers to break out of their dreams.

The rhythm feels good. Hypnotic. Energizing.

His long legs strike a mechanical pace down the silent sidewalks out to the Freedom Tower at Miami Dade College and back again.

After the ten mile, hour-long jog he soaks in the shower. The pulse of hot water on his face and head stokes his engines and he feels ready for the day.

He towels dry and dresses in a cool brown linen and silk suit with light brown shirt and tan loafers, no socks. When he's done, he sits in the kitchen and checks his e-mail and phone messages.

No word from Zoe.

She'd promised to mail him some research that she'd done and she hasn't. He's sure she must have gotten his late night text.

Now he regrets sending it. It was foolish and weak.

He reads the morning newspapers online and for breakfast cooks an egg-white omelette and forks it down with freshly squeezed OJ and thick black Colombian coffee. In the background is the constant chatter of CBS news. Like the print press, the bulletin is packed with stories about the dog attacks, about increases in strays on the street, and there's a couple of people from an animal shelter in the studio with a pair of cute pups to adopt. The shelter owner says the stray problem has become so bad that they're full-to-bursting and will have to euthanize any animal brought in if they don't find a home for it within twenty-four hours. The studio fills with aaws and sighs.

Just after seven Ghost switches the set off and heads to the office.

The cleaners have been in, but the section being used as an Incident Room still stinks of burritos and beer. It used to be a crash area for cops working overnight shifts, and he guesses the smells will never go away.

He logs on to his computer and sees there have been two more dog incidents overnight. A tax official in Santa Rosa got bitten to death in his sleep. Fortunately for his wife, they'd had a falling out and he'd been banished to a spare bedroom. She managed to get herself and their child out of the condo before the Yorkshire terrier could attack them.

A Yorkie?

Ghost takes a minute to check the size of a terrier. From memory he knows it as a "toy" dog. A tiny, scraggy runt of a thing. The detail he finds online confirms it. They are tiny. Six to nine inches tall and only about seven pounds in weight. He can't begin to think how a dog that small could become that dangerous.

The other incident seems more plausible. Over in Marion a stray bulldog has attacked a group of people coming out of a nightclub. It killed a twenty-six-year-old man and injured two women in their twenties.

Ghost sits back and weighs it all up.

From what he's seen on the news and the statewide incident log in front of him, there have now been close to thirty dog bites and fifteen fatalities in Florida in the last three days. He walks over to a large electronic operations board in the corner of the room—the type that allows you to write on it then prints copies of whatever you've scribbled. You can also call up Internet pages and download data from police servers.

He splits the screen and on one side makes a list of the fatalities, starting with the most recent.

> Sunny Budrys—Santa Rosa, Florida
> Ken Egan—Marion, Florida
> Fran Ennis, Josh Whitting, Clive and Susan Dixon—
>   Merritt Island
> Officer George Jennings —Montgomery Correctional
>   Center, Jacksonville
> Ellen McGonall, Pete and Lizzie Cooper—Lake Jackson
> Kathy Morgan, Matt Wood, Alfie Steiner—Key Biscayne,
>   Miami

On the other side of the screen he calls up a large map of Florida and marks in the locations of the attacks.

There seem no obvious geographic connections.

He ponders them again.

Santa Rosa is about as far north and west as you can get, while Merritt Island and Key Biscayne are a long way south and east. Jacksonville is back north and east, Marion more north and central, and Lake Jackson central but a bit south of Marion.

He takes a felt pen and marks them in.

They still mean nothing.

He adds the main nonfatal bites, the ones that needed surgery and resulted in dogs being destroyed. Big crosses now highlight Cape Coral on the southwest coast, Port St. Lucie back on the eastern seaboard, and Ghost—his namesake county, back up on the northwest tip.

Still nothing.

He goes back to his desk and e-mails a friend in the national crime statistics department to see if any other states are experiencing sudden rises in dog-related injuries and deaths, then goes back to the map.

The spread of locations irritates him.

If they were rape or murder scenes, he'd speculate on where the offender might strike next. Orlando. Tampa. Fort Lauderdale. The Everglades. Daytona Beach.

Those would be the most likely places. They are all tourist magnets, big centers with shifting populations made up of every nationality you can name.

He figures that for some reason the dogs have avoided these spots. But that doesn't make sense. There are more of the animals out there than in any other parts of Florida, so if there's a random virus, it should be showing in these places rather than down in Key Biscayne and remote places like that.

Jacksonville too.

He looks at the correctional center and sees it's way north of the city center, out past the airport in Four Creeks State Forest. Jacksonville itself is the biggest city in Florida, with more than three-quarters of a million people living there and another half million within easy commuting distance.

But aside from the incident at the prison—no dog deaths or even bites.

The more he looks at the puzzle the more puzzled he becomes. In the hope of finding a little clarity, he focuses on the breeds that caused fatalities.

Bulldog
Yorkshire terrier

Labrador
German shepherd
Rottweiler
Wirehaired pointer
Pit bull/Staff mongrel

Aside from the Yorkshire they're all big dogs. From previously Googling the Yorkshire terrier, he already knows it's Miami's second most popular dog, just behind the German shepherd and ahead of the rottweiler.

His mailbox pings and he gets almost a childish rush of excitement when he realizes it's a note from Zoe.

SORRY DIDN'T REPLY LAST NIGHT. FELL ASLEEP
AFTER HAVING DRUNK TOO MUCH!
ATTACHED IS PROMISED RESEARCH, HOPE IT HELPS.
JUDE IS AWAY FOR A FEW DAYS—HOW ABOUT I COOK
DINNER FOR SAY 8PM?
Z

He mails her back.

THANKS FOR ATTACHMENT. DINNER SOUNDS GREAT.
HAVE A GOOD DAY X

Before hitting Send, he deletes the kiss. Then adds it again. Having put one on the text he sent last night, he thinks it would now be strange to leave it off.

Time slips by. Around 9:00 A.M. the office starts to fill up. First in is Sergeant John Tarney, a mountain of a twenty-eight-year-old, transferred from SWAT. There's not a better guy to have riding shotgun on a hairy late-night bust, but he's barely sociable before noon. JT needs coffee, pints of it, before he can even grunt out a good-morning.

Forty-two-year-old, Bella Lansing manages a brief hello, before darting to her desk and applying the makeup she rushed out of the apartment without putting on. She came into Special Ops from Vice, where she was a sergeant facing a disciplinary charge for kicking a pimp in his testicles after he asked her if she had a daughter he could have sex with.

Ghost grabs the empty coffee cup off his desk and heads to the pantry just as Annie Swanson appears from the main corridor. Gwen Harries is less than a yard behind her.

All the good feeling from his morning run completely disappears.

A CIA agent breathing down his neck is the last thing he needs.

68

Police HQ, Miami

*A*nnoyed at being distracted from his research, Ghost settles Gwen Harries in a meeting room while he quickly pushes a pile of tasks his team's way.

He asks them to chase up the crime statistics center for a reply to his early morning mail. Then he wants them to contact the FBI and the National Criminal Justice Reference Service and compile an overview of all dog attacks in the last month and last six months. Next on their to-do list is contacting animal shelters, health services, and the National Centers for Health Statistics at the CDC, the Centers for Disease Control.

Having given his not inconsiderable orders, he reluctantly rejoins the CIA agent and puts down a printout of the map of Florida that he'd been working on. "This shows all the major dog-related attacks. Anything jump out at you?"

She holds it by the corners, as if doing that somehow focuses her concentration. "They're all over the place. Like a damned epidemic."

Ghost winces. "Not really. If this were a virus like rabies then it would spread in local clusters—animals passing it in their saliva to other animals they come into contact with and humans catching it through bites. You would see two, three, four incidents all within walking distance of each other." He taps the map. "Miami is the only place we get any cluster."

Harries sees what he's driving at. "And that was right at the beginning. The earliest incidents were here. Maybe there was contact between the Miami dogs or the Miami owners with people or dogs from these other places dotted all over the map?"

"You mean like a dog show?"

"Could be. Maybe your 'pretty secretary' could check for us?" The emphasis conjures up all manner of critical undertones.

"Annie's a *detective*, not a secretary." He tries not to be annoyed by the crass remark and refocuses on the board. "Contact from a show, or such like, would account for the spread, but it still doesn't explain why there's only one incident in places like Santa Rosa and Marion. And why there is only one in Jacksonville." He draws a big circle around the area with his finger, "There's almost a million and a half people in this area, but just the one incident at the jail."

"So we can probably guess it's not passed from dog to dog."

It's Ghost's turn to go on the offensive. "Shouldn't you guys be consulting health experts—in both the animal and human world—to work out what the hell is going on here?"

"We are. I heard this morning that the dog files have been kicked upstairs. Some bigwigs in Washington are scrutinizing the cases."

"About time." He leans over her map from the opposite side of the table and points as he talks. "Orlando, Tampa, Fort Lauderdale, and the Everglades will be hit next."

"Why so?"

"Just because they haven't been so far. If this is the epidemic we both fear it is, then I bet my badge they're next."

69

Police HQ, Miami

A pack of killer hounds gathers around the edges of Ghost's desk, murderous rottweilers, Alsatians, pit bulls, Labradors, and even that tiny terror, the Yorkshire terrier.

In a spread of ten-by-seven color prints they don't look so dangerous. By now he can match every jaw to every victim, and his imagination has repeatedly revisited the awful last moment of each and every life.

He's still shuffling through the postmortem and toxicology reports on both dogs and humans when his desk phone rings. It's the captain's secretary, Patsy Howell, a pasty slab of a woman in her forties with skin like lard and a heart of gold.

"Ghost."

"Hello, Lieutenant, he's back. I just spoke to him and he says he can give you five minutes but it has to be now."

"Thanks, Patsy, I'm on my way over."

She's not finished. "Just so you know—he's in a bad mood. A very bad mood."

"Great."

He hangs up and hurries down the corridor to the captain's block.

Patsy looks up knowingly from her desk. "Good luck," she says, and tells him to go straight in.

Ghost opens the office door and catches Cummings bent over his cluttered desk devouring a giant *frita*—a massive bun with a beef patty, shoestring potatoes, a field of lettuce, and half an onion spilling from it.

The big captain looks up without even a flicker of shame, "Sit down, Ghost—and make this quick. Aside from some serious eating I need to do, I got the freaking chief of police wanting me in his office in two hours' time. Christ knows what bad news he's been cooking just for me."

Ghost pulls up a chair and can't help but shoot a disgusted look at the grease and barbecue sauce dripping onto the splayed wrapper beneath his boss's chin.

"What?" He drops the burger and glares at him. "You're about to tell me how many calories it has? How bad it is for me? Don't even think of it. You start behaving like my wife and I swear I'll punch you out. You know what I had for breakfast? That crap that rabbits have. *Oats*. She made me eat *oats* and sultanas. Jesus Christ, a man can't start work on a bowl of rabbit food."

"Apparently not."

The captain wipes his mouth with a white paper napkin and guiltily wraps up the burger. He takes a cool slug from a bucket of Coke then sits back. "So what's so important that you want to make my shitty day even shittier?"

"Dogs. And not the kind that come with ketchup and mustard."

"Very funny."

"We need to do something about these attacks. If we don't take proactive measures then a lot more people are going to die."

Cummings can't believe he's being troubled with this crap. "Ghost, what is it with you? You see problems everywhere—that's *your* problem. Listen, for decades people have been dying from dog bites. There's nothing new in that."

"Not at this rate, not in this city—"

He cuts off the rant before it gathers momentum. "Okay. Some kind of awareness campaign wouldn't be a bad idea. I'll get the pencil heads in Press and Communications on it."

"I was thinking more of extra neighborhood patrols. Increase our presence in tourist spots. Beef up the armed response teams, keep them on standby, cancel holidays—"

"Stop. Stop. Stop." He leans forward on the desk and smiles pityingly. "Have you got a stash of lottery cash in your desk drawer that you're looking to share?" He smiles sarcastically. "C'mon, have you? Coz if you have, then can you give your famished old friend here a few hundred thou' to pay for all that overtime, extra details, new recruits?"

Ghost ignores the sarcasm. "Civil protection shouldn't be a matter of money. It's—"

"Bullshit." Cummings picks up his wrapped *frita*. "Don't act dumber than my burger. My budget is more busted than a drunk at a Vegas table, and I'm not about to fuck it up any more because some people got bit."

"*Killed*, not bit. People were *killed*. Men, women, and children. And more are going to *get* killed if you don't do something about it."

"You ruin my fuckin' appetite. That's what you do." The captain throws the remains of his food, basketball style, into a waste bin a yard away and glares at Ghost. "On your way out, take a look at the wall map and the crime stats all over it like a hooker's rash."

Ghost gets to his feet.

Cummings berates him all the way to the door. "Drugs and gangs kill more innocent people every week than your damned dogs do in an entire year. If we ain't got more money for fighting that, then we sure as hell don't have it to go collaring Lassie and Rin Tin fucking Tin." He waves his hand dismissively. "Damned rabbit food. Feed that to the dogs, the fuckers will be too weak to bite anything."

10

Eisenhower Executive Office, Washington DC

Less than an hour after Pat Cornwell briefed Press Secretary Jay Ashton, he ushers two more White House staffers into his office.

Dr. Marlon F. Gonzalez, Director of the White House's Office of Science, and Chairman of the President's Council of Science Advisors, is an intense medical academic in his mid-fifties. He is small with a large shock of Einsteinlike hair and a brain quicker than the CERN accelerator.

Forty-three-year-old Katy Chimes, a professor turned politician, the duly elected head of the U.S. Department of Health and Human Services, is the opposite. Even before she slips on Louboutin stilettos she stands an Amazonian five-eleven, and the pixie-cropped brunette is still fit enough to play a mean game of volleyball.

Cornwell briefed them on the phone last night and has called them in to give him and Brandon Jackson, the President's appointed security advisor, the benefit of their expert views on how real the Chinese threat could be.

Gonzalez folds his hands as though in prayer, then talks in a gentle, almost reverential tone. "Weaponizing animals—particularly canines—is something we've looked into doing ourselves, but have never seen through. The initiative floundered because of lack of support, lack of budget, and lack of expertise. But from what I've been able to find out from those who were involved in our brief attempts, the short answer is yes, it's entirely possible to genetically or biomechanically provoke dogs into attacking humans. The main problem would be controlling them."

Cornwell is already frowning. "You need to go slow for me. Explain the first part—genetic or biomechanical."

"By genetic I mean to imply that their DNA would have been altered, possibly in a laboratory to promote extra aggression. It could be triggered by maturity of the animal—hitting puberty. But this is hugely difficult for a third party to control with any degree of precision. By biomechanical I mean that the dog is given some drug—through injection or food ingestion—that affects it. To use a crude analogy, it could be like giving bodybuilders excessive testosterone and causing so-called 'roid rage.'" He thinks over the latter scenario. "This again is very difficult to control—the party would have to individually inject dogs, or personally ensure they were fed the correct amount of drugged food or liquid at the correct times."

Don Jackson feels he has information that will help. "The vet reports show excessive levels of adrenalinelike substances in the blood but not the stomach. That would suggest injection rather than digestion, wouldn't it?"

"It would," Gonzalez agrees.

Katy Chimes has some deeper doubts. "I get the science, but really, could the Chinese do it? I mean, if *we* couldn't see a project like that through, then why could they? The Chinese might be masterful copiers and technicians, but they're not noted as being creative, or being great innovators."

Gonzalez looks horrified. "With all due respect, you forget China's Famous Four inventions—the compass, gunpowder, printing, and papermaking. Without these our world today would be remarkably different."

The VP doesn't want an academic debate to derail his briefing. "Let me understand the basics—are we agreed that the creation of weaponized dogs is actually possible?"

Gonzalez smiles. "In genetics, anything is now possible. Here in the U.S. we're spending more than five billion dollars a year on genetic testing—it'll be nearer twenty-five by the end of the decade. Molecular biotechnologists can grow limbs and organs like we once grew tomatoes. Hell, even the Austrians have been growing cerebral organoids—minibrains, if you like. It's the same in China; they're *pouring* resources into this area. But to weaponize dogs they would need geneticists with an intimate knowledge of the canine genome, people who would be capable of very sophisticated cell engineering, gene synthesis, and the like. The project we started focused on manipulating the dog's somatotropin levels—this is the growth hormone produced naturally in animals. We found there were ways of raising it and sustaining that rise so you got much bigger and far more aggressive animals."

Jackson jumps in again. "These dogs weren't extraordinarily large. Strong and relentlessly aggressive, yes, but not overlarge."

Cornwell drills a finger into an itchy ear. "I want to go back to Katy's point. It's at the crux of our dilemma. Could the Chinese really do any of this?"

Jackson throws a curveball. "Even if they couldn't, they could have bought the expertise in, sir. The Koreans and Russians are very scientifically advanced and have no scruples about helping

China. I'd rule out Japan, though. Their relations with Xian Sheng are worse than ours."

Cornwell accepts the point and moves on. "Dr. Gonzalez, you mentioned control. I got the feeling you had more to say when I interrupted you."

"Yes, Mr. Vice President. If we imagine these dogs to be weapons, then like all such devices they must have a trigger. The question is whether that trigger is biological, technological, or psychological. If biological, then geneticists will have had to further alter the genome, so that at a certain stage of maturation the dog becomes distressed, cannot function, and becomes enraged. If technological, then we are talking about some micro-implant, some nanodevice that can be activated to cause similar distress and resulting aggression. If psychological, then perhaps as pups the animals have been abused or exposed to something that makes certain people seem more predatory to them than they actually are, so they feel instinctively inclined to attack upon sight."

Jackson sees room for optimism. "If there's a trigger on the weapon, then I guess there is also a safety lock. What might that be, Professor?"

Gonzalez shrugs. "I admire your simile, but there might well *not* be one, Director Jackson. Again, it's something we struggled with in our research. In the end we had to accept that some weapons, like hand grenades, only have a trigger, and when it is pulled, there is no Off switch, no going back."

11

The Everglades

*T*om Watkin used to camp at Long Pine with his dad when he was a kid, and he feels warmly nostalgic returning with his eight-year-old son Perry.

They've left his wife and Perry's older sister Lucy-Anne back at home for a couple of days and brought their bikes, canoes, and fishing rods to what has become a sacred spot for the thirty-five-year-old schoolteacher.

The high Florida sun penetrates the canopy of tall slash pines as they trek through sweet smelling grass and gather dead wood for a campfire.

Tom finds himself pointing out the same things his pa did a quarter of a century ago and posing pretty much the same loaded questions. "D'you know how big the Everglades are, Perry?"

The freckle-faced youngster looks up and takes a wild shot at it. "As big as Disney World?"

Dad shakes his head. "Bigger."

Now Perry is in trouble. Disney World is so huge that when he went, they spent three full days walking around and he still hadn't seen everything. "Big as *two* Disney Worlds?"

Tom laughs and pulls the kid tight to him. "Let me tell you. The Glades cover more than a million and a half acres—and that's only half the size it was a hundred years ago. It's made up of ten thousand islands. Almost a quarter of a million acres of sugarcane is grown out here and almost eight million people depend upon the Glades for drinking water. So, it's really important that we respect this place, that we don't damage things and we support all the efforts to keep it for generations to come."

Tom is about to go back more than ten thousand years and tell Perry all about the ancient people of the Glades, about the Tequestas and Calusas, the Indians and the Spanish, about hurricanes and shipwrecks, when he spots a small black and white Alsatian puppy watching him, head cocked to one side with a puzzled look in its eyes. "Hi little fella; where'd you come from?"

The puppy bounds toward Tom as he drops into a crouch to lure him over and allow Perry to pet him. "You're a lovely little guy, aren't you?"

The boy puts his hand on the little dog's soft head. The puppy licks his arm and makes him laugh. "Hey, that tickles."

Father and son are both on their knees spoiling the dog—when eighty pounds of unseen Alsatian slams into them.

Tom feels like he's been hit by a fallen tree. Pain explodes in his neck, like someone's driven four six-inch nails through his skin.

Perry picks himself up and is thinking of crying. Partly out of shock and confusion. Partly because he went facedown into the rough dirt and feels like his face has been rubbed with glass paper.

Then he sees his father. Lying on his back. A big dog on his chest. Biting lumps out of his face.

Perry screams.

Blood bubbles through holes in his dad's throat.

The young pup scampers from Perry's side and disappears into the vast darkness of the Glades, leaving the young boy frozen by fear.

72

New York

*D*anny loses track of time as he watches his capture program snare snippets of the highly confidential digital data stream.

Man, this is a big fish.

As big and exotic as shutting down the PlayStation Network or opening up the private bank accounts of the main directors of J.P. Morgan, and he had his talented hands in both those ventures.

He'd spotted the traffic a long time back. A blip of astonishingly encrypted code, unlike any he'd ever seen before. To 99.999 percent of Internet users and even 99 percent of all hackers and crackers it would have gone unnoticed.

But to Danny the shark, it was like blood in the water, or a fluorescent flare spelling out his name in a big black cyber sky. Once spotted, he logged its shape and form and determined to chase it to the ends of the earth.

Then it vanished.

Painstakingly, he worked on what few fragments of encryption he'd captured. He replicated them, much as a forensic scientist uses advanced PCR kits to create fuller DNA profiles from ancient specks of century old human genes.

Gradually, he developed a program that was a hacker's equivalent of an automated speed camera with facial recognition, staked it out there on cyber superhighway, complete with capture net, and waited. Eventually the code recognition software picked up the unique profile of the encryption, locked on, and loaded in the big fish.

Now an invaluable copy is wriggling inside his portable hard drive and begging the critical question of him.

Can he crack it?

Can he break all the locks and codes and booby-traps that whoever wrote the software built in there to protect its secrets? He's damned sure he can.

Zoe's ring tone blasts out from his phone.

This time he answers it. "Hey, sis, you need to start with sorry, then grovel your way uphill from there—and believe me, it's a long way, a very long way to forgiveness."

"I'm sorry. Danny, I *really am* sorry." She sounds like she's in a cab or someone's car because the signal distorts almost as though she's talking underwater. "I left messages on your answering service straight away saying I was sorry. What I said—all that stuff about Jenny being a gold digger—it was just a sisterly reaction. It was stupid. I don't know this girl from Eve and—"

"Sounds like you don't know me either."

"Don't be like that. I do know you and I *care* about you."

"Then care that I'm happy. That I've found someone, Zo'. Someone I'm ready to take a chance on. Christ knows, we deserve a chance, don't we?"

Zoe knows that her silence gives away the fact that she's not sure how to answer him. She certainly can't see her taking a risk on Ghost.

Can she?

The thought throws her for a second. "Danny, give me Jenny's number and I'll call her. Tell her what a protective sister-bitch I am and how I'm really happy you're both going to be married."

"But you're not, are you?"

"Not yet. But I'm going to be. But listen—if you screw this up, big brother, then I'm going to come to New York and kick your ass so bad you'll never sit at a computer again."

13

Coral Way, Miami

*C*ooking dinner isn't something Zoe normally does. Not for guys. Mostly not even for herself.

Not unless you count warming up plastic-wrapped food in a microwave, in which case she should have her own TV show. In her most ambitious moments she's boiled pasta and chopped vegetables to go with meatballs. But she's never gone the whole hog and done the "follow a recipe and put linen on a table" crap.

At least not until now.

Tonight she's making an exception. After that rooftop spread Ghost put on, the least she can do is cook some fish with a few little side dishes and open a bottle of wine.

Jude has a stack of books on a shelf above the cooker, and she's found a recipe for "Asian Salmon Bake with Creamy Miso and Sake Sauce." A quick scout around shows there's enough stuff in the freezer, fridge, and vegetable basket to have a go at it.

Zoe does her prep first. She tracks down bottles of vegetable and sesame oil and measures out what she calls "the doses." Next, she gets a board and chops green onions, cloves, and garlic, then defrosts a hunk of salmon from the icebox. Making bread crumbs is trickier than she thought, and she manages to add some grazed knuckle to the grated bread.

She needs a chair to root in the alcohol cupboard above the fridge. There's rum, whiskey, port, brandy, Cointreau, Southern Comfort, gin, and vodka.

Everything except sake.

Vodka will do.

Won't it?

She measures out the quarter cup that the recipe asks and then freezes. From the back of her mind comes a memory of baking with her mother and the young Zoe taking a sip of water from mom's cup. Only to find it wasn't water. It was vodka. Then there'd been the instant recollection of how many times Mom had drunk water from a cup. How many times it mustn't have been water but booze, the vodka that eventually would ruin her life.

Zoe throws the alcohol in the sink. The smell of it freaks her out, has her heart racing like a bolted horse. She takes the bottle and empties all of it down the sink, shakes it to get all the drops out, then runs the tap. The odor is still there. That insipid stench that was always on her mother's lips.

She takes time out from the kitchen, sits in the living room and stares into the cream nothingness of the opposite wall. But nothing is not what she sees. The past is there, in all its vividness.

She's a child again. Baking brownies with her mother. Pulling on oven gloves so she can carry them over to where her father and Danny are excitedly waiting with eyes closed. "No peeping," shouts her mama, and they tiptoe in together, Zoe concentrating hard on not dropping the precious food. "Okay, now you can look." And they do. Their eyes sparkle with the joy of the moment, the smell of the fresh baking, and Dad is even clapping. "They're amazing, honey—yummmmmm."

Zoe shuts her eyes and feels the pain shoot through her.

All that was before "that" day. The day no one ever talked about. The day that was so bad they sent her to the psychiatrist to get over it.

Zoe's in trouble now. Lost on a sea of unlocked memories. Swept out into vast stormy waters of pain and fear. She tries to stay calm. Takes long, slow breaths. Counts the time in, the time out.

Her hands reach for her phone.

Her mind is sinking in the ocean of thoughts.

Her fingers find the speed dial as her pulse quickens.

Her mouth is filling up, but not with saltwater—with vodka.

"Hello."

She stares at the phone and listens to her brother's voice.

"Hello."

She feels herself rise above the waves.

"Zoe? Is that you?"

She coughs. Spits out all the choking vodka. Splutters like she's been dragged up onshore.

Her finger finds the touch screen and the big red button that ends the call.

With any luck Danny will think she just rang him by mistake.

It's happened before.

Plenty of times.

74

Long Pine Key Camp, The Everglades

*B*y the time Ghost and Harries have driven out to the camp, the death toll has risen to four.

As well as Tom Watkin and his son Perry, the dog also killed senior citizens Baz and Bess Bradbury. The old-timers had been standing hand in hand, staring at the lopsided heart and shaky names they'd carved in a towering pine when they were teenagers.

The uniforms have already evacuated the camp and a team of police marksmen is hunting down the dog. Ghost is there to pick up the investigative pieces and see whether there is a crime to investigate or whether the incident was just an unavoidable tragedy.

He and Harries walk from the roasting air into the chill of the main camp building and see a huge bald guy in pinstriped pants shouting at a young female officer.

"What's the problem?" Ghost steps between them and shows his badge.

The man is a couple of inches bigger than him and isn't deterred by a glint of shield. He jabs a fat forefinger into Ghost's rock-hard chest. "*You're* the problem. You guys need to do your jobs and make this country safe again. These motherfucking dogs roaming around—"

"Calm down." Ghost takes his shades off, knowing how distracting the sight of his eyes can be. "What's your name?"

"Bradbury. John Bradbury." He can't help but be mesmerized by the lieutenant's pink pupils. His voice is naked now, no clothes of anger and rage, just the raw flesh of grief. "It's my mother and father who got killed out there."

Ghost puts his hand on the big guy's shoulder. "Then I understand why you are so upset, but it's not this lady's fault. We're very sorry for your loss—it's a terrible thing to happen, and you're right, it shouldn't have. Now come over here and sit down while I find out what progress is being made."

Bradbury allows himself to be led to some chairs on the opposite side of the reception area. The woman officer nods a thank-you to Ghost and sits down next to the grieving son.

Harries's phone rings.

She stares at the number display, recognizes it as the head office and finds a quiet corner to take it.

A flash of light by the door comes from sun hitting the lens of a TV camera. Somehow the press have rounded the cordon and are inside.

Ghost recognizes the reporter as Carlo Affonso from CBS.

The journalist talks as he strides toward him. "Lieutenant, we're live on air at the moment, what can you tell us about this latest tragedy?"

Ghost spots the flashing red light on the camera. The guy's not lying. They're live and he's got to say something or else look stupid.

He chooses his words carefully. "I'm afraid there's little I can say at this stage. I'm sure you understand that we need to speak first to the families of the deceased—it wouldn't be right for them to be learning about this incident from the news."

"Can you confirm that four people are dead, Lieutenant?" Affonso holds up his notebook with the back of it to the camera so only Ghost can see. "These are the names I was given, but since you've not yet spoken to the relatives, I won't read them out loud."

Ghost glances at the reporter's page. His information is good. So good that someone in the force, maybe even in his own unit, must have tipped him off. "Yes, I can confirm we're looking at four fatalities. No other injuries."

"But you haven't yet caught the dog?"

"We will. And quickly. Marksmen and trackers are out there right now."

Carlo moves to a deeper vein of questioning. "Can you tell us, Lieutenant, why are so many people around here getting attacked by dogs, and what are the police doing about it?"

Now that the heat is being turned up, Ghost wishes he'd just thrown the guy out. "There are no easy answers here. At the moment, we don't know why these dogs are suddenly becoming vicious, and until we do, I think pet owners and anyone coming into contact with a dog in a street or park has to treat such animals as genuine threats."

The reporter scents an opening, "Are you saying people should be frightened of the dogs they have at home?"

Ghost sees the trap. He's not going to tell people to be scared, but he does want to warn them of the dangers. "Responsible dog owners already know dogs *can* kill and *do* kill. Dozens of Americans die each year because of dog bites. Always have. Probably always will. But we have to remember that these animals are descendants of wolves. If you have a dog in your house, then you're feeding and petting a modern day wolf, so take care."

Carlo looks stunned. He's got more than he expected. "And the police—do you think the police and the sheriff departments should be doing more to warn and help people?"

Captain Cummings's words ring in Ghost's ears. He knows he has to be cautious or else he'll get chewed up worse than a quarter pounder with extra cheese. "We always try to do more and we should always try to do more—that's what policing is about—and prevention is better than cure. If people take care with the dogs, if they don't take risks by letting them get hungry, overheated, or stressed during this really hot spell, then I'm sure that will help." He flashes a final smile before he adds, "If you don't mind, I need to get back to the job now? Thank you."

Ghost walks away and leaves Affonso doing a wrap-up to the camera. He finds Gwen Harries by the door looking stressed. "Don't you have to get force clearance to do that kind of thing?" she asks him.

Ghost frowns. "If you can. The top brass understand that if you have a live camera shoved in your face, then you deal with it. It just looks bad if you stick your hand over the lens and say no comment."

She nods. "Makes sense. Listen, I have to go. Something has cropped up. I have to pull out quick."

"Okay." He can tell she's holding back on him. "Is something wrong?"

Harries bites her lip. "I shouldn't tell you this, so it didn't come from me, all right?"

"Then don't tell me."

"After that interview you've just done, you need to know. The call I got was from Washington. NIA Director Brandon Jackson and the President's own press officer are about to brief police chiefs and all response agencies that no one should raise public concern about dog attacks. All CIA, FBI, and government staff are banned from talking to the press about the attacks or any potential threat from dogs."

"Why?"

"That information is classified and I really can't tell you." She nods toward the departing camera crew. "You've just made national news at exactly the time the White House wants national silence. Congratulations, Lieutenant."

75

Coral Way, Miami

Zoe is staring at the dried-up, overcooked fish bake and is consoling herself by opening a second bottle of wine when Ghost finally rings the doorbell.

"Sorry," is the first thing he shouts through the intercom.

She leans somewhat drunkenly against the wall and buzzes him through, without answering. Cooking has never been her strong point and she knew right off that cooking for a man might be a bad idea. It turns out that cooking for one who would call at the last minute and say he'd be two hours late was a very stupid one. While she's waiting for him to climb the stairs, she refills her empty glass and pours one for him.

Ghost comes through the door looking so embarrassed and tired that her anger all but disappears. "Jeez, you look like hell. Here, I'm sure you need this." She holds out a glass for him.

"Thanks, I feel like hell." He kisses her and takes the wine. "Sorry again, this damned dog problem—it's so out of hand." He produces a lavish bunch of flowers from behind his back, an arrangement of stargazer lilies and white roses. "To make up for being so ridiculously late."

"They're beautiful."

"As are you."

"I wish." Zoe carries them to the small kitchen area. "Beautiful is something that certainly can't be said for the food." She puts the flowers on the sink drainer and flips down the oven door to show him the tray of incinerated fish. "Are you hungry enough to eat that?"

"It looks fine," he lies.

"Yeah, sure it does."

He puts an arm around her waist and pulls her close. "I didn't really come here for your culinary skills, so we could just skip the food and go straight to bed." He kisses her neck. "In truth, I'd just as soon *feast* on you." He bites her playfully.

"Vampire!" Zoe pushes him away from her in mock horror. "Get out now, or I'll beat you to death with the overcooked fish."

He kicks the oven door closed, "You don't frighten me. I'm ten thousand years old and now I've decided to have you—so have you I must." Ghost sweeps an arm under her legs and effortlessly picks her up.

"No, no, you beast!" Zoe protests melodramatically, and laughs as he carries her to the bedroom.

He kisses her to shut her up and then lowers her lovingly to the soft mattress. The urge to feel her naked against him has his head swimming. Her hands are around his neck and her mouth is drawing the life out of him.

And then everything changes.

The buzz of a phone kills all the passion in the room.

"Ignore it," she says breathlessly and unbuttons his shirt.

He kisses her and tries.

It stops.

Ghost slips out of his shirt. Her hands feel cool as they roam his skin, find his taut chest muscles as he bends over her, fingers brushing his hard nipples, electrifying his body.

The phone.

The damned phone—*again*.

He looks toward it. Makes the mistake of seeing the display. Annie.

He kneels up. Away from Zoe. "I have to take it."

Her eyes tell him to go ahead.

"Walton." He steps away from the bed and listens.

Zoe watches him. Seeing him half naked in the twilight of the room makes her only want him even more. But the seriousness filling his face tells her the night is over. She gets up and walks past him. Heads straight to the kitchen.

Ghost walks in a few minutes later. His shirt is fastened and tucked back into his trousers. "I'm sorry. I have to go."

"I know." She's busy filling a carrier bag with drinks and snacks. "I'm coming with you."

"I don't think you'll like where I'm going. There's been another death."

"I gathered that," she says almost curtly. "Here, take these; we may as well eat on the way."

76

Coconut Grove, Miami

*T*he new death scene is only ten minutes away. En route, Ghost and Zoe snack on packs of potato chips and slug black currant water.

Between mouthfuls Zoe checks her camera, which Ghost was far from happy about her bringing along.

They park under street lighting at the end of the suburban road, get out and slap the doors closed. The night air is fresh with the smell of wisteria as they walk toward the flashing lights and taped-off scene. Ghost whispers Zoe a warning. "You shouldn't be here, especially with that camera, so I'm cutting you no more slack than I would a press photographer. You stay on the public side of the line. Okay?"

"Fine by me, but just for the record, that's no way to charm yourself back into my bed."

He laughs. "I'm afraid bed is the last thing on my mind right now." He looks across to her. "Are you really sure you want to be here?"

"Are you sure you want to be here?"

"This is my job."

"And mine is photography. Photojournalism means being around things as they happen, catching the moment, and this dog stuff seems very much to be dominating the moment—especially our moment."

He turns his attention to Annie, who's heading his way. "Hi, what's the latest?"

The detective's eyes are on Zoe, who's already dropped back and is filming Ghost and her. "Hey, back the fuck off with that camera, or you'll need a surgeon to remove it when I've finished with you."

"She's with me," Ghost explains.

"She's what?"

He tries to explain. "She, er—came with me. She's a kinda friend."

"Kind of?" Zoe lowers the lens and smiles. "He means the kind he was about to fuck, when you rang."

Annie's eyes widen and she looks toward Ghost.

He lets out a sigh and lifts the tape. "Let's talk, while you show me the scene."

Annie ducks beneath the tape and Zoe follows.

"The other side," Ghost says firmly to her. "Or better still, go home and I'll call you later."

"No way, José." She smiles and clicks the camera full in his face. "Man, you look sexy when you're mad."

He blanks her and returns to Annie.

"That's a wild one," she says as they head to the house.

Ghost ignores the comment. "Tell me about the victims."

"Still making sense of it. Young woman and old woman, both dead in the kitchen. Mother and daughter, from the look of pictures in the living room. They've both virtually been skinned by a dog, and it's chewed through wrist and ankle bones."

"Animal still free?"

"No, sniper shot it. Neighbors heard the screams and called

the cops. Dispatch sent the dog squad and a sniper." She raised her hand and pointed to a man with an Alsatian standing partly down the side of the house. "That's a Sergeant Lyndon, he'll tell you about the dog. All I know from looking at it is that it's a big one."

Ghost veers over to the cop, a broad-shouldered man with a little neck and a shaved head. "Lieutenant Walton," he says, and badges him. " Can you fill me in on the canine?"

"Sure. It's a GWP—"

"A what?"

"German wire-haired pointer. Beautiful thing. Least it was till they shot it."

"Big dog?"

"They're a good size, but not massive like a Great Dane, about two feet high and I guess sixty, sixty-five pounds." His expression changes. "You won't believe the damage it's done. It's like someone rolled a tank through there."

"Thanks." Ghost headed toward the kitchen to see for himself.

The cop had been right. The room was devastated. Cupboard doors, a kitchen table, and chairs had been smashed into firewood. There were spilled food, drinks, and sauces all across the brown-tiled floor. And then there were the bodies. Or rather, what little remained of them.

Annie Swanson put her hand to her mouth and had to rush into the yard to hurl. The women's faces had been all but eaten off. What clothing was left on their bodies was soaked in blood and hung in tattered rags from bones broken and almost entirely stripped of flesh, muscle, and sinew. Blood had pooled and cloyed in the corner of the room, where the women had been pinned down and killed. Ghost could see where they'd slipped, grabbed with bloody hands at worktops, fallen, and were dragged. He could see the animal's paw prints across the tiles, where it had slithered in the remains of the two women.

He walked outside and took a breath of fresh night air. Moments like this made him realize how precious life was. How it could be snuffed out in just one fateful minute. Across the tape he could see Zoe, snapping shots that were meaningless—close-ups of dog handlers, faces of frightened residents, uniform cops standing in the blinking red and blue lights of their cars. "Zoe!" he shouted.

She turned and saw him.

"Come here." He waved her over.

She pointed Ghost out to the cop by the tape and he let her under. Seconds later she was at his side.

"You wanted to see what this is all about—take a look. Take a long look and snap whatever photographs you want—the world should see this shit."

77

Nian Command Center, Beijing

A seventy-inch flat-screen monitor in the operations room shows a map of Florida peppered with hundreds of multicolored lights. Green indicates the whereabouts of weaponized canines that are "untriggered." Amber signifies animals that have been activated but are yet to reach viable levels of aggression. Red denotes more than a dozen dogs across the state that have already gone into attack mode and killed or caused serious injuries.

Refreshed after a few hours sleep, General Zhang taps the giant screen as he strides through the room in his full uniform.

"Today, we will paint the American state of Florida red. Red with our precious lights—red with their capitalist blood."

He has the attention not just of Lieutenant Xue and Minister Chunlin, but also of more than a dozen other members of the command team who are hanging on his every word.

"Already in Washington they are learning to fear us. To fear each and every one of you." He smiles like a proud father. "They don't know your names, or your faces, but they see your shadows as you guide our dogs to the throats of their citizens, and slowly, day by day, they are learning obedience. Until now we have been merciful. Controlled strikes. As surgical as smart bombs. Domestic dogs triggered in specific areas to do maximum damage in minimum time."

He sits on the edge of Xue's desk. "But not anymore. Now, I want you to activate all the weaponized dogs that the Americans call strays. The dogs they have turned their ignorant backs on. The outcasts of society. Those packs that roam the streets of the state's top ten cities."

"General, please keep in mind that breed by breed and size by size the activation time on each canine varies. The lag between us triggering the aggression and the dog actually becoming violent varies from six hours to sixteen hours."

Zhang had forgotten the gap was so large. "The smaller the dog, the quicker the response?"

"Yes. Terriers can be triggered much faster than the big dogs, the rottweilers and Alsatians."

Chunlin can't help but voice his concern. "We cannot escalate to this level without pacifiers. It would be reckless and—"

Zhang cuts him off. "As I told you last night, such military decisions are now down to me." Zhang glares at him. "We are past the point of waiting for scientists, Minister. Time is now of the essence. When the pacifiers are available, we will deploy them. But I will wait no longer."

The minister turns his back on the room so that his words are only heard by Zhang and Xue. "General, even in combat there are rules to be followed and lines not to be crossed. Unleashing packs of wild, uncontrollable dogs is tantamount to widespread civilian slaughter."

Zhang's face is empty of emotion. "A campaign like this has no rules, Chunlin. It is invisible. It does not even exist. Our soldiers wear no uniforms. They fly no flags. Instead, they sit innocently on the enemy's rugs and blankets and beds, and they lick at their palms when they are petted and fed. Or, the abandoned ones lie in the animal shelters waiting to be euthanized." A flicker of warmth comes into his dark eyes. "Imagine the surprise of the Americans when they find how many of them we control, how many we took on as 'charitable acts' and we are now able to open the doors of. Those dogs will run riot. They will do more than bite the hand that didn't feed them. They will rip out their ignorant throats and hearts."

18

Coral Way, Miami

*I*t's 5:00 A.M. when Zoe and Ghost get back to Jude's apartment.

They shower together. Not out of desperate sexual need but because of the urge to psychologically rinse away the scene that still lingers on them.

Wet and wrapped in towels, they tumble into bed.

The room is dark but dawn is already breaking on the other

side of the curtains. Ghost can see enough to tenderly hold Zoe's face as he kisses her. He feels guilty about exposing her to the carnage, to dragging her into his world.

They start to make love. So slowly it's almost as though it's not happening. Each caress is as healing as it is arousing. They shared a trauma together and now they're helping each other recover.

"Open your eyes." Zoe reaches up and tenderly touches his lids. "Let me see you."

At first he doesn't. Years of albino awkwardness have taught him to keep them shut.

"Please," she pleads.

Tentatively they flutter open. In the shade they seem darker, more ruby than pink.

Ghost sees Zoe looking at him. Not with shock or horror. Not even with curiosity or pity. With a glistening look he can't describe because he's never seen it before.

"What you do is incredible." She kisses him softly. "You are a wonderful and amazing person."

He smothers her words with his mouth and slips slowly inside her. There's no crazy urgency consuming him, no frantic desire for release. Instead, he feels a rush of energy that's alien to him. One that dissipates the horrors in his mind, one that makes him feel as though he belongs to the woman who's so freely bound her flesh to his.

Zoe is lost. All the mental toughness she wears to face the world now lies somewhere on the floor, carelessly discarded along with her jeans and blouse and underwear. Making love now feels to her like she'd always imagined it would, long before the first frantic teenage boy ruined her dream.

Lost in love, the last of the night dies with the last of their sighs. Morning breaks around their entwined bodies, flooding through the crack in the curtain, floating in on the birdsong that drifts through the open window.

19

Starz Cawfee, Fifth Avenue, New York

*T*he all night coffee shop is packed pretty tight. A mix of night workers, party stragglers, and early starters. Two men sit in a beat-up corner booth near the banging doors of the restrooms and stacked brown boxes waiting to go out into the yard where they'll be squashed and torn and rammed into the recycle bins.

It's the least attractive spot in the joint.

Unless you need to go unnoticed.

And that's what Danny Speed and the man opposite him need more than anything.

Their meeting is the type that has to look accidental. Meaningless. Everyone has to grab breakfast, eat, and drink. It's just coincidence that the only place a law-abiding suit-wearing respectable business type like Brad Stevens can sit with his BLT and Americano opposite a scumbag cracker hacker like Danny with his chocolate muffin and full fat cappuccino.

Stevens sits so he can see the front of the restaurant and notice everyone coming and going. It's how he likes it. Mid-forties, he doesn't look anything but middle-aged. Except his eyes. His eyes look older—like they've seen two lifetimes worth of stuff you'd rather never witness in one. They're sunk in dark wrinkle pits and scurry from side to side like rats that never rest. He's round-faced and gray-haired, bagged up in a charcoal gray suit that's seen almost as much service as he has. Life's many blows are summarized on the empty finger that once bore a wedding band.

Brad picks a newspaper off the table and opens it. Columns of dire events stand raggedly between his two hands. More shit in Syria. New athletes caught doping in cycling. And this crazy dog business. Normally, he'd read it all and worry. Right now he has other things on his mind. "So, what have you got?"

Part of Danny's thoughts are still hooked on the strange call from his sister. He rang back and there was no pickup. Which is odd during the day. He'll try her again later. It's most likely nothing to worry about.

"Hey, I don't have all day—what is it?"

Danny pulls at his food as he answers. "I don't know exactly what it is. Not yet. But it's hotter than lava. The code is unlike anything I've come across. Superprotected. Teflon coated. First strands of it just shot through the standard capture programs like greased lightning."

"You're thinking it's noncorporate?"

"This is platinum grade intel that someone is protecting. Reminds me of when I cut across the VICAP feeds in Quantico and we had to move because the feds got nervy."

Stevens folds his newspaper and places it on the table equally between him and his table companion. "Sounds like a big one, Danny boy. Do you need someone older and wiser to help you haul it in?"

"I might. I've got ident trackers on it now, so I'm capturing bursts whenever they come, but I'm having real problems decoding the data. I'm trying to write something special."

"Special is why we pay you the big bucks."

Danny drops the remains of the muffin and wipes crumbs and chocolate from his hands. "I'll crack it. Trust me on that." He gets to his feet and picks his computer bag off the back of the chair.

"But if I shake up a nest of gun-toting badge-wavers with wasps in their asses you better have somewhere I can run to."

Thunder cracks as he heads outside and the bad feeling that ran through Danny's head in the coffee shop keeps on brewing all the way back to his place in Greenwich Village.

It rains all night.

Rains like it must have done when Noah decided it was time to start gathering wood and gathering companions.

In the damp, two-room rental above Kuzniaki's bakery, Danny Speed has hardly been asleep when he opens his baby blues and stares at red numbers blinking back from the bedside clock.

0305

That's no freakin' time to be awake.

He listens to the rainfall as it comes down hard and vertical, like gunfire from an angel sniper on a thick, black cloud.

Blasts of buckshot bounce off the metal tops of cars and the fat plastic garbage bags dumped at the kerb. Heaven is raising a racket loud enough to wake the dead.

His bed seems empty without Jenny.

She doesn't like staying at his place and he doesn't blame her. He doesn't like it much either. One day, they'll live somewhere like the loft down in the financial district, the place he works from. One day, soon he hopes, when he gets enough money together and stops taking risks like he does.

He lies on his left side and listens to feral dogs barking in the alley beneath the fire escape at the back of the bakery. He pictures them fighting for scraps from an overturned trash can.

The landlord's faded brown curtains don't quite fit and through the gap he watches moonlit droplets hit the pane, roll together and run in streams down the window. It reminds him of camping as a kid. Lying awake beneath Boy Scout canvas, watching storms flash and supernatural shadows climb the sides of the tent.

There's a bass roll of thunder that rattles the old casement window.

Or at least that's what he hopes it is.

But he's not taking chances.

He slips out of bed in just his CK's and slides a hand underneath a big stand-up wardrobe. Among the dust and dead flies his fingers find what he's looking for.

The moulded grip of a semi-automatic pistol.

If burglars, crackheads or any kind of liberty-takers are breaking in, then he's got a shock for them.

A forty-five-calibre shock.

Danny checks the magazine and silently unlocks the front door of the apartment.

He takes a long slow breath to calm himself and to concentrate. He puts his foot against the bottom of the wood to stop it creaking as he eases it open.

The light on the landing is out.

There's a creak on the stairs.

He presses himself to the wall and runs through his options.

He could shout a warning. Or just rush forward and fire at anything that looks like it might shoot back.

Danny hears a surge of wind and rain outside, a passing car. The downstairs door must be open.

There's a click.

Maybe the latch.

Maybe something more sinister.

He drops to the floor and spreads himself flat, arms outstretched; the Glock clasped rigid in both hands.

A figure in black is almost at the top of the stairs. The head of a second man is coming up a few steps behind him.

Danny waits a beat.

The first man reaches the top step.

Danny shoots him mid torso. It's lower than he would have liked but enough to drop the sonovabitch down the stairs.

Before the second figure can open fire, Danny puts a bullet in the middle of his head.

He scrambles to his knees and runs to the stairs.

The first guy isn't lying there. Despite the gut wound he's got his shit together and fled.

But his buddy is flat-out and dead.

Even in the blackness, Danny can tell that the prostrate shape with arms spread wide isn't ever going to give anyone any trouble again.

The young hacker walks quickly back to his apartment to pick up his phone. He needs help and needs it quick.

80

Coral Way, Miami

*G*host rises and dresses first. He makes coffee in Jude's small kitchen and watches the morning news on her TV. Middle Eastern tensions have taken over the lead spot. The tinderbox tensions of Syria, Lebanon, Israel, and Egypt all stacked like one big bonfire that constantly gets lit and doused. Straight after the international news comes an update on the dog attacks. There's a clip of him and the reporter in the Everglades where the four holiday makers died, followed by brief shots of him and Annie Swanson arriving at the scene in Coconut Grove where the two women died. The bulletin names them as twenty-four-years-old Astrid Gerber and her mother, Heidi.

Zoe appears in the doorway, wearing his shirt. "'Morning, what time is it?" She rubs a hand through mussed hair.

"Just after eight." He gets up and heads to the worktop. "You want coffee?"

"Intravenously." She gets up on her tiptoes to kiss him as he passes.

Ghost notices his shirt ride up and can't resist cupping the curve of exposed buttock as her lips find his.

Zoe's eyes slip to the TV as he finds a clean mug and pours her coffee. "What time do you have to go in?"

"I want to be there by nine." He passes the drink over.

She takes it. "Thanks. Can I come with? I can be like your own personal photographer."

"No, you can't. Last night was a one-off. I just wanted you to see how horrible it was."

She puts her drink down. "Why?"

"I don't know. I guess I wanted someone to understand."

"Doesn't that cop Anna understand?"

"*Annie.* You mean Detective Annie Swanson."

"Yeah, Detective Swansong. Doesn't she understand?"

He laughs at her deliberate mispronunciation. "I meant someone close to me. Someone I can talk to without having my guard up."

"Is that what I am—someone close?"

"I guess you can't get much closer than we got last night."

"I wasn't talking about sex. I've had sex with people and been in a completely different world at the time."

"Neither was I. I was talking about a closeness to the heart and soul, not just the genitals."

"Genitals?" She laughs out loud. "What a crazy word. Who the hell decided that was a good name for such a great part of the body?"

They're standing face-to-face. Inches apart. It's killing Ghost not to kiss her, sweep her into his arms and carry her back to bed. This time it would be fast and frantic. Last night's need for tenderness has been supplanted by raw animal attraction.

Zoe reads his eyes and smiles. "I have the time if you do."

He hesitates.

She doesn't. She tilts her head and presses her lips against his. Lets her breath moan inside him, lets her body take control of his.

"I've got time," he says, breathlessly. "Nothing is more important than this. Than you."

81

The White House, Washington DC

*P*at Cornwell and Jay Ashton flank Clint Molton as they sit in front of the flat screen and watch a recording of the early news.

Ashton hits pause as the item finishes. The press secretary is eager to exonerate himself from what looks like an early break in strategy. "I'd like to stress that this particularly wild and noisy horse bolted from the stable *before* Don Jackson and I held the multiagency briefing." He points at the freeze frame of the pale-skinned, sunglass-wearing detective. "David Caruso there has really set the cat among the pigeons."

Molton can't help but smile. "Horses, cats, *and* pigeons— that's a lot of mixed metaphors even for you, Jay."

"Perhaps it is, Mr. President. My apologies. But believe me, the print media are already pumping police stations all over the country for comments about the dangers of dogs. This Walton guy is fanning the flames of speculation, he's potentially our worst nightmare."

Cornwell is staring at the head-and-shoulders shot of Ghost on the TV. "I sure hope his boss tears his smart-ass balls off."

Molton looks surprised. "For what? For being right?" He points at the screen. "The guy *is* right; we should all be damned scared. And given how little this lieutenant knows about what really is going on, his comments are disturbingly smart. Instead of ripping his balls off for trying to save lives we should bring him into the fold and have him help us."

Cornwell can't believe what he's heard. "You're joking, right? Tell me you're joking, Clint."

"No, I'm not. Think about it for a minute."

Ashton is already ahead of the VP. "There might be kudos in appointing a cop who's been on the front line of these attacks to be part of a presidential task force. If this issue captures more of the public attention and our opponents start throwing criticism around, then having him inside the tent is better than having him outside."

Cornwell's not convinced. "I prefer we just have his captain rip his balls off and tell him to shut the fuck up."

Molton turns to his old friend. "Pat, I never go to war with the good guys—you should know that by now. I like the task force idea, talk to Don and make it happen." He eases himself out of his seat and stretches. All the traveling and sitting are screwing up his spine. His doctor says he should take more exercise, start doing yoga, but given his timetable the best he can manage is a few stretches and a walk around the desk. "And get this cop on board. He's smart and very recognizable, we don't want someone like that becoming the face of the opposition, the sound bite the media turn to every time they want to whip us."

Cornwell throws up his hands in defeat. "Done. Now can we talk about the real reason we're here?"

"Sure." Molton settles behind his desk. The *Resolute* desk, named that because it was made from the planks of HMS *Resolute* and gifted to the U.S. by Queen Victoria. "You think we should call a Joint Chiefs of Staff and tell them of Xian's threats."

"I do. They're being battered blind by the Middle East machinations, what with NATO, the UN, and public opinion swinging back and forth, we've got to keep them fully in the picture."

Ashton looks horrified. "It will leak, Mr. President. Call a meeting like that and it's like mailing copy to the news desks and saying, 'Hey guys! Look, here's something fresh for you to throw your shit at.'"

Molton looks toward the VP for an answer.

"You have a duty to inform them, Clint," Cornwell says. "The Joint Chiefs and the National Security Council too—though I'm sure Don has already unofficially done that. You can't hold back on a threat to the nation. If we really take this weaponized dog threat seriously—and we're starting to behave like we do—then we *have* to tell our military commanders and our closest colleagues in government. We can't just keep this between ourselves and the CIA."

The President touches the rich old grain of the desk. *Resolute*. A word meaning "firm in purpose or belief; characterized by firmness and determination."

He looks up. "Call it, Pat. Get them and the NSC together for a meeting in the Situation Room as soon as agendas allow. Have Don put together a briefing package to illustrate proof of threat. Jay, have a communications strategy in place before we sit down with them, I don't want their heads of media in the loop, and let's all pray that this is an enormous waste of everyone's time."

82

New York

*D*anny knows the score.

When serious shit happens you phone a friend. You grab what you can and you run.

Run fast.

He throws basic clothes in a gym bag plus the backup drives from his computers and puts the load in the panniers on his motorbike. He sends quick text messages to Jenny and his crew with excuses for quitting town, then ditches all his phones, even the one he uses for legitimate calls and family.

Danny thrashes the Kawasaki all the way downtown to the loft.

Moving quicker than a burglar, he disconnects the cables to the backup computers he and the other hackers had been using and stuffs them in a rucksack, along with a couple of bottles of water and some cereal bars on his desk.

Within half an hour he's crossing the Brooklyn Bridge, watching harbor lights disappear in his wing mirrors as he nervously checks to see if he's being followed.

Danny parks up on wasteland off Furman Street, the bridge to the right of him and lower Manhattan gleaming straight ahead.

Ten minutes later a black Lincoln rolls to a stop and the trunk pops open. Danny puts his rucksack and gym bag in the cavernous space, closes the trunk and gets in the passenger seat.

Brad Stevens shakes his head with exaggerated disapproval.

"I'm not your housekeeper, Danny boy. God did not put me on this earth to run around cleaning up your almighty messes."

"Who would you have had me call?"

"You did right to call, it's just the middle of the night is my time for sleeping. Funny that, eh?"

"Ha ha."

"There's a new phone and number for you in the glove box. We'll put a trace on your old cell and restore the number when we know it's safe. Until then don't call anyone you don't want to end up dead."

Danny pulls a white iPhone out of the glove box. "White? You think I'm the kind of guy who uses white phones?"

"You are today." Stevens glides the Lincoln off the dirt and heads south down Montague and out on to Columbia. "No sign of the bleeder you mentioned. He must have got away. I had his friend Mr. Stiff moved, though. And your place is being stripped and cleaned. How many bullets did you fire?"

"Just the two."

"Not too much paint and plaster needed, then. Did you collect the shells?"

"You think I'm stupid?"

"Just 'cause you're a cracker doesn't mean you're smart."

"Hacker not cracker. There's a difference."

"Being?"

"Crackers are assholes, evil cyber vandals that screw things up for no reason. Hackers have reasons, you know—like the common good."

"Yeah, sure. Your common good being personal profit."

Danny's not in the mood for a wind-up. "Fuck you, man. You pay the bills, you get the company benefits. I'm just the skateboarder hanging on to the back of your big old bus."

"Glad you know your place. Any more shit like this and the bus won't be stopping for you anymore. Did you get everything you needed out of that flea pit?"

"Pretty much. Won't be sad to see the back of it."

"What are you going to tell the rest of the crew?"

"Texted them already. Said our IP masks were compromised and the Wall Street loft isn't safe. They'll know we need to stay low and relocate. They'll be cool." Danny looks out the windshield as the Lincoln filters onto the Brooklyn Queens Expressway. "Where we going?"

Stevens smiles broadly. "You're in luck. We've got a vacation home for you out at Breezy Point."

"Breezy? You're freakin' kidding me. I hate the ocean. I can't even swim. Man, I'm gonna die of boredom out there."

"Is that a promise?"

PART FOUR

I do not know with what weapons
World War III will be fought, but World War IV
will be fought with sticks and stones.

ALBERT EINSTEIN

83

$\mathcal{T}$he high-pitched whine of an electric motor and the deep rumble of rubber wheels echo through the tunnels of the underground bunker as Hao Weiwei and his son Jihai wheel three heavily sedated pit bull terriers in a caged motorized cart to the testing zone.

Hao is ready to try again.

A new serum, split into three separate and slightly different doses.

A new hope.

As usual, Tāo and Péng help maneuver the dogs through the airlock of the central cell and into three separately petitioned areas. The PBT is a breed banned in many U.S. states and countries worldwide. It's universally recognized for being astonishingly strong and devastatingly aggressive.

This is the ultimate test.

The microchips of all three animals have been successfully triggered, and prior to being heavily sedated, they were showing advanced signs of intense aggression.

Starved and taken away from their recognized environment, they should, when they wake, become even more hostile.

Hao is confident his newly adjusted serum will be able to calm and control them.

He knows General Zhang is hoping that too. It is what the military leader needs in his fight against American aggression. So much so that the general has told him that his patience is being tested and if he doesn't produce success in the next few days he will be "replaced."

Hao also fully understands the endless meanings of the word "replaced."

Quickly but meticulously, the scientists go about their final chores, electronically measuring, weighing, and photographing the sleeping animals before drawing blood for testing and taking final pulses.

Once the sedated dogs are left in their isolated spaces, Jihai removes the motorized cart, locks all the doors, and gives Tāo the instruction to check the controls on the remote video cameras mounted inside the glass cell.

Recording machines clink and whir into action as time-coded footage begins to be gathered on all three fawn and white dogs. Seeing them asleep, it's easy to imagine them as pets, and even an untrained eye would spot striking similarities between the cute trio and at least assume they're from the same litter.

But few would guess that they are clones. Bred to the point of deadly aggression.

Péng raises his chunky arms, slips the canisters of serum into the overhead atomizers, and gives his colleagues a knowing nod.

Hao presses a button on his master control terminal and a clock on the outside of the glass cell resets to zero.

As soon as the dogs wake, the experiment may begin, and one way or another he knows it may well be the last time he is in charge.

84

Coral Way, Miami

*R*eluctantly, Ghost leaves Zoe in bed and goes into work. He's shocked how quickly the heavenly postcoital endorphins fade and the tension of the dog investigations once more creeps into his bones, muscles, and mind.

"Captain is after you," says Annie Swanson as he enters the office. "Didn't look like he wanted to give you good news either."

"Cummings is allergic to good news, he's never allowed it anywhere near him."

She looks him up and down. "You're dressed like you were yesterday."

He tries to ignore her observation. "Did he say what he wanted?"

Annie frowns as she puts together the floating pieces of what she can remember about last night. "Did you go home with that photographer woman?"

His eyes widen behind his shades. "That's none of your business."

"Oh wow."

Ghost drifts away. He hadn't expected to be quizzed on his private life. Hadn't left time to go home and get changed after he and Zoe returned to bed. He curses himself all the way to his captain's office. Normally, he keeps his private life far removed from work. This time he's slipped up.

Up on the top corridor he walks past the captain's open door to talk to the boss's secretary when Cummings catches his eye.

"Ghost! Get your freaky ass in here."

He doubles back and sticks his head around the door. "You bawled for me, Captain?"

"Yeah, I did. I bawled." He points to a chair. "Sit while I bawl some more."

Ghost takes a perch.

"Late last night I get a call from Graham Gate—you know who that is?"

The name is familiar but Ghost can't place it. "Governor's office?"

"No. You're miles off. Gate is the President's chief of staff. They saw you on CBS, mouthing off about these flaming dogs—"

"Captain, I had a camera pushed in my face, I thought it better—"

"Think of shutting up while I finish what I got to say."

The two men stare at each other until Ghost manages a suitably submissive look.

"Anyways—despite the whole police world getting briefed yesterday *not* to say shit that might scare the public about dogs, you do. You go tell the world that Fido the family pooch is really a freakin' monster who's gonna bite them to death while they sleep in their beds."

"I'm sorry, but what I said was—"

"For Christ's sake, listen and don't talk!"

Ghost raises his palms in defeat.

"Seems you touched a nerve. God knows how." Cummings searches his table for a scrap of paper. "You're to ring this guy on this number in Washington. Apparently the President wants to put together a task force to address the canine challenge, and they want you on it."

Ghost takes the scribbled note and stands up with a smile on his face.

"Do *not* smile. Do not fucking even think of smiling in my office." He eyeballs the lieutenant like only captains can. "And most of all, do not screw this up, Ghost. The chief of police has made it clear to me that my ass is your ass. If there's cause to rip you a new one, then I get one as well—a two-for-one offer that I do not want to take up—you follow me?"

"Like a puppy, Captain."

"Bad analogy." He throws a thumb at the door. "Now get the fuck outta here—and remember what I said, no screw-ups."

85

Weaponization Bunkers, North Korea

A hundred ten minutes click by on the laboratory clock.

All three pit bulls are twitching, waking, moving.

Wobbly and groggy, they haul themselves upright.

Two head instinctively and unsteadily to the water bowls in the corners of their cubicles. The third stands its ground close to the glass and adopts an aggressive stance. Its lips curl back and intense black eyes fix on the watching scientists.

Hao checks his computer monitors and sees the dogs' heart rates rise as they become more and more alert. The trigger drug is still strong, riding buoyantly through their bloodstreams, touching nerves and piquing anxiety levels. That part of Nian has always been good, but today he needs to be able to reverse it. The serum he's been working on must neutralize the aggression and kill it permanently, not just for minutes like the sedatives have done.

All three dogs start barking.

They lunge at the glass and snap their teeth. They're ready to fight for any scraps of food, more than ready to kill if necessary.

Hao types in the computer keystrokes that activate the canisters of atomized serum. Each has a slightly different chemical modifier and all have been constructed to be absolutely harmless to humans.

Within ten seconds Dog One becomes tired. He stops jumping and barking, flops on his side and licks comfortingly at his short coat. The response is good and all the scientists feel encouraged.

Dog Two, the one held in the middle section, remains highly alert but no longer aggressive. His ears are bent upward like bat wings and he paces territorially and quickly. He's no longer snapping or biting but still looks like he might go for anyone who invaded his personal space.

The third dog is motionless but still upright. It is as still as a statue, like it's been sprayed with quick-drying cement. Its head is cocked toward the other two terriers, its dark eyes glassy and fixed.

Hao is pleased. To lesser and greater degrees all three are responding. And the deviances in behavior seem to correspond to what he'd expected from the different doses of administered serum.

There is hope.

He knows the genealogy of all the dogs, and this one in particular. The pit bull was created centuries ago when the British crossed terriers and bulldogs. Later, there was more collaborative interbreeding with kennel clubs in the United States, and so the American PBT was created. Initially it was well regarded and even widely used in the police services. Then its natural aggression began to surface. A series of vicious and fatal attacks on people, mainly children, changed its image irrevocably. He thinks it ironic that the Nian project is dedicated to exploiting America's mistakes in developing interbred aggression.

If the serum can pacify a pit bull it can pacify anything.

86

Coral Way, Miami

Showered and breakfasted, Zoe uploads the photos to her Mac-Book. They seem even more shocking than when she'd taken them. The scene had been more like an abattoir than a kitchen, but after the initial shock she'd concentrated on taking the stills and somehow that process shielded her from the full emotional blast of the carnage. Now there was no such protection. The close-ups of the victims' faces—what remained of them—stings her eyes with tears. She can't help but imagine what horrible deaths they endured. Being bitten to death must surely count as one of the cruelest and most agonizing ways to die.

Who were they?

The question burned in her mind. Ghost had said they were a mother and daughter. She'd jotted their names down at the time. Astrid Gerber and her mother Heidi.

She sits back from the computer and studies a full-length shot of the ripped and ravaged torso of the younger woman. She looks little more than a collection of meat bones you'd get from the butcher shop for your dog.

Zoe flips down the lid of her Mac and gets up from her chair. She's seen enough. More than enough. Her mind is clear now. She knows what she has to do. Knows she has a duty to the memory of the women she'd photographed.

Jude left her the keys to her Nissan, "in case of emergencies," and while she'd never imagined using it, she now finds herself gratefully picking them up and wandering outside to the car. She takes a minute to familiarize herself with the controls and then sets the satellite navigation.

Twenty minutes later she's back at the scene where the two women died.

She locks the car and looks at the quiet avenue. It's as though nothing had ever happened. The police and emergency vehicles have gone. So too is the fluttering tape that kept the public and press away from the death scene. There's just a lone cop standing on the doorstep. Zoe looks around and sees a male photographer taking shots from across the road. A middle-aged reporter is going from house to house, without getting much joy. Residents are barely opening their doors more than a crack for him. She feels hugely disappointed. Her aim in coming here was to find out more about the two women, put together the stories of their lives, make them more than just statistics.

Her eyes drift back to the house where the women died, and she recognizes the cop from last night. A good-looking rookie who'd turned up just as she and Ghost were leaving. She walks down the driveway and pins on her best smile. "Hello again, don't tell me you've been here all the time?"

The cop has been watching her since she parked. His eyes have been all over her blue jeans, imagining what a shape like that would look like free of denim. Now he's hooked by the glint in her eye. "Just about to come off shift if you want to buy me a coffee."

Zoe hits him with a cheeky smile, one that's laid legions of men helpless. "Yeah, I'd like that. Listen, can you help me out first?"

"I can try."

"Remember that lieutenant I was with last night, the tall guy?"

"Yeah, freaky one wearing shades in the middle of the night."

"You got him. He's sent me back to get some more shots." She lifts her camera. "Seems I screwed up. Didn't get the full set."

He frowns skeptically. "The stiffs have long gone."

Zoe flinches. "Yeah, I know. It's not those that I missed. It's the interiors—the rooms. Seems I should have shot those."

"Why?"

She shrugs. "Damned if I know. That's why I didn't shoot them last night." She moves closer to him. Cuts his personal space in half. Watches his eyes dilate as she lowers her voice and *confides* in him. "Listen, I don't get these shots, then I get dumped, know what I mean? I'm only on probation and I'm one chance beyond my last chance. Can you let me in? I need ten minutes, that's all." She steps back and gives him her best little-girl-lost look.

The rookie glances around. The reporter is just being let into a house and he's waving his photographer over. There's no one else out and about. And there's actually almost an hour until his relief is going to be here. He plunges his hands into a jacket pocket and produces the keys. "Use the back door and be quick. You get caught and we'll both be looking for new jobs."

87

Police HQ, Miami

*G*host dials the White House.

It's something he never imagined doing.

"Aaron Davies." The voice is young but sounds as though it's irritated at being distracted from something far more important.

"Aaron, this is Lieutenant Walton of the Miami police. My captain said I should call this number in relation to the task force the President is putting together."

The staffer knows exactly who he is. "Let me see if Mr. Gate is free to take your call."

There are twenty seconds of dead air, then Davies comes back on line. "I'm putting you through to Mr. Gate."

A deeper male voice booms out, one that's known decades of late night drinking and smoky rooms. "Lieutenant Walton?"

"That's me. How can I help?"

"Thanks for calling. The President has asked Vice President Cornwell to establish a task force to investigate the recent spate of dog attacks and see if remedies need to be applied. They want you to attend a video briefing—" He pauses while he glances up at his office clock. "—in just over an hour's time. My office will fix it with yours."

"What do they want from me?"

"Your views, Lieutenant. I understand you've not been shy in sharing them with the media and the nation at large, so I trust fitting in the President of the United States isn't a difficulty."

"Of course not."

"Eleven o'clock it is, then."

Ghost is left with a dead phone. He types a note in his electronic diary and a heads-up to Force Admin, copied to Cummings's secretary in case the captain wants to join.

When he looks up, Swanson is at the edge of his desk. "Yes, Annie."

"Dispatch has called in another dog attack. It's a really bad one."

He shakes his head in dismay. "Christ alive, this is relentless."

"What do you want me to do?"

He realizes he has to delegate. Something he's not that great at. "Okay. Get John Tarney and Bella Lansing out of their hammocks. See if Bella can drive comms from here. I'll raise SWAT, and if push comes to shove, then the President is just going to have to wait for his face time."

88

Weaponization Bunkers, North Korea

*T*he once motionless dog in the third section finally moves.

Hao becomes nervous.

The animal breaks from its studious trance and darts like it is possessed by an insane and powerful demon. It crashes from wall to wall in the glass cell, banging so hard it leaves smears of blood at every point of impact.

The scientist feels all his hopes fading.

The dog runs and lunges harder, faster, and more powerfully than anything he has ever seen.

It leaps into the glass partition that separates it from the middle dog and hits it with such a tremendous force that it tears it from its floor mount. The screen comes down with a clatter and instantly all three dogs are jumping and snarling.

"Father!" Jihai shouts in concern.

"Wait. We have to wait and learn."

Dogs Two and Three are inches apart. Bred to fight, they give in to the genetically enhanced urges building inside them.

Dog Three circles and then jumps.

Two tries to fend it off with its paws and teeth but is knocked over. It manages to flip back onto its feet but Three bites a flapping curtain of bloody skin from its face.

The squealing and snarling booms from the speaker system in the lab.

"Okay, administer more serum!" shouts Hao. "Do it now!"

Jihai triggers the hypotrajectors.

The pit bulls rage on regardless. Their brute aggression is sickening to watch.

"Their adrenaline levels are off the scale," warns Jihai.

Hao knows there is nothing more he can do.

Even the dog in the first partitioned cubicle is now bounding hard at the glass.

It's as though the chemical pacifier has actually aggravated the problem rather than solved it.

Reluctantly, he readies himself to use the ultimate control, a volley of lethal darts loaded with a cocktail of quick acting barbiturates, including pentobarbital sodium and phenytoin sodium. "Load with the terminal darts."

Dog Two breaks from a potentially lethal neck bite and finds its feet. The cell floor is already spattered with blood as the third animal lunges and bites again. This time it lands a tight grip on Two's face and shakes viciously as it tries to throw the animal off balance again.

Jihai has witnessed innumerable animal experiments but never anything as sickening as this. He turns again to his father. "Can we fire? Put them out of their misery?"

Hao must see the full effect of the serum. "Not yet. We must wait."

The dogs lock jaws.

For a moment it looks like Two is strong enough to defend itself. Then there's a stomach-turning crunch of breaking teeth. Dog Three powers its head down and rolls its bleeding sibling onto its back.

Two kicks frenziedly but can't get free.

Three sinks its teeth into its neck and shakes its powerful jaws.

The dying terrier gives off a whine like a broken steam kettle.

The cell is smeared floor to ceiling in blood. Severed ears, tongue, skin, and fur lie everywhere.

Three lifts its scarred and wounded head. It stares defiantly at the watching scientists, eyes glistening with evil defiance.

89

Coconut Grove, Miami

Zoe moves quickly from room to room, feeling more like a burglar than someone on a heartfelt mission to create a lasting memory of those who died. The rooms upstairs tell an entirely different story to the ones beneath them. A pretty bedroom of peach pink above the raw and bloody kitchen hosts a double bed that's yet to be made. She can see that only one side has been slept in. Only one nightstand has a book and glass on it. Only one pair of slippers is kicked off near the bed legs.

Numerous photographs by the windows, on the dresser top, and over the makeup table summarize the life of a blond middle-aged woman who is no longer with a handsome dark-haired man with whom she apparently spent most of her adult life. Across some of the shots a spindly blond girl with gawky looks grows from ugly duckling to ravishing young woman.

Zoe flips several pictures onto the bed and shoots them without a flash to avoid glare off the glass. At the back of her mind burn the images of the mutilated bodies she photographed in the dead of night.

She puts them back and moves quickly to the next largest room. From first glance it's clear this was where the younger woman slept. Fashionable shoes, purses, and worn clothes lie untidily on the floor or are draped over the back of a chair or full-length mirror. There is a smell of too much perfume. The dressing table is littered with blingy jewelry and enough cosmetics to open a store.

Zoe feels most uncomfortable here. From the pictures she's seen and the clothes around her, the dead woman is roughly the same age, height, and weight as herself. A shiver sends her out to the stairs and down to the study. She knows she has to work quickly now. She pulls a drape, so the cop can't see if he walks down the side of the house, and fires up the big Mac on the desk. While its drive is spinning into life she opens a cupboard and goes through the alphabetically listed hang files.

Under P she finds the passports of Astrid and Heidi Gerber, B gives her their birth certificates. She was right, the girl was twenty-four and listed herself as a model. File M holds Heidi's marriage certificate to a man named Jan, and D discloses he died just a year ago.

D throws up something else too.

A whole file marked DOG.

"Hey, you finished in there yet?"

The cop's voice spooks her and she spills the file. "Yeah, I'm on my way." She turns her back to the door in case he comes in, empties the papers from the hanger and photographs as many of them as she can, including a set of photographs of a puppy and accompanying certificates that declare a wirehaired pointer called Schotzie once won numerous awards for being Best in Breed and "Demonstrating Outstanding Obedience."

90

South Beach, Miami

*S*creams spray from Lummus Park. People scatter and the bleached white sand that borders the long evergreen strips and blue water bay is already stained red.

A growling Alsatian stands rigid-legged and scans the pounded dunes.

It's already bitten its female owner to death. Two boys and their mother lie dead on the nearby grass. Ten yards behind the dog, a man with a bite wound to his leg hobbles into traffic and is hit by a motorbike.

Two police marksmen send a volley of shots through the sunlight.

The dog drops on the sand.

Open-mouthed, it twitches and jerks as more bullets riddle its long, soft fur and more white becomes red.

Barely a block away two black Labradors cut loose.

The remains of their owner, a forty-year-old male teacher, are spread over the blistered sidewalk near the Bentley Hotel.

Parents grab children and run. It's a free-for-all. The old and young collide and jostle as the air sparks with hysteria.

The two dogs snarl and snap as they charge the back of the fleeing crowd.

The Lab on the left brings down an old woman with a fuzz of white hair. The one on the right takes a child of eight out of the hand of his young mother.

Traffic backs up like it's a national holiday. Blaring horns join the orchestra of chaos. Ghost ditches the Dodge and runs against the flow of fleeing people.

He sees solid blue uniforms up ahead, cutting into the multicolored kaleidoscope of panicking citizens. Officers with guns drawn and hands outstretched.

There's a crack of gunfire and a crescendo of screams. The crowd parts and a veteran cop fires again and again, two bullets finding the head and shoulders of one of the dogs.

The other is nowhere to be seen.

New screams and a fresh outbreak of chaos point to where it is.

There's a piercing shriek from the panicking mob in front of Ghost, a cry so intense it is clearly linked to pain and not just fear.

He jumps onto the hood of a parked BMW then clambers on the roof.

The screaming crowd clears.

A teenage boy is on his back, swinging punches at the other dog's snarling jaws.

Ghost hasn't got a clear shot. And even if he had, from this angle the bullet could go straight through the Lab's head and kill the kid.

He jumps down.

The teenager's hands claw helplessly at the savage dog's head, trying to knock it away. In desperation, he jams a fist in the savage vise of teeth to protect his face.

The animal crunches down on the smooth bone and salty skin.

Time is running out.

Ghost drops flat into the dirt and puts his trust in his own skill and nerve.

The first shot pings through a vertebrae in the dog's spine, and it loses its hold on the boy.

The second goes straight over its teeth and down into its gut.

It's dead before it even topples off the teenager.

Away to his right, a wail of sirens breaks above the noise of shouting people and blaring car horns.

Across the street, Ghost sees paramedics loading a gurney in an ambulance. He shouts to them as he runs, "Hey, hey!"

One of the medics, a guy in his thirties, turns toward the running cop.

Ghost pulls up in front of him almost breathless. "I have a young guy down and hurt over there." He points to Ocean Drive as he tries to recover from the sprint. "Just the other side of the grass. He's been bit real bad. Huge wound to the abdomen, looks like a damned shark bite, and I think he's been caught on the upper thigh as well."

The paramedic looks up into the van where his colleague is. "I've got this new one," he says, then pushes the gurney and the injured man on it the last few inches into the van. "You go back with this guy and get me assistance from the crew up on Eighth."

His buddy gives him the thumbs-up and the medic grabs a bag and joins Ghost.

As they head across the road, an emergency services radio crackles.

"All units, we have two more dog attacks in the South Beach area. One at Flamingo Park and Pool and one at West Avenue opposite the Jason Schaffer. We've requested police and dog handler backup. You are urged to proceed with extreme care."

91

Coconut Grove, Miami

Zoe effortlessly brushes off the rookie. Before he can even say anything, she pulls on her worried face and hits him with a story about being called back to the office by her boss. To take away the pain, she gives him a slip of paper that only later he'll find out is not her number but that of Judy's local pizza store.

She drives a little over a mile before she takes a left off the main drag and pulls to the side of the road. With the engine off she pushes back the seat of the Nissan and settles down to do some work.

From her purse she pulls out a small red notebook and yellow felt tip pen. She powers up the Hasselblad and flicks through thumbprints of the shots. Last night Ghost had told her to take photos in the house, let the world see the full horror of what happened. Well, she intends to do that. But not gratuitously. Not just for the sake of having pictures published and maybe earning a buck or two from a news agency. She wants to do something with more meaning—more resonance. The camera in her hands holds prints that amount to twenty years of Astrid and Heidi's lives. There are shots of the young model as a teenager. Of her mom and dad getting married. There are even shots of the dog that killed them as a puppy. And that, in Zoe's mind, is the real story. How two lovely and loving women can end up killed by the family pet.

The snaps she's taken of Schotzie's documentation aren't artistically brilliant but they are revealing. There's a breeder's certificate. Vaccination confirmations. Proof he's been microchipped and his owners registered in case he got lost. On top of that are awards from the numerous discipline courses he'd completed and breed shows he'd been entered in.

Zoe thumbs through her digital images and examines the shots she'd taken of the dead dog. It was very obviously the same animal as the one pictured winning things, but it also seemed completely different—more so than just the bullet wounds the police marksman had put in its head and body.

She made notes in her book and spent time ordering her thoughts and working a plan of action. She'd have no trouble finding a magazine, newspaper, or TV channel to take her finished work—of that she was sure. So she could afford the luxury of starting at the beginning. Going back to Schotzie's breeders and the kennel where he was born.

92

Weaponization Bunkers, North Korea

Jihai sees his own worried reflection in the cell glass as he studies the last two dogs. The display of raw violence has shaken him, Péng, and the young researcher Tāo.

It's one thing to work on cell structures and DNA profiles, it's entirely another to see a mutated beast rip the throat out of a sibling.

He turns to his father. "End this now." He points to the middle dog. Its gums and jagged rows of murderous teeth are smeared with blood and flesh. There are deep wounds to its snout and left eye. "Put the creature out of its misery."

Hao Weiwei glares at his only son. "*I* will decide if or when this experiment will be terminated, now go back to your position."

Jihai fixes his father with one final stare of defiance before walking away.

Hao reruns the events of the last hour in his mind.

The third dog, the most aggressive one, actually received more of the atomized modifier than the others. The middle dog, the next highest dose, and the first dog the least. It's possible that his modification formula is inverted, that the chemicals he believed would induce the animals' genomes into emitting messages of passivity actually did the opposite.

By returning to the labs and reversing the formula, he might finally create that elusive serum to pacify the dogs.

He looks again at the two remaining animals and decides to try to prove his point. If he now exposes the first dog to multiple doses of the serum, it should become as equally aggressive as the third animal.

Hao looks to his son. "Dispense a double dose of serum into the first cubicle."

Jihai's eyes grow wide and he hesitates.

"Now!" His father's face reddens. "Do as I say!"

93

Flamingo Park, Miami

*T*he scene at Flamingo is almost as bad as Lummus.

Three already dead. Six more badly bitten. Another five are being treated for shock.

On top of that, there are multiple crush and fall injuries sustained as the whole world seemed to panic and run into each other like headless chickens.

Ghost posts SWAT teams in a moving box formation, gradually shifting inward from Twelfth and Fifteenth, and Meridian and Michigan. Uniformed officers filter civilians out of harm's way and direct paramedics into safe zones.

The lieutenant calls Tarney on his radio. He's sent the young sergeant west to chase down a big dog that's already killing over there. "How's it going, John?"

"Bad. We've got one dead—a guy in his early twenties—and there's a middle-aged woman with severe bites to the face and neck that could be fatal by the time she reaches the ER."

"What kind of dog?"

"Retriever, I think." He talks as he walks and there's a lot of background noise. "I haven't seen it yet. Eyewitness said it went into the tennis center, that's where we're going."

"Okay. Update me when you can." Ghost clicks off and focuses on the scene in front of him. His unit have spotted another dog and are spreading out.

He can see it now. To the side of the aquatic center. A Labrador shaking something the size of a doll in its mouth.

A sniper drops into a kneel-and-shoot pose in front of him and looks down the sight of his Remington 700. "Holy shit, Lieutenant—it's got a baby."

Ghost taps his shoulder. "Take it out."

The sniper doesn't need telling twice. The Remington twitches and the animal shudders from the shock of the bullet.

The sniper clicks back the rifle's bolt and fires another round.

Now it goes down.

The marksman lifts a hand, one eye still on the telescopic sight. "Clear."

Ghost and team slowly advance on the dog. Several weapons stay trained on its lifeless body. No one is taking chances.

A couple of the married men flinch as they come up close to the bloody bundle of rags. Someone guesses the tot was a year old, certainly no more than that.

Ghost turns around and looks to the crowds in the distance. Somewhere back there is a mother with her life about to change forever. No mortician he knows has the kind of skill that can make that child presentable enough to be seen by the woman who brought it into the world.

Above him comes the clacking of helicopter blades. He doesn't need to tilt his head to know it's a news crew.

He hopes the President gets to see their pictures.

Hopes it turns his political stomach enough to ensure this proposed task force has enough money and men to be more than just a vote-winning gesture.

94

Cutler Bay, Florida

Zoe travels east along 211th Street until she hits 112th Avenue, then turns south toward the junction with the 216th. Just beyond Goulds Park she see signs for WPK, the kennels where Schotzie was born and sold.

The Nissan passes through a rusty mesh fence and pulls up outside a filthy whitewashed single-story building that looks like it might once have been a series of small industrial units.

As she gets out of the car she hears the sounds of dogs barking behind walls. From the darkness of an open door a small man in his sixties with a dyed black beard and long greasy black hair trudges out. He's vigorously chewing gum, like he's recently given up smoking, and wiping his hands on a cloth. "No dogs. Sorry, honey. I'm afraid we're sold out."

Zoe can feel her heart banging. "What about those I can hear?"

"Yeah, they're all sold. Waiting for owners to take them away."

She takes the camera from around her neck. "Can I show you something?"

"Sure." He moves up close so he can look at the screen she's turning his way.

"This is a bill of sale saying you sold a puppy to a woman named Heidi Gerber. Do you remember it? She was an attractive woman in her late forties, early fifties. Might have had a very pretty daughter with her, around my age."

"I kinda remember them. More than a year back." He steps away from the camera and looks up at Zoe. "What of it?"

"You been following these dog attacks in the news?"

"Much as anyone."

"The dog you sold bit that woman and her daughter to death last night."

Zoe watches the breeder's Adam's apple rise and fall as he swallows a chunk of fear. He tries to shrug off the implication. "Ain't nothing to do with me. Them dogs were good when I sold them."

"Them? You sold more than one to the Gerbers?"

"No. Not to the women, to—"

A man in his thirties interrupts. "What's goin' on here, Pa?" He's tall and broad, has his father's long crooked nose and buzzed ginger hair.

"Young miss is asking about them dogs you bought last year, the wirehaireds."

Zoe is puzzled. "I thought you bred the dogs here?"

"We do," says the younger man. "These were offered to us as pups. A reputable source."

Zoe reaches for her notebook. "Can you tell me who?"

"What's it to do with you?" He looks at her camera. "Are you from the press?"

She doesn't answer him. "One of those dogs ripped apart two women last night. Pretty much chewed every ounce of flesh off their bones."

The old man looks worried. "Josh, I told you it weren't no good idea."

"Quiet, Pa." He steps toward Zoe. "You need to be leaving now, 'fore I throw your ass off our land."

Zoe looks down at her camera monitor and thumbs through the shots. She turns the screen around and holds it up for him to see.

He slaps the camera away. "Get out now!"

The camera tumbles to the ground. Something inside Zoe snaps. A combination of outrage that her precious camera's been treated like that and building anger over the death of the Gerbers.

She steps forward so she's only inches from his face. His breath smells of strong coffee and cigarettes. She half turns and drives an elbow deep into his stomach. She completes the spin by delivering a dropkick just under his neck.

He falls flat on his back like a felled tree.

She dips low and picks up the camera.

The big guy starts to sit up.

"Just look," she demands, thrusting it into his face. "Look at what that damned dog did and tell me what you know."

His father breaks his silence. "Like I said, the pointers weren't ours. We didn't breed them. They came from a shelter."

"A shelter?" Zoe is confused. "What's a shelter doing with

thoroughbreds like that? They usually just get mongrels, don't they?"

The son gets to his feet, his eyes on the mutilated bodies staring out at him from the camera display. "The guy said they'd taken in more than four hundred dogs of different breeds that week. Out of that batch, there were a hundred puppies born, and we took twelve of the wirehaired pointers. They looked good dogs."

Zoe takes her camera back and loops the strap over her neck. "Who's the guy and where can I find the shelter?"

He brushes dust off his pants and tenderly touches his neck where she's kicked him. "The guy we dealt with is named Chen. I don't know his last name. He works at the county shelter over on North West Seventy-fourth."

Zoe writes it all in her book.

"I got a feeling his bosses didn't know what he was doing. He said he was sticking his neck out by just touring around looking for homes for the pups, but it was either that or they got euthanized that night."

"You got records of the people you sold the dogs to?"

"Of course," says the old breeder.

Zoe digs in her jeans and pulls out Ghost's card. "You send them all to this cop." She looks toward the son. "Believe me, you don't want him coming down here. Send the details right away and I'm tell him how helpful you've been. Hold something back and I'll see the world gets pulled down on your miserable heads."

95

Weaponization Bunkers, North Korea

*O*nly two dogs remain in the experimental cell.

Within sixty seconds of the canisters being triggered, the first animal shows signs of responding to the atomized serum. Its lip curls and it lets out a ferocious snarl.

Wild-eyed, it runs and hurls itself at the one remaining partition in the cell.

The screen comes down. The big dog falls then staggers to its feet.

It's face-to-face with Dog Three.

They rush at each other.

Teeth break as they collide.

The back legs of the two animals slip and skid on the blood-soaked cell floor. They pull and push at each other, creating a slow circle of death.

Hao looks across at his son and Péng and Tāo. They are all at their stations, hypotrajectors positioned above the two dogs and trained down on them.

Dog One twists its powerful jaws, and Dog Three's neck bends and cracks painfully. One flips it onto its side and instantly goes for the front of its throat.

Jihai winces as the dog opens up the other's windpipe. The fight goes from its eyes. It falls limply.

Dog One bites again at the open throat, teeth crunching into the top of the rib cage.

Hao mentally notes that the kill was not only faster but also more gruesome than the last. It could be that the third dog had been weakened by the first fight, or that the extra dosage may have acted as an even more powerful aggressor.

Dog One finally leaves the remains of the beaten pit bull and paces the bloody floor. The place looks like an abattoir.

Hao wonders what it will do now. Now it has won. Now it has killed everything within its domain.

He doesn't have to wait long for his answer.

It charges straight at the watching scientist.

The pit bull crashes against the reinforced glass and falls. The outer panels are much stronger than the inner partitions. There's no way it can break through.

It jumps again at the front wall and the whole panel of glass bows.

Hao looks towards Jihai. "Finish the creature."

His son checks the position of the hypotrajectors and presses the command keys. Two darts of lethal poison hit the soft flesh of the animal.

It flinches as its skin is penetrated, then cranes its neck toward the nearest dart but can't reach it.

Astonishingly, the dog gets to its feet.

"Again!" shouts Hao. "Fire again!"

Two more fatal doses hit the animal. For a second it only flinches, and then it gazes vacantly at the humans beyond the glass.

Just as it looks as though it's about to fall, it bounds, springs like it's been shot from a cannon.

Hao backs away in fright.

He needn't have bothered.

The dog hits the glass with a sickening thud and slides to the floor. It's used up the last of its preternatural strength. The last of its life.

A long, bloody smear leads from the point of impact to the still twitching corpse.

96

South Beach, Miami

Sergeant John Tarney leads the three-man SWAT team into the Jason Schaffer complex, a picturesque tennis center off West Avenue squeezed between apartment blocks and clusters of long established palms.

There's blood on the baseline.

Over in the far corner, nearest the backdrop of blue water and distant islands, he sees the crouched shape of the dog.

It has something trapped against the fence boards just a yard or two from the gate.

The big sergeant puts a whistle to his lips and blows.

The retriever jerks its head and turns.

Now the marksmen can see what's on the other side of it.

A middle-aged man in tennis whites.

Only they're not white anymore. They're soaked red and he'll never chase another backhand return.

The dog's face is dripping in blood and eviscerated flesh.

It stares at the new humans, then dips its head and bounds toward them.

It's covering the court with astonishing speed.

The marksmen fan out and raise their weapons. Tarney stands over the shoulder of the crouching middle sniper, his own Sig 226 drawn and settling for a shot.

His first bullet misses.

The dog is ten yards away and still gathering speed.

A Remington cracks to Tarney's left.

Five yards.

A rifle sounds to his right.

Still the dog closes.

Tarney shoots it clean in the throat as it starts to jump.

Three more shots sound out.

The golden retriever hits the court and tumbles; its legs awkwardly break its speed and bring it to a crumpled halt.

The sergeant leaves his team to deal with the animal and runs to the injured man.

Up close he can see that the dog has bitten chunks out of his face, neck, arms, and legs.

Tarney lifts a limp left arm and pulls back the blood-spattered wristband.

There's no pulse.

He drops it and looks around. The guy must have been playing with someone. Had they gotten away? Were they injured as well?

Now he sees it.

A smear of blood around the bottom of the gate.

He pulls back the latch and walks outside. There are dried drips of red on the pathway leading to the locker rooms. He follows the trail in and out of the shade.

A woman is lying facedown on a patch of grass, her tennis skirt torn and lumps of flesh missing from the top of her thigh. A cloud of flies buzzes around the glistening wound.

Tarney swats them away and turns her over.

She's unconscious but doesn't seem to have sustained any other bites.

He checks her neck for a pulse.

Nothing.

He tries her wrist.

Nothing.

The woman appears to be in her early forties. She's trim and athletic, well tanned and probably exercised regularly. None of which have prevented her from dying of a heart attack after being bitten and chased.

Tarney walks back toward his unit and feels deflated as he calls Ghost. "We got the dog but there are two people dead. One male, one female."

"Coroner is already on the way. You okay?"

"Yeah. No injuries here. Not physical ones, anyway."

Ghost knows what he means. There's nothing worse than doing your best, then finding out that people still died. "Clean up there, get someone to do the IDs and inform the relatives, then meet me at the station house. We're not done yet. Dispatch has another two incidents—both on this side of the city."

97

Weaponization Bunkers, North Korea

*J*ihai backs a motorized flatbed trolley up to the front of the glass cell where the three dead dogs are still lying.

Tāo and Péng enter the antechamber, and Jihai wheels the trolley in for them and then steps back.

They close and seal the door behind them and wait for the sound of a computerized bleep before pressing the lock and entering the inner cell.

The two scientists are dressed in white biohazard suits complete with hoods, helmets, boots, and gloves. They've brought shovels, brushes, body bags, buckets, and morgue sprays with them, in order to clean up the mess.

First they shift the two inner partitions to one side and prop them against a far wall so they can move around more freely.

Next, Tāo photographs the dogs, both in wide shots and close-ups. There is already video footage, but Hao wants the stills for the postmortem reports and reference files that he compiles after every test series.

Péng unzips a black plastic body bag and lays it down alongside the first animal they come to. It has the number 3 sprayed in blue paint on its side. "You get the back legs, I'll get the front, and then we lift on three."

"Okay." Tāo shuffles around the back and gets a grip. "Ready."

"One. Two. Three."

They swing the pit bull into the middle of the bag and let it drop.

Péng twists its legs around to fit inside the bag and then zips it up. "On three again—but this time onto the trolley."

Tāo gives him the thumbs-up and they repeat the entire process with dog number 2 and a fresh bag.

"Two down, one to go." Péng lays out the final bag and grabs the front legs while Tāo takes the back.

They give the dog what is now a well-rehearsed swing and drop it on the black plastic.

The dog suddenly lurches upward and snaps. Its strong pointed teeth sink through Péng's boot and then find the bone of his shin.

"Fuck!" He jumps back but the dog still has a grip.

Tāo smashes a shovel down on its head but it still holds onto Péng's leg.

The scientist falls backward and bangs his head on the door to the antechamber.

Tāo keeps on hitting the animal. He swings the shovel with all his might.

Then he gets his brain in gear and instead of wielding yet another wild blow, positions the sharp corner of the shovel into the neck wound and pushes with all his strength.

The dog releases Péng.

But Tāo isn't taking any chances. He drives the dog all the way into the corner of the cell and leans against the shovel until he fatally widens the wound in its neck so it's like an open hinge.

The dog goes totally limp.

He drops the shovel and rushes to Péng, who is still sprawled on the floor and in shock. "Are you all right?"

Péng nods. "The boots protected me. I'm fine. I think I was more terrified than anything." He leans against the cell wall and gets to his feet. "It didn't hurt me that badly, but it surprised me and knocked me clean off balance."

They both glance across at the grotesquely beaten and wounded corpse.

A dog that came back from the dead.

They open the airlock and decide to get Péng treated before finishing the clean-up.

98

Miami-Dade Animal Services, Miami

More than three hundred dogs a day press their sad, abandoned faces to the cold cell bars of the animal shelter and hope their cutesy act results in someone adopting them.

They've got five days to pull it off.

After that . . .

The manager, Monique Clabbers, doesn't want to think about it.

She wishes she could bundle them all into her truck and take them home with her. The fifty-year-old already has five dogs, and her husband Bo says that's the limit. Not that he has a say in the matter, and after twenty years of marriage he really should know better than to mutter such foolish nonsense.

Monique already has her eye on a sixth.

He's a cute little boxer who has that glint in his eyes that just breaks your heart and tells you he's already part of your family and all you have to do is pick him up and snuggle him and everything will be fine.

And tonight it will.

Because once the busiest day she's ever known comes to an end, Billy the Boxer is coming home.

She'll tell Bo it was the least she could do. More than two hundred dogs were dumped on them today. Way, way more than they can handle. And no offers of adoptions. As far as she knows, it's the same at every other public shelter, plus all the private ones like Abandoned Dogs of the Everglades and her friend's No Kill sanctuary over in Tampa.

When Monique came in this morning there were twenty different dogs already tied to the building. Left by people too ashamed to look her in the eye. On top of that, her ER room is full of dehydrated dogs that have been abandoned and just left to dry up in the sun.

She really doesn't know how people can be so cruel.

Her office door swings open and front desk receptionist Marjorie Bollas is flushed as she says, "I'm sorry, Mrs. Clabbers, this young woman is looking for Chen and—"

Zoe pushes past and enters the room. "She's going to say I'm being rude—I prefer to call it insistent."

Monique puts down a stack of documents she was just about to file. "How can I help you?"

"A guy named Chen who works here sold dogs to a breeder over in Cutler Bay."

"That's impossible." She looks toward her colleague at the door. "It's okay, Marjorie, you can leave us." She waits for her to go and then turns her attention back to Zoe. "We don't *sell* dogs. We're a shelter; we take in the abandoned and ill-treated. Of course we accept donations from new owners, but they're modest and we certainly don't deal with breeders."

"Well, your Mr. Chen dealt with these breeders. I've just come from there and they named him without any prompting—why would they do that if it wasn't true?"

Clabbers looks shocked. "I don't know. I have no idea. Perhaps they got his name wrong."

"Unlikely. Chen ain't exactly as common as Smith or Jones in this neck of the woods, or even Lopez or Hernandez, for that matter. Anyway, I'd like to speak to him—get to the bottom of things."

The face of the center manager hardens. "Who are you? Do you have some ID I can see?"

"You got a pen and paper?"

Clabbers reaches for a pad on the desk and grabs a felt-tip from a mug filled with pens and pencils.

Zoe takes them and writes on the pad. "I'm working with this lieutenant," she says, and passes the information over. "Call him and he'll vouch for me. I'm following up on the deaths of Astrid and Heidi Gerber, who were killed last night in their own home by their dog, a wirehaired pointer."

Monique studies the name and number. She picks up the phone, dials, and listens.

A voice message plays in her ear. *"This is Lieutenant Walton. I'm busy and can't take your call. Please leave a message and I'll get back to you, or if it's an emergency call the main Miami police number—"* She hangs up rather than go through another sentence of numbers and who to call. "Li Chen is not here today. He's been on holiday and should have come back a few days ago but hasn't."

Zoe takes out her notebook and writes down his full name. "Could you call him, so I can ask him some questions?"

Monique nods. "I don't think he's around, because I've tried both his landline and cell phone."

Zoe notes the numbers as the manager punches them into her desk phone.

"Not there." She hangs up. "I'll try his cell."

"What exactly does he do for you?" Zoe asks, again noting the number.

"A little of everything." The manager hangs up. "No luck, I'm afraid. Li is a real help to us. He does everything from helping with collections, to vaccinations, deworming, microchipping, and even the difficult stuff." Her face turns sour. "Unfortunately; we have to put a lot of animals to sleep. Li would even help with that. What did you say he's done?"

"Sold wirehaired pointer pups to a breeder about a year ago, maybe more. He told the kennel guy they were going to be gassed if he didn't find a good home for them."

She shakes her head. "I know every animal that's been through here." She puts a hand on the top of her computer screen. "We have records from the very first day we opened, and I can tell you we've never had a single wirehaired pup in. Never."

"That's strange."

"Perhaps someone's been lying to you."

"Perhaps. I'd still like to talk to Mr. Chen. Could you give me his home address?"

She hesitates. "No. I'm not comfortable doing that. You can call again, or leave me your number and if he's come back I'll ask him to speak to you."

"That's not good enough. The dog he sold to those breeders killed two women and had to be shot dead. How much time do you think you should give it before your saintly Mr. Chen turns up? Another day? Another death? Can your conscience really live with that?"

"I don't really understand why you want to see him. Those ladies dying had nothing to do with Li, not even if he sold—or more likely gave a puppy or two away. What do you expect him to say to you?"

"That's a good question. To be honest, I really don't know. I'm just chasing down anyone who had any kind of connection with the dead women. Unless I ask a question, I'm not likely to get an answer, am I?"

Monique Clabbers capitulates. She rips off another page from her pad, writes on it and passes it to Zoe. "If you find Li, then please ask him to call me. We're hugely understaffed and really need his help."

99

Weaponization Bunkers, North Korea

*H*ao is troubled.

He's concerned about why the experiment failed. And worried

about the injury to Péng while the dog was in some bizarre death throe.

The chief scientist finds him showered and sitting on his metal bunk in just his slate gray boxers. He's examining a small but angry looking puncture wound and a red graze where the pit bull's teeth sank through the rubber lab boots and caught his anklebone.

"Are you okay?" Hao has known Péng most of his life and witnessed many cuts and bruises sustained in play with his own son.

The young man looks up from his surprisingly painful injury. "Yes, sir. I am fine." He's embarrassed to be caught making such a fuss. "It is nothing. The boot protected me. Just a little cut."

"Let me see."

Hao bends and inspects it. "There's some swelling around the bone. Does it hurt when you walk?"

Péng gets to his feet and puts weight on it. "Only a little."

"Good. Go see Dr. Chi, the unit medic, and have him look at it. When did you last have your booster shots?"

Péng tries to remember. "Five, maybe six months ago, sir. I have the papers in my locker."

"You should be infection free, but it is still best you go. Never take chances with dogs; they're a cocktail of poisons. And not just rabies."

"I know, sir." He's keen to show off a little of his zoonotic knowledge. "*Leptospirosis, Salmonellosis, Toxocariasis, Brucella canis.* I don't want any of them."

"It's unlikely you'll have any. The test dogs will all have been screened prior to being fitted with the aggressor chips." Hao leaves him to finish dressing and goes back to the main part of the bunker, where Jihai and Tāo are still cleaning up.

Poisons. Test Dogs. Screened.

The words jigsaw together in his mind. Things that previously made no sense now fall into place.

He'd missed something.

In all of his experimental revisions he'd overlooked one obvious factor.

"Jihai. I want all three dogs immediately for postmortem. Tāo, come with me. I want you to get an unchipped dog from the bunker pound and inject it with a chip I give you."

The two men set about their work, and Hao heads back to his lab.

If his hunch is right, then he finally knows what's wrong.

But it may not all be good news.

Especially for Péng.

100

Miami

Ghost is struggling. Resources were scarce to start with, now they are spread way too thinly. He sits in his car and calls Cummings. "We need extra support, sir, and we need it fast."

"No can do, Lieutenant. I've got a bank raid going off downtown and a hostage situation breaking from a bungled drug bust in the east of the county. You need to do what you've got to do with what you've got. There ain't no more coming."

Ghost resists the temptation to correct his boss's bad English. "That's just not possible, sir. We need at least one more tactical unit, maybe two. Perhaps the Sheriff's Office—"

"Don't even think of finishing that sentence. We manage our own affairs. You're a Miami cop, act like one."

"Sit—"

"And what the hell were you doing missing a conference call

with representatives of the President of the United States? I've just had my ass chewed by the chief—"

"With all respect, sir, I'm too busy saving lives to talk to anyone, even if it is the damned President."

"Oh, are you, Mr. Superfreakinghero?" The captain's rage boils down the line. "Tell me, Lieutenant, were you born with no brains or did years of self-induced stupid practices simply make them disappear."

"Sir—"

"Don't sir me. I told you before, I don't give a flying fuck about these dogs."

"I need a copter, extra men, and more weapons on the ground."

"Jeez, you never give up do you?"

"I try not to. We're getting fresh incidents every couple of hours—"

"Then get off the phone. I'll see what I can do. You try my patience, Ghost, you really do. And when you've wrapped up out there, get your ass into my office so I can show you how mad I really am at you missing that presidential call."

101

Charles Hadley Park, Miami

The address Zoe has been given for Li Chen is less than three miles from the animal shelter where he works.

She pulls the Nissan to a halt in a secluded back street beneath the cover of overhanging pines. After a final check of the number, she walks up to a neat detached house in the corner, with a short driveway and a patch of lawn that's not been cut for a week or two.

Zoe rings the bell and listens for movements inside. The fact that there's no car on the driveway has already given her the feeling that no one is at home. She rings again. This time she leaves her finger on the buzzer so it would drive anyone inside crazy and have them running to the door within seconds.

Nothing.

She turns and looks at the street. There are a lot of cars in driveways; someone is bound to have seen her. She goes next door and rings the bell.

A white-haired old lady with big black glasses cracks the door open with a chain still on. "Yes!" she shouts. "What do you want?" She touches her ear to adjust her hearing aid.

"I'm looking for Li Chen."

"Don't shout. Goodness." She adjusts the aid again.

"I've rung his bell," continues Zoe, "but there's no answer."

"They've gone away. Been away more than a week now."

"They?"

"He and his wife. They've gone on vacation."

"Any idea when they'll return?"

"Eh?" She touches her ear again. "Damned batteries."

"When will the Chens be back?"

"What did you say?"

Zoe shakes her head. "Never mind. Thank you." She smiles and walks away. Goes straight back to the Chens' house, down the side and around the back. The drapes are closed even though the yard is shaded. That strikes her as odd, maybe the act of someone wanting to hide something.

A misspent youth with her brother Danny and years of martial arts suddenly becomes useful. Nothing subtle. No picking locks. No jimmying window frames, just a well-placed dropkick near the door handle. At first the wood holds. Enough to tell Zoe it's bolted top and bottom as well as locked in the middle. The second and third kicks are more forceful. The locks still hold but the wood doesn't and the door bangs open with the timbers in splinters.

As she steps over the mess, she knows she's crossing a line. Breaking and entering is probably a step too far for even Ghost to be able to smooth over. But this isn't about him or pursuing a line of inquiry that he's plainly too busy to pursue. It's about Astrid, Heidi, and what caused a pet so obedient it won countless awards to turn on them. She's sure the answer lies somewhere down the link from the dog to the breeders to the shelter to Chen.

Zoe shuts what's left of the door and slides a wooden kitchen table back against it. If someone comes, she wants at least a warning. The kitchen is bare. She flips open the cupboards.

Cans. Packets. Jars. Sauces.

Nothing untoward but she takes pictures anyway.

She pulls open drawers.

Dish cloths. Cutlery. Fast food menus. Leaflets of local attractions. Again pretty uninteresting, but she still snaps them before heading upstairs.

At the top she sees four doors. A quick look reveals a small bathroom and what she assumes are three bedrooms. The first one she tries is completely empty. No bed, desk, carpets, or drapes. The second has a single bed in it. The cover is back. It's unmade. The mattress is memory foam like hers at Jude's. She can just make out where the occupant slept. She runs her hand over the impression. He—she assumes—was medium-sized. No taller than her. The pillow has a dent in it. She lifts it to eye level. Sees several short black head hairs. Where the pillow was, there's another indent in the mattress. Shallower than the body shape. Barely there. Her fingers trace it. It's less than a foot long. Thin at one end, fatter at the other.

A gun?

She takes photographs and wonders if her imagination is getting the better of her. Too many episodes of *NCIS, CSI,* and *Criminal Minds.* She opens the closets. Male clothes. Three shirts, a couple pairs of black jeans. Beneath the rail she sees a pair of black boots. Not fashionable. Thick-soled, metal-toe-capped. Maybe for work in the animal shelter. Maybe not. There's a chest of drawers with virtually nothing in it. A pack of unopened, plain briefs, socks, a rolled-up belt. And an ordnance map of Miami. She's peaked in guys' sock drawers before and found hidden literature, but never a map. She opens it up, sees it's dated this year but seems much older because it's so worn at the folds. There are no marks on it, no messages, no easy answers to any of her questions.

Zoe's mind is swimming with thoughts as she goes into the next room. It's the biggest. A large double bed dominates the floor. It's been neatly made. There's no obvious sign of life in here. She pulls back the cover, lifts the pillow. A nightdress. Lemon. Long and cotton. Plain not sexy. She moves it.

Another indentation.

Remarkably similar to the one in the other room.

Did Mr. and Mrs. Chen sleep in separate bedrooms with guns under their pillows? That doesn't sound like too good a marriage to her.

She checks the closets. They're almost as bare as the other ones. Two dresses. Two blouses. Three pairs of shoes. Two flats. One high heels.

And a pair of black boots. Nice. So far as she can see, that's the only thing the couple have in common. There are no photographs in here. No makeup. Nothing personal. The rooms feel like a hostel rather than a home. There is no hint of a relationship, let alone a marriage.

Zoe drops to her knees and looks under the bed. The wooden floor is dusty and there's nothing there. People stack stuff in closets and under beds, but not the Chens. Maybe they put it all in a suitcase and left for a long holiday. Perhaps she's grasping at straws. The boots seem sinister, but then again, many people buy hiking or hobby stuff together. There's probably an innocent explanation for everything.

She walks back downstairs, discounting the ordnance map as just Chen's desire to get to know the area. To do his job better. Maybe there wasn't a satellite navigator in his vehicle.

She tidies up in the kitchen before she leaves. Shuts the cupboard doors. Closes the drawers. Puts away the leaflets. As she does, she looks more closely at them. Now she sees more than just a random selection of local attractions:

Disney World
Flamingo Park
Aqualand
Crandon Golf Course
Universal Studios
Key Biscayne
The Everglades
Bill Baggs Park
Cape Florida Park

Her heart jumps when she sees another leaflet. One that might explain why the Chens are not at home.

102

Weaponization Bunkers, North Korea

*T*he remains of the three dead dogs are laid out on the cold gray steel of the draining gurney in the bunker's makeshift mortuary.

Dressed in full protective suit, Hao carries out rough autopsies while Jihai runs postmortem DNA analysis and toxicology tests.

Rough autopsies because Hao has a very good idea of exactly what he's after. He drains what's left of the body fluids, then excises, photographs, and weighs the remaining organs.

He cuts through fur and flesh and retrieves each of the three microchips, the tiny technological and biological bombs that when activated made the animals uncontrollably aggressive.

He cleans and opens them, then carefully siphons off each of the minuscule chambers, putting sample droplets of the aggressor serum on slides.

When he's done, he calls Tāo to clear the waste away and send it to the surface for immediate incineration.

He washes, changes, and takes the slides back to his laboratory for inspection and toxicology testing.

In the cool, white surroundings of his laboratory, he puts a tired eye to the magnifying glass and expects to see a familiar picture; a chemical painting that has hung in the gallery of his mind since he first started work on the Nian project some three years ago.

He's shocked.

The canvas is the same. Many of the colors and brush strokes are familiar.

But there are differences.

Huge differences.

Hao sits back from the scope and takes in the enormity of what he's just seen.

The reason for his failure.

It's clear now that he hasn't been able to formulate a pacifier because partway through his experiments the microchips and the chemicals within them were changed.

Without his knowledge.

He thinks through the process of deception. Handlers in the dog pens would have been unaware of any differences when they shot the chips under the animals' skins. From the outside, the chip canisters looked identical. It is only what was inside that has changed. They'd been filled with a serum dramatically altered from the one he'd been working with.

The new one, probably only introduced in the last few months, doesn't only enrage the dogs, it makes them poisonous.

He understands now why the North Korean scientist who invented the basic aggressor hadn't been involved in developing the pacifier. Zhang had already set him to work on creating a second strain.

The poisonous one.

He goes to the tox machine and waits impatiently for the results. Eventually there's a beep and they come through. He reads it on the screen and then prints out a hard copy to study in detail. As though only having a physical copy will truly confirm what he's just read.

The dog had excreted a modified form of TTX—tetrodotoxin, a lethal poison that can cause paralysis and death.

He can't believe it. It's there in black and white but he can't believe it.

Hao sets the machine to repeat the testing.

But the nagging doubts that Jihai had raised in his mind are now screamingly obvious and he feels foolish. Foolish and used in the way that only experts of his age and reputation can.

Shameful and angry.

Twice short-listed for Nobel prizes, he had an international reputation as a brilliant and peaceful man.

Zhang has made a mockery of that.

The general no doubt set him to work on finding an antidote to the aggressor solely so he could stay ahead of the West and develop even more powerful and poisonous strains.

He'd been played.

The question now was, what should he do about it?

103

Bicentennial Park, Miami

*D*owntown residents are used to hearing screams from the massive Big Top that dominates the giant park.

Only they're usually ones of joy.

They're nothing like this.

Ten seconds ago more than two thousand animal lovers were excitedly caught up in the annual Dog Breeder's Fair, a hugely popular event for both members of the public and professional breeders.

Now there's bedlam.

Dozens of show dogs have gone crazy. They are attacking each other and anyone who's not been fast or lucky enough to escape from the forty thousand square feet of tent.

Ghost and his team are already there, getting a verbal brief on what the venue is like. There's a tunneled entrance into a tented circle that contains more than fifty stalls. There are merchandising concessions running around two-thirds of the enclosure and a "backstage" area behind large black drapes where the animals' cages and organizers' desks are located.

The lieutenant takes a call from Tarney. "Go ahead, John."

"Just got a heads-up from Control. They've managed to call in a police helicopter from the Everglades to help track any strays that break from the site."

"Good. Cummings is finally cutting us some slack."

From the back of the vehicle that Annie drove over, Ghost hands out HK416s, the close combat rifle developed by the U.S. Delta Force and the German manufacturer Heckler & Koch. "Once we go in there," he points across to the big canvas, "nothing with four legs comes past us and gets out. We start at the back, then we work down to the middle and front. Don't get distracted and drawn away. Keep shape and focus. Anything gets out, it *will* kill, and we can't allow that."

His team take their guns and automatically check them. While they're readying themselves, Ghost heads toward Lydia Andrada, a tough-as-rocks uniform sergeant who is shouting orders to her crowd control teams.

"Lyd. Any chance some of your linebackers can open us a route into the tent and then keep us clean of civilians? The sooner we get in there, the better."

The thirty-seven-year-old checks him out in his combat black. "Yeah we can do that, but rather you than me, Ghost." She cups a hand and bawls across to one of her men. "Hey, Bellios, get a unit and come play Moses. You need to part the crowds and walk Lieutenant Walton and his team into the zone."

A young black sergeant the size of a pro football player nods. "You got it, skip." He turns to his men. "Kowolski and you guys, follow me."

Ghost leans close to Lydia so she can hear him above the screaming crowds. "Any idea of casualties, how many dogs, and what to expect in there?"

She leans back. "Eyewitnesses say forty or so dogs. Most of them are fighting each other. Some of the bigger ones chewed on the crowd too. Bit the shit out of people sat out front in the center of the tent. We haven't got anyone out yet so don't know numbers."

"Never sit at the front of anything," says Ghost ruefully. "A lesson I learned early in life."

"Agreed. I'm a backseat girl myself."

He lets the innuendo slide. "Breed of dogs?"

"Everything. Boxers, bloodhounds, even those Labradoodle-doers that are all the fashion."

"You mean Labradoodles."

"Maybe I do." She shrugs. "They're all just wool rugs with teeth to me. I hate dogs."

He laughs. "Your men ready?"

She locks eyes with her sergeant. "You up, Bellios?"

"I was *born up*, skip."

Ghost nods. "Then let's go."

Bellios and his uniforms disperse the crowd using megaphones and sheer physical presence. Even in the face of panic, people obey a pack of 250-pound policemen shouting at them.

Ghost halts his men at the entrance, a covered tunnel that leads down into the Big Top, most likely the place where tickets were bought and checked. He divides them into two groups and sounds a final warning. "Do *not* put yourselves in danger. If necessary, we back out, regroup and go again. No heroics. You can't warn or negotiate with an animal, you can't buy time or gain an advantage, so shoot on sight. Okay. Go."

Rick Diaz, the marksman who killed the dog at Flamingo Park, is briefed to peel left with Max Kweller. Ghost is going right with Zander Stolly, the unit's rookie.

Dog growls and human moans curdle the air as they walk the last few feet of the dark tunnel.

Red and green spotlights, abandoned mid-show by the tech crew, are crawling back and forth in the shadowy space ahead of them.

Ghost is first in.

He climbs the wreckage of information desks, concession stalls, and broken seats. All the noise is coming from a central show area where banked seating has been arranged to form a performance ring.

Ghost takes steps up to the back row and looks down.

Shit.

It's like a scene from ancient Rome. Lions versus Christians. Down in the sawdust of the small arena, people stand back-to-back beating away snarling dogs with folding chairs from the front stalls and bits of apparatus from the show.

Ghost counts six, maybe seven dead bodies in the ring, several of them still being savaged by large dogs. There are canine corpses too, small spaniels and terriers that have been torn to pieces.

To the left of him, Diaz's HK spits out a burst of bullets and takes down two boxers at the back of a pack. Kweller catches a wirehaired pointer with a single shot. A surgical hit that would have won him applause back on the range. Both men instantly move down a row of seats, their eyes never leaving the humans battling for their lives.

On the far right side of the ring the body of a grandmother is being torn apart by two more wirehaireds. Ghost takes out the dog chewing on her face and Stolly picks off the other.

A massive Alsatian jumps from beneath a set of seats in front of Kweller. It bounds over the young male body it's been biting and heads their way. Diaz tracks it and catches it with his second burst.

Another leaps up the terraces, eyes huge and yellow teeth bared. Kweller drops his HK to waist level and sends a chain saw of bullets across its midriff.

Now there are more of them. Coming from every direction. The gunfire has attracted their attention, like cracking a stick on a hornets' nest.

Ghost and Stolly sprint along their rows. They've got to be careful not to catch their colleagues in a cross fire.

A pointer jumps Kweller.

Just before it hits his chest he gets off a burst from the HK, but the dog still flattens him, cracks him into the seating and jars his back.

A mastiff the size of a horse gallops toward Diaz. He sees it out of the corner of his eye as he tries to help his partner but knows he won't get his gun up in time.

Ghost shoots it from ten yards away.

Dogs are pouring out of the ring now. Sprinting up the aisles and heading toward his men.

The people who were trapped see their chance and run for the exits.

Run for their lives.

"Stay tight!" shouts Ghost. He turns and pulls hard on the rifle trigger. His 416 can cough out more than eight hundred rounds a minute, and he's thinking he might need all of them to get out of here alive.

The first wave comes pouring in.

Stolly screams at the top of his voice and rakes automatic fire into the onrushing dogs. A wild release of tension that betrays his inexperience.

Ghost picks off dogs on the right perimeter, ones lumbering in late but every bit as vicious and deadly as the frontrunners.

Kweller and Diaz stand side by side and systematically mow down everything with fur that moves on the left perimeter.

The sound of the guns is deafening. The spotlit air fills with smoke, flying fur, and sprays of blood.

Finally, the shooting stalls to a stutter and Ghost shouts, "Cease fire!"

Stolly can't stop.

He's holding the rifle but has no control over it.

It's jumping in his arms as he relentlessly shoots into the body of a long-dead dog.

"Stolly!" Ghost puts his hands on the youngster's rifle. "Stop!"

The kid is wild-eyed and traumatized, but loosens his finger from the trigger and lowers his weapon.

Ghost puts an arm around him and pulls him close to his chest. "You did well, Stolly. You did really well."

104

Weaponization Bunkers, North Korea

The second tox tests confirm the findings of the first. Hao was right. The wild dogs fitted with the new microchips had secreted tetrodotoxin, a deadly and virtually undetectable neurotoxin that blocks the conduction of nerve impulses along nerve fibers and axons.

TTX is essentially a "cork" pushed into the vital channels down which nerves send messages. Once blocked, the body starts to shut down, leading to paralysis, respiratory failure, and death.

The scientist remembers, as a student, learning that creatures such as the Japanese puffer fish can host the toxin without risk to itself, because the protein of the sodium ion channel underwent mutations that changed the amino acid sequence and made the channel insensitive to tetrodotoxin. That single point mutation in the amino acid sequence rendered it immune to the poison.

The same was being done with the dogs.

On his desk are the newly completed DNA profiles that prove as much. There are changes in the base sequencing and clear signs of mutation.

Hao realizes the implications of what he's uncovered.

Once beta testing has finished, the Nian project would supply General Zhang with the world's deadliest covert weapon.

One that would be welcomed with open arms into the homes' of unsuspecting families.

It would be petted. Loved. Trusted.

Then when activated, it will kill with just a single lick.

The thought sickens him.

The toxin is so hard to trace that millions could be killed before scientists discovered it, let alone developed a mass antidote. To the best of Hao's knowledge, no one in the world has yet developed one. Though he doesn't for a moment doubt that Zhang has teams secretly working on that as well.

Teams no doubt led by Jong Hyun-Su. The Korean scientist who invented the Nian program but didn't develop it.

Hyun-Su was linked to Korea's World Stem Cell Hub and is an expert in theriogenology—the science and practice of animal reproduction. The hub was initially hailed for its brilliance and was thought to have been the first lab in the world to clone a human embryo.

Then the truth came out.

Results had been faked. The hub's leader had embezzled millions of dollars in funds and grants. As a result the whole enterprise was shut down.

While the WSCH's claims on cloning people were discredited, their work on animals and the creation of the first cloned dog escaped relatively untarnished, as did the reputation of Jong Hyun-Su, widely regarded as one of the brightest and most maverick talents around.

Hao carries these thoughts with him as he heads to the medical bunkhouse to check on Péng.

He finds the young scientist lying in a shivering, cold sweat, babbling and swiping out at nonexistent people and objects.

"How long has he been like this?" Hao asks Jihai, who sits alongside Péng.

"I'm not sure. I came to check on him and found him like this."

"Send for Dr. Chi. Did Péng go to him as I instructed?"

"Yes. Chi said there was nothing to worry about."

Hao doesn't have a lot of time for the doctor. He's in his late sixties, maybe early seventies, and should have retired years ago.

"He just put antiseptic on the cut and gave him an antirabies jab," added Jihai. "The usual immunoglobulin."

Hao looks at the feverish youngster and rules out such an infection. "Rabies wouldn't manifest itself so quickly. The earliest known cases of symptoms appear in days, but it's usually weeks before there are prodromal signs like this." He thinks of what else it might be. "I suppose he could have had a severe reaction to the jab, but that should have been spotted after earlier immunizations." He turns to Jihai. "When Chi has seen Péng, check that Tāo has prepared the new dog and meet me in the testing bunker. I need one more serum run and I need to do it quickly."

105

Bicentennial Park, Miami

Shafts of sunlight stream through bullet holes in the Big Top and pierce a thick gray cloud of gun smoke.

The place has been shot to bits.

The tactical team's 416s reduced row after row of chairs to junk wood. Lights, drapes, props, and signs have all been destroyed.

There are no more growls and snarls, just the moans of the brutally injured. Nevertheless, Ghost's men stay on alert and shadow paramedics from casualty to casualty. From uniform units outside the tent he's heard that about four dogs have broken free, so he's radioed Tarney and directed him and the other unit to help track them.

At the back of the tent, Ghost finds three families who crawled into separate dog cages and locked themselves in. They're shaking with fear and the kids have soiled themselves.

He also finds six dead men and women. From their badges, he can see they are a mix of breeders and event organizers.

As he looks around he realizes that Lydia Andrada was right. The front row got it worst. Ghost counts eighteen dead, including two people in wheelchairs and what he guesses is two of their helpers. He walks the periphery of the Big Top and hears a thumping noise. It's coming from inside a metal crew box about eight feet by four, the type used for stage lighting.

He stops and listens.

There's another bang. Like an animal moving around.

He cocks his rifle, puts his boot heel against the edge of the lid and kicks it open. He's just in the mood to kill another of the fuckers.

There's no dog.

Just an elderly couple wrapped in each other's arms.

The man's bald and liver-spotted head cranes up and around like a turtle. "Is it over?"

"Yeah, it's over." Ghost slides his rifle out of the way and sticks a hand inside. "Let me help you out."

The old guy takes it and struggles and groans his way up. Together they help his wife, a slip of a woman in her seventies, with a girlish smile that no doubt broke hearts half a century ago.

"Are you okay, ma'am?"

She steps out of the box. "Yes. I'm fine." She straightens out her dress, conscious of showing too much leg.

Her husband takes her hand and holds tight as he takes in the carnage around them. "There was a girl," he says. "A young woman who helped us in there. Black hair. Is she all right?"

Ghost doesn't have a clue. "Most people got out safely. I'm sure she's fine. Now let's get the doctors to check you over."

The wife points off to her right. "There. That's her. I recognize her shoes, they're like my daughter's."

Ghost spots a blue sneaker and bare ankle. They're sticking out from beneath a pile of broken wooden chairs and a jumble of torn backstage drapes that cover a woman's face and upper body. He figures she tried to climb to safety, no doubt with dogs snapping at her heels.

There's blood all over the floor and no sign of movement. He walks closer and stands on something. Part of dog's jawbone.

Smashed clean out. Whoever she is, she put up a hell of a fight before they got her.

He pulls off the broken chairs and carefully unwraps the drape wound around her so he can see.

His heart catapults against his ribs and every breath of air is sucked from his lungs.

It can't be.

But he knows it is.

He's staring at the body and his mind is willing it to be someone else.

Anyone other than Zoe.

106

Weaponization Bunkers, North Korea

One dog. One dose of serum. One last try.

Jihai brings a fresh shih tzu into the containment cell, injects it with the drug-loaded microchip, and once outside immediately activates the aggressor serum.

Hao would rather have used a larger dog and waited six to twelve hours before the activation but there isn't time.

Now he and his son have to sit patiently on stools in front of the glass and watch for signs of aggression before administering the pacifier. "How is Péng? What did Dr. Chi say?"

"He is much the same." Jihai can't keep the worry from his voice. "Chi thinks he just has a cold virus and the bite is coincidence. Could that be?"

"It is possible." Hao doesn't add that he thinks it highly unlikely. He turns to his son and does something he has never done before.

He takes him into his confidence.

"What you said to me about our work here—"

"I meant no disrespect, Father—"

He pats down the interruption with his left hand. "I know. As you said, you spoke as a scientist." He pauses reflectively. "And you might be right."

"About what?" He looks to the dog in the containment cell. "About the animals being part of an attack program?"

Hao nods. He finds it hard to speak. He feels foolish about how he has been betrayed and deceived. "I would never knowingly bring shame to our family. To my name or yours. Not shame of this historic magnitude."

Jihai looks shocked. "The deaths in America—you think they could be from our dogs?"

Hao doesn't move. He doesn't speak. But his silence says everything.

The little shih tzu suddenly jumps at the glass and begins yapping furiously as soon as it gets to its feet.

Jihai steps from his stool and starts for his workstation. "It is ready."

"Wait." Hao grabs him by the arm. "Promise me one thing." He glances at the snarling, crazed dog jumping in the cell. "Please, do as I say. No questions. No delays. Whatever I ask of you in the coming hours or days, just do it. Our lives and our names may depend upon it."

Jihai bows his head. "I promise."

Hao smiles. "Now let's work."

The shih tzu hits the glass again. It lands and sets its tiny legs wide beneath a silky curtain of long brown and white hair. Its lips are curled back. Tiny teeth bared as aggressively as it can manage.

Hao realizes he is pinning the largest hopes of his life on one of the smallest dogs in the world. He checks his monitor readings then looks at Jihai. "Release the serum when you're ready."

The young scientist triggers the atomized chemicals.

Both men hold their breath as they watch.

The tiny dog leaps once more.

It barks.

Then walks.

Walks not bounds.

Hao and Jihai exchange glances.

The barking stops.

The dog tilts its head back and opens its mouth.

No bark. Just a yawn. A disdainful sucking of air.

Then it sits and grooms.

Tāo burst into the room. "Professor! Péng has stopped breathing."

107

Miami

*T*here's a pulse.

That's the best he can hold onto.

A pulse.

Feint and weak but paramedics say it's there.

Zoe is alive.

Bitten up bad. Unconscious from a head injury and loss of blood from multiple bites.

But alive.

Ghost can barely function because of the shock. He takes the Hasselblad from around her neck as the medics finish up and lift her onto a gurney. Something drops from her jeans as they wheel her away. He picks it up. It's a pocketbook with a thin pen jammed in it. He slips it into his jacket and follows the crew outside.

He wants to go with her to the ER but knows he can't. Personal pain has to be buried for public good. There are operational ends to tie up, police business to be done, instructions to give. And there's Cummings and all his rot. All his anger at missing the great presidential phone-in.

"You okay?"

The voice is Annie's. She's old enough to already know the answer.

"Yeah, I'm good. The woman the medics just took, she's my—" His hand grasps at the air as he tries to find the right words for what Zoe is to him.

"Girlfriend?" suggests Annie.

"No," he answers. "She's not that. It's not a good word."

"Then what? Friend?"

He looks at her. "No. She's my love."

Annie's not sure she heard him right. "Your what?"

He gets himself together. "Her name is Zoe. Zoe Speed. She's the civilian who stepped in and stopped the Citibank robbery the other day." He takes a deep breath. "I want to be kept up to date on how she is. Have someone check on her condition every hour." He corrects himself. "Every half hour. Any change in her state, you let me know. Doesn't matter who I'm with or where I am. Okay?"

"You got it."

He has a flashback of pulling back the blood-soaked drape that she was tangled up in. That first glimpse of her face. Eyes shut. Just like she was this morning when she was sleeping, when he kissed her beautiful head and left her there in her friend's spare bed.

Now he sees the wounds.

Awful bites to her arms and legs. The gaping hole in her side. The flash of white hip bone through the sticky red gore.

He'd held her head in his hand and felt wetness in his palm. Pulled it away and looked, hoping it wasn't what he already knew it was.

A terrible head wound. Blood and swelling. A bad combination.

After that he'd gathered up the drape and made a soft pad to lay her on while he called the paramedics. Shouted at them like he was falling off the edge of a cliff and needed them there within a split second to save him.

Now they've come and gone. She's in their hands. And maybe God's.

"Boss."

Annie is staring at him. She's holding up a radio, "Captain Cummings is on the line. He says he needs you back at base. Right away."

108

Weaponization Bunkers, North Korea

*P*éng is close to death.

The monitor hooked to him is beeping alarmingly and the small, birdlike form of Dr. Chi is spread over his big chest carrying out CPR. A last resort that is unlikely to restart the heart but could keep oxygenated blood flowing, delay tissue death, and avoid permanent brain damage.

Chi looks up at the stream of concerned people who've just flooded into the medical bunkhouse. "Someone pass my bag from over there."

Jihai grabs a large, saggy brown leather carryall and brings it over.

"Open it," says Chi, still keeping up the compressions. He looks around. "Does anyone know CPR?"

"I can do it," says Tāo. "I have done it before."

"Take over."

Tāo slips into position, expertly rests his palm on Péng's chest and strikes up a steady and regular rhythm.

Chi half empties the bag. Bandages, thermometers, a metal box, all tumble across the floor. He ignores them and finds what he's after. A short plastic tube and a scalpel.

Everyone realizes what he is about to do.

Chi will cut into the neck and insert a tracheostomy tube into the wound.

One slip of that shaking old hand and the young man is dead.

"Have you done that before?" Jihai sounds skeptical.

"I'm a doctor." He glares at him defiantly then turns to Tāo. "Okay. Step away from the patient."

Tāo shifts to one side and Chi moves surprisingly quickly. He shuffles pillows under Péng and tilts his head back.

Unhesitatingly he cuts with the scalpel.

There's a spurt of blood as he creates the stoma, the hole in the neck and windpipe.

Chi feeds the single cannula tube in, secures the neck plate, and wipes away the blood. He then places his hands on Péng's chest and repeats the CPR.

There's a blip on the monitor by the bunk.

A sign of life.

Eyes swing to the screen and watch the HR climb.

Twenty . . . forty . . . sixty . . . eighty . . .

It stops at eighty-five.

Jihai smiles. "He is all right?"

"No. He is not all right. He is alive. That is all." Chi turns to Hao. "Unless he goes to a hospital right now, this man *will* die."

"I will go to my office and call Beijing for the authority for the transfer. Can you contact the military hospital aboveground and prepare them for the intake?"

Chi nods. "I will do it right away."

Jihai can't help but ask the question. "Is it rabies? Is it rabies after all?"

"I don't know," concedes Chi as he heads to the exit.

Hao doesn't answer.

But he does know.

He knows exactly what's wrong with Péng. The poison affecting him is rare and deadly. Whatever they try to do for him, he is going to die.

109

Breezy Point, New York

Locals call it the Irish Riviera.

It got the name because it has the second highest concentration of Irish-Americans in the country.

Danny thinks it should be called Dullsville.

Breezy is a summer getaway out in Queens, hanging over the western end of the Rockaway peninsula like a fat man's belly. It attracts walkers, golfers, fishermen, nature nuts, and no end of old-timers who want to sit and stare at sunsets and remember shit from their youth.

The area is a select five hundred acre cooperative owned mainly by the kind of rich residents who complain to the cops if you play your music a single decibel louder than their TV. The exception to the rule is the surfers who hang out on the beach and at least bring some life and color to the place.

Stevens has settled Danny in a big four-bedroom family home and even delivered the Kawasaki. If he's asked, Danny has a cover story that he's a rich Internet entrepreneur who's burned out and needs a rest.

The kitchen is stacked with groceries and there are enough pizzas in the deep freeze for him to set up in competition with Domino's.

The only thing he doesn't have yet is new equipment, and hopefully that'll be arriving soon. It's going to take him an age to get back on the trail of that Jackpot data stream.

Danny watches for the delivery van from a window with a view of the Rockaway Inlet and the local security force that patrols his street so regularly they've worn their own groove in it.

While he waits he calls Word, Kayoz, and Right. They're cool about the shutdown, especially when he tells them "the man" is going to pay them for the next month anyway.

He juggles the phone in his hand and thinks about his next call.

Jenny.

He has to tell her why he's disappeared.

And why he's not going to be around for a while.

110

Police HQ, Miami

*T*he journey back from the Big Top is a blur, and Ghost is still in a trance when he walks into Cummings's office.

The big captain isn't alone. He's sitting with his boss, Major Bob Martinez, and the force press officer, Scott Young.

Martinez has a face that looks like a kid has drawn it, almost perfectly round with red cheeks and black dots for eyes. He gets to his feet and extends his big soft hand. "Good to see you, Ghost. You're doing a great job."

Ghost knows he doesn't mean a word of it. The guy's been a full-time politician for thirty policing years. People say the first thing he did when he came out of the womb was shake the hand of the midwife who delivered him, then kiss himself on the head while his father took pictures.

"Take a seat," says Cummings curtly. "Reason I'm not ripping you a new ass is that word's come down from the governor's office that we're going into a State of Emergency. Seems you're not alone worrying about these freaking dogs."

"Glad to hear it."

"Shut your mouth and listen. The President is apparently on a plane and heading to Florida for a press conference. National Guard and all the shit that comes with it is being called out. Special Ops will be at the front of the multiagency initiative and the White House wants you to take the lead locally, along with an operational hotshot from Jacksonville—" He looks to Martinez for the name.

"Vasquez. Antonio Vasquez."

"He'll help coordinate resources and back office with our people and units in Orlando, St. Petersburg, etcetera. So you and he best get on. On top of that, we've got the President landing 'round about now, so you best not stand the man up twice."

It's Scott Young's turn to chip in. "He's going to make a live address to the nation from here. Probably from our press studio." He couldn't look prouder.

The remark touches a nerve with Ghost. "It'd be better if he did it from the morgue—maybe then the whole damned country will know what's really going on."

"Enough." Martinez halts him. "The President has had the *cojones* to call a State of Emergency and he's promised us whatever resources we need to make our cities safe. In return, he expects us to step up to the mark, and *I* expect you to watch your mouth and honor this force when you meet him. Do you understand me, Lieutenant?"

Ghost doesn't answer. He just stares into the major's cold blue eyes. Right now he doesn't want to be here. Doesn't want to meet the President. Certainly doesn't want to head up any national initiative with some pen-pusher from Jacksonville.

Cummings tries to defuse the tension. "He understands, *don't you,* Ghost?"

"Yeah, I do." He gets to his feet. "I understand that I'm the wrong man to do this."

"Sit down," says Martinez wearily.

Ghost doesn't stop until he gets to the door. "I have a friend dying in the hospital. She's destined to be one of the sixty-plus people killed this week. You just made me realize it's more important that I'm sitting there with her than being here with you." He looks across to Cummings. "I'm leaving my badge and gun on your secretary's desk. I'm done. Not just for now. For good."

III

Weaponization Bunkers, North Korea

$\mathcal{T}$he monitor in Hao's office shows the shih tzu is still in a calm and controlled state, curled up like a ball of silk in the corner of the containment cell.

The pacifying serum has worked perfectly.

The scientist feels a sense of vindication—plus a simmering annoyance that new chips, with new serum, were introduced without his knowledge.

He dials Beijing on an encrypted line and finds that both Zhang and Xue Shi are unavailable to take his call.

Lack of contact with them leads him to realize he's at a crossroads.

His loyalty to his country and party lie in one direction, while family honor, self-preservation, and the lives of Péng, Tāo, and his son Jihai lie in a different direction.

He sits at his computer, enters the Project Nian database and registers the code that declares the experiment has been completed and the pacifier perfected. He then pulls up various authorization forms that have been previously granted for a variety of purposes. He copies and pastes the signature of General Zhang onto a new document—one that authorizes Péng's transfer to the military hospital aboveground. He types in security codes and numbers that will come back with only one digit wrong when the guards run them through their systems. It's the kind of mistake anyone might make. An admin slip-up.

A glitch that might buy valuable time.

Hao prints off a copy and examines it

It isn't the best forgery in the world.

But it will do.

It will have to.

That and the sight of a dying man with a tube cut into his neck may seem authentic enough even to Korean guards.

The phone on the lab wall buzzes.

He picks it up, knowing it is Jihai.

"Father, where are you?"

Hao takes a deep breath. "I cannot come with you."

"Father?"

"I will tell you why in a moment, but it is important Chi doesn't hear. Do you understand me?"

Jihai backs away from the doctor and gurney where Péng is lying. "Yes, I do."

"Good. Wait at the gatehouse where you are and in a moment the guards there will receive from me the authorization documents you need to go to the military hospital. Once you have Péng inside an emergency room, there is something you must do."

"What, Father?"

"Remember you promised me that for the next day or so you would do as I ask, without question?"

Jihai is momentarily fazed. "Yes"

"Then listen to me and do not react."

Jihai turns away, so the others can't even see his face.

"Everything you said about the dogs was correct. Everything and more. I have the proof. Now this is what you must do. Be clear, Jihai, you *must* do this—not just for me, but for you and for the eternal good of our name . . ."

112

Jackson Memorial Hospital, Miami

*W*hen Ghost was a kid he went to Jackson to see specialists. He remembers going to a restroom and getting freaked out by all the cockroaches that swarmed his feet when he sat in a stall.

Twenty years later the place looks spotless but the image remains in his head. He talks to a triage nurse and learns that Zoe is still there. Because he's with Miami police, she says he can wait in a staff room.

He takes a cup of coffee from a machine and wishes he hadn't. It tastes like hot water poured on soot. He sits and lets his mind idle. Through the fog of worry comes a memory of the notebook that fell from Zoe's body as she was wheeled away. He takes it out and looks at it. The first page is marked with today's date, and then under it he sees the names and home address of Astrid and Heidi Gerber. His first thought is that Zoe was trying to work out where to place the photographs she'd taken at the house, then he sees what looks like a shot list marked Dog.

> #30-33: Vaccination
> #34-42: Puppy shots
> #43: Bill of Sale for pup

The information throws him for a second. He flicks through several other pages and sees references to Breeder, Animal Shelter, and Chens.

For a moment Ghost becomes pure detective. He loses emotional involvement and puts together the jigsaw. Zoe had gone back to the Gerbers' house and dug into the history of the family and dog. It had taken her from there to the kennel that sold the family their dog and then for some reason to an animal shelter and a place called Chens. He knew Miami intimately and couldn't think where that might be. He supposed it could be a store or name, but that was equally unfamiliar.

Inevitably, he loses focus and remembers finding Zoe unconscious in the Big Top. The wounds he saw were bad. Severe enough to have killed most people outright. It hits him that someone should be told she's here in the hospital, fighting for her life.

But who?

Who should he call and what are their numbers?

Ghost starts to realize how little he knows about her.

There's her friend Jude, but she's away somewhere. And she has a brother Danny in New York.

Those are the only ones he knows about.

There'll be numbers for them on her phone, and that's probably in her clothes, in a pocket. If it was in a purse, then she's lost it, because she didn't have one when they put her in the ambulance.

He recalls that she has a father too, but he has no idea where he lives and he knows her mother is dead.

Dead.

The word sticks as it skims across the surface of his mind.

Zoe probably *will* die.

Given her injuries, it may be the merciful thing.

But he hopes not. Maybe it's selfish, but he hopes not. More than anything he wants to see her sit up in bed and talk to him. He'll look after her. Whatever state she's left in, he'll take care of her.

Ghost feels like he's making a promise to God—he'll give the rest of his life to Zoe if only she's allowed to live.

He stands up and knocks over the last of the cold coffee at his feet.

There's a paper towel holder on the wall and he rips out a fold of rough green paper and mops it up. He throws the tissues in a bin marked NO SPIKES and turns on the TV.

President Molton's face fills the screen and a big caption in the top left corner says LIVE. The President isn't in the make-shift studio at Miami Police HQ but out at Bicentennial Park, the white canvas of the Big Top flapping behind him.

Ghost can't stop himself from turning up the sound.

"My sympathies, those of my administration and the nation at large, go out to everyone who lost loved ones today—be they in the tragedy here at the Bicentennial Park or anywhere across the country. Tonight we pray for their souls and we pray too for the speedy recovery of the many who were injured." The camera catches Molton's dark eyes in close-up, and Ghost can see that whatever the man is, whatever his politics, he's at least sincere in his grief.

"The test of a government and the test of a nation is how we react to tragedies like today and how we work together to try to prevent them from happening again. I believe we must do so with common sense and precautionary planning—not with paranoia and panic. We have always known that dogs can be dangerous, just as we have known that they can be a loving part of our lives."

The camera shot slowly tightens on Molton as journalists sense he's moving toward a stronger section of his speech, the part most likely to make their headlines.

"Over the years, America has faced a catalogue of animal-related threats and overcome them all—H5N2 Avian flu, foot and mouth disease, H1N1 Swine flu, and even rabies. I have confidence that our scientists are close to identifying what this new threat is and exactly how we should combat it. In the meantime, we are taking immediate action to eliminate strays from our streets and we will be opening special dog safety shelters in all major cities. These will be secure depositories, where you can safely leave your animals and have them cared for by the state until we are sure we have eliminated any potential risks of them being affected. As I just said, the choice is yours. One in four households in America has a dog, and it is your choice whether you wish that dog to remain with you or to bring it to one of the temporary homes we plan to open within the next twenty-four hours."

The staff room door opens and a nurse walks in. One he hasn't seen before.

"Lieutenant Walton?"

He hits mute on the TV. "Yes."

"Your friend is out of surgery. Dr. Kinsella is just scrubbing up and then she'll come and speak to you."

"How is Zoe?"

The young nurse flinches. "As I said, Dr. Kinsella will talk to you."

113

Weaponization Bunkers, North Korea

The back end of a typhoon is turning into a tropical storm.

Dr. Chi holds the intubation tube in place as they walk Péng's gurney out of the calm safety of the bunker network into the jaws of the murderous wind.

Jihai and Tāo lean and push.

At first it's a struggle to keep the blanket from blowing off, then it becomes a battle to stop the gurney itself from blowing over.

Through the stinging rain they make out some of the one million North Korean soldiers who guard the 150 miles of DMZ.

Beyond them, somewhere out there in the gray swirling storm, are half a million South Korean and American troops.

Jihai shouts at an inquisitive guard who has broken from his rigid, storm-defying stance to investigate their presence. "I've a sick patient." Fluttering in his hands are the falsified authorizations that Hao faxed through to the admin post manned by exit guards.

The soldier can barely read them.

He looks first at the injured man, then at the number of personnel authorized to exit, quickly counts and waves them on.

The tempest lashes them.

They bend double and push. It feels like they're climbing a steep hill while being hosed down by a fire crew.

Soaked and red raw from the biting wind, they reach the guarded blue hut of the medical block.

Jihai steps forward again. The papers his father gave him are now sodden and in danger of tearing. "I am a Chinese scientist, from the research establishment in the bunkers, and I have authorization for my colleague to receive emergency medical treatment in your hospital."

The guard is a young soldier, not a veteran, but he is not giving in that easily. "Give me the papers and your ID." He waves a black-gloved hand toward the others. "I need to see all of your IDs."

Jihai takes his from around his neck, passes it to the guard and rushes back to the gurney. "Give me your IDs cards, quickly. He won't admit us without them."

"Ridiculous," mumbles Chi as he pulls the chained picture ID from around his neck. Tāo collects Péng's and hands it over with his own.

The guard takes the collective stack from Jihai and walks from person to person checking the photographs. He seems oblivious to the torrential rain.

As soon as he sees Péng's opened throat, he glances at the picture and shouts to his colleagues to let them through.

The gurney bumps over boards in the entranceway and then leaves long wheel tracks on the corridor.

Everyone sighs with relief at being out of the storm.

Chi checks on Péng.

Jihai and Tāo watch nervously as he takes the pulse and rolls back his eyelids.

"He's alive," says the doctor. "But he's not conscious. He's in a coma."

114

Jackson Memorial Hospital, Miami

*D*r. Rosa Kinsella looks as if she's worked a day and a half without a break. And that's because she has. A shortage of staff and a bad road traffic accident stretched rotations to breaking point even before the wave of dog injuries.

After *another* two hours in surgery, the thirty-six-year-old brunette is still in scrubs as she walks into the staff room to give the waiting policeman the bad news.

Ghost can already read it in her eyes. He gets to his feet and readies himself.

She can tell what he's expecting. "It's not *that* bad. She is still alive—but only just."

"How 'just'?"

"Life support just."

The words leave him hanging. He can't find the right questions to ask and finds himself sitting down.

Kinsella leans on the wall next to him. "Zoe's body suffered immense trauma from the multiple bites and she lost a massive amount of blood—about five pints in all. But that's not the most serious part." She raises a right hand to the right side of her head. "She suffered a fracture to her skull. Most likely fell hard on the floor or against something and there's been internal bleeding. The bites alone would be bad. The blood loss from just one of those wounds could kill some people, let alone the complication of the head injury. Put them all together and, well . . ." She deliberately lets the sentence fall away.

"How long?" He takes his tinted glasses off and rubs tired eyes. "How long before her chances disappear of making a full recovery?"

"We're not there yet." She tries to sound more positive than she is. "Not by a long way." She misses a beat as she notices his albinism. "Do you know who Zoe's next of kin is?"

He realizes she's being practical rather than insensitive. "She has a father and a brother. I don't have numbers but I can find them." He gets to his feet again. "I need her phone. I think it must have been in her clothes."

"I'll have one of the nurses look for you. You going to go home now? You look dead on your feet and there's nothing you can do here. We'll treat you as her surrogate decision maker and call you if there's any change."

"Actually, I'd like to sit with her for a while, if that's okay? Seems wrong just to walk out of here without seeing her."

Kinsella nods. The guy's in love, she thinks. He believes that somehow holding her hand is going to work magic. They all do. Unfortunately, it never works.

115

North Korea

*H*ao's words are ringing in Jihai's ears.

"Run. Escape. Save yourself and tell the world the truth."

He'd gripped the phone in shock and still feels as dazed now as he did when he left the bunker and entered the eye of the storm.

"Péng is already as good as dead, and Zhang will kill us all when he discovers we know about the poison dogs."

The news had rocked his world, thrown him completely out of orbit. He and Péng had been friends since they both learned to speak. Since the death of his mother, Jihai's only living relative had been his father.

Now he was being told to do something that would mean he'd never see either of them again.

And if he hesitated, then he might be killed.

It was one thing to have suspicions and doubts. But to have them validated and turned into a matter of life, death, and honor was something else.

Now the questions come. The biggest he has ever faced.

Even if he could desert his dying friend—and he's not sure he can—what about Tāo, and how could they escape?

He forces himself to think.

The DMZ is long but narrow, and the hospital less than a ten minute run into sanctuary in South Korean and American hands. But a million North Korean troops lie between the two points. Could he really evade them?

Others have done it.

Done it for years.

But in a storm like this?

They'd done it in the depths of winter and the height of summer. Done it because they were determined to. Because they *had* to.

And others have been killed.

Shot down by guards in the lookout towers. Caught on barbed-wire fences and riddled with machine-gun fire.

Jihai tried to stay positive. The smart ones had gotten away. They had headed for the demarcation line, made it to Panmunjom, the abandoned village where the cease-fire was signed, where the JSA—the Joint Security Area—is and, bizarrely in this land of extreme contradictions, where tourists are even bussed in to witness the tension between the only divided country in the world. Or they made it into Daeseong-dong, the only civilian habitation within the southern portion of the DMZ. The military demarcation line lies just a few hundred yards west of the village. While the DMZ is under the administration of the Allied Control Commission, the residents of Daeseong-dong are considered South Korean civilians and subject to South Korean government law.

If he could get there, he'd be safe.

Dr. Chi is talking animatedly to medics. Finally, Péng's gurney gets wheeled into what passes as an emergency room. From the look on the faces of the Koreans, he suspects that all they are doing is isolating him, making sure that whatever has made him ill doesn't infect their soldiers.

A look around tells him that security in here is lax, to say the least. Sick army personnel are in beds, chairs, wards, showers, changing rooms, and there are uniforms and weapons everywhere.

If he's going to make his move, he has to make it now.

116

Beijing

The briefing note trembles in President Xian's hands.

He puts it down on his office desk and stares at his fingers as though alien creatures have attached themselves to him.

He's never been nervous in his life.

Nothing has ever hit him so hard that he could not control his own body.

But the note from his intelligence services has done that.

It's not so much what it says, but the fact that he has to read of such an important event, rather than be told in person.

That fact alone means more to him than the event itself.

It signifies that he is no longer the most important person to tell. The person who must know before anyone else.

It means his position is not unassailable. And people know it.

The ones outside his room, waiting to come in, they know it.

He looks down.

His hands are shaking even more.

He presses them on the camphor wood and closes his eyes.

Now he is walking the slopes of Dragon Bone Hill with his wife and child. The air is cool and fresh. Carried on it are the smells of plum blossom, camellia, and tree peonies. He sees the wonder in young Umbigo's face and feels the love in Suyin's hand as she takes his.

Xian opens his eyes.

His fingers are still.

The trembling is gone.

He holds down a switch on his desk and talks to his secretary. "Show them in. And bring us some tea."

The president stands. In his mind he hears the words of Sun Tzu, China's greatest tactician: *Pretend inferiority and encourage his arrogance.*

The door opens and Zhang enters. A step behind him is Lieutenant Xue Shi.

"My heroes." Xian beams warmly and embraces each one in turn. "What incredible victories you are achieving. Sit, sit. Come." He ushers them to the softly furnished area that is reserved for visiting dignitaries.

They settle on the plush leather sofas and Xian continues his gushing approval. "So tell me about it. How you managed to get the great bald eagle to bow before the dragon and declare a State of Emergency in Florida."

Zhang feels awkward. He'd expected the president to be annoyed. It was the effect he had hoped for. Not this effusive praise. "We have been systematic in the deployment of the Nian dogs. All has gone exactly to my plan."

"Our plan, comrade."

Zhang concedes the point. "Indeed. Our plan." He wonders if the president would be so quick to use the plural if he knew the full extent of what the plan was.

Xian picks up the intelligence briefing. "I shall have this framed. A moment of history." He puts it down and smooths it out on the desk. "Of course it wasn't news to me." He watches his general's eyes and sees a twitch of tension, the lips press together in annoyance. "Do you know how I knew, Zhang?" He positions his smile just the right side of smugness.

The general remains silent.

"The President told me." Again he sees a twitch in his under-ling's eyes. "I believe he is ready to talk."

"Did he say as much?"

Xian raises an eyebrow. "You meant to ask, 'Did he say as much, Mr. President, sir?' This chair and my position are not yet yours, so please remember the courtesy I am owed."

Zhang dips his head and respectfully acknowledges his mistake.

Xian continues with his lie. "Molton called me personally. Before his announcement to the American media. I thanked him and he asked if we could come to 'an accommodation.' I told him I would think on the matter."

General Zhang wants to ask what his president has decided, but to do so will show a swing of power again.

Silence sprouts and slowly festers between them.

It's broken by a knock on the door.

Xian's secretary brings in a tray of green tea. No one speaks while it is served. The secretary bows and leaves the room.

The president picks up his cup. "So let us talk strategically. Outline for me your proposed next moves and I shall decide how best to respond to President Molton."

117

Jackson Memorial Hospital, Miami

*T*he light, the air, the electronic noises and the smells of the hospital bedroom, all give Ghost the creeps. He guesses it goes back to his childhood when he spent so long in clinical waiting rooms and examination suites. He's never been good at waiting. Boredom multiplied by fear always makes for bad karma.

He takes a break and retrieves Zoe's Hasselblad from his car, then grabs hot chocolate from the machine in the hope that it's more palatable than the coffee. He opens up Zoe's notebook and tries to match the numbers and descriptions to the thumbnails he pulls up from the camera's memory chip.

Ghost is shocked to see the inside of the Gerbers' house. He knows she didn't take those pictures last night because she never left the kitchen. He casts his mind back and remembers that this morning, when he asked her what she was going to do with the photographs she'd taken, she answered that if anything she hoped to tell the story of the two women "with some sense of perspective and feeling." Maybe this was her attempt to do that. She must have charmed her way past the cop on duty, got into the house, and then begun her photographic investigation.

He breaks from the lists, descriptions, and images to hold her hand and watch the monitors. Zoe's motionless face depresses him. The thought of losing her is growing more painful by the hour. He kisses her hand and tries to distract himself with her research.

The combination of camera and notebook prove to be as intriguing as they are revealing. They offer the sequential explanation that *Chens* is not a town, place, or store. It appears to be a home of a man named Li Chen who worked at a Miami animal shelter and lived near Charles Hadley Park. From the photographs, Ghost sees Zoe is something of a serial housebreaker. Apparently, she got into Chen's house and took a whole series of shots. There are no other people in the stills and as far as he can make out there is nothing of significance in the photographs.

The next sequence of shots, taken forty minutes later, is at the dog show. There are close-ups of breeders' signs. He flicks through and gradually works out that she's only picked out those concerned with wirehaired pointers.

The final shots show a pointer on the center stage suddenly savaging its proud owner. Ghost guesses Zoe then forgot about photography and tried to get the hell out of there, or more likely—knowing her—focused on helping other people around her.

"Hell of a story," he says to the unconscious woman in front of him. "I just hope you wake up soon, honey, and can fill in those missing gaps." Ghost turns the camera off and puts it on her nightstand. He grabs a spare pillow from the bottom of her bed, takes her hand again, and settles down for what he suspects is going to be a long wait.

118

North Korea

*J*ihai walks to the doorway from where Tāo is watching Chi and the Korean medics attend to Péng.

He touches the young researcher's arm to get his attention and gives him a clear and firm instruction. "You stay with the doctor. I'm going back to help my father."

Tāo nods obediently.

Jihai walks the corridor and pushes open a door.

It's a shower block.

He can see steam billowing from around a corner and there are hospital gowns, shoes, and clothes everywhere.

But no uniforms. No weapons.

There's a window to the outside world, but even through the frosted glass he can see the verticals of the iron bars.

There are drains in the floor. But they are far too narrow to fit into and he guesses they simply run waste out into the earth, or into one of many self-contained septic tanks.

The steam is rising in front of him. It hits the ceiling and then bleeds away. There is no air-conditioning and there are no vents, but the steam is swirling upward.

Jihai stands on a wooden bench and puts his hand to the big ceiling boards. They are loose.

Raucous laughter comes from the showers. It sounds like some play fight. He hears three voices, maybe more.

Jihai's knowledge of Korean is good and he can make out words.

They are calling each other names. Fooling around. They're distracted.

He stretches and pushes the board.

It lifts.

But he's not tall enough or strong enough to be able to flip it back, find a joist, and haul himself up. If he stacks another bench on top of that, then the men will be suspicious when they come out of the shower.

He glances around.

In the far corner there are two toilet stalls. If he went in one of them he could climb on top of the lavatory and might be able to reach the ceiling.

More laughter spills from the showers.

But he'd have to cross the soldiers' line of sight. And then he'd either have to wait until they'd gone or make the climb with the risk of them spotting him.

A few feet to his left there's a steel bucket, a mop, some dark cloths, and a long rubber floor wiper for shifting excess water.

He takes off his white laboratory coat, folds it up and puts it in the bucket. He rolls up his shirtsleeves, grabs the cleaning equipment, takes a deep breath and heads to the stalls.

His heart is hammering as he comes level with the men. He can feel strange eyes on him, checking him out. Custom dictates that lowly cleaners keep their heads down, show respect for their betters, so he does exactly that.

One of the men says, "It's only a cleaner. Don't worry. Don't stop. He won't say anything."

Jihai keeps on walking.

The farthest stall is in the corner.

He slips inside and turns.

Through the steam he catches a glimpse of the men. Two of them are kneeling. The third has his hands spread against the wall.

The last thing they're paying attention to is him.

119

Beijing

Xian watches Zhang and Xue Shi leave.

Watches their backs all the way to his door.

Watches the door close and then listens to their heavy military footsteps fall on the boards of the corridor.

Only now does he look down.

His hands are not shaking. But the thunder in his chest tells him that he is coming to the end of his days and shaking or not, power is slipping from his fingers.

His lie about Molton telephoning him and being ready to talk has only delayed matters. Put off the inevitable. Bought a little time.

A day or two.

A week at the most.

Unless Xian can discredit or remove Zhang within the next seven days, he will find himself out of office and possibly even dead. The world's press would be given some rubbish about a heart attack, or cancer that had been kept quiet. Few would know how the assassin had struck. Most likely poison. Or a surprise attack by someone who can snap his neck quickly and not leave marks that can't be covered up by a new uniform for the state funeral.

If he is to survive, then so too must Molton. And that means they must talk. Even if he initiates the call.

Xian looks at the secure phone on his desk and wonders if he should pick it up.

The alternative is unthinkable.

He's sure that Zhang is pressing on without the safety net of having pacifying agents to sedate the weaponized dogs.

Within forty-eight hours Florida will be like an abattoir.

Then Zhang and Xue Shi will target the major cities. New York, Chicago, Los Angeles, Houston, Philadelphia, and Dallas. Finally, he will release the dogs of war in Washington—the seat of government—the ultimate humiliation.

The phone swims into Xian's view again and the urge to pick it up is hard to resist.

But he knows he needs to reflect. Think things through.

Strategize.

This, after all, is the beginning of his biggest battle.

120

Weaponization Bunkers, North Korea

*H*ao Weiwei sits in the cool, white surroundings of his laboratory and feels a sense of loss that he has only known once before. The time his wife died.

The end is near.

The end of his work. End of his time as a parent to Jihai.

End of his life.

When Zhang and Xue Shi realize that he knows about the poison dogs, they will have no choice but to "remove him" and any others they suspect he may have told.

They will all be as dead as Péng.

His fingers pause on the computer keyboard. He's at the place where he's worked for the past three years and loyally completed the tasks given him. Now he's teetering on the brink of what would be regarded as treachery.

All the tests that he has run have automatically been downloaded onto a main computer in Beijing. He's sure that at first no one will notice exactly what has happened, but they will eventually. Officials in the intelligence service will have certain alert programs in place, and once that software picks up the data he has run, then all eyes will be on him and his team.

As he accesses the restricted administration sections of the master computer, he thinks of his only son.

He remembers holding him for the first time. Struck by how light and tiny he was. How soft his skin felt. How beautiful he smelled. What joy he experienced to have brought life into the world.

Jihai will go on to be a great scientist. Of that he has no doubt. Which is why Hao is doing what he's doing.

And when he's finished, then he's going to remove the military pistol from the locked metal cabinet beneath his desk and do the honorable thing.

121

Beijing

Zhang and Xue Shi sit alone in an office adjoining the Operations Room.

The general's mood has been black ever since they walked out of the meeting with President Xian. He cracks the knuckles of his fingers as he reflects on the meeting. "The old fool is making one desperate effort to cling to power. I doubt there is truth in his claim that Molton has called him."

"I can get Chunlin to check his call records."

"We cannot trust Chunlin." Zhang's face is dismissive. "No matter. If they haven't yet spoken, they will. Xian will call Molton and suggest a meeting. It will be his last attempt to get the Americans to accept the deal."

"The level of attacks planned for the next twenty-four hours will bring the Molton administration to its knees," Xue says. "He will be begging to accept."

"Have our other friends prepared their surprise?"

Xue Shi smiles. "They have. Turmoil follows turmoil."

Zhang drums his fingers on the table while he thinks. Everything is going according to plan. He can taste victory, but he wants it to be *his* victory and not Xian's. "The moment Xian goes to meet Molton is the very instance when he feels strongest—and is therefore at his weakest. As these 'great leaders' prepare for diplomacy, we must rattle the sabers of war so loudly that they cannot hear themselves speak."

"The second phase dogs?"

Zhang is pleased by the thought of the havoc they will wreak. "How many of them can be activated?"

Xue Shi is unsure. "I will need to check. Not that many. Ten, maybe twenty."

"And these are on the East Coast?"

"New York and Washington."

"And the pacifier for the phase one dogs? Not that I care. I want to know solely in order to keep Xian under the illusion that we are still following his orders."

"Weiwei was close. I received a message that he had called, just as I was leaving to join you for the meeting."

Zhang stands up and heads for the door. "You need to prepare to close that unit down. Jong Hyun-Su can handle things from here. Don't leave any loose ends."

122

North Korea

*J*ihai takes the bucket and mop with him.

He slides back the boards, sits in the roof space and listens intently as the men dry and dress.

Only once do they mention him.

A man with a deep voice asks, "What happened to the cleaner?"

There's a pause and then a lighter voice answers. "His things are gone. I guess he's left."

That's it. He's out of their minds. They talk of how hungry they are. How ugly a particular sergeant is and how they're not looking forward to going back on duty.

He's forgotten.

The door bangs shut and the shower block falls silent.

Sitting in the dust and dark he thinks of his father and wonders what he's doing. Whether he is planning his own escape. How he will try to do it.

Jihai has a simple plan for himself.

Wait.

Wait until the black of night joins forces with the storm and he can make allies of them both.

Wait until the vast number of men on duty falls and much of the camp drifts into sleep.

Wait for his one slim chance to get out of here alive.

123

Breezy Point, New York

It's late evening by the time the FedEx van finally arrives with Danny's new computers, modems, relays, and peripherals.

Two surly New Yorkers unload them in the hallway, even though he wanted all of it upstairs.

By the time he's finished the shifting, he's glistening like a roasted hog.

It takes the rest of the night to get everything cabled up and online.

The only good news is that Brad Stevens has had the house fitted with ultrasecure satellite broadband that has upload and download speeds more than a hundred times faster than anything commercially available.

The bad news is that he can't call anyone and no one can call him.

Until he gets clearance from Stevens, he's unable to communicate with either Jenny or Zoe, the only two people who really matter to him.

Just after midnight he completes the setup and celebrates with a grilled cheese sandwich and a cold beer. Then he turns in before he collapses from stress and tiredness.

He's asleep within seconds of hitting the sack.

In his dreams he hears the click of his finger on the trigger. The explosion. The zip of air. The dull thud of bullet through clothing. The muffled agony. The tumble down the wooden stairs.

Danny wakes in a sweat.

He's soaked. It's like he's showered in wet salt.

He swings his legs out of the strange bed and pads into the kitchen to get some water.

There's a bleep.

And another.

Bleep. Bleep. Bleep.

It's his computer. Sending out an alert.

He rushes to the back room to check.

Jackpot.

He's found it again.

He's back on the tail of the elusive code.

124

North Korea

*H*ao is completing his final tasks when Dr. Chi and Tāo return.

The army issue pistol is in his hand, the door to the metal cabinet still open and a suicide note on his desk.

Chi looks at him suspiciously. "What are you doing?"

He slides the safety catch back on the gun and avoids the question. "How is Péng?"

The doctor's eyes answer before he does. "Critical. They have given him morphine." He glances toward young Tāo and then back to Hao. "He will die peacefully." He looks distressed. "I have no idea what is wrong with him."

"He's been poisoned." Hao sees no point pretending any more. "He was bitten by the dog and it secreted a neurotoxin into his blood stream."

"Neurotoxin?"

"Tetrodotoxin."

Chi looks confused. "How?"

Hao doesn't have the strength of spirit to explain in full. "There was a new batch of microchips sent for implanting. They contained a different serum. One that had been adjusted so it converted the dogs' saliva into something toxic."

Tāo steps closer to the two men. "What does this mean?"

"It means we cannot continue. I came here in the name of peace. To create a way to protect our country, not to attack others. I am shutting down the program."

Chi rushes him.

Hao is caught unawares and the gun goes off.

The doctor lets out a primeval cry and falls to his knees.

Blood is pumping over his white medical coat, surfacing like a giant poppy from the middle of his stomach.

Hao is traumatized by what he's done. His eyes are glued to Chi, who is already going into shock.

The doctor slumps sideways, cracking his head on the tiled floor. His eyes and mouth are splayed open.

Tāo is crouched in the corner of the room. His back is against the wall and he too looks shocked.

Then Hao sees why.

The bullet has passed straight through Chi and hit the youngster.

"Oh no. Tāo. Tāo." He rushes to him.

The researcher is holding his chest, and it's instantly clear that the shot went up through Chi and caught him in the worst possible place.

Hao puts his arms around him and guides him to the floor.

"Don't—let—me—die." Tāo's eyes are filled with pain and fear. "I—don't want—to—die—"

"It's okay," lies Hao. "You'll be okay." He leans over him and takes his hand. "Lie still, don't tense up."

He feels Tāo grip his fingers. Grip hard. Then slacken.

The boy lets out a splutter and his body spasms.

He's gone.

Hao stands up and looks at the blood on the white floor. Looks at the two crumpled bodies. And he looks at the gun.

He'd meant to shoot himself. An honorable end to the dishonor he'd been tricked into. He'd planned to end it all with just a single bullet, and instead that one shot has killed two innocent people.

He sits in his chair and raises the weapon. His eyes take in one last look of his office. A lab coat of Jihai's behind the door, a photograph of him on the wall, and the dead bodies of Chi and Tāo.

As he slides the cold barrel into his mouth he has a final thought.

One that might just save his son's life.

125

Jackson Memorial Hospital, Miami

*T*he last thing Ghost notices is the rhythmic beep of the life support machines and the dull green glow of lights on the other side of Zoe's bed.

After that sleep comes.

It scoops him up and transports him to an unblemished land of parks and rivers. The sun is golden and a cool wind blows Zoe's dress tight to her body as they walk the banks of a river and decide where to sit.

The click of the door handle wakes him.

A big male figure stands in the frame, bright corridor lights burning in the background.

"Lieutenant Walton?"

He peers out from the shade and reaches for the sunglasses he put on a bedside cabinet. "Yeah."

The man steps into the small room and takes a pace to one side. "Stand for the President of the United States."

Ghost isn't together enough to make sense of what's happening and he's still sitting and staring when Clint Molton walks in.

Now he tries to get up.

"Mr. President."

Molton waves him back down. "Sit. I need to do the same." He pulls over a chair near the door and turns to the protection officer who walked in before him. "We're fine; you can leave us, thanks. I'm in no danger from this man."

As they're talking, Ghost can't help but listen for the machines and look across at the dials and monitors. He doesn't understand the readings but their positions and sounds are familiar, and familiar means good. He glances at his watch.

Ten past midnight.

He's sitting with the President at ten past midnight.

Molton waits patiently for him to finish his scanning of the screens then smiles. "This your lady?"

"I hope so." He remembers his manners and belatedly adds, "Sir."

"Forget the formalities. How's she doin'?"

"Not so well." He looks across at Zoe's pale motionless face, the mask that's helping her breathe, and the tubes and drips that are keeping her alive. "But they say she's stable."

"That's good. She'll be okay." He puts his hands on his knees and looks across at her as though she were one of his own family. Then he turns back to Ghost. "My sister got hit by a bus, under the Loop in Chicago. Spent two days in a coma. My mama sat there every minute worrying. Soon as I walked in the room I knew Connie was going to pull through. She did. Recovered just fine. I know your lady's going to do the same."

"I hope you're right, sir." He can't help but add the formality. "But I guess you didn't come here at this time to discuss patient welfare."

Molton nods. "In a way I did." He's been carrying something in his hand, something chunky wrapped in a plastic bag and rolled short and tight. He pulls it up and hands it over. "This is yours, I believe. Your badge and gun. I was at your station house talking to your captain and I asked to see the guy who ducked out of a video date with me—"

Ghost starts to explain, "I'm sorry, I—"

"No need to apologize. I know what you've been doing. And how you've been doing it. The Vice President and I saw you on TV yesterday—and again today. Forgive my language—you kick ass. You say what you think and you do what you know needs doing. I need ass-kickers like you. I've always needed them, now I need them like I've never needed them before." He looks across at Zoe. "She's in good hands, Lieutenant—the best there is, from what I'm told. Now I need the best of people to help me and America fight the war we're facing." He sticks out his right hand. "Will you help me—Lieutenant?"

126

Beijing

Lieutenant General Xue Shi puts the phone down and looks at his notes.

He's learned from past experiences that bad news is best told quickly.

Such knowledge doesn't, however, dispel the trepidation he feels as he enters the briefing room for a routine update and prepares to recite the contents of the call to General Zhang and Minister Chunlin.

"I have just heard, General, that Hao Weiwei has killed himself, his son, and the unit doctor as well."

"What?"

"It is correct. A night patrol found them dead in the laboratory. The doctor and Weiwei's son had been shot in the body and in the head from close range. Their faces were so badly blown off that guards only recognized them from the name tags on their lab coats. Weiwei had done the same to himself. He'd put a pistol in his mouth and shot himself."

"Such loss." Chunlin can't hide his shock. He'd known the scientist and had thought of him as an admirable man. "What possessed someone as bright and honorable as him to do that?"

"There were factors." Xue Shi gives Zhang a knowing look.

"Leave us." The general opens the office door. "Leave us, and speak of this incident to no one."

The minister feels indignation and anger boil up as he rises from his seat and walks out.

"What did he know?" asks Zhang as Chunlin closes the door. "What brought on this 'noble' act? For make no mistake, that is how the idiot scientist will have seen it."

"He knew about the poison dogs. His suicide note condemned the Nian project as 'morally reprehensible and beyond the boundaries of evil.'"

"He always had such limited vision."

"The shooting happened just a few hours after one of his team was transferred to the military hospital in a coma and then died."

"Transferred? Who authorized such a transfer?"

"I don't know. It should have been me, or you, but I gave no such permission."

"Then Weiwei faked it."

Xue Shi completes the picture. "That's why he was calling us. He was seeking authorization."

Zhang is anxious to contain any possible damage. "Let us be clear about things. Weiwei acted without authority. He faked your approval and jeopardized our country's safety. Lose the suicide note. Have it destroyed. Can you trust the commander?"

"Probably not."

"Then have him and anyone else who saw the note returned to Beijing to report to us. And see to it that they never make it. For the moment, nothing must throw us off course. We cannot have Xian or senior members of the party casting any shadows of doubt over us."

127

The White House, Washington DC

*T*he security staff patch the encrypted call from the Chinese leader through to Pat Cornwell.

"President Xian, I'm afraid President Molton isn't in Washington tonight. Can I be of help to you?"

There's a pause before he answers. "No. When will he be back?"

"It's the middle of the night here, sir. The President is in Miami and will make an early morning return to the capital. He could call you on the secure line from Air Force One in about four hours, say seven P.M. Beijing time. Would that be suitable?"

There's a heavy pause before he answers. "Yes. It is suitable."

"Can I tell him what it's about, sir?"

The line is already dead.

Cornwell holds the buzzing phone out to demonstrate his surprise to Don Jackson, who's sitting a few feet away. "And good night to you too, Mr. President."

Jackson had been listening on a loop. "What do you think he's going to say to Clint?"

The VP puts the phone back on its cradle. "More threats, I imagine. Might even try to increase their ridiculous demands."

"Do you think we should call him and wake him?"

Cornwell rubs his tired forehead. "Let the poor bastard have what little sleep he can. He was dead on his legs when he left here."

"Yeah. Not a good time to be President. I'm going to head to my office and check on how the Army and the National Guard are getting their acts together."

"I'll come down and see you later."

Jackson raises a hand as a goodbye and walks out.

Cornwell settles down to his own to-do list. Come first light he wants police and sheriff's offices working with military units to hunt down strays across Florida and "dispose" of them. He wants a one-to-one with this freaky new guy that Clint has put in charge at the Florida end of things. And he wants fresh press initiatives to keep the media at bay.

For a short while he zaps across the news channels to see if he's missed anything and to try to get a feel for the mood of the country.

It's not good.

Channels are starting to move on from the scene of disaster reporting and are beginning to get more analytical. In turn, the average Joe is starting to ask smarter questions when a microphone is shoved in front of him. The big one is simple: What the hell is going on?

The Vice President wishes he knew.

It's still dark when he takes a rare cigarette break and downs another espresso. He's had much more caffeine than his doctor recommends. Too much stress as well.

Standing in the cool courtyard, he reflects on how he'll be disappointed when Air Force One returns from Florida and he's no longer calling the shots.

The VP flicks away the low tar butt and ambles back inside, his head still mixing up his personal ambitions to run for the next presidency with the current problems the country is facing.

The idea of secure containment areas for all dogs—or "safe homes," as Jay Ashton is publicly branding them—was his, not

Molton's. And it's a smart one. For now, dog owners will have the choice of putting their mutts in containment, but in the next few days, maybe even sooner, the government will make it compulsory. After that, it's almost inevitable that *most*, maybe *all*, of the dogs will have to be destroyed.

Cornwell has already got Ashton and his spin doctors working on some cock-and-bull story about the dogs being infected with a rabieslike virus that justifies the culls. Rabies scares everyone shitless. Just one shout of the word and people will be grabbing shotguns and shooting their own dogs.

Around dawn he wanders down to the Situation Room.

Lights are burning in all the offices and a much bigger watch team than normal is putting together the "Morning Book," the daily compilation of new reports from intelligence agencies plus diplomatic cables and a summary from the State Department.

Cornwell finds Jackson at the far end with a duty officer and intelligence analyst, working his hand deftly across a state-of-the-art Telestrator. The monitor screen always reminds Cornwell of the one sports commentators use when they draw rings around players and highlight offensive and defensive runs. Only down here, Jackson is working on a mix of 3D maps, live satellite images, and graphic overlays of where attacks have taken place.

"How's it going, guys?" The VP gives them an encouraging smile as he approaches.

Jackson answers on everyone's behalf. "We're just reviewing the implications of the decision to focus our National Guard and hit team resources around the areas where there have been the most damaging or most frequent attacks."

"And?"

"And we're not sure the Joint Chiefs have made the right decision."

"Go on."

Jackson swipes a finger down the east coast of Florida and leaves a dotted white line on the screen. "Miami keeps getting hit. We've had multiple kills at Lummus Park, Jason Schaffer, Flamingo Park, Key Biscayne, Coconut Grove, and South Beach. But not here." He runs a finger around the Miami city center. "There's not been so much as a bark in the middle of town, which is why we only have a small patrol allotted to give cover here." His hand moves up the map. "Same over at Jacksonville. Nothing in the center. There have been no attacks there, and we just have a couple of crews doing watch-and-see deployed here." He sweeps his hand across to Santa Rosa. "This is countrified. Way, way away from a center of population. And we had deaths here and over in remote places like Merritt Island and Millers Landing."

Cornwell starts to get the picture. "You believe the big cities are going to be targeted? You think our armed resources are being pulled wide to the rural areas, then they're going to strike at the centers with a wave of weaponized dogs?"

Jackson takes his hand off the board. "I'm certain of it. The question is not really where they'll hit us, but when."

Cornwell sees his point. "Strategically it fits. If I were running an attack campaign, I'd build things up. Smash the small, soft targets during the first stages of political negotiations, then when talks start to disintegrate, hit a densely populated area to prove your power."

"Exactly. Our problem, sir, as you know from the briefing earlier today, is that we don't have resources to instantly cover all the areas at risk for all of the time."

Cornwell winces. "A-fucking-ghanistan. We should have been out of there years ago."

Jackson doesn't even mention that his latest intel shows

troubles rising there as well. "Which brings us back to our dilemma, Mr. Vice President. Have the Joint Chiefs done the right thing by deploying units to rural areas in preparation for more rural attacks? Or, have they bet wrong? Will the next wave be the big cities? It's your call—and I'm afraid you have to make it right now."

"Then we stay as we are. Doubts are always going to raise their heads, Don. We have to learn not to be distracted by them and stick to our guns. The Chiefs thought long and hard about this strategy, so we're sticking to it."

128

Jackson Memorial Hospital, Miami

*T*he presidential visit puts some energy into the antiseptic air and makes the early morning hours pass more quickly.

Once Clint Molton leaves, nurses flit into Zoe's room more attentively than ever. Naturally, during their visits they are keen to ask Ghost what the President had said and what he was like.

Around 3:00 A.M. the excitement fades and the lieutenant is left on his own again. Occasionally, he picks up Zoe's camera and notebook and imagines what she had done with her last day, from the moment he left her flushed pink from their lovemaking to the second he found her bloodred and unconscious.

Life seemed so fragile.

Letting her accompany him in the Gerbers' kitchen had been a mistake. The horror of the scene had touched her. He'd seen it in her face at the time. Her whole being had blotted up the violence and emotion spread in front of her. He guesses she only survived true trauma because she'd had her camera. The lens became a shield. It objectified things. Allowed her to see the two women as critical objects, to be framed properly, correctly focused, and diligently captured. But afterward she probably had craved a sense of balance, needed to find perspective for the photographs, something to validate them as more than proof of her journalistic voyeurism. He knows that if he'd stuck to rules and regulations, she'd have stayed on the other side of the tape and the chain of events that brought her to this ER would never have begun.

He tells himself not to feel guilty. That life is packed with awful twists of fate and that's just how things are. But he doesn't believe a word of it. He *is* to blame. And if she dies, it will unquestionably be his fault.

Looking at her pocketbook, it seems to Ghost that Zoe risked her life for a story. Her first true piece of photojournalism. Sadly, she had gotten lost along the way. If her intention was to tell the world about the heartfelt relationship between mother and daughter, then she'd have been better going back to the village school they'd both attended, or asked in the clothes stores where they shopped together, or even gone down to the local gym where they regularly cycled side by side on spinning bikes. His office had found all that stuff, from house-to-house inquiries as they looked for someone who knew family or friends who could identify the bodies.

Ghost taps the red book on his knees. He finds it intriguing that Zoe took almost the same direction that he would have had he been treating the dog as a murder suspect and not just a dumb animal. She'd sought out *its* antecedence and *its* known contacts. Tracked down its last movements and identified all key events in its life.

He could see that she'd found the kennel where the Gerbers

bought the dog, but after that several things puzzled him. Most of all, what was the connection to the shelter? To Chen? And why had she left Chen's house and gone straight to a dog show—one that fatally ended with the animals turning on the audience?

129

North Korea

*S*tanding on the apex of the roof, Jihai sees moonlight through a crack in the timbers.

He walks a thin joist and through other cracks spots flood-lights, horizontal rain, and blackness.

No one has entered the shower block for several hours, and he's beginning to feel that now is time to make his move.

He tiptoes back to the board where he made his entry and prizes it up with his fingers. It's heavy and awkward to move but he manages to slide it across as gently and quietly as possible, then grabs the cleaning equipment and lowers himself down onto the top of a toilet in the farthest cubicle.

A motion sensor triggers a light, and for a moment he thinks the door opened and someone came in.

As quickly as possible he replaces the board, puts the cleaning equipment back in the corner, and slips his white lab coat back on. If he's caught, there's a chance he can still explain his presence with the papers in his pocket and his friend in a bed a few doors away.

Péng is on his mind as he slips out of the shower block into the corridor.

The place looks deserted.

Three doors are open to his left and three to his right. He can't resist walking by to take a look.

The first room he comes to is a nurses' station, and two male nurses look questioningly at him.

He tries to drift by but one of them shouts after him. "Hello."

Jihai knows there's no point running. They'd raise the alarm within seconds.

He turns, pulls the faked authorization papers out of his pocket and speaks in his best Korean. "I've come for the sick scientist. The one brought in earlier from the research bunker."

The small dark-haired male nurse has red eyes and looks as if he's just woken. "Come for him?"

"Yes. Where is he?"

"I'll show you." He leads the way around the corner, past several more rooms and then around another corner. "In here." He pushes the door open.

Jihai hears the buzz of flies.

The lights come up and he sees three steel gurneys. All are covered with white sheets.

"The one on the right," says the nurse unemotionally. "He was last in."

Jihai is not sure what to do. He feels compelled to look but at the same time wants to remember his friend as he was.

He walks to the gurney and pulls back the sheet.

Pain hits him like a plank across the face.

Péng is there. But he isn't. All the laughter and light that made him a best friend was gone.

"Yeah, this is him." Without thinking, Jihai slips the brake off and spins the gurney around.

The nurse stands back so he can push his way through the door. "Where are you taking him?"

"His family will come from America. I must take his body to Panmunjom to be collected for burial. You know about Chinese burial rituals, yes?"

The look on the young nurse's face shows he doesn't.

"Do you not believe in God and a life after ours?" Jihai asks.

He looks offended. "I am Shaman. My mother was a *mudang*."

"That must have brought great honor to your family." Jihai bows his head respectfully. "This man here is a Taoist—" He touches Péng's shoulder. "—and he must have a special burial. Just as your mother spoke to spirits, so too must his family. They must begin the ceremony to free his body from the demons that seek to prevent him rising to heaven." He adds a layer of lies. "And it must happen within twenty-four hours or else he will be damned—as will anyone who prevented the ceremony taking place."

The nurse picks up the implication. "I am not stopping you. Take him."

Jihai takes a chance. "I need your assistance. I need you to show me how to get to the Joint Security area so the body may be picked up by the Americans."

"I can take you to the guards at the gate," says the nurse, "but not until my shift finishes."

"When is that?"

He glances at his watch. "Six hours from now."

"Not good enough." Jihai steps forward. "There will be a diplomatic and religious incident if I don't get this body to the pickup point within the hour."

130

Beijing

*X*ian is relieved to find that he has a late night visitor to his office.

He looks across the top of his newly poured whiskey as Minister Chunlin sheepishly heads toward the chair on the other side of his expansive desk.

"Would you like a drink?" He holds up the expensive liquor that Molton had given him as a gift.

"I would, Mr. President. Thank you."

Xian takes a glass from the cabinet behind him, unscrews the Macallan and pours a generous measure. "Why did you not contact me about the State of Emergency?" He passes the glass over. "And why do you come to me now?"

"Thank you." Chunlin takes the whiskey. "I did not know of the American announcement. Xue Shi has circumvented most of my senior reports and cut off my principle communication sources. I am becoming isolated from my own operatives."

Xian takes a jolt of the whiskey. His instincts were right. Power is shifting. Only it is moving faster than he had suspected. "How does Xue Shi control your own people? Do they not have loyalty to you?"

"They do. But they have loyalty to their own lives. On a daily basis they see Zhang's ruthlessness and they rightly fear for themselves and their families."

Xian swirls the whiskey in the glass and peers at its rich, fiery colors as he thinks things through. "And you, Geng, have you come to fear him too? Do you sit with me now at his bidding?"

"No." The minister looks hurt. "He has forbidden me to talk to you."

Xian feels his temper rise. "Then in being here you put yourself at risk."

"I still have friends. There is still loyalty." He drinks a little and draws breath, a sigh of relief at being able to let out some of the fear inside.

The president tops up their glasses, "I am pleased to hear that there is some immunity to the disease of treachery. Fear of death can turn the staunchest of allies into the worst of traitors." He looks into Chunlin's eyes.

"I would never betray you." His voice rings with indignation.

Xian wants to believe him. Their history is strong. "So what is so important that you risk your life in coming to me?"

"There has been an incident in North Korea that Zhang has forbidden me to talk to you about."

"Go on."

"Hao Weiwei has killed his son, a doctor, and himself."

"No." Xian looks shaken. "I know the man well. He is one of our brightest brains, our most distinguished scientists."

"Was, Mr. President. He killed himself and left some kind of suicide note. I do not know the contents but I suspect they explain the reason for the shootings."

"I am sure they do." He reaches for the phone. "I will call Zhang to account, immediately."

Chunlin puts a hand on the receiver. "Please forgive me, Mr. President. It would be better if you didn't."

Xian glowers at the impertinence. Then he softens. Chunlin obviously has a plan. "Why? What have you in mind?"

"A way, Mr. President, a way to use this to ensure that the ambitions of General Zhang and Xue Shi do not ruin the reputation and future of our country."

131

Bristol, Liberty County, Florida

*T*hey come from the south.

Out of the Apalachicola Forest, west of where it bumps into Lake Talquin, east of Sheppard and north of Mystic.

Out of the place where some claim Noah built his ark.

Out of the dead of night, the pits of darkness.

They come with slobbering jaws, haunted eyes, and the thunder of a cattle stampede.

More than a hundred weaponized dogs are hurtling toward the small, sleepy town of Bristol.

It's barely 7:00 A.M. and its thousand citizens are only just stirring. Early starters wander in the moist morning air. They are expecting nothing but another day as placid as the last in the Florida panhandle.

Emily Stokes straps her two children into their car seats and thinks about her long journey west to visit her mother in Pensacola. The two aren't getting on and a heart-to-heart is in the cards.

She looks down the road toward the Baptist Church. There's something on the blacktop rolling her way, like a two-foot-high tidal wave. Emily squints and struggles to make out what it is. Old Mrs. Emmings is doddering around down there, getting her newspapers from off the lawn where that stupid Ryland kid threw them from his bicycle.

"Dear God."

The words are as close as the thirty-five-year-old has ever come to a profanity.

Priscilla Emmings has been knocked down by what looks like a giant pack of dogs and they're trampling right over her.

Emily rushes to the front door of her tidy three bedroom home, shuts it, and runs back to her car.

Two-year-old Jade greets her mother's return with a familiar statement. "I want to pee-pee, Mommy."

"You'll have to wait until we're at Grandma's, honey." She looks out of the Chevrolet window. The dogs are less than a hundred yards away. Too near to take the kiddies out and into the house and maybe even too close for her to get off the short drive and head down to the 20 and out of town.

She decides to sit it out.

Four-year-old Henry gets excited and points. "Look at all those doggies. Wow!"

"Yeah, let's wait a minute and watch them." She turns and gives her children a reassuring smile.

They're close enough now for Emily to see their shapes and sizes. They look mainly mongrels, dirty. Black-and-whites with shaggy coats, bit, by the looks of things.

She locks the door. The central locking clunks and the kids sense a change in the air.

"Want a wee, Mommy."

"Watch the doggies, honey."

Emily starts the engine. They're only twenty yards away and she somehow feels safer if she can at least move the car.

Now that they're closer, they look like wolves, a massive pack of charging wolves.

Jade starts to cry.

"It's okay, baby."

But it isn't.

A wild dog crashes into the passenger side of the car. Another hits the trunk. A third crashes into the back fender.

The thumps are frighteningly loud. And more and more are happening. It's as though the car is being hit in a multiple pile-up.

Both kids are crying.

There are so many dogs now that they're blocking the light at the windows.

Emily can barely see as she slips off the hand brake and screeches off her strip of asphalt.

A huge Alsatian hits the windshield.

Henry screams.

The Chevy's wheels bump over dogs hit by the front bumper.

Something hits the driver-side window, and despite trying to stay calm, Emily shrieks.

Another dog hits the cracked windshield.

Its paw juts through.

Dangles through the crack like a monstrous limb appearing through a lake of ice.

Emily floors the accelerator.

The dog's leg doubles back and breaks. It falls from the windshield and she can see road.

Open road.

Escape.

132

North Korea

*J*ihai stares imploringly into the eyes of Shin Kung, the nurse.

He's the son of a *mudang,* a form of Shaman priestess, he must have seen his mother fall into trances, communicate with spirits, cast spells, and tell fortunes.

Jihai hopes to turn the experience to his advantage. "You have been brought up to respect the dead. To know that they have their needs. What would your mother say to you if you told her that you turned your back on me and my friend's needs?" He grips the cold metal gurney where Péng lies. "Would she approve? Or would she think you had discredited your family and especially her." He sees the words have struck home. "Help me. It is fate that I have found you. Ten minutes of your time will mean an eternity for my friend."

Shin nods. "I will help." He walks to the side of the room and removes a new body bag from the stacks on a shelf. "We must cover the corpse. The weather is still severe." The nurse hands the bag to Jihai. "You begin to put him in this. I will get his medical papers."

Jihai takes the plastic cover and feels his heart start to race. Every step toward freedom brings with it a greater fear of capture.

Rigor mortis has set in on Péng's corpse and the stiffness makes it difficult for him to do much more than get half the body into the zip-up.

Shin returns with a brown A4 envelope and two greatcoats. He folds the envelope and places it in the pocket of one. "The storm is still raging and there are no waterproofs, but these will protect us a little. I have told my colleague I am going to help you take the body to the gatehouse and he is calling the guards and telling them to expect us."

Jihai feels another surge of apprehension. He'd believed his best chance at the gates would be the element of surprise. It had worked coming into the hospital, and with Shin in tow it might have worked again. But if the guards contact their military superiors and Beijing is called, then his plan will collapse.

"Lift please." Shin is tugging the bag underneath Péng.

Jihai puts his arms under his old friend and heaves him up while the nurse shuffles the bag under.

Shin makes the final adjustments and passes the scientist a coat. "Follow me. We go out through the rear of medical center."

They push the gurney down several corridors and Jihai sees a number of other people working. No one questions the sight of two men with a body bag. They are just glad it isn't them having to push the thing.

Shin knocks down the metal lock bar on two rear doors.

The wind rips them out of his hands and flings them hard against the outside of the building.

Jihai has to help bolt them into the floor.

The rain is still torrential. It comes unseen out of the blackness of night and then like millions of thrown stones bounces off the puddled road leading through the camp.

The two men push the gurney out into the savage storm, apply the brake and rush back to shut the doors.

Within seconds their hands and faces are whipped raw.

The wind is soon behind them, but the downpour penetrates their coats. Their necks and backs soon become soaked.

The blacktop is full of potholes and every ten yards or so a wheel of the gurney dives dramatically and the two men have to stop and lift it out of the craters. More than once they have to reposition the body bag to prevent it from slipping to the ground.

Up ahead Jihai sees the intense whiteness of searchlights and the shadowy outline of meshed gates, coiled barbed wire, watchtowers, and guards.

"Nearly there," says Shin with a sense of relief. "We're nearly there."

133

Miami

*F*lorida's morning sky is a delicate swirl of soft pinks and pale blues.

Clint Molton can't imagine a more peaceful view in the world than the one he is enjoying from Air Force One.

But all that is about to change.

He takes a final look out of the window as the plane straightens up and noses its way toward Washington. The secure phone is in his hand, and in a second it will connect him to his nemesis, the leader of the People's Republic of China, the man who is dragging him and his country to the brink of ruin—or the first shots of war.

Better that than occupation, he thinks. Giving in to Xian's economic demands would be no different than having twenty-five percent of Congress run by the Chinese.

If it wasn't for the thought of casualties—millions of casualties—he'd already be fueling up the warplanes and sighting the missiles.

And it may still come to that.

Seeing the dead and dying last night in Miami shifted Molton's mood. He got to thinking that it would be better for his country to fight and die than acquiesce and live under such a regime. For in his mind there is no doubt that Xian's demands are just the beginning. If he wins, then he'll be back for more, much more.

The operator on the line announces, "You're through to President Xian."

Molton takes a deep breath. "Mr. President, I believe you called my office last night. I'm sorry I wasn't available. I was visiting parents who had seen their children savagely injured or murdered, and I was visiting the morgues where lines of broken-hearted citizens lined up to identify the remains of their loved ones."

Xian is unmoved. "Death is a sight no one should see. Your job and mine is to protect life, to prolong it and to enrich it. We are fast approaching a crossroads, Mr. President, and I fear unless you and I talk more closely we may both lose our ways."

"Sir, I don't have time for cryptic conversations. Nor am I in the mood to be given final ultimatums or watch my countrymen continue to be the victims of cowardly attacks—"

Xian interrupts him. "Then I will speak plainly. Unless you and I arrange to meet in person, I will be unable to stop the military momentum that is being built. So far, only my influence has managed to restrict operational activity to Florida. Do you not think such devastation could also have been inflicted on New York or Washington? Florida was chosen because you could seal it off. Contain it and contain the curiosity of your people and your press. Now the containment is almost over, and when it ends, so too will my influence on what follows."

Molton reads between the lines. China has always been locked in a deadly balance of political power and military might. If Xian's star was falling, then General Zhang's was rising, and that thought was about as unpalatable as could be. "I will need to talk to some members of my cabinet and executive office, but what do you suggest?"

Xian senses the softening and tries not to show his relief. "The APEC conference is about to begin in Hawaii. Issues will arise and I will join it for the latter stage. It will seem appropriate for you to also fly there."

"What issues?"

"In the greater scheme of things, they will be of no real concern. Will you join me?"

Molton feels he has little choice. "And if I say yes, will your influence be strong enough to prevent any more deaths?"

"Not presently. What is in play cannot be stopped. Not until we have met."

Xian's words trouble Molton. He wants to say no. Wants to tell him to go to hell. In fact, he wants to bring hell to him, bring it in the form of air strikes all over his military bases, barracks, and weapon stocks.

But he knows he can't.

"I'll join you."

"Be there the day after tomorrow. We'll meet in the afternoon. There may even be cause for us to dine together."

Molton is not sure he could stomach that. He puts down the phone and stares at the sky pressed to the window. The outlook is no longer so bright.

Clouds are gathering over South Carolina. The plane hits a patch of turbulence and the seat belt light comes on, along with the pilot's voice. "Bad weather ahead, Mr. President. I'm afraid we're in for a bumpy ride, sir."

134

DMZ, North Korea

*R*ain beats like ball bearings on the corrugated iron roof of the Watch Tower.

Two soldiers climb down the steep ladder and come to the locked gates topped with coils of barbed wire.

Rifles are trained on Shin and Jihai, and through the wind comes the clear instruction, "Hands up! Put your hands in the air and step forward."

The two men leave the braked gurney in the middle of the approach road and advance toward the soldiers.

Jihai sees bewilderment on the face of the first guard. He's rightly suspicious of anyone moving around outside in weather like this. The black body bag could easily be packed with explosives.

Shin is keen to do the talking, and Jihai is more than happy to let him. "I come from the hospital," he explains. "We called in advance. The body back there is of a scientist that has to go to the Joint Security Area for collection by the Americans." He turns his head toward Jihai. "Where are your colleague's parents flying in from?"

"New York," answers Jihai. "New York State."

The guard is still suspicious. "Papers."

One hand in the air, Shin slowly removes Péng's medical papers, including his ID card and certificate of death, from the pocket of his greatcoat.

The guard inspects them all. Rain pours over his round, steel helmet and spills onto the documents. He shakes them and pushes them into his own pocket. "Now show me your identification."

Shin dips into an inside pocket.

"Slowly!" The guard's eyes grow large.

The nurse carefully hands over the photo ID.

The guard holds it next to Shin to check the likeness. When he's satisfied, he pockets it. "Now him."

Jihai feels his stomach growl and his heart cramp as the guard approaches.

The soldier sticks out a gloved hand. "Papers."

He unbuttons the greatcoat and pulls a chain from around his neck containing his plastic ID photo card.

"Chinese?" The guard looks confused.

Shin tries to help. "They do research. In the bunkers."

"What research?" The guard addresses the question to Jihai.

"It is confidential, between your government and mine. I am not cleared to discuss it with you."

A gust of wind tears across the open fields and pushes everyone sideward.

The gurney topples.

Péng's body bag hits the soaked ground and splatters mud and water upward into the white light of the search beams.

The guard shoves Jihai's ID into his pocket with the other documents, steps to one side and points his rifle at the Chinaman. "Go and unzip that bag."

Jihai turns and is blown again by another gust. He staggers like a drunk toward the corpse of his friend, rain now soaking every inch of him.

He kneels on the sodden blacktop and pulls the zipper down.

"Further," shouts the guard. "All the way down."

He does as instructed.

The soldier walks a long arc, his gun now trained on Péng's lifeless torso, while other guards fix their sights on the two visitors to the gate.

The guard has seen enough death to recognize when it is real or not. "How did he die?"

"Virus," shouts Jihai. "Some highly virulent unknown virus. We don't think it is contagious."

The guard forgets about carrying out a closer inspection. "Get him back on the wheels and bring him through. I will check on your papers and your clearance."

Jihai takes a risk. "We are in a hurry. We need to proceed immediately."

The guard's big eyes stare into him. "There is no immediately. I need to check before you go on."

135

Situation Room, The White House, Washington DC

*N*IA director Brandon Jackson stands at the back of the Situation Room. Senior intel analyst Rhona O'Brien is at his side. The forty-year-old redhead has worked with him for almost a decade on some of the Agency's biggest operations. They're watching live feeds of the latest attacks at Bristol, dogs still arriving from the Apalachicola Forest.

The town's tiny population is under siege.

Shopkeepers lie dead in their doorways.

Homeowners' remains are spread across their lawns.

A look across the monitors shows that the situation is as bad in Sanderson and Kingsland, Palatka and Ocala, Eustis and Pine Hills.

There are more than thirty new deaths and at least that number again in casualties.

"The Joint Chiefs were right," says Jackson. "Those murdering sons of bitches are not done out in the sticks. Cornwell made a good call in not pressing for a switch to the cities."

"It's what he gets the big bucks for. Making the good calls." O'Brien scratches a hand through long coils of her unruly hair. "What I hate about all this is that we can never be ahead of the game. You can't see the enemy until it's too late. Do you know what I mean?"

"I do. One dog looks as friendly as the other—until it turns."

"Exactly. And that means the rapid response teams are always going to look less than rapid. No one can get called until someone gets bit."

They both fall silent and watch the screens. Over in Bristol, activity is now little more than a clean-up operation. Guards and local police are working together to get people off the small streets and into the safety of homes or buildings. "Wet" crews are scraping human remains off the blacktop. Covering corpses. Taping off areas. Shifting dog carcasses. Doing their best to restore an illusion of normality.

Jackson's tired, but his mind is still racing with facts and figures, guesses, second guesses, and fears. He points at the monitor. "That town has a population of what, eight, nine hundred people?"

"Maybe a thousand." O'Brien finishes her zillionth cup of coffee and drops the plastic in the bin.

"So, let's do the math. Four people per household, that's two hundred and fifty homes. On average, one in four homes has a dog, that's seventy-five dogs—max—in the whole town." He bites at a thumbnail while he thinks. "I saw forty, maybe fifty dogs get shot there. I'm sure I did."

"Your point?"

"Too many dogs. I bet there are still sixty dogs alive in Bristol. We saw at least twenty or thirty being controlled or shifted by the National Guard or their owners. I bet the weaponized animals were strays, somehow guided there and forced to attack the town."

She raises an eyebrow. "I'll get autopsies on some of the dogs. But how the hell can a dog be controlled like that? I can't even get my pooch to piss where I want it to."

Almost on cue a monitor changes shots. The image is gray and out of focus, but there's no mistaking what it is.

A pack.

Jackson and O'Brien walk down the room to take a closer look.

"Where is this?" She taps the screen and addresses one of the young analysts sitting at a curve of tracking desks.

"It's Old Town, in northern Florida, I've just flagged it as a potential incident. Alerts have gone out to the police, sheriff, and the National Guard."

"Well done," says O'Brien. "Let's hope they get there in time."

They both know it's unlikely they will.

"I've also called emergency service in Gainesville," the analyst says. "We need to get copters in to airlift any survivors to their hospitals."

Any survivors.

The two veterans know the kid used the right words.

On screen, dozens of people in Old Town are gathering in a field and erecting tents for some kind of fete. Kids are fooling around, chasing each other, throwing balls and having a good time.

No one has a clue what's heading their way.

Packs of dogs.

Dozens of strays.

Coming in from all corners of the compass.

The analyst punches up different pictures on his screens and digitally refocuses the images.

Jackson watches helplessly as a group of five kids, no older than ten, stand playing twenty yards from oncoming dogs.

"Come on, move!" he shouts, as though he has supernatural powers and can be heard through the glass. "Come on—get the hell out of there!"

A young girl turns her head and one of the ribbons her mother tied comes loose.

Too late.

The pack is on them.

The children are knocked down by more than a dozen dogs.

There's no sound coming from the monitor screens, so Jackson can't hear the screams, but he knows they are there. Knows from his own kids' howls just what they will sound like. Imagines they are being heard clean across the fete site, because by the look of things every adult he can see is freaking out and rushing toward the danger.

More dogs are joining the fray.

They're pounding toward the spill of blood and rip of flesh. Drawn by the scent of violence.

Jackson sees adults writhing on the ground. Men on their backs with dogs on their chests. An old woman is facedown in the dirt. A lurcher has her spread-eagled and is chewing at her legs and back.

The NIA director has seen bad shit in his time, and counts this right up there with napalm victims drowning in seas of orange fire and dismembered babies being found in the aftermath of missile attacks.

He looks across the room, and there are half a dozen monitors all telling similar stories. All showing their own horrific silent movies.

136

Beijing

Ten thousand miles from Don Jackson's spy screens in Washington, General Zhang, Lieutenant General Xue Shi, and Minister Chunlin are watching the same footage.

Zhang and Chunlin are standing behind Xue Shi at his desk, viewing the massacre at Old Town over his shoulder.

Dozens of bodies lie across the field. Men. Women. Children. The weaponized strays are killing everything in their path.

"It goes well." Zhang claps a soldierly hand on his loyal number two's shoulder. "Today's increased activities—here and elsewhere—will break the Americans."

A portly old grandfather with white hair and beard is backed into a fenced corner of the field with a young boy and girl clinging to his legs. They're facing a pack of seven snapping dogs and he's holding them off with a handgun, an old revolver drawn.

He misses with one shot and kills a boxer with a second.

Xue Shi smiles. "Four bullets left and six dogs on him—the odds are not good."

Chunlin can't help but say what's on his mind. "Now is past the point we should have been able to pacify the dogs."

The old man shoots a black mongrel.

Zhang looks at him with contempt. "Please, Minister, don't lecture me on morality. Not you of all people."

Chunlin points at the screen as the old man kills another dog. "I would never countenance this. I have never targeted a civilian in my life. Operatives, agents, soldiers—yes. Old men with children. Never."

"Be quiet and watch. Or be more useful and leave."

A Labrador leaps up on the boy's back. His grandfather jabs his old gun forward and shoots it in the head at point-blank range.

The spray of blood and bone doesn't seem to even be noticed by the remains of the pack.

"He is bold for an old man," observes Xue Shi. "Maybe he was once a soldier. But now I think he has only one bullet—and three dogs."

The grandfather fires the last of his bullets and kills a sandy-colored mongrel. He quickly stoops, gathers the children tight to his chest and turns his back on the two remaining dogs.

Zhang, Xue Shi, and Chunlin watch the silent footage and wait for the inevitable to happen.

But it doesn't.

One of the dogs inexplicably falls on his side.

The head of the second spurts blood.

Into the frame come two local sheriffs. Guns extended. Determination etched across their faces.

They climb the fence and one of them touches the hunched-up man.

He shudders with fright.

At first he thinks it's a dog. Braces himself for the pain.

But it doesn't come.

Slowly, he turns and straightens up. He sees the cops, and a smile as long as the Mississippi breaks out across his face.

Chunlin walks away from the monitor desk. "A great general once said that those who look most beaten often end up the greatest victors." He opens the door. "We would all do well to remember it."

137

DMZ, North Korea

Jihai and Shin have been left standing with the gurney at the gates.

Two guards have AKM assault rifles aimed at their chests.

Fifteen feet above them, rain still hammers on the iron roof of the open-windowed watchtower.

Silhouettes of soldiers stand out against the searchlights and starless night sky.

Jihai recognizes one of the men who spoke to them.

He has a phone pressed to his ear. In his other hand is all their documents.

Finally, he puts the receiver down, exits the box, and quickly descends the ladder to the gate.

"The lines are down," he explains. "You will have to wait."

"I cannot wait." Jihai blurts the words out. "My colleague has to be buried by nightfall. His religion demands it." He looks at the two stars on the soldier's olive green uniform. Despite the man's presence and confidence, he is only a junior officer, a *jungwi*. "If you do not let me through there will be a diplomatic incident. One involving your country, the Americans, and mine. Do you want that?"

A twitch in the lieutenant's left eye shows a sign of weakness.

"I wish now to speak to your senior officer."

The guard's tone softens. "I am the most senior officer here. Wait until we have communications back and I will talk to my captain."

Jihai looks beyond him. The gates are open. Through them, in the distance, he can see the flicker of lights.

He walks away and slips the brake off the gurney. He grips the end rails and pushes.

"Stop!" says the guard.

Jihai pauses. "You will have to shoot me. Shoot an unarmed Chinese scientist pushing the body of his dead colleague. I hope you can explain that." Jihai dips his head and pushes.

A second later the soldier shouts again. "Stop or I will shoot."

This time Jihai doesn't hesitate. He pushes hard and doesn't look back.

138

Breezy Point, New York

*J*ackpot's reappearance has kept Danny up all night.

Something has changed.

It's not as elusive as before, not as Teflon-coated, and he's been able to download endless hours of partial code. But he still can't track down the IP addresses of the sending or receiving terminals. It's like looking at a long length of digital rope without seeing who holds either end. Page after page of blue, green, and white alphanumeric instructions and reports scroll up before him, flashing their secrets but giving nothing away.

Every now and again he thinks he's close. Thinks he's picked up jump instructions, a different form of assembly language, or a vaguely familiar source code that's been adapted.

Then he gets knocked back.

But this fish isn't getting away.

Not this time.

He's spent all night matching fragments of foreign machine code with "parodies" that he's devised in the hope that the master computer might get fooled into contacting him directly.

He stands up and steps back from the action. Two out of five computers are still catching data bursts and trying to interpret them, but none are exposing the parties at either end, and none of the decoding packages are quite working. But they've not been defeated, they're still plugging away.

He takes a bathroom break and almost falls asleep on the can. Before coming back, he washes his face as well as his hands and tries to get some life back into his aching brain. He heads back to the screens and stretches tension out of his neck and shoulders before sitting back down.

Two blank screens light up with a burst of white letters, numbers, backslashes, front slashes, and all manner of symbols. At first it looks like the screens are twin feeds.

But they're not.

He realizes it now.

The one on the left is running original machine code. The one on the right is a byte code created by the interpretation software he'd been relentlessly running.

It's happening.

Danny's heart pounds. He takes his hands off the computer desk, anxious that nothing accidental stops it.

It's finally happening; the software he created is simultaneously translating the original Jackpot stream into code he can understand.

IP addresses appear. Instructions. Commands. Executions. Locations.

It's like being let out of the black hole of solitary confinement into blinding sunshine.

Danny is suddenly awake. Never have his brain cells felt more awake.

On a parallel machine he throws every hacking code he knows at Jackpot, and slowly but surely the sonovabitch starts letting him in. It spreads its legs and gives him its all—the main source computer, passwords, files, recycle bins, video folders, documents, photographs, and every other piece of cyber treasure it's ever created.

Danny's eyes stay fixed on all five fast-downloading screens as he powers up the new burner Stevens gave him.

There's a click.

Danny doesn't even wait for the hello. "I've got it. The code has opened up."

Stevens comes alive. "Derig and prepare to leave the house. I'll have a moving crew with you in ten minutes. We're going to bring you in before anyone gets to you."

139

Police HQ, Miami

*G*host stays at the hospital until dawn; until he finds a new shift of medics to grill about Zoe's condition and what might be done for her. He leaves in a mood of despondency, goes home to shower and change before heading into work.

Last night he'd walked out of his captain's office without his badge and gun, and now he feels awkward going back, even though it is following a special request from the President to serve the country.

He pats his pockets as he enters the building and calls to the old-timer on reception, "Forget my swipe card, Al. Be a buddy and buzz me through."

"Sure, no problem, Lieutenant." Al's crinkled old face smiles and he hits the button.

"Thanks." Ghost waits for the buzz then passes through the security doors. He'd shaken Molton's hand last night and agreed to help run the task force to combat the dog attacks. But now as he rides the elevator to his office, he's still wondering why the President and the NIA had been interested in the attacks right at the beginning, back when young Kathy Morgan was killed on the beach at Key Biscayne.

Something is being kept from him.

From him and the country at large.

The thought is still troubling him as he heads down to Lost Property, where he eventually finds a charger that fits Zoe's phone.

Back in the Incident Room, he plugs it in, and once the unit powers up he scrolls through the contacts. There's only one Danny listed, and though it's just 7:45 A.M., he dials the number.

The phone on the other end rings, then trips the answering machine message: *"This is Danny, I'm busy doing other stuff, leave your details after the beep."*

"Hi, this is Lieutenant Walton of the Miami police. I need to talk to you urgently about your sister Zoe. Call me back at this number."

Ghost hangs up and searches the rest of the phone's names and numbers. There's only one Jude listed in Zoe's directory, but it has two numbers—a Miami landline and the cell—so he's fairly sure this is the friend she's been staying with.

Again he gets palmed off with an answering message.

"Hi, this is Jude Cunningham. I'm really sorry I'm not around to take your call. Please leave me your details and I'll get back to you just as soon as I pick this up. Thanks for calling."

He leaves the same message as he gave Danny, hangs up and surveys the wreckage of his desk. Part of the reason he came in early was to clear things before he dives into his new set of responsibilities. There are skyscrapers of brown internal mail envelopes, and around them a multicolored settlement of Post-it notes left by various team members, secretaries, and other departments.

He's only begun to scratch the surface of the paperwork when Annie turns up. She greets him as she slips her car keys in her purse. "'Morning, how is your friend?"

He looks up from the desk mess. "Not good. She's still unconscious."

"I'm sorry to hear that." She can see he doesn't want to talk about it. "You want me to get you some coffee or water?"

"No thanks. Can you ask Sandra Teale to come in? I want to quiz her more on the pathology reports."

"Sure. I'll call her right away."

"Hang on, don't rush off." He reaches into his jacket and pulls out Zoe's pocketbook plus some scrap paper that he's scribbled notes on. "And get in touch with this animal shelter. Zoe went there yesterday. I want to find out who she spoke to and what was said."

She takes the book. "Can I ask why?"

"It seems she was following up some kind of link between the shelter and the breeders who sold the Gerbers the dog that killed them."

Annie looks surprised. "Should she have been doing that?"

He ignores the question. "I want to know what that link is and what sent her from the shelter to the home of a man named Li Chen and from there to Bicentennial Park." His thoughts wander for a moment. "It's as though she had an inclination that something bad was going to happen."

"Maybe she did," says Annie. "Anyway, I'll find out." She lifts the pocketbook as a goodbye gesture and drifts off to make the calls.

Ghost sits in silence. He doesn't like that he's given away the pocketbook. It makes him feel like he's lost a link to Zoe. He distracts himself by opening up computer access to the Police Records System and searching for Li Chen.

He finds nothing.

Not that he expected to get lucky on his first shot. No matter.

He's got plenty of other searches to perform: immigration, work permits, health insurance, tax, credit ratings, and a million other ways the government has of snooping on the average man.

140

DMZ, Korea

*T*he shot doesn't come.

Jihai counts the seconds.

Thirty.

Thirty-one.

Thirty-two.

He tells himself that if it hasn't come by now it isn't going to come at all.

His spirits rise. He's going to make it.

He's in the DMZ and they won't fire at him here. They wouldn't dare.

Through the howling wind and swirling rain, the lights of distant buildings grow brighter. This is where Shin said the main buildings were. The Peace House. The Bridge of No Return, where prisoners and spies were exchanged. The Conciliation Pavilion, where both sides still meet to discuss DMZ issues. Now it's just a matter of struggling on.

Getting there and defecting.

Telling the world what has been going on.

The front left wheel of the gurney plummets into another pothole.

Jihai is tired and barely has the strength to lift it out. He's soaked to the skin and the greatcoat is now more a liability than a help. It weighs as much as the gurney and is dragging him down.

He unfastens it and lays it across the middle of the body bag.

The plastic in front of his hand splits open.

At first Jihai doesn't understand.

Then when another split appears he does.

He's being fired at.

The wind is so deafening he hasn't heard the crack of a rifle, but the two holes in the body bag couldn't have been caused by anything else.

He runs.

He abandons his lifelong friend and runs toward the lights, weaving as much as he can, hoping that the zigzagging will make it impossible for a sniper to hit him.

It doesn't.

A bullet burns the tip of his right hand. It feels like it's been hit with an axe.

Adrenaline kicks in and Jihai keeps running.

His lungs are bursting. He's barely able to breathe. The lights are coming up fast now. No longer blurred and shapeless. He sees vertical and horizontal rectangles.

Windows.

His right leg buckles.

Only as he hits the ground does he realize he's been shot in the back of the knee. A soldier with a sniper rifle and night sight is trying to pick him off.

The lights are so close.

He tries to rise, but his leg won't take it.

He falls.

A bullet rips up a chunk of road and spatters his face.

Jihai rolls away from it.

Rolling is all he can do.

He pushes down with his right hand to turn himself and sees the ends of his middle fingers are missing.

There's no time for fear. No time for pain or self-pity. He pushes the stumps against the hard road and completes the turn.

Then he rolls again.

Rolls toward where he saw the lights.

Rolls toward freedom.

141

DMZ, Korea

*J*ihai hears voices as he bumps hard into something huge and solid.

A bullet tears apart a piece of wood above his head.

He's reached a building.

He puts his shattered hands to the board and lifts himself.

His knee shakes but he gets his balance.

Bloody fingers feel out the edge of the building.

He claws his way around it.

There are lights on either side of him. Dawn is breaking beyond the ridges of the huts that flank him.

He's face-to-face with soldiers.

Soldiers from both sides.

He looks toward the blue uniforms of the South Koreans and stretches out his arms. "Help me. Please help me. I'm Chinese and I—"

He never finishes.

The sniper's bullet roars through his back and bursts his heart.

The words stick in the young scientist's mouth, then he falls limply face first to the ground.

142

The White House, Washington DC

Clint Molton is on his way to the West Wing when he sees the ashen face of Vice President Cornwell appear in the corridor. "What is it, Pat? More dog attacks? Is that the welcome home you have for me?"

"That—and worse."

"Worse?"

"A Taliban bombing at Camp Leatherneck."

Molton goes into shock. "Damnation. How many hurt?"

"More than thirty Marines dead. I don't know how many injured. The reports are still coming in."

"Dear God. I thought this part of the world had quieted down and all we really had to worry about was the Middle East."

"It seems not." He jabs a thumb toward the door. "I was just on my way to the Briefing Room when I saw you were back."

"I'll come with you." Molton turns on his heels. "I spoke to Xian on the flight over."

"Not good news?"

"He wants to talk. I'm going to fly to the APEC conference to meet with him."

"Of course he wants to talk. Talk and up the ante."

"I don't know. I got the feeling he was being squeezed by Zhang. And not in a loving way."

"The only love that Zhang knows is war. His dogs have been

giving us hell in the last few hours. Attacks all across Florida, villages are being wiped out."

"What about the National Guard and the police?"

"Still getting their acts together. Quick to respond, slow to anticipate."

"We have to turn that around."

"I know."

They arrive at the Briefing Room. Secretary of Defense Leo Cagnetti is hunched over a secure phone finishing a call to Major General Jon Sherman, the force commander in Helmand and Nimruz.

Molton takes a seat across a small conference table. "What's the latest, Leo?"

"Thirty-nine fatalities now, sir. Six more Marines critical but stable, and around twenty more being treated for blast injuries."

"Pat, make sure we convey my condolences to their families. I will write personal notes as soon as I have all their details." He turns back to the Defense secretary. "Sorry, Leo, please continue."

"Sir, it seems we're able to treat most of the casualties on site, but some are going to have to go over to Dwyer—"

Cornwell interrupts. "Dwyer? Why not the field hospital at Bastion, it's right next door."

"The explosion took out part of Bastion, sir, damaged the section of the runway over there and they're still sweeping for secondary devices."

"Any British casualties?"

"Afraid so, sir. Four injured at Bastion and two killed inside Leatherneck. The UK's Deputy Prime Minister David Pearson was there at the time but is unhurt."

Cornwell shakes his head and shows his rage. "None of this would have happened if they'd stayed away. They knew we were at a tense point in the pull-out strategy but had to go chasing photo-opportunities because it's their damned election year."

Molton turns to his VP. "Enough. Let's talk about this afterward." He focuses on Cagnetti again. "How can I help, Leo? Have your people got everything they need out there to do their jobs properly?"

"Thank you, I believe so, sir."

"Come to me if you think I can open doors, twist arms, or speed anything up. Is there any news yet of how the Taliban bomb got through security checks?"

"We think it was plastic explosives built into the frames of a new rank of portable toilets, sir."

The President huffs out a long sigh. Taliban ingenuity and determination never ceases to amaze him. "They've come a frighteningly long way from legacy bombs and IEDs. I need the fullest details you can give me, so I can go over it with my press secretary and prepare an address to the American people."

"Yes, sir."

Molton gets to his feet. "Thanks, Leo, keep me apprised."

"I will, sir. Thank you."

The President heads out, followed by Cornwell.

"I'll talk to Prime Minister Hatfield, Pat. You need to get yourself over there, both as a mark of respect for our dead and for the British."

"What?"

Molton stops in his tracks. "We need Britain close. Especially with this damned dog problem. We need every ally we have. So just do it, Pat. Don't give me shit, just do it."

143

Police HQ, Miami

*W*ithin the half hour, Annie reappears at Ghost's desk. "Bella is just showing Mrs. Clabbers—Monique Clabbers—to an interview room—"

"Who is she?" he asks, studying yet another set of records that doesn't correspond to Li Chen.

"She's the manager of the animal shelter Zoe visited. Fortunately, she was coming downtown when I caught her on her cell."

Ghost pulls his nose off the tiny data print on the screen and tries to focus. "Okay that's good. Did she say what went on with Zoe?"

"No, the car line was too bad."

"And the vet?"

"Sandra Teale said she'd try to get in to see you within the hour."

"Thanks." Ghost stands up, "Where's Mrs. Clabbers?"

"Interview Three."

He nods and heads for the corridor.

Annie walks with him, Zoe's pocketbook in her hand. "Are there photographs to go with these notes you gave me?" she asks.

"Yeah. I'm sorry. I've uploaded them from Zoe's camera, you'll find them on my computer."

"Which file?"

"Just all over the desktop."

"Neat," she says sarcastically as she leaves him and goes back to his office.

Interview Three is situated just past the overnight detention block. The air down there has been turned fetid by the overnight intake of drunks, druggies, and the homeless. He opens the door to the room and sees Bella Lansing drinking coffee with a gray-haired woman in a black pantsuit who he guesses is the local manager of the county's animal shelter.

"Mrs. Clabbers, I'm Lieutenant Walton." He stretches out a hand.

"Lieutenant." She rises a little from her seat, shakes it timidly and sits back down.

He can see she looks stressed. "Are you okay?"

Bella answers for her. "Mrs. Clabbers is a little nervous."

"No need to be." Ghost settles in a chair opposite the manager.

"I've never been in a police station before. They are—well— rather intimidating."

Ghost smiles reassuringly. Normally he'd spend more time putting her at ease, but today time is in short supply. "Mrs. Clabbers, a woman named Zoe Speed came to see you yesterday. What did she want?"

"She used your name, actually. Gave me your number, and I called, but you were busy—"

"You're not in trouble, Mrs. Clabbers, I just need to know everything that was said between you and Miss Speed."

"Right. Well, she was asking questions about Mr. Chen—"

"Who is?"

"He's an assistant at the center. His full name is Li Chen." She opens the purse on her lap. "I wrote down all his particulars for you—his name, address, phone numbers." She hands over a slip of paper.

"Thank you." Ghost takes it and holds it between them. "Why did you do that? How did you know I'd be so interested in Mr. Chen?"

She colors and shifts in her seat. "Well, Miss Speed said he had sold some wirehaired pointer pups to the breeders who'd supplied those ladies who died the other night."

"Astrid and Heidi Gerber?"

"Yes, I think so."

"And had he?"

"I don't know. Not as far as I know. Though Miss Speed was insistent he had. She said she'd spoken to the breeders and they'd named Li out of the blue."

"And that made you think it was possible?"

"Perhaps."

Ghost could tell that Monique Clabbers was beginning to have doubts about the man. "How long have you known Mr. Chen?"

"About eighteen months." She corrects herself, "No, it's longer, must be more like two years now. Li and his wife turned up one day and we thought they were looking to *take* a dog, you know, give it a home. But actually they were volunteering to help."

"Both of them?"

"Yes, Mingyu is a businesswoman. Very bright. She makes financial contributions to our center but doesn't do any physical work. Li does, though. He's very hardworking. He's not in trouble, is he?"

"We just want to talk to him."

Bella interrupts. "Sorry, how do you spell his wife's name?"

"M-I-N-G-Y-U."

"Thanks."

Ghost continues his questioning, "To be clear, before Li Chen turned up at the center, you didn't know him at all? There were no personal recommendations or references?"

"No."

"Did you subsequently do any checks on him?"

She looks embarrassed. "Well, no—there was really no need—I mean, we haven't been paying him—he's not on our books—he's just a volunteer." A thought hit her, "Is he—you know—" She lowers her voice. "—an illegal?"

"At the moment there's no suggestion Mr. Chen has done anything wrong." Ghost doesn't mention that so far he's failed to find any records that even confirm Li Chen exists, let alone is a candidate for deportation. "Is he at work today or should I try him on these numbers you've given me?"

She shifts awkwardly in her seat. "He's not been at the center for a couple of weeks now. Said he was taking a break, but hasn't called since he was due back."

"Which was when?"

"About a week ago."

"And is that unusual?"

"Yes. Especially with Li. He's always so punctual. You can set your clock by him."

"Did he say where he was going on vacation?"

She strains to remember. "No, I don't think so. Or else I've forgotten. I'm afraid I forget a lot more these days than I used to."

Ghost reran things in his head. What the woman had just said to him. Notes he'd read in Zoe's pocketbook. His own half-formed theories on this line of inquiry. "Let me share some of our thoughts and worries with you, Mrs. Clabbers, and see if you can help us get a better idea of what is going on."

She sits up attentively.

"Zoe Speed, the young lady who came to see you, went to the Chens' home after being at your center."

"I know that, I gave her Li's address."

"Well, Miss Speed is now in intensive care after being savaged by dogs at the Bicentennial Park incident yesterday."

Clabbers clasps a hand to her mouth.

"That means there are two close connections between fatal and near fatal dog attack victims, your shelter and this man Li Chen."

Clabbers sinks back in her chair.

Bella reaches across and touches her arm reassuringly.

"I need you to tell me everything, absolutely everything that Chen and his wife have done for your shelter. Every contact they may have had with dogs, customers, breeders, suppliers. Anything and everything, no matter how inconsequential you think it is."

144

The Oval Office, The White House, Washington DC

*M*olton had thought that his day couldn't get worse.

It just has.

He knows it, just from the look on Don Jackson's face. "What is it, Don?"

Jackson takes a seat at the edge of the President's desk and puts down the briefing papers he's been given by his own watch team. "We're getting reports of an incident in the DMZ." He's unshaven, without a tie, and sounds exhausted. "A defector from the North was shot dead right on the demarcation line. Now the South have his body and won't give it back."

"Any exchange of fire between North and South?"

"Not that I know of, sir. They did find another body out in the DMZ but it had been dead for some time. In fact it was bagged and tagged."

"Excuse me?

Jackson explains. "It looks like the first man pushed the body across the zone on a gurney and got shot in the process. We're digging for intel as we speak."

"Was the shooter in the DMZ? The South Koreans are going to go crazy if he was."

"We think so. The bullet was a 7.92 Mauser that apparently comes from a Zastava sniper rifle, standard issue to the KPA marksmen. It would be accurate up to about a thousand yards, less in strong winds, and last night it was blowing a typhoon. The dead man was way beyond that kind of range when he was cut down."

"The implications of all this?"

"Well, as the Koreans never actually ended their war, the ceasefire of '53 can disappear in a blink and the two of them can go at each others' throats. Just like they did back in '69 when skirmishes essentially led to an unofficial war that essentially lasted three years and saw hundreds killed, wounded, and captured. Last known shooting incident was a couple of years back when the KPA fired on a South Korean post over at Hwacheon; no one was killed, though." Jackson slides across the papers that he'd brought with him. "These are briefing notes for when Kim Jong-un calls you, as I'm sure he will."

"You can bet a night's sleep on it."

"I'd bet my house before I'd bet any decent sleep."

Molton looks at his watch. "I've got a live press conference coming up on the Taliban bombing. Can I be sure the press won't ask me about the DMZ?"

Jackson nods. "The hacks are good but not that good. This information won't be on the streets for days. With any luck, never."

"They say bad things come in threes." Molton holds up his fingers, "Dogs, Taliban, and DMZ. Hopefully that's the lot."

145

Police HQ, Miami

*U*rgent calls drag Ghost away from the interrogation of Monique Clabbers. To his pleasant surprise, Antonio Vasquez, his new right-hand man on the presidential task force, seems smart, efficient, and focused. No sooner has he hung up than there's a call from Cummings's office for him to "swing by when he has the chance." It's an offer he won't be rushing to take up.

He's just about to take another stab at finding Li Chen through dental or medical records when Bella appears at his door. "Come in."

She settles quickly. "Clabbers said something interesting."

"Go on."

"This guy Chen carried out lots of jobs for her, including microchipping the dogs, you know, injecting those little data chips that show the dog name, owner, address, basic info on shots it's had, etcetera."

"Yeah, I know what you mean, but so what?"

"That was my reaction as well. It turns out Chen told Clabbers he and his wife had friends who manufactured the chips and he could get them much cheaper than she was paying through her regular supplier."

Ghost didn't quite see the significance. "But we're talking *data* here. As far as I know, dodgy data chips wouldn't infect a dog and drive it rabid or crazy."

"I know. Clabbers said the same thing. Anyway, she's got a big bag of the chips at the shelter, so I've asked for them to be sent here, so we can at least look at them."

Ghost thinks about the chips. It's an unknown quantity, and in his experience the unknown often held the answer to cases he's been on. "It would be interesting if those chips match ones found in our killer dogs. That really would be a coincidence worth digging into."

"Well, here's a thing . . ." Bella flips over her pocketbook. "Mingyu—Li Chen's wife—didn't just give sizable funds to this shelter. According to Clabbers, she was a leading supporter of at least half a dozen other shelters spread across Florida and beyond."

Ghost feels his heart bump. "So Chen's dodgy chips—if they are that—could also have been sent to those shelters as well."

146

East Room, The White House, Washington DC

*T*he world's press corps has turned up for the live presidential broadcast.

Molton speaks for close to five minutes, running the gamut of tones and messages. As he heads to his conclusion, the emphasis is on firmness and revenge.

"Vice President Cornwell is at this moment flying to Afghanistan. Though Camp Leatherneck is seven thousand miles from our borders, we hold the men and women who serve there near to our hearts and we are deeply saddened by today's tragedy. My sympathies and those of the American people will be conveyed by Vice President Cornwell, and he will reemphasize to the Afghan government that America's plans for troop withdrawal, our intention for the Afghan people to police their own peace, and the world's determination for this sovereign state to write a new page of history will not be destroyed."

Jay Ashton steps forward and promises journalists five minutes of Q&A. A forest of hands goes up and he points to a friendly reporter. "Go ahead, Rod."

The reporter follows protocol and introduces himself. "Rod Taylor, *New York Times*. Mr. President, can you tell us more about the size and nature of the bomb, and how it was smuggled into the camp?"

"To some degree, I can," says Molton. "Without getting too technical, we understand it was an advanced form of C4, with the type of enhanced velocity usually found in PE4. Some of you may know this is a flexible plastic explosive that can be molded into all shapes and is therefore very easy to conceal. I can't at the moment tell you *how* the C4 was detonated. When a full forensic examination has been completed I hope to give you more information."

"John Bonham, *Washington Post*. Mr. President, we conducted a flash poll of our readers today, and 80 percent of them want our troops to come home now. No delays. No waiting. How do you respond to that?"

"I agree with them. I want our troops to come home now. And I want the British troops to come home now. And more than anyone, the Taliban wants our troops to come home now. Panic withdrawal is not the answer to oppression and tyranny. It is a long-term betrayal of the Afghan people. It is a betrayal of more than a hundred thousand troops who've fought there in the name of freedom and human rights. And most of all, it is a betrayal of every single man and woman who has been wounded or laid down their lives trying to create a freer, fairer future for the Afghan people."

"Mr. President, Victoria Ashbourne, CNN. Aside from the human cost, in terms of fatalities and injuries, our experts say Operation Enduring Freedom will cost in excess of three trillion dollars by the time we've withdrawn from Afghanistan. Will it have been worth it?"

"What price do your experts put on freedom?"

The reporter is stumped.

"I suspect they don't have an answer either. The citizens of the United States have no time for fancy-mouthed financiers who think a calculator is an instrument to make a moral decision. Freedom is priceless."

Ashton scans the sea of hands. "One more question and then we have to wrap things up." He points to a woman in the front row. "Jane Dockery, Reuters. Mr. President, what's your message to the families of the American and British troops who died and were injured today?"

Molton takes a beat. "Your sons and daughters are heroes in the truest sense of the word. They have given their lives for the most honorable and selfless of all causes—the basic human rights of a perfect stranger, someone they'd never even met, to live without fear. They gave their lives so future generations can live—can live and prosper in a far better world. I am proud to be the President of those American heroes, and I know the British Prime Minister will feel the same way about the brave British troops who were injured and killed. And to those who took their lives, to the cowards of the Taliban and their accomplices, I make you this promise. We will find you. No matter how far you run, how remotely you hide or how long it takes us—we *will* find you and we will make sure you pay the ultimate penalty for your cowardice and criminality."

Molton steps back from the microphone and leaves the room.

Don Jackson catches him as soon as he walks out of public view. "Mr. President, I need a word."

"Yes, Don." He can tell from the director's face that something is wrong.

"We've just had a call from the British, and we've confirmed it with General Sir James Winnet, leader of the British forces in Afghanistan. The Deputy Prime Minister and two senior army officers have been critically injured."

"My God, how?"

"A second attack. An Afghan civilian worker stole a truck, set it on fire, and drove it into the tent where Mr. Pearson was briefing the press corps on the first incident."

"Will he pull through?"

"I don't know, sir. This is literally breaking news. The Deputy PM has a fractured skull, broken ribs, and collapsed lung. If he dies, it'll be a major victory for al-Qaeda."

147

Police HQ, Miami

It's early afternoon when Ghost gets a call from Zoe's friend Jude. To his relief, she says she's catching the next flight back. Her instant and kindly response makes him feel guilty that he's not at the hospital monitoring Zoe's every second. It also prompts him to call her brother again.

There's still no answer.

"This is Danny, I'm busy doing other stuff, leave your details after the beep."

He wonders what kind of guy doesn't check his phone for so long. "Danny, this is Lieutenant Walton, Miami Police. I've called several times and still need to talk to you about your sister. Ring me back on this cell phone number or you can get me on 305-476-5423. Thanks."

He makes a mental note to call the cops in New York City and see if they can trace him.

The urge to ring Jackson Memorial is too great. He has the direct number on speed dial.

"ICU." The female voice sounds busy.

"Lieutenant Walton, Miami police. I was there last night. Can you give me a condition check on Zoe Speed?"

The duty sister, Tessa Norton, doesn't even have to look at her notes. "Unchanged. I'm afraid there's been no marked improvement and she hasn't regained consciousness."

"Thanks." He ends the call and tries to clear his mind. He tells himself that everything will turn out okay. Zoe is a fighter. There's no doubt about that. In that dark world where she's submerged, she'll be clawing her way slowly back to the surface, and sometime soon her eyes will open and she'll gasp for breath without all those tubes and lines and monitors.

Annie interrupts his thoughts and says Sandra Teale has just been settled in his old office—a corridor away from the Incident Room that's now become home for the task force.

When he gets there he finds the forensic vet is wearing a floaty, floral, knee-length sundress and her long dark hair is down to her bronzed shoulders. Ghost can't help but notice how different she looks than when they met on the beach at Key Biscayne. "Nice to see you out of your forensic whites."

"You could see me out of everything, if you asked nicely."

The comment throws him. "Gosh. Well . . ."

She's amused at how uncomfortable he looks. "Has my directness embarrassed you?"

"No. Not at all," he lies. "Well yes, but not for the reason you think."

"No?"

"Listen, I'm very flattered by your flirtation, it's just that there is someone in my life that I care a lot about at the moment and actually she's *quite* ill."

"Oh, I'm sorry." She reddens slightly. "Now I feel both crass and stupid."

"Don't be. Unless you had psychic powers there's no way you could have known."

She completes her blush. "So, how *else* can I help you?"

"President Molton has asked me to head the Florida task force combatting the dog problem. I'd like you to work with me. I really could do with your expertise."

"At least I know you've approached me for professional reasons. I'd be honored to help."

"Thanks. One of my sergeants is on her way to the animal services shelter on North West Seventy-fourth. Do you know it?"

"Yes, I got a cat from there some years back."

"She's collecting a stack of dog microchips. I'd like you to examine them."

"Why in particular?"

"I want to see if they match the ones you found in the other dogs."

She looks uncomfortable with the suggestion. "To be honest, I didn't examine the physical chips."

"Why not?"

"Well, there didn't seem any need. I just scanned the animal bodies and read the electronic data that came up on screen. It tells you all about the owner, registration, vet, etcetera, and the manufacturer of the chip."

"You get the manufacturer's data from the scan?"

"Yes."

He pulls over a notepad. "Anything you can tell me about who made them? Anything that links our victims?"

She has to pause and think. "Well, the microchips in the Kathy Morgan, Matt Wood, and Alfie Steiner cases were all from the same supplier. All Chinese. But I've checked with other vets that have done postmortems on recent dogs shot in human fatality incidents, and they've given me different batch numbers and manufacturers for those."

"Do you know if they were Chinese as well?"

"Yes, I believe they were. But that's not uncommon. Chinese and Japanese manufacturers have gained strong footholds in these areas. Some years ago American and Swiss companies led the field, but they lost a lot of ground—mainly due to costs and the fact that we ended up with different chips and different scanners in the market that weren't compatible."

"Why did you check that?"

"What?"

"You said you have already checked with other vets on the type of microchips used in the dogs—why did you do that?"

"Well, for a variety of reasons. Firstly, just to see if they were chipped—and amazingly, all the dogs were. Then, to see if the owners had gotten their animals from the same breeders—they hadn't. And I did wonder whether they'd suffered some infection; if there was a chance that the chips had come from a contaminated area such as Fukushima in Japan. But as they were all from China, that was also a nonstarter."

"Could you go back to the animals and inspect the actual chips?"

She looks a little nonplussed. "Yes, of course. But why? I also scanned the animals for radiation, and their levels were normal."

"I'll tell you why—maybe it's nothing, but as of now, that chip is all we've got, so I want you to examine every microscopic nanoparticle of it."

"You've got it." She gets up to go. "When you get the chips, can you have them sent through to my office? I'll run microscopy on those straight away and then comparison tests on the ones in the animals."

"They'll be with you within an hour."

They exchange smiles and she leaves.

Ghost barely has time to reflect on their meeting when a direct line on his desk rings. It's Vasquez in Jacksonville.

"Hi, Antonio, what've you got?"

"Are your monitors on?"

Ghost picks the remote off his desk. "No. Hang on. No one has actually shown me how to operate these things yet." He thumbs through the buttons, powers up, and tries several sources.

A bank of five screens fills with different feeds. All of them show savage dogs on the rampage. "Where is this?"

"The last place on earth we'd want it to be," answers Vasquez.

148

Bonnet Creek Parkway, Lake Buena Vista, Florida

It's normally one of the cleanest kennels in the world. Now it's covered in blood, skin, and human organs. Staff and customers are either dead or panicking.

A Doberman snaps its jaws around the neck of a kennel worker. An Alsatian tears at the remains of the young couple that were dropping it off. Two pointers chew on the corpse of a female vet.

There are bodies spread across the concrete deck where guests arrive. More lie along the crushed granite pathways and by drinking fountains where the seniors tend to sit in the sun before they go on their way.

And there are more in the play park.

Frisbees, balls, and rubber bones lie neglected on artificial green turf that is now a sodden crimson.

A row of intermittently spurting fountains, installed to amuse the animals and keep them cool, sprays a thin red mist into the faultless blue Orlando sky. Across a water jet lies the body of a young center cleaner. Just nineteen, this was the first day of his first job.

The air fills with the sound of sirens, and cops and National Guardsmen pour into the grounds of the 27,000 feet of luxury pet center.

They're too late to save the lives of fifteen people. But maybe— just maybe—they can keep the dogs from breaching the fences and entering the land next door.

Because if they don't, then the dogs are going to run amok in the most famous and densely populated family venue in the world.

Disney World.

149

Police HQ, Miami

*G*host watches the horror unfold on his monitors. He's already sent Tarney, Diaz, and other key Special Ops leaders in helicopters to the resort. They'll hook up with locals and give strategic instructions should the situation worsen. Which it well might.

Occasionally he glances at feeds that local force techies have pulled up from the pet center's own 24/7 camera coverage.

Through a comm headset he listens to a mix of audio links to the various teams dispatched by both himself and the local police and sheriff's offices. Across from him, Bella Lansing waves to grab his attention and holds a note that says: THE MICROCHIPS ARE HERE. SAMPLES SENT TO TEALE.

He mouths the word *Thanks*.

Ghost looks down and sees his direct line to Vasquez is flashing. He removes one side of his headphones and picks it up. "What do you know, Antonio?"

"FYI—I'm getting real heat from Disney. The kind you could roast all of America's Thanksgiving dinners on."

"Sorry to hear it. You want me to get someone from the White House have them back off?"

"Would help. I gave Disney's chief of security a heads-up that we're considering a complete evac and he went ballistic. Within minutes I had the president of Disney World Attractions on one line and the group's public affairs manager on another. Expect some heat yourself, they're going to fight any attempt to close."

"Let's hope it doesn't come to that. Once my people get in there, they're going to clear everyone from the southwestern part of the Port Orleans Resort. I've already got Guard units in the center, partway down the parkway, across Sassagoula Circle and Riverside as far as the Jambo House."

"Okay. Just wanted to let you know that you had incoming political fire that I couldn't head off. Sorry."

"Appreciated. Thanks." Ghost hangs up and his eyes follow the satellite feed. There are marksmen out there now, and they're doing a good job by the look of things.

Two dogs lie dead on the freshly mown grass that forms the median dividing the parkway. On one side is the kennels and on the other Disney World.

A Guard gets off several shots and a medium-sized pointer falls to the turf on the Disney side.

From what Ghost has managed to find out, the resort is about as secure as a maximum-security prison. They've kept out ticket dodgers for decades, by using patrols and chain link that any corrections board in the world would be proud of. Today it might just save them lives as well as money.

Ghost, Bella, and Teale forget about the chips. The satellite feed has picked up a hole in the Disney fence. A deliberately cut hole. And dogs are pouring through it.

150

Disney World, Florida

Seven dogs go through the fence.

Three Labradors. Two golden retrievers. A Doberman and a boxer.

The animals' supersensitive hearing tunes in to the shrieks of joy that spill from the happy, choppy waters of Ol' Man Island, the elaborate three-acre outdoor pool complex built around a bend of the Sassagoula River.

The dogs gallop as a pack, feet drumming loudly as they hit the boards of a bridge.

The decking is full of moms and dads with kids. They're lost in their own private worlds, lazily pushing strollers, proudly carrying tots on their shoulders, dripping water onto the hot, bleached boards and wondering what drinks and snacks to order before they jump into another hour or so of fun.

Someone shouts, "Look out!"

A hairy-chested dad in red swimmers scoops up his three-year-old son.

Too late.

The Doberman jumps.

Giant paws knock the man over. He clutches at his kid as he tumbles. A blond woman at his side screams in panic but doesn't know what to do.

A retriever crashes into a Disney stroller. Knocks it clean out of a young mother's hands. Giant teeth sink into the soft face of the unprotected baby. Men nearby kick out. Some barefooted. Some in only sandals. The dog snarls and snaps. Draws fresh blood. The mother straightens the stroller and runs.

Three steps later the dog has her.

Its needle sharp teeth sink into her thigh and bring her face-down.

Two thirteen-year-old buddies run from a Labrador. Glances are thrown over bony, sunburned shoulders, skinny arms pump like pistons.

The dog reaches the ankle of the slowest boy and pulls him down.

The child puts his arms defensively over his face. The animal's teeth settle for the soft flesh of the boy's stomach.

A crack of gunfire is lost in the screams.

The Lab is thrown clear of the kid. A cop runs forward and pumps more bullets into his head and body.

A rifle sounds and a retriever tumbles. It is injured but not dead.

It gets to its feet and growls at a terrified child less than a yard away.

A second round hits it in the head. There's a spray of blood and now it's down and not getting up.

There's uncontrollable panic now. People jump off the bridge into what they hope is the safety of the water, others climb trees or leap into the river and swim for their lives.

Guardsmen and cops are on the bridge searching for dogs and for clean shots without harming anyone.

Another Lab savages a deaf and slightly drunk grandmother who'd fallen asleep on a sun lounger in the shade. It's pulling organs from her stomach when a Guardsman stoops low and shoots it in the head.

More Guardsmen flood the island.

They kill the third of the Labs and the boxer over by the shade of the terminus for the horse drawn carriages. The bodies of a young woman and her daughter lie in the bushes. A horse is on its side, injured and in pain after bolting and overturning its carriage.

The place is clear of people now. The only sound that breaks an eerie silence is comm chatter from police and National Guard radios. Word comes through—the last of the dogs has been shot at the entrance to the Muddy Rivers Pool bar.

The crisis is over.

Or so everyone hopes.

151

CIA HQ, Langley, Virginia

Ten miles and twenty minutes in a car is all that separate the White House from the George Bush Center for Intelligence, the official name of CIA HQ, where Don Jackson has his team.

The NIA director makes the journey at the urgent request of one of America's most decorated officers, Chris Parry, chief of operations of SAD, the CIA's Special Activities Division, a branch of the Agency's National Clandestine Squad.

Jackson sticks out a hand and they shake as they walk. "I need this to be good, Chris. We're jammed up bad with the Chinese, Koreans, and Taliban at the moment."

"I know." The fifty-year-old former Delta Force commander pats Jackson on the back. "I'm going to give you hope, my friend."

"If hope doesn't have nuclear capabilities, it may not be good enough."

They manage to laugh as they turn a corridor and head toward an operations room. "The cyber task force we set up on day one has been working its balls off. They've been phreaking the buildings—essentially hacking the comm and computer systems of everything Chinese, and have pulled an encrypted stream called Nian."

"Nian? What is that, an acronym?"

"No." Parry's face lights up. "The Nian is a mythical Chinese dog. Stuff of legend and horror stories, like our bogeyman or Wicked Witch of the West. Kids get told about this monster dog that comes out of hiding, attacks villages, kills people, and disappears. Sound familiar?"

"Uncomfortably so."

They enter a large briefing room filled with tired but familiar faces. Managers from the Counter Intelligence Center, the Office of Asia Pacific Analysis, the Anti-Cyber Crime Division, and the Office of Terrorism Analysis have all given up their sleep to help analysts polish the gems of information that have been dug up.

Task force leader Bill Everett steps forward when he sees his boss enter with the NIA director. He shakes Jackson's hand. "Good to see you again, sir. I'd like to introduce you to two of our people. This is Brad Stevens, one of our senior cyber crime supervisors."

Stevens looks even more baggy-eyed and gray than normal. "Pleased to meet you, Director Jackson."

They shake hands and then Everett's face lights up with pride. "And this is one of our most promising and ambitious young field operatives, the man who found the Nian stream."

Danny Speed sticks out his young hacker hand. "Glad to meet you, Mr. Director."

Chris Parry hurries things along. "Tell the director what you've got."

All eyes are on Danny. "I've captured highly secured military data flowing from North Korea to Beijing, sir, and I have broken some of the basic codes. That means the computer language makes sense and I have managed to recognize and assemble all the scrambled data so we can see folders, photographs, and video."

"But?" Jackson feels liked a coiled spring. "I know there is a 'but' otherwise I'd have heard more positive stuff earlier than this."

"There is," interjects Parry. "A butt bigger than Kim Kardashian's. Beyond the computer code is a language code, and it's not in English. It's Chinese, and not even Mandarin or Cantonese."

Everett explains further. "As you probably know, sir, about one and a quarter billion people in China speak Mandarin, and another seventy million Cantonese. We now have to work through the lesser languages—Wu, Yu, Min, Jin, Xiang, Hakka, Gan, and Pinghua."

Jackson rolls his eyes. "Isn't there standard software to translate that?"

"Not that makes sense. We can't afford errors, and those flip-up programs are full of mistakes. We've got our best linguists all over this."

Jackson nods. "You said video?"

Danny nods. "Yes sir. There seem to be years of lab experiments."

"We're prioritizing the latest ones," adds Everett.

"It was this stream that got snagged and opened everything up," explains Danny. "It was as though after the final experiments were finished, someone broke the firewalls so we could deliberately get in. Until then all the programs I'd thrown at it just slid off."

Jackson looks to Parry, a glance that asks if they had an operative inside the operation, but the commander shakes his head. "Thanks, Speed. Excellent work. Thanks, Bill, I'll catch up with you later." He leads the director out to the corridor. "We ran some of the log-ins and cross-matched them with other intelligence. Two names came up, a father and son called Weiwei."

"Go on."

"They're both scientists. Well known within the international community. Especially the older one. Years back we tried to turn him but had no luck. He's a geneticist, Hao Weiwei, who was short-listed twice for a Nobel. His son was named on much of his work and published his own papers on GM crops."

Jackson is tired. "They're behind Nian?"

"Looks like they were involved at senior levels. Hence their names being on the computer access. We ran facial recognition on the scientist shot by the North Koreans. It's Jihai Weiwei. He was crossing the DMZ when the KPA shot him."

152

Police HQ, Miami

*G*host leans back in his chair, stretches and yawns. He's bone weary from too little sleep and too much worry. There's little action on the monitors now. Just a giant clean-up operation. All the adrenaline of the day has disappeared like a retreating tide. The room is filled with emptiness and sadness.

He looks to one side and sees Annie staring at him. "What?"

"You mind if I say something?" She walks closer.

"Is it advice? I'm really not in the mood for advice."

"It is." She pushes her luck. "You look awful. I can't even see beyond those superstar shades of yours but I'm willing to bet your eyes look like walnuts, and from your crumpled suit and yawning, I'm guessing you should go home and crash before you fall over or something."

He knows she means well. "Home is the last place I want to be. I'm going to make some final calls and then go to the hospital."

"Why not *call* the hospital? You can't make her better by sitting alongside her, you know. Sitting beside someone is not a form of medical treatment."

Ghost smiles. "I know." He picks up the phone. "One call then I'm going."

She nods and leaves him to it.

The call Ghost makes, however, is not to the hospital but to Sandra Teale.

The vet recognizes his number and picks up right away. "I was five minutes away from sending you an e-mail."

"I have special telepathic powers and thought I'd save you having to write."

"Well, your timing is perfect. I have you on speakerphone and I'm peering down the most powerful microscope we have, at one of those chips from the center."

He picks up a sense of intrigue in her voice. "Is there something unusual about them?"

"Oh, yes. Very much so. They're not data chips at all."

"Pardon?"

"Well, that's not technically correct. I should have said they're not *only* data chips."

"What do you mean?"

"They are drug chips. That is to say, they are filled with tiny reservoirs that are filled with some kind of drug—"

He jumps in. "That small? You can get drugs into a microchip?"

"Yes you can. Highly concentrated droplets are kept in separate reservoirs and then released at timed intervals. The technology was developed for seriously ill patients who would be unlikely to remember to take pills at the right times."

Ghost makes notes as he fires questions. "What kind of drug is in these chips?"

"Hey, I'm quick but not that quick. I've drawn some of the liquid out but still have to run tests."

"Sorry. Have you any idea what it might be? Some kind of vaccination? An antirabies shot?"

"No, I don't think so. I haven't heard of shots being given that way. There's no rabies alert at the moment. And most of all, these are really sophisticated chips, they're far too expensive to use on dogs."

Ghost falls silent.

So does Teale. She waits for a question that never comes, then asks, "What are you thinking?"

"I'm not sure. I'm trained to look for the obvious, and then when everything obvious has been ruled out, consider the ridiculous."

"Which is what?"

"That the dogs have been deliberately drugged to enrage them and make them kill. In other words, they'd been effectively weaponized."

153

Honolulu, Hawaii

The giant conference table is ringed by the rich and unfamous. Powerful men most of the world have never heard about who decide the fortunes of millions.

The gathering is an emergency session of a little known but highly powerful organization called APEC. Asia-Pacific Economic Cooperation is the key forum for protecting North America's business interests in markets like China, Japan, North Korea, and Australia, and right now its cross-border treaties are in danger of falling apart.

Ichiro Nomura, the delegate for Japan, leans into the microphone in front of him and sums up the perilous situation. "The USA has yet again delayed interest payments on its very sizable debts to my country and leaves us no choice but to consider an immediate cessation of trade unless shortfalls are remedied and guarantees given that future payments will be timely."

Tomas Reynolds, the U.S. executive, presses the red light on his desk and responds quickly. "My good friend Ichiro-san makes an unfair point. The delay in debt payment is a technical holdup of just a few days."

Nomura responds. "A few days' interest on several trillion dollars is a lot of money, Tomas-san. Do I need to remind you that 95 percent of consumers lie outside America's borders and that 40 percent fall within APEC's domain?"

"You don't. I need no such reminder."

"Or that the Asia-Pacific region buys 70 percent of U.S. agricultural exports."

Applause from other member countries drowns out the U.S. delegate's reply.

Ichiro Nomura stands, his microphone still on. In his hands is a thick legal document. "This is a contract worth two billion dollars, for the provision of transportation equipment by companies in Indiana." He tears it in two and lets the papers ceremonially flutter over the edge of his desk. "No more trade until debts are paid."

Cheers go up. Korean delegate Kim Kak-Hee turns his microphone on and similarly stands, papers in hand. "Contract for chemical manufacturing—one billion dollars." He rips it in half and half again. "No trade until debts paid."

As the applause dies down, Chinese delegate Zhiang Liu gets to his feet. "The People's Republic of China is owed more than two *trillion* dollars by the United States of America." He holds his hands up, so three contracts are seen by the table of delegates. "These are manufacturing orders worth *ten* billion dollars for companies in Ohio. It is with great regret that I do this on behalf of my country." He walks from his place and stands next to the U.S. representative, where he tears them up and leaves them on the table in front of him. "China will not trade with the U.S. until debts are paid on time and in full."

154

Police HQ, Miami

*O*nce Sandra Teale has hung up, Ghost sits in a daze.

Poisonous microchips.

It makes sense. Sounds outrageous but makes perfect sense.

But Li Chen?

Was he really an illegal immigrant who'd spent months jabbing dogs with killer chips? And who had put him up to it? A company ready to sell some antidote? Or a more sinister group?

Ghost is reminded that Zoe found something at Chen's house that sent her straight to Bicentennial Park. He mentally flicks through the images on her camera and suddenly they take on significance. Two bedrooms. Made and unmade beds. Clothes in separate closets.

These weren't the living habits of man and wife. They were signs of spies hiding out, sharing a roof and a lifestyle as a cover for their activities.

More pieces of the puzzle slotted into place. If he was right about the poison chips and the spies, then it began to explain why the NIA and President were so interested in the dog attacks so early in the chain of events. He looks at the small business card he's placed in the middle of his desk. On it is a private number. One he was told he could ring at any time, providing, of course, the occasion was important enough.

Ghost thinks it is.

He makes sure his office door is securely locked and dials it.

The voice that answers is male and well-educated, crisp and friendly. "President Molton's office. Jordan speaking."

"This is Lieutenant Walton from the Florida task force. I need to speak to the President as a matter of urgency."

Molton's executive secretary sounds surprised. "How did you get this number, sir?"

"The President gave it me in person when he was in Miami."

"Please hold."

Ghost is left in a digital void. He guesses the assistant is checking to see if the great man is around or even wants to take his call.

The next voice he hears is Molton's. "Lieutenant, how are you and how is your lady?"

"I'm fine, sir. Unfortunately, she's not so fine. Still in a coma, I'm afraid. Thank you for asking."

"I'm sorry to hear that. What can I do for you?"

"Mr. President, I'm calling you directly because I have information that suggests the dog attacks are not a natural phenomenon but a coordinated event. The result of a gang of individuals, possibly a form of terror group." He pauses to see if the President reacts and will fill in some of the many holes in his own theories.

"That's quite a statement, Lieutenant. What leads you to that idea?"

"Sir, the vet who attended several of the dog-related deaths has discovered that the microchips used to ID the animals contain chemical reservoirs that can be remotely activated. I just spoke to her and she believes the substance in the chips will have directly boosted the dogs' adrenaline levels, destabilized and disorientated them and as a consequence made them aggressive."

Clint Molton feels his heart leap. "Lieutenant, I need you—and this vet—to speak to the CIA and to my scientific advisors. And I need you to do that in person ASAP." He knows that Walton won't want to leave Miami but he has no option but to ask. "I'm going to clear a military plane to pick you both up and bring you here. The way those guys fly, it's less than a two-hour flight, and I promise to get you back right away. Is that okay with you, Lieutenant?"

Ghost wants to say no. He wants to be close to Zoe. Whatever happens. "Of course, sir."

"Good. I presume you haven't mentioned this to anyone else?"

"No, sir."

"Then please don't."

"I won't. What have the Chinese got to do with this, Mr. President?"

Molton falls silent. Finally he asks, "What prompts your question?"

"Because one of the dog shelters here employed a man called Li Chen, and I can't find any trace of him even being in the country, let alone Miami."

"Sadly, illegal immigration is not that uncommon."

"It's more than that, sir. Chen supplied those drug-filled microchips, and a woman purporting to be his wife is connected to a number of other dog shelters, spread across America."

Molton took a beat. The information filled in so many blanks, but he couldn't discuss it now. "I won't lie to you, Lieutenant, there is a Chinese dimension but I can't talk about it on the phone. Director Jackson will speak to you when you arrive. I have to go now. My office will be in touch within the next ten minutes regarding your travel."

Ghost hears the line go dead.

He stands up and picks his car keys off the desk. If he's going to Washington, then he's going to see Zoe first. He has to hold her hand and kiss her—at least one more time.

155

Beijing

"*I*n American movies they talk of the beginning of the end," says General Zhang as he sits alongside Xue Shi and points at the dogs on three monitors in the control room. "*This* is the real beginning of the end."

Computer generated graphics tell the rest of the story.

> CAM 1: New York, Central Park
> CAM 2: Chicago, Lake Shore Drive
> CAM 3: Los Angeles, Century City

Zhang folds his arms and leans back in relaxed anticipation of what's to come.

At Fox Plaza in L.A. two balls of brown wool turn from being harmless Labradoodles into murderous dogs. Their owner, a fifty-year-old former TV presenter, thinks they're having a tantrum and tugs hard on their Gucci leads.

Then they rip into her.

One dog savages her hand and pulls at her wrist and arm. The other tears a mouthful of flesh from her gym-toned right thigh. Crowds scatter along the sidewalk.

Half a block down, an Alsatian jumps a skateboarder and closes his yellow jaws around the young boy's throat.

Zhang's eyes move unemotionally to the middle monitor and he points at the scene with deep satisfaction. "Chicago. President Molton's hometown. How I would like to see his face when he learns of the deaths here." A black Doberman, the size of a small horse, brings down a businessman in a blue suit outside the Edgewater Beach Hotel. The man loses his brown leather case and claws his way up a bank of grass. The dog lurches forward and bites into his hip. He falls and the big animal clambers onto his chest. The dog is all over him and he will be dead in minutes.

Xue Shi is following the action in New York. In Central Park, off the Great Lawn, down by Eighty-Fifth Street where the edge of the reservoir rolls toward the Guggenheim, a pack of wild dogs overturns a horse-drawn carriage. The driver is lying on his side in shock as several large mongrels set on him. His passengers, a dark-haired man and red-haired woman, are kicking out at two brown rottweilers. Other walkers are running for their lives. No one is helping.

Zhang draws comfort from that.

Fear is a wonderful ally.

Florida's dog problems and the emergency measures imposed there have clearly struck terror into the hearts of all the Americans.

He sits up in his seat and turns to Xue Shi. "Tomorrow, Xian flies out to meet the American. He will buy time for himself and claim Molton is close to accepting our demands. Demands that are now ridiculously low. If he is clever, he may even persuade the American to agree to them and then ring the party chiefs with news of his triumph. Either way, I want to be ready to bring our weak leader's period of power to a humiliating end. Let him inform the council of his great diplomacy and what it has achieved. Give him that hour of false satisfaction. Then deploy the poison dogs. Let them loose and have them undermine him. Have them rip the spirit out of the Americans and destroy his credibility once and for all. Then we will take control and make more fruitful demands of Molton and his administration."

PART FIVE

"If you win, you need not have to explain . . .
If you lose, you should not be there to explain!"

ADOLF HITLER

156

The White House, Washington DC

The flight from Miami to the capital gives Ghost an opportunity to think. To live with the notion that the dog attacks were orchestrated by some militant, maverick Chinese terrorists. Maybe it went back to the Syrian crisis and the stand both China and Russia had taken against U.S. intervention to stop Assad. Perhaps it was more obscure than that. One thing he knew for certain, spying incidents happened every day and got covered up. It was more than possible that this one escalated until it was just too big and dirty to sweep under a diplomatic carpet.

By the time Ghost and Sandra Teale are shown through to a meeting room, the dog attacks in New York, Chicago, and Los Angeles have escalated.

The TV news is playing on a screen and they can see that four more New Yorkers have been killed and nine injured in Wall Street. Five have been killed and seven injured at Universal Studios in L.A., and in Chicago six people have been killed and eleven injured at Union Station.

The total across the three cities is now sixty-five dead and eighty more being treated for wounds and shock.

Their viewing is interrupted when a tall black man and two white men, walk in. A pace or two behind them is a pencil-thin woman Ghost recognizes. Gwen Harries. "Brandon Jackson, NIA director." He sticks out his hand. "And this is Chris Parry, from

Langley, and Marlon Gonzalez, director of the White House's Office of Science."

"I'm Lieutenant Walton, and this is veterinary pathologist Sandra Teale."

There's a merry-go-round of handshakes until Jackson says, "And I understand you and Agent Harries know each other."

"We do." To her great surprise, Ghost makes a point of warmly embracing her. "Good to see you again Gwen. Though I do have a feeling that you've been holding back vital information that might have helped the Miami police."

"Only under my instructions," says Jackson, noting the sarcasm. "Please sit down." He ushers them to a table behind the soft sofa area where they'd been watching the TV. "The President told me your story about the shelter, the microchips, and the Chinese couple, but I'd like us all to hear it from the two of you."

Sandra Teale slips over a file containing copies of her research. "I only did one set of copies. I'm sorry."

"No problem." Jackson reroutes the technical data to Gonzalez.

"Basically," the vet continues, "the dogs were fitted with microchips. They look like the standard kind that can act as a tracer and when scanned will reveal owner and dog details. But these were more advanced." She produces a packet of unused chips from the folder in front of her and passes them over. "They have drug reservoirs that release chemicals to make the dogs aggressive and anxious." She looks toward Gonzalez. "I can be more technical if you wish?"

"Later," says the white-haired advisor with a smile. "Let's keep this simple for the moment."

"Well," continues Teale, "this type of chip was found in all the dogs that killed people in Florida. That is, all the ones I've managed to examine or trace reports on. And it seems the same chip supplier has been used in most shelters throughout the state and elsewhere in the country." She looks across to Ghost.

He picks up the story. "I talked to the major animal shelter in the region and they got their supplies through a Chinese guy called Li Chen who worked with them." He notices Jackson and Harries exchange glances. "Does that name mean anything to you?"

"It might," answers Jackson. "Please go on."

Ghost takes that as a yes. "Turns out Li Chen distributed chips across the country, and I believe even dogs. One hound that was traced back to him was responsible for the death of a young woman named Astrid Gerber, and her mother Heidi." Now he looks directly at Parry. "But then I guess you do know about all this because I suspect you've had a tap on my phone since the first day sweet-innocent Gwen here turned up—and I guess she only disappeared from the scene once she was certain that the recording devices in my office and the trace software on my computer systems had gone undiscovered. Right?"

Jackson looks toward his colleague. "You can talk within reason, Chris."

The head of the Special Activities Division sits forward. "To a degree you are right, Lieutenant. Li Chen is a Chinese deep cover agent, a sleeper. We lost track of him several years ago. We didn't know he was connected to this case, he interested us for several other reasons which I won't go into here, but yes, we are very interested in him, and Agent Harries now has an active mandate to find him and his wife."

"Those are not their real names," Harries adds. "But they are among the ones they've used since they came into the country about half a decade ago."

Ghost is confused. "I couldn't find any records on either of them."

"We pulled them," answers Parry. "Expunged them from the system."

"Why?"

"Lots of reasons," explains the SAD chief. "They've been moving around for the past few years, living in New York but coming to Florida very frequently. They have several homes in the state and multiple identities and businesses. Li Chen has often stayed for periods in Miami, while Mingyu has done the same on the East Coast. We found that unless we followed them exceptionally closely it proved impossible to work out whether the couple were together or apart. When we lost track of them about two months ago we killed their records in the hope that it might flush them out and force them into re-registering on official sites. So much easier to look at new regs."

"But it didn't?"

"No," conceded Jackson. "Until you came across their activity, we hadn't even connected them to all the current troubles."

Ghost's interest spiked. "All the current troubles?"

Jackson sensed the cop was going to probe too far. "Lieutenant, given Dr. Teale's presence, I suggest we brief you more fully in private."

Ghost nods.

Jackson's mind goes back to the attacks he saw in Bristol, where out-of-town dogs came in from the countryside and decimated the population. "Doctor, just so I'm clear on things, could those microchip things also contain some kind of remote guidance system that forces the dogs to go in a particular direction?"

"Not at all." Sandra Teale has to hold back a laugh. "Why do you ask?"

"Well, mainly because it seems that once they've been activated, the dogs congregate and seem en masse to attack human settlements. How can that be?"

"They're hunters," explains the vet. "Deep down these animals are descended from wolves and instinctively they'll hunt in packs wherever they can smell food—or flesh, to be more precise."

The director glances at his watch. "Thanks. A simple but horrifyingly easy to understand explanation." He looks to Ghost. "Lieutenant, I suggest you go with Chris and Gwen and they'll answer the rest of the many questions you seem to have." He gets to his feet. "Doctor, perhaps you could give Dr. Gonzalez more background. I'm afraid I have to go to a crisis meeting with the President and the Joint Chiefs."

157

Beijing

Sitting opposite each other in the grand presidential office, both Xian and Chunlin are aware how momentous their short meeting is.

It may be the last time they see each other.

In a few hours' time the president will leave for the APEC summit and his critical appointment with Molton. The end game will have begun.

The minister looks frail and tired. He has expended all his energy on gathering intelligence about Zhang and Xue Shi. "The general is preparing to activate more dogs in the major American cities. Next on his list are Seattle, Philadelphia, and Detroit. The strikes are planned just as you meet the President."

"I have lost all influence with him." Xian looks despondent. "The only consolation is that the more fear he creates, the more people wish his downfall."

"You found support in the Politburo?"

"Enough. Eighteen of the twenty-five we could bank on."

"I am sure I can name the seven who would stand against us."

"I am sure you can as well," Xian manages a smile. "Four are key to the Central Military Commission."

"Of which you are head." Chunlin realizes his leader is having doubts. If he acquiesces to Zhang and steps aside, he will be allowed to leave office and live the rest of his years with his family. But if he makes a move against the general and fails, then they will all be killed. "The Military Commission will learn shortly of the incident in the DMZ. When they do, it will reflect badly on Zhang. Weiwei was his appointment. There may even be international fallout to the incident."

Xian dismisses the thought with a wave of his hand. "He will launder the blame. No doubt he and Xue Shi already have it in hand."

Chunlin grows angry. He remembers his leader when the man was full of fight and fury, guile and resolve. "I need your decision, Mr. President. I need you to tell me clearly and with no doubt in your mind or heart that you wish me to implement my plan."

Xian hesitates.

His mind is still on the safety of his family. His thoughts on safeguarding them and living to watch his son grow up and marry.

"Zhang must *not* rule," says Chunlin forcefully. "If you will not sanction a move against him, then I will make one anyway." He stands and pushes back his chair.

"Wait!"

The minister stops and his hands settle on the top of the chair.

"You must not stand alone. I will leave shortly for the meeting with Molton. When I do, I will call and send my wife and child to Guangdong. There are people there who will protect them and get them out of the country if necessary." He walks from behind his desk and stands in front of his old friend. "I thank you for your loyalty to me and to our country. I pray history remembers us as both righteous and victorious."

158

The White House, Washington DC

*G*host is surprised to find himself alone with Chris Parry in a small but stylishly furnished briefing room. "Where is the elusive Agent Harries?" he asks as they settle on green corduroy sofas.

"She sends her apologies," says Parry. "She has a very active caseload. As I believe you do, so I'll cut to the chase."

"Please do."

"The information you have given us is really useful. If substantiated, it may lead us to a way of—how shall I say this—'disarming' these dogs and saving a lot of lives."

"I'm glad to help in any way I can."

"We know. And we're grateful for you coming at short notice, especially given your personal circumstances."

The allusion to Zoe makes Ghost feel sad. "Your boss said you needed to brief me more fully, in private."

"I do." Parry sits forward, tries to create a closer bond with the cop. "Neither you nor Sandra Teale can speak to anyone about the evidence that you gave us. Not now. Not tomorrow. Not ever. Do you understand?"

"No. I don't. In fact, every day there is more and more about this bloody mess that I *don't* understand. And as far as I can remember, buddy, you don't have the power to quite so easily interfere with my freedom of speech, so if you want compliance and help, you better quit the strong-arm shit and brief me responsibly."

"I'm not in a position to do that."

"Then we're done here." Ghost gets to his feet and towers over Parry. "Now, if you've got nothing else to say, I need to get back to Miami to see someone who really matters to me."

159

The White House, Washington DC

*T*he crisis meeting is held in the Situation Room. The President and the Joint Chiefs of Staff are there in person. The leaders of the Army, Navy, Air Force, Marine Corps, and National Guard Bureau, and other senior commanders watch and listen on a video link to the Pentagon. On another feed from CIA HQ at Langley is the operational task force led by Bill Everett and the heads of the Counter Intelligence Center and Office of Terrorism Analyses.

Vice President Cornwell is on a feed from a presidential plane heading to Camp Dwyer in Afghanistan.

Around the table with Molton are his senior executive advisors and Attorney General Jan Saunders.

NIA director Don Jackson is on his feet by a digital summary board that shows maps, death figures, and totals for injured people. "The attacks of the last twelve hours have been swiftly countered by police and National Guard units. Our response has been good and we have been alerted to more incidents. The President is preparing to fly to Hawaii to attend a meeting there with President Xian of China, and it is likely that this will happen amidst more canine assaults, probably in more of our major cities. We have deployed units in Dallas, Houston, Seattle, Philadelphia, Phoenix, Detroit, and of course we've redoubled cover in the cities hit today." He looks toward Molton.

The President picks up. "Don doesn't want to say it, and neither do I. But I think we're a day away from declaring a nationwide State of Emergency."

Groans break across the room.

"Listen up." Molton falls back on his old political language for controlling unrest. "We still have diplomatic channels open, diplomatic options, and our intelligence services are making up ground—rapidly. Right, Don?"

"Yes, Mr. President. In a moment we'll split into a smaller group and I'll brief the Security Council members more fully on the progress made in the last hour."

The door to the Situation Room opens and Jordan Taylor, the executive secretary, enters. "I'm sorry for the interruption. Mr. President. I have the Prime Minister of Canada on a phone for you in the breakout room. He says it's urgent and cannot wait."

"Excuse me." Molton gets to his feet and follows his assistant into a side office.

The President's heart sinks as the Canadian leader, Jacques Bastin, is put through to him.

"Mr. President, I call you to express the deep sympathies of the Canadian government, the Canadian people, and of course myself and my family."

"Thank you."

"It is terrible. We have watched it, of course, on the television, and it is unbelievable. I hope by now that the worst is over?"

"We are hoping so as well. The Army and National Guard are working with the police and sheriff departments, backed by multiagency support, and I'm sure normality will soon be resumed."

"It is encouraging to hear that . . ." Bastin takes a diplomatic pause. ". . . but until that moment Canada feels it must close its borders to the United States."

"I beg your pardon?"

"There is concern here that your diseased animals may end up in Canada, and this cannot happen. So, until we are certain that you have mastered your difficulties, there will be no entry to anyone with an American passport, or any citizen other than a returning Canadian."

"You're being ridiculous. You can't close five thousand miles of border."

"Perhaps not, but we have to try. And with respect, protecting a population is not ridiculous; it is a governmental duty, and one you seem to be failing in. I wish you and your people well in tackling this menace. *Au revoir.*"

Molton throws the receiver at the phone cradle. America is becoming a world pariah and he's had enough.

160

Beijing

*O*n a patch of grass in the courtyard of the city's famous garrison—the place that is the home of Wishu, the martial art better known to the western world as kung fu—a fight has broken out.

Soldiers gather around the two combatants and cheer them on.

It is a bloody and quick affair. An older warrior defeating a young upstart with a brutal flurry of blows.

General Zhang shows the crowd his triumphant fist and then licks blood off his knuckles.

The beaten young man lying in the dirt behind the guarded walls of the army camp knows better than to get up.

He needs to be a gracious loser.

This is how the monthly ritual goes. Zhang fights three recruits. One round apiece. The two men who do best receive privileges. The one who performs the worst is sentenced to a twenty-mile hike.

Zhang stages the fight for all manner of reasons. He believes it shows the men he is as tough as them. Is one of them. He thinks it creates an unassailable bond with grassroot soldiers. But more than that, it teaches them the art of war.

Dare they beat him?

Some are certainly fit and big and strong enough to do so.

But none ever have.

They are learning deception. How to lose when they could win. How to do it convincingly. How not to talk about it afterward, because those who deceive must never give away their true characters.

From far across the courtyard, in the shadow of a doorway, Minister Chunlin watches as the two bare-chested fighters bow to each other out of respect. Deception is on his mind as well. And what better place to see it played out?

Fresh blood steps forward. A young recruit named Luo Kai. He has a body hewn from granite and feet and hands the size of car wheels.

The two men take their respective stances in the sharp sunshine.

They shuffle left and right to find an opening, a chink in each other's tactical armor.

Kai's physical prowess seems nature's way of making up for his lack of intelligence. Every troop has its big dumb ox, and he is it.

Or at least that's what he wants them to believe.

Zhang doesn't even see the blow coming.

A front kick so hard and fast that it smashes his lips against his teeth and fills his mouth with blood.

His head throbs with rage.

Anger courses through every nerve and sinew as he tries to counter and attack.

Kai hits him with a pile-driving center punch, stiff-armed and loaded with enough raw power to drop the general flat on his back.

A huge grin fills his innocent face and he pumps a fist in the air.

There is no cheer, though. No noise at all from the crowd. All eyes are on the general as he gets to his knees and puts his hand to his face. He looks at the blood then wipes it on his chest and stands.

"Come on," Zhang beckons his opponent with his left hand. "Is that the best you've got?"

Kai advances cautiously. He knows what to expect.

Zhang turns to the side, his bodyline a thin target, his foot ready to strike like the head of a cobra.

Then the crowd sees it.

The trailing left hand. The glint of steel. The flash of a blade.

Chunlin sees it too. And it makes him smile. It's what he expected. What he told Kai to expect. The young Goliath was pointed out to him years ago when the boy was first conscripted. Since then he's been one of the minister's protégés.

Zhang lunges, and the tip of the knife cuts across the man's muscled stomach.

There's a sound of shock from the crowd.

Kai doesn't even touch the blood. He knows now he has to get up close. Seize the knife and make what happens next look like an accident.

Zhang fakes a lunge with the knife, then wheels around and slams a kick into his opponent's side.

Kai counters by grabbing Zhang's ankle and rolling forward.

Zhang is thrown off balance.

For a second he is on his back and exposed.

Kai knows he should drop a knee on the knife arm. Break the wrist and see the fingers lose their grip on the steel.

He doesn't.

He misses. Misses by a fraction.

Zhang slices upward and cuts into his side.

Kai rolls away.

Cut twice, he's now bleeding heavily. He stands. Shakes his hand in surrender and bows his head.

Zhang throws his bloodied knife into the earth and goes to the beaten man. He raises Kai's hand in shared victory and the crowd roars.

The general turns so no one else can hear. "Get that stitched up then call my office. You have the makings of a true warrior. I could use a man like you."

Chunlin is too far away to hear what is being said. But he knows enough to smile. Zhang is as inevitably drawn to brutal power as a moth is to a flame.

He will want time alone with Kai. The opportunity to talk man-to-man.

It will be an auspicious meeting, of that Chunlin is certain.

161

Situation Room, The White House, Washington DC

*W*hen Molton reenters the room, the size of the group has been slimmed down to only members of the Security Council.

Video screens on the monitor wall are playing satellite footage of new dog attacks in New York. Paramedics and helivac teams are attending injured people out at Liberty Island.

The President glances at the feed as he sits back at the table. The monitors are so full of horror at the moment he can no longer spare the time to stop and stare. "Canada is closing its borders, that's what the call was. The biggest unguarded border in the world is about to get guarded."

Pat Cornwell shakes his head on the link from Afghanistan. "Expect the Mexicans to follow suit. After all our efforts to keep *them* out, they're not going to be able to resist turning the tables."

Molton looks to Jackson. "Carry on, Don. Before I stepped out of the room you mentioned progress. I'd really like to hear about progress."

"Yes, sir. Lieutenant Walton from the Florida task force has provided us with information that we're working fast on. He's discovered a link between a known Chinese operative, killer dogs in the Miami region, and the supply and distribution of drug-carrying microchips to a network of shelters across the U.S."

Molton makes notes as he talks, a habit from his days out "on the stump" in Chicago. "What does Gonzalez say about all this?"

"He's confirmed the viability, Mr. President. We have some of the chips and they're in the labs being analyzed as we talk."

Pat Cornwell asks the question everyone's thinking. "How do they get triggered?"

"They're a form of RFID—Radio Frequency ID—and they could be set off from anywhere in the world," says Chris Parry almost dismissively. "The dogs' positions will show up on a computer map and an operator will simply type in a trigger command to a local relay that will use radio waves to set them off. Guys over at MIT have been developing an advanced system for humans with Alzheimer's or schizophrenia—they can remotely deliver more than twenty drugs through a chip and monitor patient response. Mercedes and Lexus have chips in cars that do diagnostics, they contact service centers and remotely tell owners when they're heading for a breakdown before the part fails. This dog stuff is simple, now that we know what it is."

Molton looks exasperated. "If it's so simple, why didn't we get this before?"

"They'll have been running cryptographically altered rolling codes and CRA—challenge response authentication."

No one answers.

Finally, the VP has a stab at it. "We have been chasing our tail. That's why. It's all happened so fast we've been struggling to set up response teams and not put enough resources into detection."

Jackson feels affronted. "With respect, sir, that's not quite true. Since day one we've been working hard on the intelligence side and have made a significant breakthrough."

Chris Parry takes his cue. "We have captured highly encrypted data running from North Korea to Beijing. It's called the Nian program. Nian is a mythical monster from Chinese folklore.

"Yesterday, pretty much around the time of the incident in the Korean DMZ, the firewalls momentarily came down. It was enough for us to prise open the door and pull a load of stuff out.

We have decoded most of it. Normally, you would then be faced with recognizable characters and languages. We were not. We encountered Chinese characters—and to make matters worse, not the most commonly spoken version of Chinese. Linguists have now successfully determined that the inner code, as we call it, is written in Gan, or Jiangxinese, as it is often known. This is a language spoken by only about thirty million Chinese. We have found several experts and they are transcribing the data that we have, but there is a final complexity and perhaps the most awkward one of all. The data relates to advanced genetics and related formula. So we have had to draft in genetic scientists to work with the specialist translators to ensure everything is accurately translated and makes sense."

Jackson adds a footnote. "Two leading Chinese scientists, Hao Weiwei and his son Jihai, were named as accessing that computer. Hao had administrator privileges to the database. We've pulled video showing tests on dogs. Experiments in which the dogs become aggressive and go crazy. Strange thing is, he seems to be using some kind of drugs to pacify them."

"Or maybe make them worse," adds Parry. "Until we break down the data we won't have a clear picture."

"I think it's clear enough," says Molton. "This amounts to proof that the Chinese and North Koreans colluded in the creation and control of weaponized dogs that have been set upon innocent American people. It's an act of war. And I don't need the Attorney General to tell me whether I have the right to strike back or not."

"Right doesn't come into it," says Cornwell. "The big problem is *might* not *right*. We launch a preemptive strike on China and North Korea, they both have the nuclear firepower to fight back and cause millions of deaths. Head-to-head with just China and we would be seriously outmuscled in a conflict. They have about two and a quarter million regular troops with the same again in reserve. We couldn't muster three million in total."

"We wouldn't stand alone, Pat." Molton sounds indignant. "The USA has some strong allies who would unhesitatingly stand with us."

"China too." Cornwell can't help but fight his point. "The North Koreans could put maybe nine million troops into the battlefield. Russia could add another two. That's a combined force against us of around fifteen million troops. And I haven't even gotten into the financial power of the likes of Russia and China. We are $14 trillion in debt, Clint, and we're in no position to go to war with those bankrolling us."

Molton is annoyed by the outburst and the open challenge to his authority. "Well, thank God that Great Britain didn't do that kind of math when they declared war on Germany in 1939. Damn it, Pat, I'm not going to be bullied, and I suspect the American public feel the same way." He turns to Jackson and Parry. "I'll go see Xian at this godforsaken APEC summit, but only to buy some breathing space. If you can't give me more than just hope, then by the time I come back you best prepare for war. For I sure as hell will go to Congress with that as my preferred option."

162

Miami

*T*he predawn light is charcoal gray when the military plane from Washington touches down in Miami. Ghost had called Jackson Memorial just before takeoff and he calls again as soon as he arrives.

The same female ward nurse tells him what she told him just over two hours ago. "There's no change in Miss Speed's condition, sir."

No change.

He'd never thought that those two innocuous words could prove so painful.

Ghost drives straight home. Showers. Changes. Makes coffee and starts his computer. He double-clicks an icon he hasn't used in a long time and waits for it to load.

The trip to Washington taught him a lot. Much more than Jackson, Parry, Harries, and all the other spooks had expected him to learn. The big picture is still far from complete, but now he can see most of it and is kicking himself for taking so long to work out what is happening. China and the U.S. are apparently locked in some kind of secret war, and the President and his pals need it to stay secret, presumably until they win it. Meanwhile, innocent, unsuspecting people are being killed while the politicians posture and pontificate over their power plays.

Ghost takes a swallow of his freshly brewed coffee and hears his stomach growl with hunger. There is plenty of food in his refrigerator, and the thought of Eggs Benedict and perhaps a side of smoked salmon is enticing, but he's too wound-up and too busy to indulge in any culinary activity.

A look at his watch says it's still way too early to ring the media. Most of the hacks that he knows are either sobering up from last night's drinking and socializing or else still at it. Later in the day he'll call one of them. Maybe the guy from CBS. He'll hand over Zoe's pictures, one of the microchips that contains the drug reservoir, details of Li Chen and his wife, and he'll sit back and watch the whole damned bonfire of deception go up in flames.

A bleep bleeds from his computer. The software has loaded.

He looks at the screen and doesn't see what he'd expected. Not at all. He takes a final hit of his coffee and grabs his smartphone from where he'd been charging it.

On the way out he takes a jacket from the closet by the door, and from behind a metal panel built into the wall collects two Glock 22 pistols, spare magazines, and several boxes of extra ammunition.

163

Beijing

Army nurse Tan Fei secures the suture thread, gently drifts an antiseptic wipe across the sown-up wound, and then softly pats a padded dressing over the injured man's rock solid mass of abdominal muscles.

Her dark eyes register more than just job satisfaction as she looks into the soldier's face. "You will need to take care not to split it open or get the wound dirty. Come back and see me in one week."

Luo Kai snakes a big hand around her tiny waist. "I need to come back earlier than that."

Tan fights back a smile. "A week will be sufficient." She wriggles free of his grip and puts scissors, suture thread, and needles in a steel tray.

He sits up on the medical center's rough bed and fastens the buttons on his white uniform shirt. "Do you have something for the pain—like a kiss?"

The nurse feels her pulse race. "A big man like you shouldn't need anything."

"Well, I do." He stands and pushes his shirt inside his trousers. "I need a dose of you. Once a day and three times a night."

"Come back in a week. Let us see if you still have any pain then." Her eyes touch his as she drifts away from the privacy of the cubicle and joins the mass of other medics.

Kai smiles as he puts on his tie and dark green jacket. He can wait a week for a woman like that. No problem.

He walks out of the treatment center and into the corridors. Ahead, beneath a ceiling-mounted old brown clock, he sees Minister Chunlin waiting for him. His mentor. His shortcut up the ladder of success and away from the snakes of common soldiering.

Chunlin smiles and pats his shoulder. "Well done today. He will call you later. You will get but a few minutes alone with him. Make every second count."

"I understand." Kai feels the minister touch his jacket and then he's gone.

He knows what has been slipped into his pocket.

Understands, fully, what he has to do with it.

164

Washington DC

*C*lint Molton knows history is in the making as he and Don Jackson board Air Force One.

He's acutely aware of the importance of what's about to happen, how his actions in the next twenty-four hours will shape the future of the world's two biggest superpowers.

Before the plane even powers up, he holds a lengthy conference call with the Vice President, the Secretary of Defense, and the Joint Chiefs of staff, during which they agreed to reset the country's defense readiness condition to its highest level since October 22, 1962.

DEFCON 2.

Not since the Cuban missile crisis has the country been one step away from nuclear war. Even back on September 11, 2001, the USA only reached DEFCON 3. Throughout the entire Cold War, U.S. ICBM sites were never at a state of alert higher than DEFCON 4.

Molton thinks of the hundreds of people moving into action at the national Military Command Center inside the Pentagon. The secret meetings that will be held over the next hours in the war rooms, the coded messages going out to the battleships, nuclear submarines, and fighter planes. Over at Raven Rock in Pennsylvania there'll be similar activity at what White House insiders call the "Underground Pentagon." The top secret facility, sometimes just known as Site R, houses emergency operations centers for the Army, Navy, and Air Force, and runs almost forty specific communications systems for the defense bodies.

The big Boeing thunders down the runway and lifts effortlessly into the clear Washington sky. A screen in front of Molton tells him he's nine hours away from landing in Hawaii.

Twelve hours—720 minutes—away from his meeting with Xian.

165

China

*T*wo hours into the twelve-hour flight to Hawaii, sixty-year-old Xian Sheng, President of the People's Republic of China, breaks from the mass of paperwork spread before him in the office area of the customized Air China 747 and takes the call he's been waiting for.

Minister Chunlin's voice is calm and measured. "Zhang has just called for him. The meeting will happen at the end of the day."

"Keep me informed."

"Please ring when you land. I hope to have the best of news for you by then."

166

Miami

*G*host follows a very special GPS system on his phone as he drives out of Miami. He guns the old Dodge so hard he's sure he's in for a steep repair bill and a whole pack of speeding tickets by the time he's done.

He winds down the window in the hope that the morning air will keep him awake and turns on the radio for the latest news. Most stations are full of through-the-night phone-ins and breaking reports about the latest dog attacks. It saddens him to learn that there have been more deaths in New York, Los Angeles, Chicago, and across Florida.

More deaths.

It's the ubiquitous phrase that all news readers have adopted.

In total, thirty-one towns and cities have now been hit by what the media is calling the Dog Bite Epidemic. Deaths have risen to more than five hundred, and there are over a thousand injuries.

Ghost tunes in 100.3 FM and finds WIOD News radio is running an interview with the Canadian prime minister about the border closure. They follow that with a sound bite from the president of Mexico saying his country will make a decision on border closure in the next twenty-four hours. There's a report as well on the orders that U.S. businesses have lost at APEC, and interviews with families of soldiers killed in a bomb blast in Afghanistan.

Ghost turns it off.

Today is going to be a bad day. In a few hours they'll be expecting him at his desk. Looking for him. Readying themselves to control and silence him. Make him compliant.

It isn't going to happen.

He isn't going to be there.

Ghost heads west, out of the city. More than thirty miles down Highway 41 at speeds close to 140. Only as he clears the main turn to the Monument Lake campground does he take his foot off the gas and start looking for the road that will take him into Big Cypress, almost three-quarter-million square acres of open parkland.

A glance at the GPS says he's almost at his destination. He slows down as he hits a track and snatches the smartphone from its dashboard mount. Sometime back, out of good practice, he'd diligently entered all the contact details of Agent Gwen Harries. Now he dials her cell.

Four rings play out. He knows she's looking at her caller display and wondering why on earth he's contacting her at seven in the morning.

Finally, she picks up. "Harries."

"You know where he is, don't you, Gwen?"

Her shock shows in a long silence before she answers. "I'll call you back. Now's not a good time."

"No need," says Ghost. "I'll be with you shortly."

167

Washington DC

*A*fter a sleepless night worrying about the events of the coming morning, Sheryl Molton is almost relieved that the time has come to face her fears.

The two children, Jack and Jane, are similarly anxious and both have been crying. Though everyone understands what has to be done, no one wants to do it.

Sheryl's driver pulls the armor-plated SUV over to the curb and two protection officers slide out and scan the streets.

Four other armed men slip from government vehicles in front and behind the First Lady's car and complete a 360-degree security ring before giving a signal that it's safe for her to get out.

Sheryl's dressed down for the day. Black pumps and slacks, a white hoodie, and her hair up in a chignon. If not for the G-men, she'd look almost like any other mom in her forties going to the shops or making the school run. Only she isn't. She's the First Lady, setting an example to the nation by taking the family's pet dog to a secure depository where it will stay behind bars until all the horror of the dog attacks and uncertainty is over.

So many cameras flash as she pops the trunk and gets Emperor down that it's like being caught in a sudden electrical storm.

The red Tibetan mastiff jerks his head from right to left and tugs hard against the silver choker lead. The lights, loud noises, and strange surroundings all seem to make him nervous.

A TV cameraman sees the chance of a great low-angle shot and hangs his lens over a roped-off line. He swings it an inch off the floor and toward the million-dollar dog, his eye focused on the monitor frame as it fills with the animal's majestic head and vibrant coat.

Emperor sees the camera late, coming at him like a strange, predatory animal.

He pounces.

The newsman drops the equipment and the dog lunges for his arm.

Sheryl Molton tugs on the lead but the pup is too powerful.

Teeth find wrist bone.

A security man steps forward and tries to get between the dog and the cameraman.

Emperor bites at the new limb that's thrust into his face.

The crowd is screaming now. Other photographers are breaking the press line to get better angles. Police struggle to push them back.

Emperor jumps and barks. A big noise from a big dog.

He snaps and growls.

"Shoot it!" someone shouts to a cop. "Shoot it before it hurts someone!"

A G-Man takes the lead out of Sheryl's hands and pulls hard.

The dog goes to ground. Head to floor so it doesn't get strangled.

Sheryl falls to her knees next to it. "Emperor. Hey boy, it's all right." She puts a hand to his head.

The dog sees her out of the corner of his black eyes and starts to snap.

Then holds back.

She strokes him and he yields.

"It's okay boy. It's all okay." Sheryl covers him with her body and rubs at his face and ears until she feels him relax.

She puts her hand back and retrieves the lead. Getting to her feet, she turns to the security men. "Thank you. We're fine now."

Her heart is bursting through her ribs as she crosses the road to her shelter. Somehow she holds it together.

168

Pacific Ocean

Air Force One skims over the world's biggest ocean, the vast and empty stretch that amounts for almost half of the planet's seawater and a third of its total surface.

The worried face of the President of the United States is pressed to a window and stares out at the geographic enormity beneath him.

Clint Molton wants to daydream on the adventures of Spanish, Dutch, and English explorers. Of Charles Darwin's epic voyage here in HMS *Beagle* and of the U.S. struggles to take Guam and the Philippines from Spain. He wants to contemplate Japan's domination of the region in the early 1940s and the immense battles of the Second World War that saw them comprehensively defeated by the U.S. Pacific Fleet.

He wants to think of anything other than the news he's just been given.

Philadelphia, the fifth most populated city in the country, is in chaos. It has been overrun by packs of murderous dogs that in the last hour have claimed sixty lives and injured a hundred more.

Philadelphia, the City of Brotherly Love. So called because its name came from the Greek words *adelphos*—brother and *philos*—loving.

Now it is the City of Fear.

The security missive laid on his lap says shoppers are under attack from hoards of mongrel hounds at Rittenhouse Row, the high-class blocks of major brands off Walnut Street. It details the bedlam that's broken out at Reading Terminal Market, where wild pit bulls rampaged into restaurants and savaged unsuspecting diners. And it chronicles how tourists have been killed by dozens of strays at Independence Hall in the National Historic Park, where the nation's iconic Liberty Bell hangs.

The watch team report also mentions the start of attacks in Houston and Dallas, down the banks of the Trinity River. Hurt and angry as those assaults make him, they don't for a second raise the same level of pain as Philadelphia.

Philly is a psychologically debilitating blow.

It's where three centuries ago the Declaration of Independence was signed. Where the America of today was born and baptized. Where the Founding Fathers met during the American Revolution, and where the nation's capital was, while Washington DC was under construction.

The attacks here feel like an attempt to wipe out history, to add monumental insult to the monstrous injury that has already been inflicted.

A presidential aide crosses the plane. "There's a call being routed to you from the Oval Office, sir."

"Thank you." Molton picks up a receiver in the armrest. "Hello."

The voice is that of his executive secretary, Jordan Taylor. "Mr. President, I don't know how to say this. I just call from the Dog Protection Depository in Washington, where your wife was—"

He jumps to the worst conclusion. "Is she all right?"

"Yes, sir. The First Lady is just fine. But I'm afraid your dog, Emperor, has been shot."

"What?"

"Apparently, there was an incident while transferring him from the presidential vehicle and then another one after Mrs. Molton had left him."

"Go on."

Jordan reads from his notes. "'The animal had been sedated and was being checked over as part of a routine admission, when it woke from a seemingly placid state and bit two male attendants. One needed four stitches to a hand, the other was badly mauled on the arm, shoulder, and face.'"

"Dear God—is he in the hospital?"

"Yes, sir."

"Then you must get me a contact number there so I can ring him. And for the other attendant as well."

"Yes, sir, I will." Jordan hesitates. "Mr. President, the dog was shot with a pistol by a police officer, and he—well, the dog is still alive. The manager of the unit wants to know if he has your permission to destroy him."

For a second Molton thinks of his family and their attachment to the family pet. Jack isn't going to understand all this. Not one bit. He swallows hard and gives the only answer he can. "Permission granted, but no one speaks about this until I've handled it with my family."

169

Big Cypress National Preserve, South Florida

*T*he former Seminole settlement is riddled with rugged tracks and trails far too dangerous for the Dodge.

Ghost parks and jogs deep into a dark maze of swampy forest. He's way off the beaten track. Far from the open water where airboats skim and miles of boardwalks lead tourists around more cultivated areas. Every ten steps sees a change of terrain, from dry to wet, from gluey mud to hard ground. Around him he knows there are dozens of reptiles, everything from gators to geckos. His right foot goes down in an unseen hole and a brown water snake wriggles away from him.

Half a mile of energy-sapping swamp leads to trees, bushes, brambles, and finally a narrow track that winds up to higher ground.

The GPS on Ghost's smartphone leads him to three Army ORVs, camouflaged personnel carriers, adapted swamp buggies, driven deep into a copse of evergreens. From this moment he knows hidden eyes and guns are trained on him. He walks with his hands held high above his head, fingers spread wide, to show without a shadow of doubt that he's not carrying a weapon and isn't a danger.

A female voice hushes out an angry reassurance to her colleagues, "He's a cop. He's with me."

Ghost lowers his arms as Gwen Harries approaches. She's in combat blacks and her face looks like a thunderstorm about to break. "What the fuck are you doing here? And how the hell did you find me?"

"One good bug deserves another."

"What?"

"The surprise hug I gave you in Washington. It wasn't a sudden rush of affection. I slapped a transparent tracer on the back of your ID. It was on top of your purse."

A burst of gunfire from off in the distance cuts short the volley of outrage she was about to hurl at him. "Keep back and don't get in the damned way."

He follows her into a cluster of trees. "That's Li Chen, I presume."

"And his wife. They're holed up in a shack we've been watching. It's why I left early."

Ghost slides up against a tree. Harries is still talking, but he's not listening. His mind is playing over the connections between Chen, the killer dogs, and Zoe lying in a hospital bed fighting for her life. He slips his hand beneath his jacket and pulls out one of the Glocks.

More gunfire breaks out. Short bursts of automatic fire. A Mac-11 or maybe an Uzi. He places it 150, maybe 200 yards away. Close to Harries he sees men in black start to spread out and move in on their prey. It should be over quickly now. He'll have the satisfaction of looking into the faces of the pair who've brought death to Miami, then he'll head to the hospital.

A loud explosion throws water, soil, and busted tree branches high into the air.

More gunfire follows.

Smoke bombs.

More automatic fire.

Ghost edges toward the action. He gets the feeling the Chens are putting up more of a fight than Harries and her chums expected. Another explosion goes off to his right, and he instinctively peels left. His brain tells him the CIA unit will be drawn to the action and it might be a ruse. Chen could be putting on a show to draw the fire while his accomplice heads in the opposite direction.

The hard ground quickly becomes swampy and he starts to have doubts. The gun battle still wages off to his right but there is nothing but stink, slime, and silence out here.

And a gator.

He's seen enough not to get easily spooked, but this is a big boy and the sudden noises have left the gator with his mouth open, and he's not looking for his teeth to be cleaned.

Ghost levels the Glock and pumps a shot down its throat and another in the side of its head as it lurches left. If it hadn't been so close and the circumstances had been less tense, he might have given it a chance to back off and find a watery hole to disappear into.

He watches the gator spasm. Way beyond it, another big reptile moves. Seems at first he's stumbled into a nesting area, then he sees fresh movement and makes out a human form.

The distant figure is exposed. Out in the open. Vulnerable.

It's about a hundred yards away, and Ghost can't make out whether it's male or female.

A single gunshot rings out. The bullet slashes water just a couple of feet from him. Whatever the sex, the person behind the weapon is a good shot. And the single shot means either they're testing distance or have limited ammo.

He has no option but to fire back. He's just as exposed as the shooter, and diving for cover is not an option in this stretch of gator-strewn swamp. The G22 jerks in his hand. He's firing high and left to allow for the distance and a slight breeze coming in off the Atlantic.

Two more shots hit the swamp near him. Barely a foot away.

Ghost shifts to his right and returns fire. This time he sprays and prays as he empties the rest of his fifteen round mag.

The figure's still standing.

Ghost goes for the second Glock.

A bullet thumps his shoulder.

The impact spins him. Drops him on his side in the swamp. Mud and water fill his mouth. For a second his head fills with bouncing lights. Adrenaline pumps through his body. Masks the pain. He reaches into his waistband. Finds the second gun. Not that it matters. The shooter will be far away by now.

He gets to his knees and looks across the swamp.

A Chinese man is twenty yards away and closing in on him. A gun dangles from his right arm.

Ghost raises his pistol and fires.

The shot misses.

Chen lifts his weapon, and Ghost knows his time is up. He always thought he'd realize the moment when it came. And now is that moment. He closes his eyes and hears the shot ring out.

170

Beijing

General Zhang sits in his silent vice presidential office. He reflects on his forty years of life, how after starting with so little he now stands on the edge of so much.

His family come from Ningxia, a bleak and barren autonomous province that has been christened the poorest place on earth. It is one fall of rain short of being a desert, with little sanitation and the barest of crops to feed a near anemic population.

His father was the first of the Zhangs to move away from the area, to trek across China and enlist as a full-time soldier. The toughness of his father's upbringing laid the basis for him to develop into a brutal and much feared professional soldier. He rose through the ranks and married a young secretary from Beijing named Jin Leung. Two years later they had him—their only permissible child.

In his young, formative years he witnessed brutality. His father beat his mother and she in turn would beat him. He grew up knowing only that you had no control over your life unless you were ruthless, duplicitous, and strong.

All traits that he recognizes now in the big soldier being shown through to his office to sit with him.

"How are your wounds?" Zhang pours whiskey from a decanter and hands a glass to Luo Kai.

"I have no wounds, only lessons, General." He takes the tumbler and puts it on the edge of the desk but doesn't drink. Alcohol has never touched his lips and never will.

"Where did you learn to fight so well?"

"Foshan, sir. Where I was born. A school with historic connections to the great master Yip Man."

"You learned Wing Chun, I can tell from your style."

The soldier smiles. "You have great powers of observation, General."

"You are correct. I do." He leaves the desk as he talks and walks around the other side so he can stand behind the muscled soldier. "But you can never know so much that you shouldn't seek to learn more. So I asked about you, soldier. Inquired as to your suitability to serve me."

Kai turns around to see him. "I am honored—"

"Face the other way! Look at me only when I tell you."

The young man turns, so he stares only at the wood walls behind the great general's desk.

Zhang paces. His strides cause the wooden boards to clump and squeak.

Kai hears the door open. More feet rush into the room.

Metal slides on metal.

The unmistakable sound of rifles being cocked.

"Stand up." Zhang barks out the order. "And spread your hands on the desk."

He does as he's told. His mind on the tiny item that he concealed on his body, the one which if discovered will lead to his death.

The general keeps his distance.

He stays far behind and off to one side of the dangerous young soldier. Far enough back for the man to be cut down by several soldiers should he suddenly turn and try to kill him. "Cuff his hands behind his back. Manacle his feet, then search him."

The four soldiers set about their tasks. Two keeping their weapons sighted on Luo Kai's head, the others applying the restraints.

Once the prisoner has been secured, Zhang walks back in front of him, pulls his pistol, drags Kai's head up by his hair and puts the gun in his mouth. "You are an assassin. Everything about you betrays the fact. It is in your eyes and the steadiness of your hands. It is in your faint praise and the fearless odor of your young skin. And it is in the fact that you keep the regular acquaintance of people like Minister Chunlin." He stares into the man's wide and now frightened eyes. "My only interest in you is how you intended to kill me."

171

Big Cypress National Preserve, South Florida

*T*he extra pain never comes.

Ghost is on his knees in swamp water waiting to check out of a life he's loved to the best of his abilities. But the bullet to the heart or head never arrives.

He opens his eyes and sees figures running into view from the right. There's no sign of the gunman. Of Chen. Now he sees Gwen Harries. She's at the front of the pack, a gun held in clasped hands. She's pointing her weapon at the ground some fifteen yards from him and others are joining her.

She shot him. Harries shot Chen. His brain finally makes the connection. The sneaky, duplicitous CIA agent who he never had time for has just saved his life.

He gets to his feet and almost falls over. Pain has come now. Arrived like a sledgehammer blow to his left shoulder. He eases the muddy jacket off and sees his shirtsleeve is soaked in blood.

"You best get that cleaned and stitched." Harries is only a couple of feet away from him. She glances back to where her colleagues are. "Chen's dead, unfortunately. I didn't have time to shoot selectively."

"Not too unfortunate for me." He pulls the bloody shirt off his skin and tries to locate the exact point of entry. "Thank you for saving my life."

"You're welcome." She can see what he's trying to do. "Let me help." She loops a finger into the tear above his biceps and rips the sleeve wide. "You're lucky, it's outer shoulder muscle, through and through, not bone."

"I don't feel so lucky."

"You will when you reminisce. People like Chen are trained assassins. He came to finish you off because he only had limited ammunition. The firefight back at the shack left him low because his 'wife' used most of what they'd stashed when she made her covering run. Let's walk back, there's some morphine in the ORV, a shot of that will see you right."

Ghost is glad to be pulling his feet out of the stinking swamp water. His suit is pretty much ruined but he couldn't give a damn. A few yards from dry ground his cell phone rings. He has to stop to fish it out of his pocket and instantly smears mud over the display. It's no doubt someone from the task force wanting to know when he'll be at work.

"Walton."

"Lieutenant, this is Jude, Zoe's friend."

"Jude. Are you in Miami already?"

"Arrived a couple of hours back. I'm at the hospital."

The pause told Ghost something was wrong. "What's happened?"

"Zoe's back in surgery. She's taken a real turn for the worse."

172

Pacific Ocean

*P*resident Molton talks first to the doctors at Washington Memorial, then to Tyler Hutchins, the male attendant whose hand was bitten by Emperor.

After giving his apologies and wishing him the speediest of recoveries, he speaks next to Ashton Stephens, the forty-four-year-old who was more severely hurt.

"I'm told that you've suffered some very nasty injuries, Mr. Stephens, and I'm extremely sorry that my dog did that to you."

"Not your fault, Mr. President. I been reading the news. I know these poor dogs are goin' crazy and it ain't no one's fault but Nature's for turnin' them that way."

"All the same, I'm very sorry. Are you in a lot of pain?"

"Not right now, but I think I will be when the drugs wear off."

"Doctors tell me the attack to your face isn't as bad as first feared."

"Your dog bit me mostly on the top of the skull, coz I stuck my head down when he went kinda mad. I had a heap of stitches in there and he scraped a lot of hair off but they say it'll grow back."

"I'm relieved."

"Me too, sir. My face won't nothin' to shout about to begin with—couldn't have done with him makin' it any worse."

Molton's relieved the guy has a sense of humor. "Glad you can joke about this, sir. Please rest assured that my family will be living up to its responsibilities, so don't hesitate to talk to my aides about making proper compensation claims and us picking up your medical bills. And don't worry about time off work. Whatever you lose because of the attack, I'll make it up to you."

"I appreciate that, Mr. President. I have five kids and my wife was laid off from her night job two months back."

"Sorry to hear it. Five kids—my, that sounds like a real handful."

"It is, sir. Five girls too. All of them princesses."

"I'm sure they are. Mr. Stephens I have to go now, but I'll call you again in a few days' time to see how you're getting on. Meanwhile, if you need anything, then please call my secretary and we'll do what we can to fix things for you."

"Thank you, Mr. President. God bless you and God bless America."

Molton hangs up and instantly dials his wife.

Sheryl picks up on the second ring, delighted to get an unexpected call. "Hi."

He hits her with the news right away. "Honey, the dog has had to be put down." He waits for it to sink in.

She wants to believe she hasn't heard him right. "Emperor?"

"He bit two guys at the depository, one of them badly."

"Oh my God. He was jumpy and scared when I got him out of the car. Clint, there were a zillion cameras going off in his face, the poor thing was frightened to death."

"Doesn't matter, Sheryl. He savaged two people and a cop had to shoot him to protect the public."

"What do I tell the kids?"

"The truth. It's the only way they'll make any sense of it."

Silence hangs heavy on the line.

"You okay?"

"Yeah," she answers. "I'm just thinking back to when he nipped Jack. Maybe we had a lucky escape."

"I know. I've been thinking the same thing." Molton doesn't add that he's also been wondering if the canine "present" from Xian had been meant to attack and kill him and his children.

"I'm going to go and tell them now, Clint." Her voice sounds strained but focused. "I won't sleep tonight if I don't do it straight away."

She hangs up.

For a moment the phone dangles in the President's hand. He realizes he's just urged his wife to tell the truth to his kids, yet that's what he's not done with the American public. As much as he'd love to blow away the smoke screen of lies, he knows he can't. There'd be domestic panic and global instability on a scale never seen since the Second World War. For now, he has to keep quiet. Keep his silence and hope America prevails.

173

Big Cypress National Preserve, South Florida

*G*host lets one of Harries's agents carry out battle zone surgery on his wound. They shoot him full of morphine, dig out the slug, wipe it clean, and stitch him up. Nothing pretty, but within the half hour he's nursing a dressing and is back on his feet.

Harries insists he's not fit to drive and has a copter airlift him from the big park all the way back to Jackson Memorial. She promises to take care of the Dodge and not fill it full of bugs and tracers.

Ghost gets directions from the hospital's front desk and heads to the surgical wing. He sees a desolate, blond woman sitting on a plastic chair, near a low table full of magazines. Her head is down and she seems to be staring a hole in the floor but he knows it's Jude Cunningham.

"How is she?" he asks gently.

Jude raises her head and her face fills with shock. First, because she didn't hear or see him approaching. Second, because of his filthy, ragged state. His suit is covered in dried mud, his shirt ripped and his shoulder patched with bandages and sticky plaster. "I don't know. She's been in there for nearly three hours now."

Ghost grabs a chair and pulls it up close. "What's wrong with her? I mean, they said she was stable. I wouldn't have left her alone here if I'd thought she was going to get any worse."

"I haven't been able to find out." The medic in her takes over. "Head injuries are often complicated. I suspect there's been bleeding."

"Shit." He stands and starts to pace nervously.

"What happened to you?" she asks. "You fight some dogs as well?"

"Not a dog, a bullet. These days bullets are less dangerous."

The door opens and a nurse appears. She looks toward Jude. "They've just finished. The surgeon, Dr. Brook, says he'll come and see you as soon as he's scrubbed up."

"How is she?" Ghost and Jude ask in unison.

The nurse smiles weakly. "Best I leave it to Dr. Brook to tell you." She makes her exit before either of them grills her further.

174

Beijing

They strip him bare. Search every inch of his uniform. Every fold and sewn edge of cloth, where a garrotte or spike might be hidden.

They rip the dressing from his wound.

They ram fingers deep into his anus.

But they find nothing.

The soldiers kick the back of his legs and force him down to his knees at the side of the general's desk.

"This very moment my men are arresting Chunlin," Zhang tells Kai. "I know you serve him. I know you have been patronized and favored by him. I knew it the moment you were chosen to fight me. Did the pair of you not think I would have you checked out? You are a pair of fools. Now tell me, how were you supposed to kill me?"

Luo Kai says nothing.

"It is getting late and you are keeping me from my pleasures."

Zhang puts a hand to the man's knife wound and digs his fingers through the stitches. Digs until he can feel the wetness of blood and the meat of his sinews and muscles. "Be honest and I will be merciful." He twists with his fingers and works them back and forth in the wound.

Kai fights an urge to scream.

He locks off his thoughts. Hovers them in a space of nothingness.

Zhang senses he is fighting the pain. He frees his blooded hand, rests it on Kai's forehead and slams his steel toe-capped boot hard into his testicles.

The young soldier doubles up.

His hands are cuffed behind his back so he can't even touch the injured area. He falls coughing and spluttering to the wooden boards of the office.

"Hold him up." Zhang pulls paper from a printer to wipe the blood from his hands.

Two soldiers struggle to straighten Kai. His muscles are locked up in pain and they don't have the strength to force him upright.

Zhang can't believe their incompetence. He strides over and forces his thumb into the soldier's right eye socket. "Threaten a man's eye and you control his body. See how it now yields."

The young soldier is panting now. It's no longer possible to keep the pain out. A stream of fire is burning its way from his reopened wound to his ruptured testicles. His heart is hammering its way close to the point of arrest.

Zhang holds his head up and screams at him, "Tell me!"

Then he punches him.

Hits him so hard, Kai's lips burst and his jaw breaks.

He moves his tongue in the sea of blood swimming in his mouth.

It's gone.

Zhang sees the blood and saliva, tooth bone and drool, spatter on the floor and he feels a deeply sadistic surge of power and excitement.

In the middle of the mess is a lump.

Not a tooth.

Something more interesting.

He bends down and picks it up.

An elliptical glass bead. Small enough to have been concealed as a filling in a tooth. Filled no doubt with something deadly.

175

Jackson Memorial Hospital, Miami

The morphine has all but worn off. Ghost is feeling the pain, a deep throb like someone is sliding a hot sword in and out of his wound. He steps into the corridor and makes a series of calls. Things he's been putting off. People he's been putting off. He calls Vasquez over in Jacksonville then sends an e-mail on his phone to Annie, listing a whole bunch of things that need to be done quickly, quietly, and confidentially. Finally, he asks her to buy a new shirt and bring a pile of stuff to the hospital from his desk so he can tie up loose ends.

When he returns to the waiting room, Jude Cunningham is fighting sleep in a chair. Her head is resting against a blue plaster wall and the sun is busting through a side window and illuminating one side of her face.

The door creaks open and a tired looking surgeon comes in and lets it bang shut behind him.

Ghost breaks from his trance and looks across the dull room. Jude slowly gets to her feet.

The medic is in his late thirties, well-tanned, dark-haired, and slim. But for the bags under his eyes he'd look a picture of good health.

He fastens the blue suit jacket he's clearly just changed into from his operating room scrubs. "Lieutenant Walton?"

"Yes." He gets up from the back-aching, black plastic seat. "This is Zoe's friend Jude."

"Jude Cunningham." She offers a hand and the nervous suggestion of a smile.

"I'm Nathan Brook, I've just finished operating on Zoe."

"And?" Ghost takes a worried breath.

"We won't know for a while. She's had major surgery and we need to see how that plays out." He studies the cop and the woman in order to work out how technical he should get. "Do you know what an epidural hematoma is?"

"I have a medical degree," says Jude in a nonboastful tone. "It's a bleed in the brain, between the dura mater and the skull." She says it for Ghost's benefit more than anything. "It's a bad place to have a bleed."

"It is." Brook adds a little more info for the cop. "The dura is the tough outer membrane of the central nervous system. It surrounds the brain and spinal cord and is responsible for keeping in the cerebrospinal fluid. The blow to Zoe's head caused a buildup of blood there and it reached a point where it could have killed her."

"Could have?"

"Pressure was building up in the intracranial space, compressing delicate tissue and causing what we call a brain shift—a type of hernia in the head. We think we've relieved it."

"Thank God for that," says Jude.

"Is it common?" asks Ghost.

"No. Not at all. Which is why we were worried. The condition is present in only 1 or 2 percent of head injuries, and when it does manifest it often proves fatal."

Ghost feels as though he's sinking. Every question he asks brings an answer laden with new terrors. "But she's okay now, right? You've fixed everything."

The forced smile says things are not that simple. "We had to perform a type of decompressive craniectomy. In layman's language, we took out part of her skull in order to remove the etiologic mass and relieve the pressure. If we hadn't, she'd have died. Or at best, the risk of permanent paralysis and possible brain damage would have been very high. She's a long way from being okay, Lieutenant, a very long way. But the next few hours will tell us which direction she's heading in." He checks his watch. "I'm going to have to go to another operation now. But I'll check on her when I'm done and if there's any improvement I'll let you know."

176

Beijing

*T*hey're coming for him.

Geng Chunlin knows they are.

The fact that he hasn't heard from Luo Kai means that the young soldier has been discovered.

Zhang is probably torturing him. The thought makes him wince. The brute is without mercy and will mix humiliation and cruelty in measures that even he wouldn't think of sanctioning.

Chunlin thinks it is unlikely that Kai has been killed. Just as it's unlikely that he will be. The general will want them alive for a show trial, for a way to discredit President Xian and as justification for his planned coup.

He thinks for a moment about his old friend and leader, destined to touch down soon in Hawaii. Once he's out on the blistering blacktop of the runway, he will be desperate for good news and will try to contact him.

The minister picks up his cell phone and removes the data card. He walks to the corner of the office and squeezes it between the corner joint where the skirting boards of two walls come together.

He throws the carcass of the phone into a bottom drawer and begins to shut down his computer. Zhang's men will find nothing incriminating on it, but he doesn't want to make life easy for them. Let them search. Let them waste their precious time.

Chunlin takes out his pistol and puts it on the rectangle of white blotting paper in the middle of his desk. He pushes back his chair and takes a book from the shelves behind him. It's a gardening manual, dedicated to the creation and care of miniature landscaping. The minister has always had a soft spot for paying attention to the tiniest of details.

The office door opens and six armed soldiers march in. At the front is Senior Colonel Lie Han, Xue Shi's right hand man. "Minister Chunlin, I have a warrant for your arrest for crimes of treason."

He swings his legs down and puts a piece of paper in his book so he doesn't lose his page. "I presume you have no objection if I bring this with me?"

177

Jackson Memorial Hospital, Miami

*T*he door to the waiting area opens. An Hispanic nurse, coils of sumptuous black hair tied back, enters with an expressionless look on her face. "Dr. Brook says you can see Zoe now. Please come with me."

Ghost and Jude virtually jump from their chairs and follow her a short stretch down a doglegged corridor to a sign saying ICU. "She isn't conscious, but her vital signs are stable again. So don't expect too much."

"Is the surgeon coming back?" asks Jude.

"I think so." The nurse stops as they reach a small single ward just a few yards from an operating room. "Here you go." She pushes a blue door and holds it for them as they enter the darkened room.

Jude's eyes fall on the vital signs monitor. Systolic 129. Diastolic 75. They're okay. Not perfect but fine for someone in her condition. Her heartbeat is high, though: 110 . . . 112 . . . 110. She looks from the screen to the drips, the stands, the ventilator, and the other monitors—all the paraphernalia of critical illness.

Her friend is lying on her back, head turned to the right, black hair on the pillow, mask to her mouth, tubes plastered to her arms. Sodium, potassium, and sugar are dripping from bags into tubes and then needles into veins. A Foley catheter runs discreetly from the bladder, a nasogastric tube from her stomach.

Ghost stands at the foot of the bed feeling empty. It breaks his heart to see Zoe like this. The stitches on her arms and legs, the dressing to her skull where they cut to release the swelling. This is not the vibrant, full-of-life woman he fell in love with. As he walks down the opposite side of the bed to Jude and takes Zoe's tiny, pale hand in his, he has an acute sensation that he's losing her. Her fingers feel lifeless. Corpselike. He's picked up the limbs of enough cadavers to know the sensation. Instinctively, he slides his thumb and forefinger down her wrist and feels for a pulse.

He's tired and his lack of expertise means he finds it and then loses it again.

It was so faint.

He searches once more and this time seems unable to locate it.

A monitor in the corner of the room lets out a loud warning bleep.

Jude has been watching the screens and is already a move ahead of him. She hits a red button by the bed.

A green jagged line on a screen near Ghost goes flat. Numbers disappear and hit zero.

The doors burst open.

The surgeon rushes in, concern etched into his brow. "Out. Out. Get these people out."

Nurses push Ghost back to the door. He sees Jude asking questions. Overhears someone say, "She's crashed. Her heart has stopped."

178

Beijing

*T*he bank of video monitors in the Nian Operations Room shows coast-to-coast chaos in the United States.

Xue Shi's tired but vigilant eyes take in the live feeds and the glowing maps on his computer showing the devastation the dogs are wreaking. He'll be glad when this mission is over. When he can grab precious sleep and the rewards for helping Zhang take over the presidency.

The Chinese satellites show that the U.S. Army's lead teams are still trying to round up and kill the last of the attack dogs in New York's Central Park, Wall Street, and downtown areas. In Los Angeles, Bel Air and Glendale police are pursuing a mix of pointers, labs, and boxers that have killed more than a dozen of the wealthy residents and injured close to twenty.

Across the monitor bank, the lieutenant general watches the National Guard fight a rear-guard action through Burleson Park in the north of Dallas. The bodies of dozens of locals and tourists are strewn across the grass, playgrounds, and picnic sites as marauding dogs rampage eastward toward the North Central Expressway.

In Dallas itself, shoppers are under attack in the Main Street area and the Historic and Arts districts. Traffic is at a standstill and paramedics are caught in the gridlock.

In Houston, four Alsatian guard dogs have been activated at the Mission Control center and have already killed two members of the International Space Station ground crew.

A pack of strays is attacking visitors leaving an antiques show in the George R. Brown Convention Center.

In Seattle, the first of a whole series of planned attacks has just begun. Sniffer dogs down at the dockside are attacking port workers. Across town, two kennel maids are being savaged to death by Labradors at a nearby animal shelter.

A message flashes on his computer. An alert he's been waiting for. He picks up the phone and dials General Zhang's private cell phone.

"Yes."

"I have the results from the laboratory. The glass capsule that Luo Kai had in his mouth contained polonium."

"Polonium-210?"

"Yes, General. The specially coated glass would have contained it, but once broken, the uranium would have proved deadly."

179

Beijing

*T*omorrow he will deal with Geng Chunlin. Until then the odious man can sweat and rot in a dark cell full of cockroaches and rats.

The world will be a very different place in twenty-four hours.

President Xian will have returned from making a fool of himself in Hawaii. The Americans will be broken. And he—Fu Zhang—will be assuming the presidency and total control of the People's Republic of China.

It will be his world.

His in the way that only the great emperors of bygone China have ever known.

Absolute rule.

Not only of China, but soon, also of the other biggest super-powers in the world.

Starting with America.

True power.

Global power obtained through global fear.

Fear is the energy of power, like that uranium they tried to poison him with. Maintain the fear, and the power is regenerated over and over again. And once started, it only needs a little here and there to keep it running.

He slips off his robe and steps into the bathwater.

It is not as he wished.

He'd asked the private butler at the Raffles Hotel to run a tub that was tepid and filled with soothing herbs and oils. Any hotter and it inflames the scars on his chest.

But this is not tepid.

Far from it. When he sees the old fool he will hold him down in it and teach him what tepid is.

The anger rouses him. Acts as a perfect pick-me-up for the playmates that his soldierly contact is bringing around for him.

Special playmates.

Ones he needs to relieve all the excitement that's been building tensely inside him. His desires need to be met. The anger and rage need to be vented through his sexual potency. Women need to understand him and fear him just as much as men.

He runs cold water until it is the perfect temperature and slides into the bath. He thinks for a moment of what he will do with Luo Kai when the bigger issues are settled.

Maybe he will have him fight some dogs.

That really would be something to watch.

The young soldier was so fast and powerful, Zhang knows he could easily have killed him. But then he'd have been arrested. Or even shot. Hence the ruse with the poison. In war the clever moves often turn out to be the clumsiest.

Yes, he'll have him fight the dogs.

One at a time.

Until gradually he is worn down. Then he will send in the tiniest Chihuahua to finish him off.

The thought is delicious.

Zhang steps out of the deep tub and pulls on a terry-cloth robe. He is ready for his playmates now. Ready to rip at their bodies like a Nian dog

180

CIA HQ, Langley, Virginia

*D*anny Speed is dead on his feet.

There doesn't seem a moment when he isn't being asked a question by a code breaker, geneticist, analyst, scientist, or fellow CIA operative.

Chris Parry catches the young New Yorker falling asleep in front of a screen at a hot desk terminal. He slides a chair alongside him and offers words of encouragement. "We're close, Danny. Really close. You've done a brilliant job and the linguists have completed 80 percent of the translations. We already have enough to have sent the scientists wild, and plenty for the strategy teams to build patterns, models, and mapping software."

Danny can tell this isn't the start of a backslapping pick-me-up. "But you have a 'but,' sir?"

"Yeah, I do. You're a smart kid, so I think you know what it is, don't you?"

He nods. "I do. But I can't explain it. The walls just came down. For less than an hour the normal security barriers just dropped, like someone deliberately opened up the master computer in North Korea and let us rifle through their safe."

"That's the problem. If this is false information and we act on it, then they win. And I mean, end game win, not slight loss in a bigger battle win. This would be the kind that there's no coming back from."

Danny runs things through in his head. Just as he'd been doing for the past twenty-four hours. "I didn't change capture codes. Didn't do anything different than I had been doing. The only real change in practices was me relocating from New York to Breezy Point."

"That wouldn't have done it."

"Sometimes a reboot on hacking codes has an effect."

"Not like that."

Brad Stevens wanders their way and joins them. He looks even more tired than he normally does, and that was never a good place to start from. He waggles a piece of printout paper. "This is interesting."

Parry smiles. "I'm always interested in interesting, Brad."

"There was an outgoing coded message, nonmedical, not scientific, and incomplete, so it didn't get top priority from our team. One of the linguists has just completed the translation and now the fragments take on greater impact. It says, 'I am Hao Weiwei. My son Jihai and I are scientists but first and foremost we are men of honor and peace. We were told Nian was a defensive project, dedicated to discover an antidote to an evil invention of the West. Only when I discovered tetrodo—' That's where the message was cut off."

Parry takes the piece of paper, and as he reads it for himself, puts some of the pieces together. "Jihai was the scientist who caused the standoff in the DMZ." He looks at Danny. "And both he and Hao had administrator access to the terminals, right?"

"Right. We've been through that connection, though, haven't we?"

"Not in quite this light." Parry gets some of the bigger picture now. "It's an honor thing. Hao found out that the dogs' program was going to be an offensive operation so he disabled the firewalls during the time his son tried to escape, that's how you got the data burst that you did."

"Makes sense," says Danny.

"They'd have picked it up in Beijing," adds Stevens. "Then they'd have shut him down double-quick."

"Probably." Parry puts a finger on the printout. "That's why he never finished the message." He turns to Danny. "What's tetrodo? Does that mean anything to you?"

"Not a thing." Danny types it into a search engine on the computer in front of him. "There are some hits here. It's the name of an iTunes podcast on e-learning. There's a rock band by the same name. And . . ." He pauses. "Shit. You'd better see this. There's a thing called tetrodotoxin. It's a deadly neurotoxin that is regarded as undetectable unless you are looking solely for it, and even more worryingly, it's incurable."

181

Air Force One

The pilot announces that the presidential plane has been cleared for landing and they expect to be on the ground in Hawaii in ten minutes' time.

Clint Molton is deep in thought, mentally rehearsing his conversation with Xian and trying not to think about his children and how they will have taken the news about Emperor being destroyed.

Don Jackson picks up the flashing phone and takes a call

from the leader of the CIA's cyber squad. "I'm hoping this is good news, Chris."

"The best you'll have had today." The former Delta Force commander looks back at the teams of code breakers, translators, geneticists, scientists, and operatives who have been toiling relentlessly on the data streams that Danny Speed captured.

Jackson sees clouds hit the windows of the 747 and swallow the plane in their strange foam and dulled light. "Give me the headlines, we're coming in to land."

"We have a complete decode. One that actually makes sense to linguists and scientists. We have the chemical composition of the adrenaline booster, we have the antidote—what they call a pacifier—and most important of all, we have the full range of RDIF frequencies for all the weaponized dogs."

Jackson feels elated. He touches Molton's arm to break him from his thoughts and switches to speakerphone. "Chris, I've just conferenced in the President. You were saying that you believe you now have the full collection of parts, everything there is on Nian?"

"We think so. We've got computer programs up and running. The batch codes and ID numbers of the dogs' RDIF transponders tally with activated dogs."

"We need teams on the nonactivated ones, the ones that could still do damage."

"Already on it. National Guard and Army have their intel people digging into our data and are redirecting as we speak."

Molton feels something he's not felt for a week. Optimism. "That's great work, Chris. Don will talk to you when we land. I'm going to need certain data sent to me so I can show Xian he's a busted flush. Can you have someone prepare key and conclusive extracts that will leave him in no doubt?"

"I'll look after it personally, Mr. President."

"Thank you. And tell the team, well done."

"I will, sir."

Jackson hangs up and turns to the President. "For the first time we can be proactive. We can literally go get these bitches and sonsofbitches before they so much as snarl at anyone."

182

Jackson Memorial Hospital, Miami

Ghost takes a call from Annie Swanson. She's done everything he asked. Dealt with all the paperwork and made the calls he told her to. Now she's in the hospital reception with the change of shirt and other stuff he wanted.

He leaves Jude in the waiting room and rushes down to meet her.

Annie's eyes grow wide when she sees the state of her boss. "Holy shit, you look bad. What happened?"

"Long and unimportant story." His eyes fall on two large plastic carrier bags in her right hand. "Is that everything I asked for?"

"It is." She offers the bags. "Can you manage?"

"I'm fine. Thanks."

"Let me help. I'll walk with you to the waiting room."

"No," he snaps. "Sorry. No thanks. You've done enough, now get out of here and keep Cummings and the White House off my back for as long as you can."

She nods. "You're sure you don't want me to stay?"

"I'm fine."

She presses out a smile and sadly turns and leaves.

Ghost's phone rings as he trudges back to Zoe's bedside.

Annie, he imagines. He's forgotten something. Or else she has.

Caller display shows a number that's not hers.

"Walton."

"Lieutenant, this is Danny Speed. You left a message for me about Zoe."

Ghost walks away from the bed. "What the hell took you so long?"

He matches the cop's anger with his own. "Never mind that, how is my sister?"

"She's—" The word sticks in his mouth. "She's dying, Danny. She's in Jackson Hospital in Miami and has just come out of surgery. I don't think she's going to be alive much longer."

183

Honolulu, Hawaii

*P*resident Xian's plane touches down perfectly on the Reef Runway, one of the four magical landing strips suspended in the sea in front of Honolulu's spectacular cityscape.

After a brief delay, he steps off the plane and into the shimmering heat of another tropical day. There is no pomp and ceremony to this visit. It is as low key as his administration has been able to manage, though a necessary contingent of bodyguards and flunkies is already out on the blistering blacktop.

A soft trade wind blows across the open area, and to one side he can see Hickam, the naval and air base that forms a vital part of the United States Pacific Air Command.

Suited bodyguards usher him toward the bulletproof Mercedes that will be driven by his trusted driver to the APEC conference hotel.

Once inside the air-conditioned cocoon of tan leather and walnut, he calls Geng Chunlin.

There is no answer.

He waits a few moments then rings again.

Still there is no pickup.

He tries his direct line office number and it just rings out.

Xian ends the call and replaces the car phone.

The minister's plan has failed.

As he feared it might.

He feels isolated. More alone than he has ever felt in his life.

Xian calls his wife.

Suyin picks up on the second ring. "Hello."

"I have just arrived in Hawaii. Where are you?"

"We are in Guangdong."

"Good. How is Umbigo?"

"He is fine. He is sleeping like an angel." There is tenderness in her voice. "He misses you and wants to know when you will join us."

"He is a good boy."

"What shall I tell him?" The question is as much for herself as her son.

Xian realizes he may never see either of them again. That once his meeting with Molton is finished, he's likely to be seized by Zhang's men as soon as he reenters China. "Tell him I love him and I am always with him and always will be. No matter where I am and no matter where he is. Our hearts are as one. Just as yours and mine are."

The president hangs up before she can press him further. Before she can say things that will touch his soul and weaken his resolve. The shadow of the towering hotel falls across the front of his Mercedes. He turns off his phone, puts it into his pocket and prepares for what he has no doubt is the final official meeting of his life.

184

Raffles Hotel, Beijing

Zhang's lascivious eyes linger on the two dark-haired hookers.

"They will do." He passes an envelope to former Colonel Huan Lee. "Have they brought the clothes I ordered?"

"Of course, sir."

"Then have them change and then you get yourself out of here."

Lee hurries the young girls toward the palatial bathroom in the Presidential Suite. "They will change and then come out for your pleasure." He bows and leaves.

The general can barely contain his excitement as he hears them giggling in the bathroom.

They won't be soon.

They'll be sobbing and begging for mercy.

His mercy.

They come out together, shaking the handfuls of glittering tinsel as they pump the air and twirl seductively in their cheer-leader costumes. One in lemon, one in red. Complete with matching pom-poms.

Now he gets to choose.

There's not much between them. They're both late twenties. Real women, not girls. Curvaceous but not fat. Hair cut short, much like his mother's was when she burned him.

They introduce themselves. The first is Min, a name meaning quick. She has a confidence in her dark eyes that marks her out as a watcher, one to be tied up so she can witness the suffering of the other.

The second, slightly smaller girl is clearly in awe of him. She tells him she is Jing-Wei, the name for a small bird.

"You." He points at Min. "Sit on that chair. Put your hands behind your back. You have been chosen to watch."

Fear creeps into her eyes as she does as he says. Her heart thumping as soon as the rough rope touches her soft wrists and ankles.

Zhang turns to Jing-Wei. "Bird, come here."

The pretty courtesan steps forward.

The general punches her. A blow so hard it breaks her nose.

Before she can even scream he slaps a hand over her mouth and pushes her onto the bed.

Jing-Wei's blood runs from her nose over his fingers. He looks across to the other woman and lustfully licks it away, his excitement rising with her pain.

185

Kahala Hotel, Honolulu, Hawaii

Presidents Molton and Xian are now in the same palatial building but still haven't met.

They're in separate suites, each costing their respective countries a cool ten thousand dollars a night.

On the floors below, tensions are running high between the two security teams, with Chinese and American protection officers almost standing nose-to-nose at every set of elevator doors, emergency exits, and stairwells.

The final session of the APEC summit is in full swing in the hotel's vast, pillar-free ballroom, where delegates sit beneath luxurious venetian glass chandeliers, overlooking a tropical lagoon. There are whispers that Molton and Xian are in the hotel and that there will be a dinner tonight. Perhaps some form of historic announcement.

The leaders of the world's two biggest superpowers have agreed through their offices to meet in the more modest Kianoa Boardroom. Agents from both countries have already had it electronically swept and sealed. Protection officers are posted outside to ensure total security.

The President of the United States pulls himself out of a luxurious couch where he's drinking iced coffee and puts on the jacket to his tailor-made black suit. He straightens the knot of his dark gray tie under the collar of his crisp white shirt and shakes the cuffs out of the sleeves. He breaks the tension by standing inspection straight in front of his NIA director. "So, how do I look, Mr. Jackson?"

"Just like a G-Man, sir. You want to accessorize with a service issue Glock?"

"I'll pass on that." He points to the TV. "Turn it on please. Let's take one last look at the world before we go downstairs."

Jackson takes the remote and clicks it on. "There won't be good news, Mr. President."

"I know that. I want to remind myself of the suffering before I enter that room and rip Xian's heart from his body."

186

Raffles Hotel, Beijing

*T*he white sheets and white carpet are spattered with Jing-Wei's blood.

The hooker's nose and jaw are broken and her shoulder dislocated from when Zhang held her face down on the bed and almost choked her to death.

The general throws the tattered remains of a cheerleader costume at her as she lies sobbing. "Get cleaned up and get out." He points to the bathroom and turns his attention to the other girl.

Min has been hanging her head for the past ten minutes. Trying not to see what was going on. Trying not to accept that it would be her next. That every scream that came from Jing-Wei's throat would soon echo in her own.

Zhang's lips and his left eye twitch with excitement as he stands naked before her. "Now you."

He grabs her by the head and pulls her across to the bed so only the back legs of the chair scrape along the carpet.

Min struggles to breathe and fears he may break her neck or strangle her.

Zhang steadies the chair and swings a punch at her face.

Min unclasps her hands from behind the back of the chair and darts forward.

The force—and the fact that she has somehow untied herself—takes the general by surprise.

He crashes into a table and hits the floor.

The general's eyes light up. Aggression. Nothing turns him on more than the rush of a fight.

He slowly gets to his feet and smiles at her. "Now I am going to hurt you. Hurt you so badly you will wish I had ended your life."

He leaps forward and lands a high kick against her right breast. Almost in the same moment he spins and plants the full force of his left foot against her face.

Min doesn't feel any pain. She's been trained not to. The Chinese Special Ops agent times her move immaculately. She slips inside his secondary swirl and with both hands loops the length of the rope he'd tied her up with around his neck.

Only now does Zhang realize he's not beating up a defenseless courtesan.

Only as Min's knee sinks into the small of his back and her grip tightens the garrotte does he know he's made a mistake.

A fatal one.

She holds on tight. Hangs tough, as he bucks his body, swings elbows, kicks, and tries to roll.

They tumble across the floor.

Zhang plants his feet against a skirting board and drives himself back against her.

Min crashes into the bedside cabinet but holds on. The rope is wrapped white-tight around her fingers and knuckles.

Zhang starts gagging. Choking. Spluttering.

Min strains even harder. She can see his skin coloring. His eyes bulging.

The general kicks. His heels bang on the floor. His legs spasm.

She continues to pull. Holding her breath and straining for all she is worth. Way beyond the point when he's stopped making a noise. Way beyond the moment when his body goes totally limp.

Only when his bowels give way and the stench hits her nostrils does she unclench her fists and fall back exhausted.

The agent, one of Chunlin's finest, quickly catches her breath and rolls away from beneath the corpse.

The bedroom door opens and former Colonel Huan Lee surveys the wreckage. "It is done?"

She straightens her clothes and wipes blood from her skin. "See for yourself."

He walks over to the body. Zhang's face is beetroot red, the rope still tight around his neck. He spits at the general and rubs the spittle in with the sole of his shoe. "For me, my country, and Minister Chunlin."

187

Kahala Hotel, Honolulu, Hawaii

*U*nder the scrutiny of Chinese security, Don Jackson enters the boardroom a few minutes before the President.

He hooks a state-of-the-art CIA laptop to the room's AV system and shields his fingers as he logs onto the Agency's secure VPN. He quickly checks that both sound and vision are working on the flat screen built into the wood-paneled wall.

Everything's good to go.

The NIA director ducks out of the room just as both leaders are walking side by side toward it. They cut an almost perfect picture of cordiality.

Molton stands to one side and allows Xian to enter first. "Please, after you."

The Chinese leader acknowledges the courtesy with a gracious nod. He thinks it good that the American has learned subservience; it will serve him well in the future.

Molton shuts the doors behind them. He sees that Jackson has set up the TV system and computer link that he needs. "In the interests of time, President Xian, I'd like to start by showing you something." He flips up the top of the laptop and hits the exterior AV key. A live feed to CIA HQ in Langley appears on the big boardroom screen. "This is Chris Parry, who heads up one of our Special Operations teams. Chris, can you hear us?"

Parry straightens up and pushes a finger in his ear to secure the connection pod. "Yes, sir. We can hear you just fine."

"Chris, please walk President Xian through what you and your colleagues have recently discovered."

"My pleasure, sir." Parry presses a key and the feed reduces his head and shoulders to only half a screen. "President Xian, you should be seeing some video playing now. This is encrypted footage we took from secure drives located in North Korea, those computers were in constant connection with your military base in Beijing."

The Chinese president watches footage of dogs going wild in the bunker laboratories in North Korea. There's a fast fade to black and then their dead bodies are inspected and removed by men in white lab coats.

The picture freezes and Parry picks up his commentary. "Those two men there, sir—they are Hao Weiwei and his son Jihai. I'm sure you know them—they are renowned Chinese scientists. The son was shot dead in the Korean DMZ, and I understand there are still tense discussions between the North and South about the return of his body and that of another dead scientist who was also found in the DMZ."

Molton watches Xian like a hawk. Judges his responses. Reads his face for signs of nervousness or anger.

The Chinese leader stays impassive. Decades in front of party committees and military councils has taught him to give nothing away.

"If you look at the top of the screen, sir," continues Parry, "you'll see data from what we understand is a venture called Project Nian. The numbers you see are the latest map locations of all the weaponized dogs in the United States. The CIA and the Army are rounding up the animals as we speak. We also know, sir, about the tetrodotoxin and the work done with this particular poison." The last sentence is something of a bluff, but Parry's face doesn't hint at how little the Americans have actually discovered.

The cell phone in Xian's trouser pocket rings. He reaches it and turns it off. "My apologies."

"Please, take it if you wish," says Molton graciously.

"I have cut it off."

"As you wish." He motions to the monitor. "I'm not sure if you need to see any more of the footage. In summary, we have all the information we need to destroy Nian, to make America safe again, and to publicly implicate China in atrocities that in their sickness go beyond the worst of many war crimes."

Xian's phone beeps with a message. In order to buy a little thinking time he takes it out.

The screen says: ZHANG IS DEAD.

He checks the number and sees it is Chunlin's.

For a moment his mind is in a whirl. His elation at the general's death is a heady contrast to the humiliation Molton is putting him through.

"Please, excuse me, for one moment."

The American nods and moves away.

Xian walks to the other side of the large room and triggers the phone's voice-mail service.

Chunlin's voice comes online. "It is done. There were complications but Zhang is dead."

It's all the confirmation he needs.

He turns the phone off, returns it to his pocket, and walks back to Molton with a diplomatic smile on his face. "Mr. President, may we speak now without the virtual presence of your colleagues in Washington?"

"Of course." He leans in front of the camera on the monitor. "Thank you, Chris. Stay on standby."

"Yes, sir."

Molton flips down the computer screen and ends the connection. "We are alone."

188

Jackson Memorial Hospital, Miami

*G*host and Jude have run out of things to say. They sit in the antiseptic gloom of the room and listen for any clues that the machines and Zoe's breathing may offer. The agony of waiting is occasionally interrupted by the arrival of a nurse who checks to see that everything is working, scribbles on clipboard notes hung on Zoe's bed, and then disappears again.

"Who was it," asks Jude, "who said patience is a virtue?"

"It's idiom."

"Who?"

"It's an idiom; a mangled, mongoloid phrase that's taken on meaning over the centuries, you probably can't pin it down to one single person."

"Right." She looks at him and tries to take stock. He seems

brighter and odder than any cop she knows or has even seen on TV. They're supposed to be simple souls, verging on caveman but maybe a bit vulnerable. This guy isn't anything like that. He's probably about as smart as they come and more complex than a Rubik's cube. One thing for sure, there's no doubting his devotion to Zoe. His eyes never leave her, and that wound in his shoulder must be torturing him. "Hey, you want me to go get you some painkillers for your wound?" She gets to her feet just as the door opens.

A nervous young man walks in. He glances at both Jude and Ghost, then at the bed. "I'm Danny, Zoe's brother."

"Lieutenant Walton." Ghost shakes his hand and reads the worry on his face. "They've operated and she's stable. We're waiting for her to come around."

"Jude Cunningham."

Danny shakes quickly and bends over his sister. He kisses her forehead and winces from the sadness of seeing her flat out and tubed up.

Ghost and Jude give him space. Let the shock sink in.

He finally turns and asks the questions they knew he would. "What happened? Why is she like this?"

"She was attacked by dogs," explains Ghost, "one of a number of people hurt at a public show."

"Dogs?" Danny finds it hard to bury his fury. "What was she doing at a dog show?"

"A long story," Ghost says. "Basically, she was following up some information that she thought might help solve the canine crisis that's been sweeping the country."

Danny falls silent. It seems horribly ironic to him that he was keeping his dog-related work secret and so was she.

"The bites were relatively minor," adds Jude, "but there was a complication with the head injury and they had to operate to remove a blood clot."

"But she'll be okay, right?" He looks to them both. "They said she'll be okay, didn't they?"

"I'm sure she will." Jude gives him a smile that's meant to be reassuring.

Danny stares at Ghost. "How could you let this happen to her? I thought the cops were supposed to be looking after everyone."

Ghost doesn't have an answer. In his mind, Danny is right. He should have looked after her. Should have kept her and all the other good people of Miami safe.

Zoe coughs.

It sucks all the noise out of the room.

She splutters. Her eyes screw up. She swallows painfully. Moves her lips.

"Sis?" Danny puts his face inches away. "Zo', are you awake?"

Her eyes open.

She blinks.

Then they close again.

189

Kahala Hotel, Honolulu, Hawaii

*B*oth men are standing. Only a few feet away from each other but culturally a whole world apart.

Neither is inclined to sit at the large conference table spread out in the boardroom and bring matters to a head.

The Chinese leader looks out at the dying light of the Hawaiian day. "President Molton, can I have your word that whatever is said in this room is just between you and me, unless we both agree otherwise?"

The American's face is set as hard as Mount Rushmore. "Sir, you and I have run out of undertakings. Say what you want to say."

Xian tries to soften him. "I would appreciate a final confidence with you."

Molton takes a beat. Reluctantly, he nods his consent.

"Are you familiar with the writings of Georges Clemenceau?"

"A little. The War Minister for France during the First World War."

Xian smiles. "Yes. The inappropriately named 'Great War.' Clemenceau said, 'War is much too serious a matter to be entrusted to the military,' and he was right. Nian was the cause célèbre of my vice president, Fu Zhang. He won sufficient political power in the party to take it forward. Zhang and Nian are now both—how shall I put this—no more."

The American President understands the implication. "I am relieved—on both accounts. But, with respect, it doesn't alter what has been done—or the country responsible for doing it."

"I understand your point." Xian takes a pace away from the American as he talks. "You are seeking reparations. Compensation for the damage and loss of life."

It's at moments like this that Molton most hates politics. Right and wrong reduced to dollars and cents. "I would like the families of victims to be substantially compensated for their loss, for what has been done to their lives. Money will not take away their heartache but it may help them going forward."

Xian ponders for a moment before responding. "The Chinese government would be willing to make a fund of five hundred million dollars available for them."

"One billion."

Xian stares into his counterpart's eyes.

Money.

The very thing that had driven them to the brink of war is now bridging the divide between them.

And they both know it.

Xian gives a considered nod of consent. "One billion—on condition that we agree on a public statement saying a manufacturing fault in the microchips caused an allergic reaction in the dogs."

Molton sighs. He knows he can hardly go public with a story that his administration suspected China of something worse but were powerless to do anything about it. "I might be able to live with that. But what about our outstanding debts?"

Xian realizes it is time for compromise. "We already have arrangements in place for them, do we not, Mr. President?"

"We do. And America will honor them. Providing China also uses its influence to reinstate the business orders that have been threatened at this APEC meeting."

Xian smiles. The American is a good negotiator. He looks at his watch. "We have a few hours before the closing dinner of the conference, I will arrange it by then." He puts out his hand.

It pains Molton, but he takes it. "There is a lot to rebuild, Mr. President. Starting with trust."

"Everything begins and ends with trust. Who better to build on what little is left than we who almost lost so much? We have been to the brink and seen the bodies in the pits below the edge of our feet. I never want my country to see war."

"Nor do I."

The Chinese leader heads for the exit. "Your new puppy, the Tibetan I gave you, I hope he is still proving agreeable and has not misbehaved in any way."

Molton gives a disappointed sigh. "Unfortunately, he didn't work out as we hoped."

"That is a great pity."

"Yeah, it is. We kinda had a soft spot for him. Kids *loved* him and we really wanted to make him fit in and become part of the family." He stops and turns to his counterpart. "I'm afraid he just got unmanageable—even vicious."

Xian looks offended. "The dog was pure. Part of my own litter. What did you do to him?"

"We did what was best." Molton's face is cold and emotionless, his stare set in steel. "Once he turned on us, we shot him. Then for safe measures, we burned his carcass and trashed the ashes." He motions again to the door. "After you."

190

Jackson Memorial Hospital, Miami

Zoe's room is cleared of visitors.

For twenty minutes it's a case of medics only.

Ghost, Danny, and Jude prowl the corridor like caged animals as the doctors and nurses crowd around her.

"This is good, right?" asks Danny. "I mean, they're in there because she regained consciousness."

"It's good," confirms Jude. "But don't go expecting too much too soon. Sometimes people with brain injuries mumble and talk nonsense for a while. They can come around right away and be fine, or they can take days to get back to anything like normal."

The debate is cut short by the appearance of Zoe's surgeon,

Dr. Brook. To everyone's relief, there's a smile on his face. "I'm very relieved to say that the patient is responding well and looking good."

A chorus of sighs comes from Ghost, Jude, and Danny.

"That's not to say she's out of the woods or going home anytime soon. But she's conscious and talking. We've given her a glucose boost and some water and so far so good."

"What does that mean?" asks Danny. "Why the caution?"

"Surgeons are always cautious," interjects Jude.

"You're right. It's because we have to be." He looks directly at Danny. "Swelling, major trauma to the brain, cranial bleeds, they're all survivable, but only with great care. Surgically we've done all we can. I really do think we're over the worst. But now she needs to rest and her body has to help us out and repair itself." He guesses what's on all their minds. "That means you can see her, but I don't want her overstimulated. So here are the rules: Only one person at a time, a limit of a couple of minutes each. Then I want you all to get out of the way, so she can rest properly and we can monitor her." Brook looks pointedly at Ghost. "Seems some folks could do with a change of clothes more than most."

"Point taken."

"Good. Then sort yourselves out and please leave Miss Speed to us, as quickly as you can."

Brook disappears and Ghost is left with Danny and Jude. "You guys go first. I need to at least wash up." He walks away before they can argue. In truth, he wishes they weren't even here. Wishes he could have all those precious few minutes with her just for himself.

Ghost finds the restrooms and uses a wall machine to buy a disposable toothbrush and a razor. There's no hot water but he manages to soap up, shave, and then scrub his teeth. He strips off the remains of his tattered shirt and pulls on the new one Annie got him. It's too baggy in the body. Too short in the sleeves. And made of cotton too rough for him to even consider cleaning the Dodge with.

He tells himself beggars can't be choosers. Rolls up the cuffs and tucks the vast white spread of cloth into his muddied trousers.

A look in the mirror shows he looks better. At least from the waist up. It shows something else as well. A strange nervousness in his eyes. He stares for a moment at himself and tries to work out what it is. Fear? Excitement? Love?

All of those things.

Ghost throws the old shirt in a receptacle and walks back to Zoe's room. He's a corridor away when his cell phone rings. If the display wasn't flashing a number he'd only dialed once in his entire life he'd ignore it.

"Hello, this is Lieutenant Walton."

A young male voice says, "Please hold on, I'm putting you through to the President of the United States."

Ghost finds himself standing up straight, almost as though he's being seen.

"Lieutenant?"

"Yes, sir."

"I'm in Hawaii at the moment but have been apprised of your injuries and your efforts to help us. I just wanted to say thank you."

"There's no need, sir."

"There's every need, Lieutenant. The information you gave us has helped enormously. My teams are sure within a day we will have eradicated these dogs problems—and I'm pleased to say our

international difficulties with China have been very cordially re-
solved."

"I'm really pleased, sir."

"How are you and how is your lady friend, Miss Speed?"

He half laughs. "Well, it's fair to say we've both looked health-
ier than we do right now. But she's out of her coma."

"I told you she'd pull through. I'm delighted. Delighted for
both of you. My office will be in touch. When you're fully fit, I
want you both to come to the White House for dinner and get as
fat as Thanksgiving birds."

"Thank you, sir."

"No, America thanks you, Lieutenant . . . *Icarus* Walton."
There's amusement in his voice. "That's a very fine name by the
way. Very fine indeed."

The President hangs up.

Ghost is left stunned. Not so much by the call but that the
name he has gone to such lengths to keep secret is now known to
the most powerful man in the world.

He turns the corner and sees Jude and Danny outside Zoe's
room. Their faces are animated. "She's good, bro', real good," announces Danny, as though they've known each other for years.

"Go on in," says Jude, pleased at the way he's tried to clean up
for her friend. "She's been asking for you."

From a chair, Ghost grabs the carrier bags Annie had brought
for him and enters the room.

Zoe looks up from the bed. A smile cracks across her pale face.
"Hi."

He hurries to her side. Bends low. Kisses her gently.

A tear runs down her cheek as she feels his warmth. This is what
she'd dreamed of. In the dark depths that had sucked her down,
she dreamed of this strange and wonderful man holding her again.

Zoe finds herself sniffling as they break.

Ghost plucks tissues from a box by the bed and gives them to her. "How you feeling?"

She mops her eyes and blows her nose. "Like a pack of dogs almost chewed me to death."

He laughs at her humor. "Shit, you had us worried. *Really* worried."

"Sorry."

He dips down and lifts up the carrier bag. "Here, I brought you some stuff."

She frowns. Partly from the pain in her head. Mainly from confusion. "What's in it?"

He tips the belongings onto the bed. Files. Prints. Her Hasselblad.

Zoe's eyes spark up. "My camera."

"And prints of the shots you took before you were attacked." Ghost steps away with the Hasselblad and takes several snapshots of Zoe.

"Please, not while I look like this."

"Especially while you look like this. You couldn't look more beautiful to me." He sits on the bed and puts the camera down near her hands. "You don't know this yet, but you're going to be famous. The most famous photojournalist in America."

Zoe humors him, "Sure I am. I told you that when we first met. Chief photographer at Reuters, a Manhattan loft the size of a football field."

"I remember. Well, my sweet, beautiful, crazy lady, you are going to show the world the pictures you took—the ones at the Gerbers' home, the shelter, and the Chens', then you're going to tell the story of how you saved the greatest country in the world from the greatest threat this side of a nuclear attack."

Zoe isn't really listening. She's stretched an arm to the empty carrier bag and is shaking it. "Something's missing," she says sadly.

"What?"

"The house key you offered me. If that invitation still stands, I'd like to take it and hang around awhile—a very long while."

About the Author

SAM MASTERS is a pseudonym of an author who has written seven books, including a bestseller sold in more than forty countries.